ECHO PARK

ALSO BY MICHAEL CONNELLY

Fiction

Nonfiction

ECHO PARK

A NOVEL BY

MICHAEL CONNELLY

DOUBLEDAY LARGE PRINT HOME LIBRARY EDITION

LITTLE, BROWN AND COMPANY
NEW YORK   BOSTON   LONDON

Little, Brown and Company
Hachette Book Group USA
1271 Avenue of the Americas, New York, NY 10020

The characters and events in this book are fictitious. Any similarity to real persons, living or dead, is coincidental and not intended by the author.

Lyrics from "It's Just Work for Me" copyright © 2005 by Ry Cooder, Hi-Lo Shag Music (BMI), from the album Chávez Ravine. Used by permission of Ry Cooder.

ISBN-13: 978-0-7394-7570-6

Printed in the United States of America

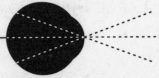

This Large Print Book carries the
Seal of Approval of N.A.V.H.

This is for Jane Wood — who keeps Harry Bosch well fed and close to the heart. Many, many thanks.

ECHO PARK

THE HIGH TOWER
1993

It was the car they had been looking for. The license plate was gone but Harry Bosch could tell. A 1987 Honda Accord, its maroon paint long faded by the sun. It had been updated in '92 with the green Clinton bumper sticker and now even that was faded. The sticker had been made with cheap ink, not meant to last. Back when the election was a long shot. The car was parked in a single-car garage so narrow it made Bosch wonder how the driver had been able to get out. He knew he would have to tell the Forensics people to be extra diligent while checking for prints on the outside of the car and the garage's inner wall. The Forensics people would bristle at being told this but he would become anxious if he didn't.

The garage had a pull-down door with an aluminum handle. Not good for prints but Bosch would point that out to Forensics as well.

"Who found it?" he asked the patrol officers.

They had just strung the yellow tape across the mouth of the cul-de-sac which was made by the two rows of individual garages on either side of the street and the entrance of the High Tower apartment complex.

"The landlord," the senior officer replied. "The garage goes with an apartment he's got vacant, so it's supposed to be empty. A couple days ago he opens it up because he's got to store some furniture and stuff and he sees the car. Thinks maybe it's somebody visiting one of the other tenants so he lets it go a few days, but then the car stays put and so he starts asking his tenants about it. Nobody knows the car. Nobody knows whose it is. So then he calls us because he starts thinking it might be stolen because of the missing plates. Me and my partner have got the Gesto bulletin on the visor. Once we got here we put it together pretty fast."

Bosch nodded and stepped closer to the garage. He breathed in deeply through his nose. Marie Gesto had been missing ten days now. If she was in the trunk he would smell it. His partner, Jerry Edgar, joined him.

"Anything?" he asked.

"I don't think so."

"Good."

"Good?"

"I don't like trunk cases."

"At least we'd have the victim to work with."

It was just banter as Bosch's eyes roamed over the car, looking for anything that would help them. Seeing nothing, he took a pair of latex gloves out of his coat pocket, blew them up like balloons to stretch the rubber and then pulled them onto his hands. He held his arms up like a surgeon coming into the operating room and turned sideways so that he could try to slide into the garage and get to the driver's door without touching or disturbing anything.

He slid into darkness as he moved into the garage. He batted spider threads away from his face. He moved back out and asked the patrol officer if he could use the Maglite on his equipment belt. Once he was back in the garage he turned the light on and put its beam through the windows of the Honda. He saw the backseat first. The riding boots and helmet were on the seat. There was a small plastic grocery bag next to the boots with the Mayfair Supermarket insignia on it. He couldn't tell what was in the bag but knew that it opened an angle on the investigation they hadn't thought of before.

He moved forward. On the front passenger seat he noticed a small stack of neatly folded clothing on top of a pair of running shoes. He recognized the blue jeans and the long-sleeved T-shirt, the outfit Marie Gesto was wearing when last seen by witnesses as she was heading to Beachwood Canyon to ride. On top of the shirt were carefully folded socks, panties and bra. Bosch felt the dull thud of dread in his chest. Not because he took the clothing as confirmation that Marie Gesto was dead. In his gut he already knew that. Everybody knew it, even the parents who appeared on TV and pleaded for their daughter's safe return. It was the reason why the case had been taken from Missing Persons and reassigned to Hollywood Homicide.

It was her clothes that got to Bosch. The way they were folded so neatly. Did she do that? Or had it been the one who took her from this world? It was the little questions that always bothered him, filled the hollow inside with dread.

After surveying the rest of the car through the glass, Bosch carefully worked his way out of the garage.

"Anything?" Edgar asked again.

"Her clothes. The riding equipment. Maybe some groceries. There's a Mayfair at the bottom of Beachwood. She could've stopped on her way up to the stables."

Edgar nodded. A new lead to check out, a place to look for witnesses.

Bosch stepped out from beneath the overhead door and looked up at the High Tower Apartments. It was a place unique to Hollywood. A conglomeration of apartments built into the extruded granite of the hills behind the Hollywood Bowl. They were of Streamline Moderne design and all linked at the center by the slim structure that housed the elevator — the high tower from which the street and complex took its name.

Bosch had lived in this neighborhood for a time while growing up. From his home on nearby Camrose he could hear the orchestras practicing in the bowl on summer days. If he stood on the roof he could see the fireworks on the Fourth and at the close of the season.

At night he had seen the windows on the High Tower glowing with light. He'd see the elevator pass in front of them on its way up, delivering another person home. He had thought as a boy that living in a place where you took an elevator home had to be the height of luxury.

"Where's the manager?" he asked the patrol officer with two stripes on his sleeves.

"He went back up. He said take the elevator to the top and his place is the first one across the walkway."

"Okay, we're going up. You wait here for SID and the OPG. Don't let the tow guys touch the car until Forensics takes a look."

"You got it."

The elevator in the tower was a small cube that bounced with their weight as Edgar slid the door open and they stepped in. The door then automatically closed and they had to slide an interior safety door closed as well.

There were only two buttons, 1 and 2. Bosch pushed 2 and the car lurched upward. It was a small space, with enough room for four people at the most before everybody would start tasting each other's breath.

"Tell you what," Edgar said, "nobody in this place has a piano, that's for sure."

"Brilliant deduction, Watson," Bosch said.

On the top level they pulled the doors open and stepped out onto a concrete runway that was suspended between the tower and the separate apartments built into the hillside. Bosch turned and looked past the tower to a view that took in almost all of Hollywood and had the mountain breeze to go with it. He looked up and saw a red-tailed hawk floating above the tower, as if watching them.

"Here we go," Edgar said.

Bosch turned to see his partner pointing to a short set of stairs that led to one of the apartment doors. There was a sign that said MANAGER below a doorbell. The door was opened before they got to it by a thin man with a white beard. He introduced himself as Milano Kay, the manager of the apartment complex. After they badged him Bosch and Edgar asked if they could see the vacant apartment to which the garage with the Honda in it was assigned. Kay led the way.

They walked back past the tower to another runway that led to an apartment door. Kay started working a key into the door lock.

"I know this place," Edgar said. "This complex and the elevator, it's been in the movies, right?"

"That's right," Kay said. "Over the years."

It stood to reason, Bosch thought. A place as unique as this could not escape the eye of the local industry.

Kay opened the door and signaled Bosch and Edgar in first. The apartment was small and empty. There was a living room, kitchen with a small eat-in space and a bedroom with an attached bathroom. No more than four hundred square feet and Bosch knew that with furniture it would look even smaller. But the view was what the place was about. A curving wall of windows looked out on the same view of Hollywood seen from the walkway to the tower. A glass door led to a porch that followed the curve of glass. Bosch stepped out and saw the view was expanded out here. He could see the towers of downtown through the smog. He knew the view would be best at night.

"How long has this apartment been vacant?" he asked.

"Five weeks," Kay answered.

"I didn't see a FOR RENT sign down there."

Bosch looked down at the cul-de-sac and saw the two patrol officers waiting for Forensics and the flatbed from the police garage. They were on opposite sides of their cruiser, leaning on the hood with their backs to each other. It didn't look like a thriving partnership.

"I never need to put up signs," Kay said. "The word that we have a vacancy usually gets out. A lot of people want to live in this place. It's a Hollywood original. Besides, I've been in the process of getting it ready, repainting and small repairs. I haven't been in any hurry."

"What's the rent?" Edgar asked.

"A thousand a month."

Edgar whistled. It seemed high to Bosch, too. But the view told him there would be somebody who would pay it.

"Who would have known that that garage down there was empty?" he asked, getting back on track.

"Quite a few people. The residents here, of course, and in the last five weeks I've shown the place to several interested parties. I usually point out the garage to them. When I go on vacation there's a tenant here who sort of watches things for me. He showed the apartment, too."

"The garage is left unlocked?"

"It's left unlocked. There's nothing in it to steal. When the new tenant comes in they can choose to put a padlock on it if they want to. I leave it up to them but I always recommend it."

"Did you keep any kind of records on who you showed the apartment to?"

"Not really. I might have a few call-back numbers but there is no use in keeping anybody's name unless they rent it. And as you can see, I haven't."

Bosch nodded. It was going to be a tough angle to follow. Many people knew the garage was empty, unlocked and available.

"What about the former tenant?" he asked. "What happened to him?"

"It was a woman, actually," Kay said. "She lived here five years, trying to make it as an actress. She finally gave up and went back home."

"It's a tough town. Where was home?"

"I sent her deposit back to Austin, Texas."

Bosch nodded.

"She live here alone?"

"She had a boyfriend who visited and stayed a lot but I think that ended before she moved out."

"We'll need that address in Texas from you."

Kay nodded.

"The officers, they said the car belonged to a missing girl," he said.

"A young woman," Bosch said.

He reached into an inside pocket of his jacket and pulled out a photograph of Marie Gesto. He showed it to Kay and asked if he recognized her as someone who might have looked at the apartment. He said he didn't recognize her.

"Not even from TV?" Edgar asked. "She's been missing ten days and it's been in the news."

"I don't have a TV, Detective," Kay said.

No television. In this town that qualified him as a freethinker, Bosch thought.

"She was in the newspapers, too," Edgar tried.

"I read the papers from time to time," Kay

said. "I get them out of the recycle bins downstairs. They're usually old by the time I see them. But I didn't see any story about her."

"She went missing ten days ago," Bosch said. "That would have been Thursday the ninth. You remember anything from back then? Anything unusual around here?"

Kay shook his head.

"I wasn't here. I was on vacation in Italy."

Bosch smiled.

"I love Italy. Where'd you go?"

Kay's face brightened.

"I went up to Lake Como and then over to a small hill town called Asolo. It's where Robert Browning lived."

Bosch nodded like he knew the places and knew who Robert Browning was.

"We've got company," Edgar said.

Bosch followed his partner's gaze down to the cul-de-sac. A television truck with a satellite dish on top and a big number 9 painted on the side had pulled up to the yellow tape. One of the patrol officers was walking toward it.

Harry looked back at the landlord.

"Mr. Kay, we'll need to talk more later. If you can, see what numbers or names you can find of people who looked at or called about the apartment. We'll also need to talk to the person who handled things while you were in Italy and get the name and forwarding address of the former tenant who moved back to Texas."

"No problem."

"And we're going to need to talk to the rest of the tenants to see if anybody saw that car being dropped off in the garage. We will try not to be too intrusive."

"No problem with any of that. I'll see what I can dig up on the numbers."

They left the apartment and walked with Kay back to the elevator. They said goodbye to the manager and went down, the steel cube lurching again before smoothing out on the descent.

"Harry, I didn't know you love Italy," Edgar said.

"I've never been."

Edgar nodded, realizing it had been a tactic to draw Kay out, to put more alibi information on record.

"You thinking about him?" he asked.

"Not really. Just covering the bases. Besides, if it was him, why put the car in his place's own garage? Why call it in?"

"Yeah. But then, maybe he's smart enough to know we'd think he'd be too smart to do that. See what I mean? Maybe he's outsmarting us, Harry. Maybe the girl came to look at the place and things went wrong. He hides the body but knows he can't move that car because he might get pulled over by the cops. So he waits ten days and calls it in like he thinks it might be stolen."

"Then maybe you should run his Italian alibi down, Watson."

"Why am I Watson? Why can't I be Holmes?"

"Because Watson is the one who talks too much. But if you want, I'll start calling you 'Homes.' Maybe that would be better."

"What's bothering you, Harry?"

Bosch thought of the clothing neatly folded on the front seat of the Honda. He felt that pressure on his insides again. Like his body was wrapped in wire being tightened from behind.

"What's bothering me is that I've got a bad feeling about this one."

"What kind of bad feeling?"

"The kind that tells me we're never going

to find her. And if we never find her, then we never find him."

"The killer?"

The elevator jerked to a hard stop, bounced once and came to a rest. Bosch pulled open the doors. At the end of the short tunnel that led to the cul-de-sac and the garages, he saw a woman holding a microphone and a man holding a television camera waiting for them.

"Yeah," he said. "The killer."

Part One

THE KILLER

1

The call came in while Harry Bosch and his partner, Kiz Rider, were sitting at their desks in the Open-Unsolved Unit, finishing the paperwork on the Matarese filing. The day before, they had spent six hours in a room with Victor Matarese discussing the 1996 murder of a prostitute named Charisse Witherspoon. DNA that had been extracted from semen found in the victim's throat and stored for ten years had been matched to Matarese. It was a cold hit. His DNA profile had been banked by the DOJ in 2002 after a forcible rape conviction. It had taken another four years before Bosch and Rider came along and reopened the Witherspoon case, pulled the DNA and sent it to the state lab on a blind run.

It was a case initially made in the lab. But because Charisse Witherspoon had been an active prostitute the DNA match was not an automatic slam dunk. The DNA could have come from someone who was with her before her killer turned up and hit her repeatedly on the head with a two-by-four.

So the case didn't come down to the science. It came down to the room and what they could get from Matarese. At 8 a.m. they woke him up at the halfway house where he had been placed upon his parole in the rape case and took him to Parker Center. The first five hours in the interview room were grueling. In the sixth he finally broke and gave it all up, admitting to killing Witherspoon and throwing in three more, all prostitutes he had murdered in South Florida before coming to L.A.

When Bosch heard his name called out for line one, he thought it was going to be Miami calling him back. It wasn't.

"Bosch," he said after grabbing the phone.

"Freddy Olivas. Northeast Division Homicide. I'm over in Archives looking for a file and they say you've already got it signed out."

Bosch was silent a moment while his mind dropped out of the Matarese case. Bosch didn't know Olivas but the name sounded familiar. He just couldn't place it. As far as signed-out files went, it was his job to review old cases and look for ways to use forensic advances to solve them. At any given time he and Rider could have as many as twenty-five files from Archives.

"I've pulled a lot of files from Archives," Bosch said. "Which one are we talking about?"

"Gesto. Marie Gesto. It's a 'ninety-three case."

Bosch didn't respond right away. He felt his insides tighten. They always did when he thought about Gesto, even thirteen years later. In his mind, he always came up with the image of those clothes folded so neatly on the front seat of her car.

"Yeah, I've got the file. What's happening?"

He noticed Rider look up from her work as she registered the change in his voice. Their desks were in an alcove and pushed up against one another, so Bosch and Rider faced each other while they worked.

"It's kind of a delicate matter," Olivas said. "Eyes only. Relates to an ongoing case I've got and the prosecutor just wants to review the file. Could I hop on by there and grab it from you?"

"Do you have a suspect, Olivas?"

Olivas didn't answer at first and Bosch jumped in with another question.

"Who's the prosecutor?"

Again no answer. Bosch decided not to give in.

"Look, the case is active, Olivas. I'm working it and have a suspect. If you want to talk to me, then we'll talk. If you've got something working, then I am part of it. Otherwise, I'm busy and you can have a nice day. Okay?"

Bosch was about to hang up when Olivas finally spoke. The friendly tone was gone from his voice.

"Tell you what, let me make a phone call, Hotshot. I'll call you right back."

He hung up without a good-bye. Bosch looked at Rider.

"Marie Gesto," he said. "The DA wants the file."

"That's your own case. Who was calling?"

"A guy from Northeast. Freddy Olivas. Know him?"

Rider nodded.

"I don't know him but I've heard of him. He's lead on the Raynard Waits case. You know the one."

Now Bosch placed the name. The Waits case was high profile. Olivas probably viewed it as his ticket to the show. The LAPD was broken into nineteen geographic divisions, each with a police station and its own detective bureau. Divisional Homicide units worked the less complicated cases and the positions were viewed as stepping-stones to the elite Robbery-Homicide Division squads working out of the police headquarters at Parker Center. That was the show. And one of those squads was the Open-Unsolved Unit. Bosch knew that if Olivas's interest in the Gesto file was even remotely tied to the Waits case, then he would jealously guard his position from RHD encroachment.

"He didn't say what he has going?" Rider asked.

"Not yet. But it must be something. He

wouldn't even tell me which prosecutor he's working with."

"Ricochet."

"What?"

She said it slower.

"Rick O'Shea. He's on the Waits case. I doubt Olivas has anything else going. They just finished the prelim on that and are heading to trial."

Bosch didn't say anything as he considered the possibilities. Richard "Ricochet" O'Shea ran the Special Prosecutions Section of the DA's office. He was a hotshot and he was in the process of getting hotter. Following the announcement in the spring that the sitting district attorney had decided against seeking reelection, O'Shea was one of a handful of prosecutors and outside attorneys who filed as candidates for the job. He had come through the primary with the most votes but not quite a majority. The runoff was shaping up as a tighter race but O'Shea still held the inside track. He had the backing of the outgoing DA, knew the office inside and out, and had an enviable track record as a prosecutor who won big cases — a seemingly rare attribute in the DA's office in the last decade. His opponent was named Gabriel Williams. He was an outsider who had credentials as a former prosecutor but he had spent the last two decades in private practice, primarily focusing on civil rights cases. He was black, while O'Shea was white. He was running on the promise of watchdogging and reforming the county's law enforcement practices. While members of the O'Shea camp did their very best to ridicule Williams's platform and qualifications for the position of top prosecutor, it was clear that his outsider stance and platform of reform were taking hold in the polls. The gap was closing.

Bosch knew what was happening in the Williams-O'Shea campaigns because this year he had been following local elections with an interest he had never exhibited before. In a hotly contested race for a city council seat, he was backing a candidate named Martin Maizel. Maizel was a three-term incumbent who represented a west-side district far from where Bosch lived. He was generally viewed as a consummate politician who made backroom promises and was beholden to big-money interests to the detriment of his own district. Nevertheless, Bosch had contributed generously to his campaign and hoped to see his re-election. His opponent was a former deputy police chief named Irvin R. Irving, and Bosch would do whatever was within his power to see Irving defeated. Like Gabriel Williams, Irving was promising reform and the target of his campaign speeches was always the LAPD. Bosch had clashed numerous times with Irving while he served in the department. He didn't want to see the man sitting on the city council.

The election stories and wrap-ups that ran almost daily in the *Times* had kept Bosch up to date on other contests as well as the Maizel-Irving contest. He knew all about the fight O'Shea was involved in. The prosecutor was in the process of bolstering his candidacy with high-profile advertisements and prosecutions designed to show the value of his experience. A month earlier he had parlayed the preliminary hearing in the Raynard Waits case into daily headlines and top-of-the-broadcast reports. The accused double murderer had been pulled over in Echo Park on a late-night traffic stop. Officers spied trash bags on the floor of the man's van with blood leaking from them. A subsequent search found body parts from two women in the bags. If ever there was a safe, slam-bang case for a prosecutor-candidate to use to grab media attention, the Echo Park Bagman case appeared to be it.

The catch was that the headlines were now on hold. Waits was bound over for trial at the end of the preliminary hearing and, since it was a death penalty case, that trial and the attendant renewal of headlines were still months off and well after the election. O'Shea needed something new to grab headlines and keep momentum going. Now Bosch had to wonder what the candidate was up to with the Gesto case.

"Do you think Gesto could be related to Waits?" Rider asked.

"That name never came up in 'ninety-three," Bosch said. "Neither did Echo Park."

The phone rang and he quickly picked it up.

"Open-Unsolved. This is Detective Bosch. How can I help you?"

"Olivas. Bring the file over to the sixteenth floor at eleven o'clock. You'll meet with Richard O'Shea. You're in, Hotshot."

"We'll be there."

"Wait a minute. What's this *we* shit? I said *you,* you be there with the file."

"I have a partner, Olivas. I'll be with her."

Bosch hung up without a good-bye. He looked across at Rider.

"We're in at eleven."

"What about Matarese?"

"We'll figure it out."

He thought about things for a few moments, then got up and went to the locked filing cabinet behind his desk. He pulled the Gesto file and brought it back to his spot. Since returning to the job from retirement the year before, he had checked the file out of Archives three different times. Each time, he read through it, made some calls and visits and talked to a few of the individuals who had come up in the investigation thirteen years before. Rider knew about the case and what it meant to him. She gave him the space to work it when they had nothing else pressing.

But nothing came of the effort. There was no DNA, no fingerprints, no lead on Gesto's whereabouts — though to him there still was no doubt that she was dead — and no solid lead to her abductor. Bosch had leaned repeatedly on the one man who came closest to being a suspect and got nowhere. He was able to trace Marie Gesto from her apartment to the supermarket but no further. He had her car in the garage at the High Tower Apartments but he couldn't get to the person who had parked it there.

Bosch had plenty of unsolved cases in his history. You can't clear them all and any Homicide man would admit it. But the Gesto case was one that stuck with him. Each time he would work the case for a week or so, hit the wall and then return the file to Archives, thinking he had done all that could be done. But the absolution only lasted a few months and then there he was at the counter filling out the file request form again. He would not give up.

"Bosch," one of the other detectives called out. "Miami on two."

Bosch hadn't even heard the phone ring in the squad room.

"I'll take it," Rider said. "Your head's somewhere else."

She picked up the phone and once more Bosch opened the Gesto file.

2

Bosch and Rider were ten minutes late because of the backup of people waiting for elevators. He hated coming to the Criminal Courts Building because of the elevators. The wait and the jostling for position just to get on one of them put a layer of anxiety on him that he could live without.

In reception in the DA's office on the sixteenth floor they were told to wait for an escort back to O'Shea's office. After a couple minutes a man stepped through the doorway and pointed to the briefcase Bosch was holding.

"You got it?" he asked.

Bosch didn't recognize him. He was a dark-complected Latino in a gray suit.

"Olivas?"

"Yeah. You brought the file?"

"I brought the file."

"Then come on back, Hotshot."

Olivas headed back toward the door he had come through. Rider made a move to follow but Bosch put his hand on her arm. When Olivas looked back and saw they were not following him, he stopped.

"You coming or not?"

Bosch took a step toward him.

"Olivas, let's get something clear before we go anywhere. You call me 'Hotshot' again and I'm going to shove the file up your ass without taking it out of my briefcase."

Olivas raised his hands in surrender.

"Whatever you say."

He held the door and they followed him into the internal hallway. They went down a long corridor and took two rights before coming to O'Shea's office. It was a large space, particularly by district attorney's office standards. Most of the time prosecutors shared offices, two or four to a room, and held their meetings in strictly scheduled interview rooms at the end of each hallway.

But O'Shea's office was double-sized with room for a piano-crate desk and a separate seating area. Being the head of Special Prosecutions obviously had its perks. Being the heir apparent to the top job did as well.

O'Shea welcomed them from behind his desk, standing up to shake hands. He was about forty and handsome with jet-black hair. He was short, as Bosch already knew, even though he had never met him before. He had noticed while catching some of the TV coverage of the Waits prelim that most of the reporters who gathered around O'Shea in the hallway outside the court-room were taller than the man they pointed their microphones at. Personally, Bosch liked short prosecutors. They were always trying to make up for something and usually it was the defendant who ended up paying the price.

Everybody took seats, O'Shea behind his desk, Bosch and Rider in chairs facing him, and Olivas to the right side of the desk in a chair positioned in front of a stack of RICK O'SHEA ALL THE WAY posters leaning against the wall.

"Thank you for coming in, Detectives," O'Shea said. "Let's start by clearing the air a little bit. Freddy tells me you two got off to a rough start."

He was looking at Bosch as he spoke.

"I don't have any problem with Freddy," Bosch said. "I don't even know Freddy enough to call him Freddy."

"I should tell you that any reluctance on his part to fill you in on what we have here came directly from me because of the sensitive nature of what we are doing. So if you are angry, be angry with me."

"I'm not angry," Bosch said. "I'm happy. Ask my partner — this is me when I'm happy."

Rider nodded.

"He's happy," she said. "Definitely happy."

"Okay, then," O'Shea said. "Everybody's happy. So let's get down to business."

O'Shea reached over and put his hand above a thick accordion file placed on the right side of his desk. It was open and Bosch saw that it contained several individual files with blue tabs on them. Bosch was too far away to read them — especially without putting on the glasses he had recently begun carrying with him.

"Are you familiar with the Raynard Waits prosecution?" O'Shea asked.

Bosch and Rider nodded.

"It would have been kind of hard to miss," Bosch said.

O'Shea nodded and offered a slight smile.

"Yes, we have pushed it out in front of the cameras. The guy's a butcher. A very evil man. We've said from the start that we are going for the death penalty on it."

"From what I've heard and seen, he's a poster boy for it," Rider said encouragingly.

O'Shea nodded somberly.

"That's one reason why you are here. Before I explain what we have going, let me ask you to tell me about your investigation of the Marie Gesto case. Freddy said you've had the file out of Archives three times in the past year. Is there something active?"

Bosch cleared his throat after deciding to give first and then receive.

"You could say I've had the case for thirteen years. I caught it back in 'ninety-three, when she went missing."

"But nothing ever came of it?"

Bosch shook his head.

"We had no body. All we ever found was her car and that was not enough. We never made anybody for it."

"Not even a suspect?"

"We looked at a lot of people, one in particular. But we couldn't make the connections and so nobody rose to the level of active suspect. Then I retired in 'oh-two and it went into Archives. A couple years go by and things don't work out the way I thought they would in retirement and I come back on the job. That was last year."

Bosch didn't think it was necessary to tell O'Shea that he had copied the Gesto file and taken it with him, along with several other open cases, when he left his badge behind and walked out the door in 2002. Copying the files had been an infraction of department regs, and the fewer people who knew that the better.

"In the last year I pulled the Gesto file every time I had a little time to work it," he continued. "But there's no DNA, no latents. There's only legwork. I've talked to all the principals again — everybody I could find. There's still the one guy out there who I always felt could be the guy, but I never could make anything out of it. I talked to him twice this year, leaned pretty hard."

"And?"

"Nothing."

"Who is it?"

"His name's Anthony Garland. He comes from Hancock Park money. You ever heard of Thomas Rex Garland, the oilman?"

O'Shea nodded.

"Well, T. Rex, as he is known, is Anthony's father."

"What's Anthony's connection to Gesto?"

"'Connection' might be too strong a word. Marie Gesto's car was found in a single garage attached to a Hollywood apartment building. The apartment it corresponded to was empty. Our sense of things at the time was that it wasn't just coincidence that the car ended up in there. We thought whoever hid the car there knew the apartment was vacant and that he'd get a decent ride out of hiding it there."

"Okay. Anthony Garland knew about the garage or he knew Marie?"

"He knew about the garage. His former girlfriend had lived in the apartment. She had broken up with him and then moved back to Texas. So he knew the apartment and the garage were empty."

"That's pretty thin. That's all you had?"

"Pretty much. We thought it was thin, too, but then we pulled the ex-girlfriend's DMV mug and it turned out she and Marie looked a lot alike. We started to think that maybe Marie had been some sort of replacement victim. He couldn't get to his ex-girlfriend because she had left, so he got to Marie instead."

"Did you go to Texas?"

"Twice. We talked to the ex and she told us that the main reason she split with Anthony was because of his temper."

"Was he violent with her?"

"She said no. She said she left before it got to that point."

O'Shea leaned forward.

"So, did Anthony Garland know Marie?" he asked.

"We don't know. We are not sure he did. Until his father brought his lawyer into it and he stopped talking to us, he denied ever knowing her."

"When was this? — the lawyer, I mean."

"Back then, and now. I came at him again a couple times this year. I pressed him and he lawyered up again. Different lawyers this time. They were able to get a restraining order reissued against me. They convinced a judge to order me to stay away from Anthony unless he had a lawyer with him. My guess is that they convinced the judge with money. It's the way T. Rex Garland gets things done."

O'Shea leaned back, nodding thoughtfully.

"Does this Anthony Garland have any kind of criminal record before or after Gesto?"

"No, not a criminal record. He hasn't been a very productive member of society — he lives off his old man's handouts, as near as I can tell. He runs security for his father and his various enterprises. But there's never been anything criminal that I could find."

"Wouldn't it stand to reason that someone who had kidnapped and killed a young woman would have other criminal activity on his record? These things usually aren't aberrations, are they?"

"If you went with the percentages, yeah. But there are always exceptions to the rule. Plus, there's the old man's money. Money smooths a lot of things over, makes a lot of things go away."

O'Shea nodded again like he was learning about criminals and crime for the first time. It was a bad act.

"What was your next move going to be?" he asked.

Bosch shook his head.

"I didn't have one. I sent the file back to Archives and thought that was it. Then a couple weeks ago I went down and pulled it again. I don't know what I was going to do. Maybe talk to some of Garland's more recent friends, see if he ever mentioned Marie Gesto or anything about her. All I knew for sure was that I wasn't going to give up."

O'Shea cleared his throat and Bosch knew he would now get down to the reason they were there.

"Did the name Ray or Raynard Waits ever come up in all these years of investigating Gesto's disappearance?"

Bosch looked at him for a moment, his stomach twisting.

"No, it didn't. Should it have come up?"

O'Shea pulled one of the folders out of the accordion file and opened it on the desk. He lifted a document that looked like a letter off the top.

"As I said, we've made it public that we're going for the death penalty on Waits," he said. "After the prelim I think he realized the writing was on the wall. He's got an appeal on the probable cause for the traffic stop. But it will go nowhere and he and his lawyer know it. An insanity defense is a nonstarter as well. This guy's as calculating and organized as any killer I've ever prosecuted. So they responded last week with this. Before I show it to you I have to know that you understand that this is a letter from an attorney. It is a proffer. No matter what happens, whether we move forward with this or not, the information contained in this letter is off the record. If we choose to ignore this offer, no investigation can come of the information in this letter. Do you understand that?"

Rider nodded. Bosch didn't.

"Detective Bosch?" O'Shea prompted.

"Maybe I shouldn't see it, then," Bosch said. "Maybe I shouldn't be here."

"You were the one who wouldn't give Freddy the file. If the case means that much to you, then I think you should be here."

Bosch finally nodded.

"Okay," he said.

O'Shea slid the paper across the desk and Bosch and Rider leaned forward to read it together. Bosch first unfolded his glasses and put them on.

Sept. 12, 2006

Richard O'Shea, Assistant District
   Attorney
Los Angeles County District
   Attorney's Office
Office 16-11
210 West Temple Street
Los Angeles, CA 90012-3210

Re: *California v. Raynard Waits*

Dear Mr. O'Shea:

This letter is intended to open discussions regarding a disposition in the above-referenced case. All statements made herein and hereafter in connection with these discussions are made with the understanding that they are inadmissible under California Evidence Code §1153, California Penal Code §1192.4 and *People v. Tanner,* 45 Cal. App.3d 345, 350, 119 Cal. Rptr. 407 (1975).

I suggest to you that Mr. Waits would be willing, on terms and conditions outlined below, to share with you and investigators of your choice information regarding nine homicides, excluding the two in the above-referenced case, and to plead guilty to the charges in the above-referenced case, in exchange for the People's agreement not to seek the death penalty on the instant homicide charges or to file charges in regard to the homicides about which he would provide information.

Furthermore, in return for the cooperation and information Mr. Waits would provide, you must agree that any and all statements by Mr. Waits and any information derived therefrom will not be used against him in any criminal case; no information provided pursuant to this agreement may be divulged to any other state or federal law enforcement agencies unless and until those agencies, through their representatives, agree to be bound by the terms and conditions of this agreement; no statements made or other information provided by Mr. Waits during any "off-the-record" proffer or discussion may be used against him in the prosecution's case-in-chief; nor may you make derivative use of or pursue any investigative leads suggested by any statements made or information provided by the defendant.

In the event the above-referenced case goes to trial, if Mr. Waits offers testimony materially different from any statements made or other information provided during any proffers or discussion, then you may, of course, impeach him concerning such prior inconsistent statements or information.

I suggest that the families of eight young women and one male victim will attain some form of closure with the knowledge of what transpired in regard to their loved ones and, in eight of these instances, be able to conduct proper religious ceremonies and burials after Mr. Waits leads your investigators to the places where these victims now rest. Additionally, these families will find, perhaps, some comfort in knowing that Mr. Waits is serving a prison sentence of life without the possibility of parole.

Mr. Waits offers to provide information in regard to nine known and unknown homicides between 1992 and 2003. As an initial offer of credibility and good faith, he suggests that investigators re-

view the investigation into the death of
Daniel Fitzpatrick, 63, who was burned
to death in his Hollywood Boulevard
pawnshop on April 30, 1992. Investigative files will reveal that Mr. Fitzpatrick
was armed and standing behind the roll-
down security fence at the front of his
store when he was set afire by an as-
sailant using lighter fluid and a butane
lighter. The can of EasyLight lighter fluid
was left behind, standing upright in front
of the security fence. This information
was never made public.

Further, Mr. Waits suggests that police
investigative files in regard to the September 1993 disappearance of Marie
Gesto be reviewed as an additional
showing of his credibility and good faith.
The records will reveal that while the
whereabouts of Ms. Gesto were never
determined, her car was located by police in a garage at a Hollywood apartment complex known as the High Tower.
The car contained Ms. Gesto's clothing
and equestrian equipment plus a grocery bag containing a one-pound package of carrots. Ms. Gesto intended to
use the carrots to feed the horses she

groomed in exchange for riding time at the Sunset Ranch stables in Beachwood Canyon. Again, this information was never made public.

I would suggest that if an agreement of disposition could be achieved, such an agreement would fall within the exceptions to California's prohibition against plea bargaining serious felonies inasmuch as, absent Mr. Waits's cooperation, there are insufficient evidence and material witnesses to prove the People's case in regard to these nine homicides. Moreover, the People's forbearance regarding the death penalty is entirely discretionary and does not represent a substantial change in sentence. (California Penal Code §1192.7a.)

Please contact me at your earliest convenience if the foregoing is acceptable.

Sincerely,
MauriceSwann, PA
101 Broadway
Suite 2
Los Angeles, CA 90013

Bosch realized he had read almost the entire letter without taking a breath. He now gulped down some air but it did not displace the cold tightness that was forming in his chest.

"You're not going to agree to this, are you?" he asked.

O'Shea held his gaze for a moment before responding.

"As a matter of fact, I am negotiating with Swann right now. That was the initial proffer. I've improved the State's take substantially since that arrived."

"In what way?"

"He'll have to plead to all the cases. We'll get eleven murder convictions."

And you'll get more headlines in time for the election, Bosch thought but didn't say.

"But he still walks?" he asked.

"No, Detective, he doesn't walk. He never sees the light of day again. Have you ever been up to Pelican Bay, the place they send sex offenders? It only sounds like a nice place."

"But no death penalty. You're giving him that."

Olivas smirked as if Bosch didn't see the light.

"Yes, that is what we are giving," O'Shea said. "That's all we're giving. No death penalty and he goes away forever and a day."

Bosch shook his head, looked at Rider and then back at O'Shea. He said nothing because he knew it wasn't his decision to make.

"But before we agree to such a deal," O'Shea said, "we need to make damn sure he is good for those nine. Waits is no dummy. This could all be a trick to avoid the needle or it could be the real thing. I want to bring you two into this to work with Freddy in finding out which it is. I'll make the calls and you will be cut loose. That will be the assignment."

Neither Bosch nor Rider responded. O'Shea pressed on.

"It is obvious he knows things about the two bait cases cited in the letter. Freddy confirmed the Fitzpatrick thing. He was killed during the riots after the Rodney King verdict came in, burned to death behind the roll-down fence in his pawnshop. He was heavily armed at the time and what is not clear is how his killer got close enough to set him on fire. The can of EasyLight was found just like Waits said, standing upright in front of the security fence.

"The mention of the Gesto case we could not confirm because you've got the file, Detective Bosch. You've already confirmed the part about the garage. Did he get that right about the clothes and the carrots?"

Bosch reluctantly nodded.

"The car was public information," he said. "The media was all over it. But the bag of carrots was our ace in the hole. Nobody knew about that except me, my partner at the time and the evidence tech who opened the bag. We held it back because that's where we ended up thinking she crossed his path. The carrots came from a Mayfair Supermarket on Franklin at the bottom of Beachwood Canyon. Turned out it was her routine to stop there before going up to the stables. The day she disappeared she followed the routine. She came out with the carrots and probably her killer as a trailer. We found witnesses who put her in the store. Nothing else after that. Until we found her car."

O'Shea nodded. He pointed to the letter, which was still on the desk in front of Bosch and Rider.

"Then this is looking good."

"No, it's not," Bosch said. "Don't do this."

"Don't do what?"

"Don't make the deal."

"Why shouldn't we?"

"Because if he is the one who took Marie Gesto and killed her and he killed those eight other people, maybe even chopped them up like the two they caught him with, then he isn't someone who should be allowed to live, whether in a prison cell or not. They ought to strap him down, put the juice in him and send him on down the hole to where he belongs."

O'Shea nodded as if it were a valid consideration.

"What about all of those open cases?" he countered. "Look, I don't like the idea of this guy living out his life in a private room at Pelican Bay any more than you do. But we have a responsibility to clear those cases and provide answers to the families of those people. Also, you have to remember, we have announced that we are *seeking* the death penalty. That doesn't mean it's automatic. We have to go to trial and win and *then* we have to do it all over again to get the jury to recommend death. I'm sure you know that there are any number of things that could go wrong. It only takes one juror to hang a case. And it only takes one to stop the death penalty. It only takes one soft judge to ignore the jury's recommendation, anyway."

Bosch didn't respond. He knew how the system worked, how it could be manipulated and how nothing was a sure thing. Still, it bothered him. He also knew that a life sentence didn't always mean a life sentence. Every year people like Charlie Manson and Sirhan Sirhan got their shot. Nothing lasts forever, not even a life sentence.

"Plus, there is the cost factor," O'Shea continued. "Waits doesn't have money but Maury Swann took the case for publicity value. If we take this to trial he will be ready for battle. Maury's a damn good lawyer. We can expect experts to cancel out our experts, scientific analysis to cancel out our analysis — the trial will last months and cost the county a fortune. I know you don't want to hear that money is a consideration here but that is the reality. I have the budget management office already on my back about this one. This proffer could be the safest and best way to make sure this man harms no one else in the future."

"The best way?" Bosch asked. "Not the right way, if you ask me."

O'Shea picked up a pen and drummed it lightly on his desk before responding.

"Detective Bosch, why did you sign out the Gesto file so many times?"

Bosch felt Rider turn and look at him. She had asked him the same thing on more than one occasion.

"I told you," he said. "I pulled it because it had been my case. It bothered me that we never made anybody for it."

"In other words, it has haunted you."

Bosch nodded hesitantly.

"Did she have family?"

Bosch nodded again.

"She had parents up in Bakersfield. They had a lot of dreams for her."

"Think about them. And think about the families of the others. We can't tell them that Waits was the one unless we know for sure. My guess is that they will want to know and that they are willing to trade that knowledge for his life. It's better that he plead guilty to all of them than that we get him for only two."

Bosch said nothing. He had registered his objection. He now knew it was time to go to work. Rider was on the same vibe.

"What is the time frame on this?" she asked.

"I want to move quickly," O'Shea said. "If this is legit, I want to clean it up and get it done."

"Gotta get it in before the election, right?" Bosch asked.

He then immediately regretted it. O'Shea's lips formed a tight line. Blood seemed to collect beneath the skin around his eyes.

"Detective," he said. "I will give you that. I'm running for election and clearing eleven murders with convictions would be helpful to my cause. But do not suggest the election is my only motivation here. Every night that those parents who carried dreams for their daughter go to bed not knowing where she is or what happened to her is a night of terrible pain as far as I am concerned. Even after thirteen years. So I want to move quickly and assuredly and you can keep your speculations about anything else to yourself."

"Fine," Bosch said. "When do we talk to this guy?"

O'Shea looked at Olivas and then back at Bosch.

"Well, I think we should have an exchange of files first. You should come up to speed on Waits and I'd like Freddy to familiarize himself with the Gesto file. Once that is done we'll set something up with Maury Swann. What about tomorrow?"

"Tomorrow's fine," Bosch said. "Swann will be there during the interview?"

O'Shea nodded.

"Maury's riding this one all the way. He'll milk every angle, probably end up with a book and a movie deal before this thing's over. Maybe even a guest anchor slot on Court TV."

"Yeah, well," Bosch said, "at least then he'd be out of the courtroom."

"Never thought of it that way," O'Shea said. "Did you bring the Gesto records?"

Bosch opened his briefcase on his lap and took out the investigation file, which was contained in a three-inch-thick binder generally known as a murder book. He handed it to O'Shea, who turned and gave it to Olivas.

"And I will give you this in return," O'Shea said.

He slid the file back into the accordion folder and handed it all across the desk.

"Happy reading," he said. "Are you sure about tomorrow?"

Bosch looked at Rider to see if she had an objection. They had another day before they needed to walk the Matarese filing to the DA. But the work was mostly finished and he knew Rider could handle the rest. When Rider said nothing Bosch looked back at O'Shea.

"We'll be ready," he said.

"Then I will call Maury and set it up."

"Where is Waits?"

"Right here in the building," O'Shea said. "We've got him in high-power on keep-away status."

"Good," Rider said.

"What about the other seven?" Bosch asked.

"What about them?"

"Are there no files?"

"The proffer, as well as Maury Swann, indicates that these were women who were never found and possibly never reported missing in the first place," O'Shea said. "Waits is willing to lead us to them but there is no prep work we can do for them."

Bosch nodded.

"Any other questions?" O'Shea asked, signaling that the meeting was over.

"We'll let you know," Bosch said.

"I know I am repeating myself but I feel I need to," O'Shea said. "This investigation is all off the record. That file is a proffer that is part of a plea negotiation. Nothing in that file or anything that he tells you can ever be used to make a case against him. If this falls apart, then you will not be able to use the information to pursue him. Is that clearly understood?"

Bosch didn't answer.

"It's clear," Rider said.

"There is one exception that I have negotiated. If he lies, if you catch him at any time in a lie or if any piece of information he gives you during this process proves to be knowingly false, all bets are off and we can go after him for all of it. He has been made quite aware of this, too."

Bosch nodded. He stood up. Rider did, too.

"Do you need me to call someone to free you two up?" O'Shea asked. "I can flex a muscle if needed."

Rider shook her head.

"I don't think so," she said. "Harry was already working the Gesto case. The seven women might be unknown victims but there's got to be a file in Archives on the man in the pawnshop. It all cuts Open-Unsolved in. We can handle our supervisor."

"Okay, then. As soon as I have the interview set up I will call. Meantime, all of my numbers are in the file. Freddy's, too."

Bosch nodded to O'Shea and threw a glance at Olivas before turning to the door.

"Detectives?" O'Shea said.

Bosch and Rider turned back to him. He was standing now. He wanted to shake their hands.

"I am hoping you are on my side on this," O'Shea said.

Bosch shook his hand, unsure whether O'Shea was talking about the case or the election.

He said, "If Waits can help me bring Marie Gesto home to her parents, then I'm on your side."

It wasn't a completely accurate summation of his feelings, but it got him out of the office.

3

Back at Open-Unsolved they sat in their supervisor's office and brought him up to date on the day's developments. Abel Pratt was four weeks away from retirement after twenty-five years on the job. He was attentive to them but not overly so. On the side of his desk was a stack of Fodor's guidebooks for Caribbean islands. His plan was to pull the pin, leave the city and find an island to live on with his family. It was a common retirement dream among law enforcement officers — to pull back from all the darkness witnessed for so long on the job. The reality, however, was that after about six months on the beach the island got pretty boring.

A detective three from RHD named David Lambkin was set to be the squad's top after Pratt split. He was a nationally recognized sex crimes expert chosen for the job because so many of the cold cases they were working in the unit were sexually motivated. Bosch was looking forward to working with him and would have liked to be briefing him instead of Pratt but the timing was off.

They went with who they had, and one of the positive things about Pratt was that he was going to give them free rein until he was out the door. He just didn't want any waves, no blowback in his face. He wanted a quiet, uneventful last month on the job.

Like most cops with twenty-five years in the department, Pratt was a throwback. He was old school. He preferred working on a typewriter over a computer. Rolled halfway up in the IBM Selectric next to his desk was a letter he had been working on when Bosch and Rider stepped in. Bosch had grabbed a quick glance at it while he was sitting down and saw it was a letter to a casino in the Bahamas. Pratt was trying to line up a security gig in paradise, and that about said it all when it came to where his mind was at these days.

After hearing their briefing, Pratt gave his approval for them to work with O'Shea and only became animated when he issued a warning about Raynard Waits's attorney, Maury Swann.

"Let me tell you about Maury," Pratt said. "Whatever you do when you meet him do not shake his hand."

"Why not?" Rider asked.

"I had a case with him once. This is way back. It was a gangbanger on a one-eighty-seven. Every day when we started court, Maury made a big deal of shaking my hand and then the prosecutor's. He probably would have shaken the judge's hand, too, if he'd gotten the chance."

"So?"

"So after his guy was convicted he tried to get a reduced sentence by snitching out the others involved in the murder. One of the things he told me during the debriefing was that he thought I was dirty. He said that during the trial Maury had told him he could buy all of us. Me, the prosecutor, everybody. So the banger had his homegirl get him the cash and Maury explained to him that every

time he was shaking our hands he was paying us off. You know, passing the cash palm
to palm. He always did those two-handed
shakes, too. He was really selling it to his
guy while all along he was keeping the
cash."

"Holy shit!" Rider exclaimed. "Didn't you
guys work up a case on him?"

Pratt dismissed the idea with a wave.

"It was after the fact and besides it was a
bullshit he-said-he-said case. It wouldn't
have gone anywhere — not with Maury being a member of the bar in good standing
and all. But ever since then I heard that
Maury likes shaking hands a lot. So when
you get in that room with him and Waits,
don't shake his hand."

They left Pratt's office, smiling at the story,
and returned to their own workstation. The
division of labor had been worked out on
their walk back from the courthouse. Bosch
would take Waits, and Rider would take
Fitzpatrick. They would know the files inside
and out by the time they sat across the
table from Waits in the interview room the
following day.

Since Rider had less to read in the Fitzpatrick case she also would finish the filing

on Matarese. This meant Bosch was cleared to study full-time the world of Raynard Waits. After pulling out the Fitzpatrick file for Rider, he chose to take the accordion folder O'Shea had given them down to the cafeteria. He knew the lunch crowd would be thinning out and he would be able to spread the files out and work without the distractions of the constantly ringing phones and chatter of the Open-Unsolved squad room. He had to use a napkin to clean a table in the corner but then quickly settled into his review of the materials.

There were three files on Waits. They included the LAPD murder book compiled by Olivas and Ted Colbert, his partner in the Northeast Division Homicide squad, a file on a prior arrest and the prosecution file compiled by O'Shea.

Bosch decided to read the murder book first. He quickly became acquainted with Raynard Waits and the details of his arrest. The suspect was thirty-four years old and lived in a ground-floor apartment on Sweetzer Avenue in West Hollywood. He wasn't a large man, standing five foot six and weighing 142 pounds. He was the owner-operator of a one-man business — a residential window-cleaning company called Clear-View Residential Glass Cleaners. According to the police reports, he came to the attention of two patrol officers, a boot named Arnolfo Gonzalez and his training officer, Ted Fennel, at 1:50 a.m. on the night of May 11. The officers were assigned to a Crime Response Team which was watching a hillside neighborhood in Echo Park because of a recent rash of home burglaries that had been occurring on the nights of Dodgers home games. Though in uniform, Gonzalez and Fennel were in an unmarked cruiser near the intersection of Stadium Way and Chavez Ravine Place. Bosch knew the location. It was at the remote edge of the Dodger Stadium complex and above the Echo Park neighborhood that the CRT teams were watching. He also knew that they were following a standard CRT strategy: to stay out on the perimeter of the target neighborhood and follow in any vehicle or persons who looked suspicious or out of place.

According to the report filed by Gonzalez and Fennel, they grew suspicious as to why a van marked on the sides with signs that said ClearView Residential Glass Cleaners was out and about at two in the morning.

They followed at a distance and Gonzalez used night-vision binoculars to get the van's plate number. He then entered it into the car's mobile digital terminal — the officers choosing to use the onboard computer rather than the radio in case the burglar working the neighborhood was equipped with a police radio scanner. The computer kicked back a flag. The plate was registered to a Ford Mustang with an address out in Claremont. Believing that the license plate on the van was stolen and that they now had probable cause to stop it, Fennel accelerated, put on the UC car's grille lights and stopped the van on Figueroa Terrace near the intersection of Beaudry Avenue.

"The driver of the vehicle appeared agitated and leaned out of the van's window to talk to Officer Gonzalez, an effort to block the officer from conducting a visual survey of the interior of the vehicle," the arrest summary read. "Officer Fennel approached the vehicle's passenger side and beamed his flashlight into the van. Without entering the vehicle, Officer Fennel was able to notice what appeared to be several black plastic trash bags on the floorboard in front of the front passenger seat of the vehicle. A substance appearing to be blood could be seen leaking from the cinched mouth of one of the bags and onto the floor of the van."

According to the report, "The driver was asked if that was blood leaking from one of the bags and he stated that he had cut himself earlier in the day when a large plate glass window he was cleaning shattered. He stated that he had used several glass-cleaning rags to clean up the blood. When asked to show where he was cut the driver smiled and then suddenly made a move to restart the vehicle's ignition. Officer Gonzalez reached through the window to restrain him. After a short struggle the driver was removed from the vehicle and placed on the ground and handcuffed. He was then moved to the backseat of the unmarked car. Officer Fennel opened the vehicle and inspected the bags. At this time Officer Fennel found the first bag he opened contained human body parts. Investigative units were immediately summoned to the scene."

The driver's license of the man taken out of the van identified him as Raynard Waits. He was booked into the holding tank at Northeast Division while an investigation of his van and the plastic trash bags carried on through the night on Figueroa Terrace. Only after Detectives Olivas and Colbert, the on-call team that night, took over the investigation and retraced some of the steps taken by Gonzalez and Fennel was it learned that the rookie officer had typed the wrong license plate number into the MDT, typing an *F* for an *E* and getting the plate registration for the Mustang out in Claremont.

In law enforcement terms it was a "good faith error," meaning the probable cause to have stopped the van should still hold because the officers had been acting in good faith when an honest mistake was committed. Bosch assumed that this was the point of the appeal Rick O'Shea had mentioned earlier.

Bosch put aside the murder investigation file and opened the prosecution file. He quickly looked through the documents until he found a copy of the appeal. He scanned it quickly and found what he had expected. Waits was claiming that typing in the wrong plate number was a custom and practice within the LAPD and often employed when officers on specialty squads wanted to pull over and search a vehicle without legitimate probable cause to do so. Though a Superior

Court judge found that Gonzalez and Fennel had acted on good faith and upheld the legality of the search, Waits was appealing that decision to the District Court of Appeal.

Bosch went back to the investigative file. No matter the question of the legality of the traffic stop, the investigation of Raynard Waits had moved rapidly. The morning after the arrest Olivas and Colbert obtained a search warrant for the apartment on Sweetzer where Waits lived alone. A four-hour search and Forensics examination of the apartment produced several samples of human hair and blood taken from the bathroom's sink and tub traps, as well as a hidden space beneath the floor containing several pieces of women's jewelry and multiple Polaroid photos of nude young women who appeared to be sleeping, unconscious or dead. In a utility room was an upright freezer which was empty, except for the two samples of pubic hair found by an SID tech.

Meantime, the three plastic bags found in the van had been transported to the coroner's office and opened. They were found to contain the body parts of two young women, each of whom had been strangled and dismembered after death in the same way. Of note was the fact that the parts from one of the bodies showed indications of having been thawed after being frozen.

Though no cutting tools were found in Waits's apartment or van, it was clear from the evidence gathered that while Officers Gonzalez and Fennel were looking for a burglar, they had stumbled onto what appeared to be a serial killer at work. The belief was that Waits had already discarded or hidden his tools and was in the process of disposing of the bodies of the two victims when he drew the attention of the CRT officers. The indications were that there might be other victims as well. The reports in the file detailed the efforts made in the next several weeks to identify the two bodies as well as the other women in the Polaroids found in the apartment. Waits of course offered no help in this regard, engaging the services of Maury Swann on the morning of his capture and choosing to remain silent as the law enforcement processes continued and Swann mounted an attack on the probable cause of the traffic stop.

Only one of the two known victims was identified. Fingerprints taken from one of the dismembered women drew a hit on the

FBI's latent database. She was identified as a seventeen-year-old runaway from Davenport, Iowa. Lindsey Mathers had left home two months before being found in Waits's van and had not been heard from during that time by her parents. With photos supplied by her mother, detectives were able to piece together her trail in Los Angeles. She was recognized by youth counselors at several Hollywood shelters. She had been using a variety of names to avoid being identified and possibly sent home. There were indications she was involved in drug use and street prostitution. Needle marks found on her body during the autopsy were believed to have been the result of a long and ongoing practice of injecting drugs. A blood screen taken during the autopsy found heroin and PCP in her bloodstream.

The shelter counselors who helped identify Lindsey Mathers were also shown the Polaroid photographs found in Waits's apartment and were able to provide a variety of different names for at least three of the women. Their stories were similar to Mathers's journey. They were runaways possibly engaged in prostitution as a means of earning money for drugs.

It was clear to Bosch from the gathered evidence and information that Waits was a predator who targeted young women who would not be immediately missed, fringe dwellers who were unaccounted for by society in the first place and therefore not missed when they disappeared.

The Polaroids from the hidden space in Waits's apartment were in the file, encased in plastic sheets, four to a page. There were eight pages with multiple shots of each woman. An accompanying analysis report stated that the photo collection contained shots of nine different women — the two women whose remains were found in Waits's van and seven unknowns. Bosch knew that the unknowns were likely to be the seven women Waits was offering to tell authorities about in addition to Marie Gesto and the pawnshop man, but he studied the photos anyway for the face of Marie Gesto.

She wasn't there. The faces in the photos belonged to women who had not caused the same sort of stir that Marie Gesto had. Bosch sat back and took off his reading glasses to rest his eyes for a few moments. He remembered one of his early teachers in Homicide. Detective Ray Vaughn had a special sympathy for the ones he called "murder's nobodies," the victims who didn't count. He taught Bosch early on that in society all victims are not created equal, but to the true detective they must be.

"Every one of them was somebody's daughter," Ray Vaughn had told him. "Every one of them counted."

Bosch rubbed his eyes. He thought about Waits's offer to clear up nine murders, including Marie Gesto's and Daniel Fitzpatrick's and those of seven women who never caused a blip on anybody's radar. Something seemed not right about that. Fitzpatrick was an anomaly because he was a male and the killing didn't appear to be sexually motivated. He had always assumed that Marie Gesto was a sex killing. But she was not a throwaway victim. She had hit the radar big time. Had Waits learned from her? Had he honed his craft after her killing to make sure he never drew such police and media heat again? Bosch thought that maybe the heat he had applied on the Gesto case was what caused Waits to change, to become a more skilled and cunning killer. If that was so, then he would have to deal with that guilt at a later time.

For now he had to focus on what was in front of him.

He put his glasses on again and went back to the files. The evidence against Waits was solid. Nothing like being caught in possession of body parts. A defense attorney's nightmare; a prosecutor's dream. The case sailed through a preliminary hearing in four days, and then the DA's office upped the ante with O'Shea announcing he would go for the death penalty.

Bosch had a legal pad to the side of the open file so that he could write down questions for O'Shea, Waits or others. It was blank when he came to the end of his review of the investigation and prosecution files. He now wrote the only questions that came to mind.

If Waits killed Gesto, why was there no photo of her in his apartment?

Waits lived in West Hollywood. What was he doing in Echo Park?

The first question could be easily explained. Bosch knew killers evolved. Waits could have learned from the Gesto killing that he needed reminders of his work. The photos could have started after Gesto.

The second question was more troubling to him. There was no report in the file that dealt with this question. It was thought simply that Waits had been on his way to get rid of the bodies, possibly to bury them in the parklands that surrounded Dodger Stadium. No further investigation of this was contemplated or called for. But to Bosch it was something to consider. Echo Park would have been at least a half hour away by car from Waits's apartment in West Hollywood. That was a long time to be driving with body parts in bags. Additionally, Griffith Park, which was larger and had more pockets of isolated and difficult terrain than the area around the stadium, was far closer to the West Hollywood apartment and would have been the better choice for a body dump.

To Bosch it meant that Waits had a specific destination in mind in Echo Park. This had been missed or dismissed as unimportant in the original investigation.

He next wrote two words.

psych profile?

No psychological study of the defendant had been conducted and Bosch was mildly surprised by this. Perhaps, he thought, it had been a strategic decision by the prosecution. O'Shea might have chosen not to take this route because he didn't know exactly where it would lead. He wanted to try Waits on the facts and send him to the death chamber. He didn't want to be responsible for opening a door to a possible insanity defense.

Still, Bosch thought, a psychological study could have been useful for understanding the defendant and his crimes. It should have been done. Whether the subject was cooperative or not, a profile could have been drawn from the crimes themselves as well as from what was known about Waits through his history, appearance, the findings in his apartment and interviews conducted with those he knew and worked for. Such a profile might have also been useful to O'Shea as an edge against a move by the defense to claim insanity.

Now it was too late. The department had a small psych staff and there would be no way for Bosch to get anything done before the interview with Waits the next day. And

farming a request out to the FBI would result in a two-month wait at best.

Bosch suddenly had an idea about that
but decided to grind it over for a little while
before acting on anything. He put the questions aside for the moment and got up to re-
fill his coffee mug. He was using a real coffee mug he had brought down from the
Open-Unsolved Unit because he preferred
it over Styrofoam. His mug had come from
a famous writer and television producer
named Stephen Cannell who had spent
time with the OU Unit while researching a
project. Printed on the side of the mug was
Cannell's favorite piece of writing advice. It
said *What's the bad guy up to?* Bosch liked
it because he thought it was a good question for a real detective to always be considering as well.

He came back to the cafeteria table and
looked at the last file. It was thin and the
oldest of the three. He put aside thoughts of
Echo Park and psychological profiles, sat
down and opened the file. It involved the reports and investigation related to Waits's arrest in February 1993 for prowling. It was
the only blip on the radar involving Waits

until his arrest in the van with the body parts thirteen years later.

The reports said Waits was arrested in the backyard of a home in the Fairfax District after a neighbor with insomnia happened to look out her window while walking through her dark house. She saw a man looking in the rear windows of the house next door. The woman woke her sleeping husband and he promptly snuck out of the house, jumped the man and held him until police arrived. The man was found in possession of a screwdriver and charged with prowling. He carried no identification and gave the name Robert Saxon to the arresting officers. He said he was only seventeen. But his ruse crumbled and he was identified as Raynard Waits, twenty-one, a short time later when a thumbprint taken during the booking process scored a match in DMV records to a driver's license issued nine months earlier to Raynard Waits. That license carried the same day and month of birth with one change. It said Raynard Waits was four years older than he had claimed to be as Robert Saxon.

Once identified, Waits admitted to police during questioning that he had been looking for a home to burglarize. However, it was noted in the report that the window he had been seen looking through corresponded to the bedroom of a fifteen-year-old girl who lived in the house. Still, Waits avoided any sort of sex offender jacket in a plea agreement negotiated by his attorney, Mickey Haller. He was sentenced to eighteen months' probation, which, according to the reports, he completed with high marks and no violations.

Bosch realized that the incident was an early warning of what was to come. But the system was too overburdened and inefficient to recognize the danger that was in Waits. He worked the dates and realized that while Waits was successfully completing probation in the eyes of the justice system, he was also graduating from prowler to murderer. Marie Gesto was taken before he cleared his tail.

"Howzit going?"

Bosch looked up and quickly took off his glasses so he could focus on distance. Rider had come down to get coffee. She was holding an empty *What's the bad guy up to?* mug. The writer had given one to everybody in the squad.

"Almost done," he said. "How about you?"

"I'm done with what O'Shea gave us. I called Evidence Archives for the box on Fitzpatrick."

"What's in there?"

"I don't know for sure but the inventory in the book just lists the contents as pawn records. That's why I'm having it pulled. And while I'm waiting I'm going to finish up on Matarese and have it ready to walk over tomorrow. Depending on when we get to talk to Waits, I'll walk Matarese in either first thing or last thing. Did you eat lunch?"

"Forgot. What did you see in the Fitzpatrick file?"

She pulled out the chair opposite Bosch and sat down.

"The case was handled by the short-lived Riot Crimes Task Force, remember them?"

Bosch nodded.

"They had a clearance rate of like ten percent," she said. "Basically, anybody who did anything during those three days got away with it unless they were caught on camera, like that kid who bricked the truck driver while a news chopper was right on top of him."

Bosch remembered that there were more

than fifty deaths during the three days of riots in 1992 and very few were ever solved
or explained. It had been a free-for-all, a
lawless time in the city. He remembered
walking down the middle of Hollywood
Boulevard and seeing flaming buildings on
both sides of the street. One of those buildings probably contained Fitzpatrick's pawnshop.

"It was an impossible task," he said.

"I know," Rider said. "Putting together
cases out of that chaos. I can tell from the
file on Fitzpatrick that they didn't spend a
lot of time with it. They worked the crime
scene with a SWAT line guarding the place.
The whole thing was pretty quickly written
off as random violence, even when there
was some stuff they should have routinely
looked at."

"Like what?"

"Well, for starters, Fitzpatrick looks like he
was a straight arrow. He took thumbprints
off of everybody who brought in stuff to
pawn."

"His edge against taking in stolen property."

"Exactly. And what pawnbroker do you
know of back then who voluntarily did that?

He also kept an eighty-six list — customers who were persona non grata for various reasons and customers who complained or threatened him. Apparently it isn't uncommon for people to come back in to buy back the property they've pawned, only to find they are past the holding period and it's been sold. They get mad, sometimes they threaten the pawnbroker, and so on. Most of this came from a guy who worked for him in the store. He wasn't there the night of the fire."

"So, was the eighty-six list checked out?"

"It looks like they were going down the list when something happened. They stopped and wrote the case off as random violence associated with the riot. Fitzpatrick was set on fire with lighter fluid. Half the stores on the Boulevard that were burned down were started the same way. So they stopped spinning their wheels on it and went on to the next one. There were two guys on it. One's retired and the other works Pacific. He's a patrol sergeant now, p.m. watch. I left a message."

Bosch knew he didn't have to ask if Raynard Waits was a name on the 86 list. That would have been the first thing Rider said.

"You might have an easier time getting to the retired guy," Bosch suggested. "Retired guys always want to talk."

Rider nodded.

"That's an idea," she said.

"The other thing is Waits used an alias when he got popped in 'ninety-three on a prowling charge. Robert Saxon. I know you checked for Waits on the eighty-six list. You might want to check Saxon as well."

"Got it."

"Look, I know you have all of that going, but do you have time to do an AutoTrack run on Waits today?"

The division of labor in their partnership had her doing most of the computer work. AutoTrack was a computer database that could provide an individual's address history through utility and cable hookups, DMV records and other sources. It was tremendously useful in tracing people back through time.

"I think I can swing it."

"I just want to see where he's lived. I can't figure out why he was in Echo Park and it looks like nobody else has given it much thought."

"To dump the bags, I thought."

"Right, yeah, we know that. But why Echo Park? He lived closer to Griffith Park and that would've probably been a better place for burying or dumping bodies. I don't know, something is missing or doesn't fit right. I think he was going somewhere he knew."

"He could have wanted the distance. You know, he thought the farther away from him the better."

Bosch nodded but he wasn't convinced.

"I think I'm going to ride over there."

"And what? You think you'll find where he was going to bury those bags? You turning psychic on me now, Harry?"

"Not yet. I just want to see if I can get a feel for Waits before we actually talk to the guy."

Saying the name made Bosch grimace and shake his head.

"What?" Rider asked.

"You know what we're doing here? We're helping to keep this guy alive. A guy who cuts women up and keeps them in the freezer until he runs out of room and has to take them out like trash. That's our job, find the way to let him live."

Rider frowned.

"I know how you feel, Harry, but I have to

tell you, I kind of come down on O'Shea's side on this. I think it's better that all the families know and we clear all the cases. It's like with my sister. We wanted to know."

When Rider was a teenager her older sister was murdered in a drive-by shooting. The case was cleared and three bangers went away for it. It was the main reason she became a cop.

"It's probably like you with your mother, too," she added.

Bosch looked up at her. His mother had been murdered when he was a boy. More than three decades later he solved the crime himself because he wanted to know.

"You're right," he said. "But it just doesn't sit right with me at the moment, that's all."

"Why don't you take that ride and clear your head a little bit. I'll call you if anything comes up on the AutoTrack."

"I guess I will."

He started closing the files and putting them away.

4

In the shadows of downtown's spires and under the glow of lights from Dodger Stadium, Echo Park was one of L.A.'s oldest and ever-changing neighborhoods. Over the decades it had been the destination of the city's immigrant underclass — the Italians coming first and then the Mexicans, the Chinese, the Cubans, Ukrainians and all of the others. By day a walk down the main drag of Sunset Boulevard might require skills in five or more languages to read all of the storefronts. By night it was the only place in the city where the air could be split by the sound of gang gunfire, the cheers for a home-run ball, and the baying of the hill-side coyotes — all in the same hour.

These days Echo Park was also a favored destination of another class of newcomer — the young and hip. The cool. Artists, musicians and writers were moving in. Cafés and vintage clothing shops were squeezing in next to the bodegas and *mariscos* stands. A wave of gentrification was washing across the flats and up the hillsides below the baseball stadium. It meant the character of the place was changing. It meant real-estate prices were going up, pushing out the working class and the gangs.

Bosch had lived for a short time in Echo Park when he was a boy. And many years back, there had been a police bar on Sunset called the Short Stop. But cops were no longer welcome there. The place offered valet parking and catered to the Hollywood crowd — two things sure to keep the off-duty officer away. For Bosch the neighborhood of Echo Park had dropped off the radar. To him it wasn't a destination. It was a drive-through neighborhood, a shortcut on his way to the Medical Examiner's Office for work or to a Dodgers game for fun.

From downtown he took a quick jog on

the 101 Freeway north to Echo Park Road and then took that north again toward the hillside neighborhood where Raynard Waits had been arrested. As he passed Echo Lake he saw the statue known as the *Lady of the Lake* watching over the water lilies, her hands palms up like the victim of a holdup. As a boy he had lived for almost a year with his mother in the Sir Palmer Apartments across from the lake, but it had been a bad time for her and him and the memory was all but erased. He vaguely remembered that statue but almost nothing else.

At Sunset he turned right and took it down to Beaudry. From there he drove up the hillside to Figueroa Terrace. He pulled to the curb near the intersection where Waits had been pulled over. A few old bungalow homes built in the thirties and forties were still there, but for the most part the houses were postwar concrete-block construction. They were modest with gated yards and barred windows. The cars in the driveways were not new or flashy. It was a working-class neighborhood that Bosch knew would be largely Latino and Asian now. From the back of the homes on the west side there would be nice views of the downtown towers with the DWP Building front and center. The homes on the east side would have backyards that stretched up into the rugged terrain of the hills. And at the top of those hills would be the far parking lots of the baseball stadium complex.

He thought about Waits's window-washing van and wondered again why he had been on this street in this neighborhood. It wasn't the kind of neighborhood where he would have customers. It wasn't the kind of street where a commercial van would be expected at two in the morning, anyway. The two CRT officers had been correct in taking notice.

Bosch pulled over and put the car in park. He stepped out and looked around and then leaned against the car as he contemplated the questions. He still didn't get it. Why had Waits chosen this place? After a few moments he opened his cell phone and called his partner.

"You run that AutoTrack yet?" he asked.

"Just did. Where are you?"

"Echo Park. Anything come up near here?"

"Uh-uh, I was just looking. The farthest east it puts him is the Montecito Apartments on Franklin."

Bosch knew that the Montecito wasn't near Echo Park but it was not far from the High Tower Apartments, where Marie Gesto's car had been found.

"When was he at the Montecito?" he asked.

"After Gesto. He moved in, let's see, in 'ninety-nine, and out the next year. A one-year stay."

"Anything else worth mentioning?"

"No, Harry. Just the usual. The guy moved house every one or two years. Didn't like staying put, I guess."

"Okay, Kiz. Thanks."

"You coming back to the office?"

"In a little while."

He closed the phone and got back in the car. He took Figueroa Lane to Chavez Ravine Place and hit another stop sign. At one time the whole area up here was known only as Chavez Ravine. But that was before the city moved all the people out and bull-dozed the bungalows and shacks they had called home. A grand housing project was supposed to rise in the ravine, with play-grounds and schools and shopping plazas that would invite back those who had been displaced. But once they cleared it all out the housing project was scratched from the city's plans and it was a baseball stadium that went in instead. To Bosch it seemed that as far back as he could remember in L.A., the fix was always in.

Bosch had been listening lately to the Ry Cooder CD called *Chávez Ravine.* It wasn't jazz but that was okay. It was its own kind of jazz. He liked the song "It's Just Work for Me," a dirge about a bulldozer driver who came to the ravine to knock down the poor people's shacks and refused to feel guilty about it.

You got to go where they send you
When you're a dozer-drivin' man . . .

He took a left on Chavez Ravine and in a few moments he came to Stadium Way and the spot where Waits had first drawn the attention of the CRT patrol as he passed on his way down into Echo Park.

At the stop sign he surveyed the intersection. Stadium Way was the feeder line to the stadium's huge parking lots. For Waits to have come into the neighborhood this way, as the arrest report stated, he would have to have come in from downtown, the stadium, or the Pasadena Freeway. This would not have been the way in from his home in West Hollywood. Bosch puzzled with this for a few moments but determined there was not enough information to draw any conclusion. Waits could have driven through Echo Park, making sure he was not followed, and then drawn the CRT tail after turning around to go back.

He realized that there was much about Waits he didn't know and it bothered him that he would come face-to-face with the killer the next day. Bosch felt unprepared. He once again considered the idea he'd had earlier, but this time he didn't hesitate. He opened his phone and called the FBI field office in Westwood.

"I'm looking for an agent named Rachel Walling," he told the operator. "I'm not sure what squad she's with."

"Hold one."

By "one" she had apparently meant a minute. As he waited he was honked at by a car that had come up from behind. Bosch moved through the intersection, made a U-turn and then pulled off the road into the shade of a eucalyptus tree. Finally near the two-minute mark his call was transferred and picked up and a male voice said, "Tactical."

"Agent Walling, please."

"Hold one."

"Right," Bosch said after he heard the click.

But this time the transfer was made quickly and Bosch heard Rachel Walling's voice for the first time in a year. He hesitated and she almost hung up on him.

"Rachel, it's Harry Bosch."

Now she hesitated before responding.

"Harry . . ."

"So what's 'Tactical' mean?"

"It's just the squad designation."

He understood. She didn't answer because it was eyes-only stuff and the line was probably on tape somewhere.

"Why are you calling, Harry?"

"Because I need a favor. I could use your help, actually."

"With what? I'm sort of in the middle of something here."

"Then don't worry about it. I thought maybe you'd . . . well, never mind, Rachel. It's no big deal. I can handle it."

"You sure?"

"Yeah, I'm sure. I'll let you get back to Tactical, whatever that is. You take care."

He closed the phone and tried not to let her voice and the memory it conjured distract him from the task at hand. He looked back across the intersection and realized he was probably in the same position the CRT car had been in when Gonzalez and Fennel spotted Waits's van. The eucalyptus tree and night shadows had provided them cover.

Bosch was hungry now, having missed lunch. He decided he would cross over the freeway into Chinatown and grab takeout to bring back to the squad room. He pulled back onto the street and was debating whether to call the office to see if anybody wanted anything from Chinese Friends when his cell rang. He checked the screen but saw the ID was blocked. He answered anyway.

"It's me."

"Rachel."

"I wanted to switch to my cell."

There was a pause. Bosch knew he had been right about the phones at Tactical.

"How have you been, Harry?"

"I've been fine."

"So you did like you said you were going to do. You went back to the cops. I read about you last year with that case up in the Valley."

"Yeah, my first case back. Everything's been below the radar since then. Until this thing I've got working now."

"And that's why you called me?"

Bosch noted the tone in her voice. It had been more than eighteen months since they had spoken. And that was at the end of an intense week when they had crossed paths on a case, Bosch working on a private ticket before coming back to the department and Walling working on resuscitating her career with the bureau. The case led Bosch back to the blue fold and Walling to the L.A. field office. Whether Tactical, whatever that was, constituted an improvement over her previous posting in South Dakota was something Bosch didn't know. What he did know was that before she had fallen from grace and been cast out to the reservation beat in the Dakotas, she had been a profiler in the Behavioral Science Unit at Quantico.

"I called because I thought maybe you'd be interested in putting some of your old skills to work again," he said.

"You mean a profile?"

"Sort of. Tomorrow I have to go head to head in a room with an admitted serial killer and I don't know the first thing about what makes him tick. This guy wants to confess to nine murders in a deal to avoid the needle. I have to make sure he's not playing us. I have to figure out if he's telling the truth before we turn around and tell all the families — what families we know of — that we've got the right guy."

He waited a moment for her to react. When she didn't he pressed on.

"I've got crimes, a couple crime scenes and forensics. I've got his apartment inventory and photos. But I don't have a handle on him. I was calling because I was wondering if I could show you some of this stuff and, you know, maybe get some ideas from you on how to handle him."

There was another long silence before she answered.

"Where are you, Harry?" she finally asked.

"Right now? Right now I'm heading into Chinatown to pick up some shrimp fried rice. I missed lunch."

"I'm downtown. I could meet you. I missed lunch, too."

"You know where Chinese Friends is?"

"Of course. How about a half hour?"

"I'll order before you get there."

Bosch closed the phone and felt a thrill that he knew came from something other than the idea that Rachel Walling might be able to help him with the Waits case. Their last encounter had ended badly but the sting of it had eroded over time. What was left in his memory was the night they had made love in a Las Vegas motel room and he had believed he had connected with a kindred soul.

He looked at his watch. He had time to kill even if he was going to order food before she got there. In Chinatown he pulled to the curb outside the restaurant and opened up his phone again. Before he had turned the Gesto murder book over to Olivas he had written down names and numbers he might need. He now called Bakersfield and the home of Marie Gesto's parents. The call would not be a complete shock to them. His habit had always been to call them every time he pulled the file to take another look at the case. He thought it was some measure of comfort for them to know he had not given up.

The missing woman's mother answered the phone.

"Irene, it's Harry Bosch."

"Oh!"

There was always that initial note of hope and excitement when one of them answered.

"Nothing yet, Irene," he responded quickly. "I just have a question for you and Dan, if you don't mind."

"Of course, of course. It's just good to hear from you."

"It's nice to hear your voice, too."

It had been more than ten years since he had actually seen Irene and Dan Gesto. After two years they had stopped coming to L.A. in hopes of finding their daughter, had given up her apartment and gone home. After that, Bosch always called.

"What is your question, Harry?"

"It's a name, actually. Do you remember Marie ever mentioning someone named Ray Waits? Maybe Raynard Waits? Raynard is an unusual name. You might remember it."

He heard her breath catch and he immediately knew he had made a mistake. The recent arrest and court hearings involving Waits had made it into the media in Bakersfield. He should have known that Irene would have a keen eye on such things in L.A. She would know what Waits was accused of. She would know they were calling him the Echo Park Bagman.

"Irene?"

He guessed that her imagination had taken terrible flight.

"Irene, it's not what you think. I'm just running some checks on this guy. It sounds like you've heard of him from the news."

"Of course. Those poor young girls. Ending up like that. I . . ."

He knew what she was thinking, maybe not what she was feeling.

"Can you think back before you saw him on the news. The name. Do you remember if your daughter ever mentioned it?"

"No, I don't remember it, thank God."

"Is your husband there? Can you check with him?"

"He's not here. He's still at work."

Dan Gesto had given everything of himself to the search for his missing daughter. After two years, when he had nothing left spiritually, physically or financially, he went home to Bakersfield and went back to work at a

John Deere franchise. Selling farmers their tractors and tools kept him alive now.

"Can you ask him when he comes home and then call me back if he remembers the name?"

"I will, Harry."

"One other thing, Irene. Marie's apartment had that tall window in the living room. You remember that?"

"Of course. That first year we came down for Christmas instead of her coming up. We wanted her to feel like it was a two-way road. Dan put up the tree in that window and you could see its lights from up and down the block."

"Yes. Do you know if she ever hired a window washer to keep that window clean?"

There was a long silence while Bosch waited. It was a hole in the investigation, an angle he should have followed thirteen years before but hadn't even thought of.

"I don't remember, Harry. I'm sorry."

"It's okay, Irene. It's okay. Do you remember when you and Dan went back to Bakersfield and you took everything from the apartment?"

"Yes."

She said it in a strangled voice. He knew

that she was crying now and that the couple had felt that in some way they were abandoning their daughter as well as their hope when they had gone home after two years of searching and waiting.

"Did you keep it all? All the records and bills and all of the stuff we gave you when we were finished with it?"

He knew that if there had been a receipt for a window washer, it would have been a lead that was checked out. But he had to ask her anyway to confirm the negative, to make sure it hadn't slipped through the cracks.

"Yes, we have it. It's in her room. We have a room with her things in it. In case she . . ."

Ever came home. Bosch knew their hope would not be fully extinguished until Marie was found, one way or the other.

"I understand," he said. "I need you to look through that box, Irene. If you can. I want you to look for a receipt from a window washer. Go through her checkbooks and see if she paid a window washer. Look for a company called ClearView Residential Glass Cleaners, or maybe an abbreviation of that. Call me if you find anything. Okay, Irene? Do you have a pen there? I think I got a new cell number since the last time I gave it to you."

"Okay, Harry," Irene said. "I have a pen."

"The number is three-two-three, two-four-four, five-six-three-one. Thank you, Irene. I'm going to go now. Please give your husband my best."

"I will. How's your daughter, Harry?"

He paused. Over the years it seemed like he had told them everything about himself. It was a way of keeping solid the bond and his promise to find their daughter.

"She's fine. She's great."

"What grade now?"

"Third, but I don't get to see her that much. She's living in Hong Kong with her mother at the moment. I went over last month for a week. They've got a Disneyland over there now."

He didn't know why he threw in that last line.

"It must be very special when you are with her."

"Yes. She is also sending me e-mail now. She's better at it than me."

It was awkward speaking about one's daughter to a woman who had lost her own and didn't know where or why.

"I hope she comes back soon," Irene Gesto said.

"Me, too. Good-bye, Irene. Call me on the cell whenever you want."

"Good-bye, Harry. Good luck."

She always said good luck at the end of every conversation. Bosch sat in the car and thought about the contradiction in his desire for his daughter to live here in Los Angeles with him. He feared for her safety in the far-off place where she lived now. He wanted to be close so that he could protect her. But would bringing her to a city where young girls disappeared without a trace or ended up in pieces in trash bags be a move toward safety? He knew deep down that he was being selfish and that he couldn't really protect her no matter where she lived. Everybody had to make their own way in this world. It was Darwin's rules out there and all he could do was hope that her path didn't cut across the path of someone like Raynard Waits.

He gathered up the files and got out of the car.

5

Bosch didn't see the CLOSED sign until he got to the door of Chinese Friends. It was only then that he realized the restaurant closed in the late afternoon before the dinner rush started. He opened his phone to call Rachel Walling but remembered she blocked her number when she had called him back. With nothing to do but wait he bought a copy of the *Times* out of a box at the curb and paged through it while leaning against his car.

He scanned the headlines quickly, feeling that he was somehow wasting time or losing momentum by reading the paper. The only story he read with any interest was a brief item reporting that district attorney candidate Gabriel Williams had picked up the endorsement of the South County Fellowship of Christian Churches. It wasn't much of a surprise but it was significant because it was an early indication that the minority vote was going with Williams, the civil rights attorney. The story also mentioned that Williams and Rick O'Shea would be appearing the next night at a candidate forum being sponsored by another coalition representing the south side, the Citizens for Sensitive Leadership. The candidates would not debate each other but would give speeches and take questions from the audience. The CSL would announce its endorsement afterward. Also appearing at the forum would be city council candidates Irvin Irving and Martin Maizel.

Bosch lowered the paper and daydreamed for a moment about showing up at the forum and sandbagging Irving from the audience, asking him how his skills as a police department fixer qualified him for elective office.

He came out of the reverie when an unmarked federal cruiser pulled to the curb in front of his car. He watched Rachel Walling step out. She was dressed casually in black slacks and blazer with a cream-colored blouse. Her dark brown hair was down to her shoulders now and that was probably what was most casual of all. She looked good and Bosch jumped back to that night in Vegas.

"Rachel," he said, smiling.

"Harry."

He walked toward her. It was an awkward moment. He didn't know whether to hug her or kiss her or just shake her hand. There was that night in Vegas but it had been followed by that day in L.A., on the back deck of his house, when everything had come apart and things had ended before they really started.

She saved him from making a choice by reaching out and touching him lightly on the arm.

"I thought you were going to go in and order food."

"For some reason they're closed. They don't open up for dinner until five. You want to wait or go somewhere else?"

"Where?"

"I don't know. There's Philippe's."

She shook her head emphatically.

"I'm tired of Philippe's. We eat there all the time. In fact, I didn't eat lunch today because everybody in the squad was going there."

"Tactical, huh?"

If she was tired of a downtown place, then Bosch knew she wasn't working out of the main field office in Westwood.

"I know a place. I'll drive and you can look at the files."

He walked back over and opened the door of his car. He had to grab the files off the passenger seat so she could get in. He then handed her the files and went around to the driver's side. He tossed his newspaper onto the backseat.

"Wow, this is so Steve McQueen," she said of the Mustang. "What happened to the SUV?"

Bosch shrugged.

"Just needed a change."

He revved the engine to humor her and then pulled away from the curb. He went down to Sunset and turned toward Silver Lake. The route would take them through Echo Park on the way.

"So what exactly do you want from me, Harry?"

She opened the top file that was on her lap and started reading.

"I want you to take a look and then tell me your impressions of this guy. I'm talking to him tomorrow and I want to have any edge I can get. I want to make sure that if anybody is manipulated, it's him and not me."

"I've heard about this guy. He's the Echo Park Butcher, right?"

"Actually, they call him the Bagman."

"Got it."

"I have a previous connection to the case."

"Which is?"

"Back in 'ninety-three I was working out of Hollywood Division. I caught a case involving a missing girl. Her name was Marie Gesto and she was never found. It was big at the time, a lot of media. This guy I'm going into the room with, Raynard Waits — he says that's one of the cases he'll trade us."

She looked over at him and then back down at the file.

"Knowing how I have seen you take a case straight to heart, Harry, I wonder, then, if it is wise for you to be dealing with this man now."

"I'm fine. It's still my case. And taking it

straight to heart is the way of the true detective. The only way."

He glanced over at her in time to see her roll her eyes.

"Spoken like the Zen master of Homicide. Where are we going?"

"A place called Duffy's in Silver Lake. We'll be there in five minutes and you'll love it. Just don't start taking your bureau buddies there. That'll ruin it."

"I promise."

"You still have the time?"

"I told you, I didn't take lunch. But I do need to go back to check out at some point."

"So are you working out of the federal courthouse?"

She answered while continuing to scan and turn pages in the file.

"No, we're off campus."

"One of those secret federal locations, huh?"

"You know the story. If I told you I'd have to kill you."

Bosch nodded at the joke.

"That mean you can't tell me what Tactical is?"

"It's nothing. Short for Tactical Intelligence. We're gatherers. We analyze raw data we pull off the Internet, cell transmissions, satellite feeds. It's actually quite boring."

"But is it legal?"

"For now."

"Sounds like a terrorism gig."

"Except more often than not we end up feeding leads to the DEA. And last year we came up with more than thirty different Internet scams involving hurricane relief. Like I said, it's raw data. It can lead anywhere."

"And you traded the wide-open spaces of South Dakota for downtown L.A."

"As far as the career choice goes, it was the right move. I don't regret it. But I do miss some things about the Dakotas. Anyway, let me concentrate on this. You do want my take on it, right?"

"Yes, sorry. Have at it."

He drove silently for the last few minutes and then pulled to a stop in front of the small storefront restaurant. He brought the newspaper in with him. She told him to order her what he was having. But when the waiter came and Bosch ordered an omelet she changed her mind and started scanning the menu.

"I thought you said we were having lunch, not breakfast."

"I missed breakfast, too. And the omelets are good."

She ordered a turkey sandwich and handed back the menu.

"My warning is that my take is going to be very superficial," she said when they were left alone. "There is obviously not going to be enough time for me to do a full psychological. I'll only be scratching the surface."

Bosch nodded.

"I know that," he said. "But I don't have the time to give you, so I will take whatever you can give me."

She said nothing else and went back to the files. Bosch glanced at the sports pages but wasn't that interested in the rundown on the Dodgers game the night before. His appreciation for the game had dropped markedly in recent years. He used the newspaper section mostly as a blind so that he could hold it up and appear to be reading while he was actually looking at Rachel. Other than the longer hair, she had changed little since he had last been with her. Still vibrantly attractive with an intangible sense of damage about her. It was in the eyes. They weren't the hardened cop's eyes he had seen in so many other faces, including his own when he looked in the mirror. They were eyes that were hurt from the inside out. She had a victim's eyes and that drew him to her.

"Why are you staring at me?" she suddenly said.

"What?"

"You're so obvious."

"I was just —"

He was saved by the waiter, who appeared and put down plates of food. Walling moved the files aside and he detected a small smile on her face. They continued their silence as they began to eat.

"This is good," she finally said. "I'm starving."

"Yeah, me, too."

"So what were you looking for?"

"When?"

"When you were acting like you were reading the newspaper but you really weren't."

"Um, I . . . I guess I was trying to see if you were really interested in looking at this. You know, it sounds like you have a lot going.

Maybe you don't want to get into this sort of stuff again."

She held up half her sandwich but stopped herself from taking a bite.

"I hate my job, okay? Or rather, I hate what I am doing right now. But it will get better. Another year and it will be better."

"Fine. And this? This is okay?"

He pointed to the files on the table next to her plate.

"Yes, but there is too much. I can't even begin to help you. It's information overload."

"I only have today."

"Why can't you delay the interview?"

"Because it's not my interview to delay. And because it's got politics on it. The prosecutor is running for DA. He needs headlines. He's not going to wait for me to get up to speed."

She nodded.

"All the way with Rick O'Shea."

"I had to push my way into the case because of Gesto. They're not going to slow down to let me catch up."

She put her hand on top of the stack of files as if taking some sort of measure from them that would help her make a decision.

"Let me keep the files when you drive me

back. I'll finish my work, clock out and continue with this. I'll come see you tonight at
your place and give you what I've got.
Everything."

He stared at her, looking for the hidden
meaning.

"When?"

"I don't know, as soon as I get through it.
Nine o'clock at the latest. I have an early
start tomorrow. Will that work?"

He nodded. He wasn't expecting this.

"Do you still live in that house up on the
hill?" she asked.

"Yeah. I'm there. Woodrow Wilson."

"Good. My place is down off Beverly, not
too far. I'll come up to your place. I remember the view."

Bosch didn't respond. He wasn't sure
what he had just invited into his life.

"Can I give you something to think about
until then?" she asked. "Maybe do some
checking?"

"Sure, what?"

"The name. Is that his real name?"

Bosch frowned. He had never considered
the name. He assumed it was real. Waits
was incarcerated. His fingerprints would

have been run through the system to confirm identity.

"I assume so. His fingerprints matched a
previous arrest. That previous time he tried
to give a false name but a DMV thumbprint
made him as Waits. Why?"

"Do you know what a reynard is? *Reynard*
spelled *R-e-y* instead of *R-a-y.*"

Bosch shook his head. This was coming
from left field. He hadn't even been thinking
about the name.

"No, what is it?"

"It's a name for a young male fox. A young
female is a vixen and the male is a reynard.
I studied European folklore in college —
back when I thought I wanted to be a diplo-
mat. In medieval French folklore there is a
character that is a fox named Reynard. He
is a trickster. There are stories and epics
about the scheming fox named Reynard.
The character has appeared repeatedly
through the centuries in books — children's
books mostly. You can Google it when you
get back to the office and I am sure you will
get many hits."

Bosch nodded. He wasn't going to tell
her he didn't know how to Google. He
barely knew how to e-mail his eight-year-

old daughter. She tapped a finger on the stack of files.

"A young fox would be a small fox," she said. "In the description Mr. Waits is small in stature. You take it all in context of the full name and —"

"The little fox waits," Bosch said. "The young fox waits. The trickster waits."

"For the vixen. Maybe that's how he saw it with his victims."

Bosch nodded. He was impressed.

"We missed that. I can do some checking on the ID as soon as I get back."

"And hopefully I will have more for you tonight."

She went back to eating and Bosch went back to watching her.

6

As soon as Bosch dropped Rachel Walling at her car he opened his phone and called his partner. Rider reported that she was finishing up the paperwork on the Matarese case and that they would soon be good to go on it and able to file charges at the DA's office the following day.

"Good. Anything else?"

"I got the box on Fitzpatrick from Evidence Archives and it turned out to be two boxes."

"Containing what?"

"Mostly old pawn records that I can tell were never even looked at. They were sopping wet back then from when the fire was

put out. The guys from Riot Crimes put
them in plastic tubs and they've been
moldering in them ever since. And, man, do
they stink."

Bosch nodded as he computed this. It
was a dead end and it didn't matter. Raynard Waits was about to confess to the killing of Daniel Fitzpatrick anyway. He could
tell that Rider was looking at it the same
way. An uncoerced confession is a royal
flush. It beats everything.

"Have you heard from Olivas or O'Shea?"
Rider asked.

"Not yet. I was going to call Olivas but
wanted to talk to you first. Do you know
anybody in city licensing?"

"No, but if you want me to call over there
I can in the morning. They're closed now.
What are you looking for?"

Bosch checked his watch. He didn't realize how late it had gotten. He guessed that
the omelet at Duffy's was going to count as
breakfast, lunch and dinner.

"I was thinking we should run Waits's
business and see how long he's had it,
whether there were ever any complaints,
that sort of thing. Olivas and his partner

should have done it but there is nothing in the files about it."

She was silent for a while before speaking.

"You think that could have been the connection to the High Tower?"

"Maybe. Or maybe to Marie. She had a nice big picture window in her apartment. It isn't something I remember coming up back then. But maybe we missed it."

"Harry, you never miss a thing, but I'll get on it right away."

"The other thing is the guy's name. It could be phony."

"How so?"

He told her about contacting Rachel Walling and asking her to look at the files. This was initially met with resounding silence because Bosch had crossed one of those invisible LAPD lines by inviting the FBI into the case without command approval, even if the invitation to Walling was unofficial. But when Bosch told Rider about Reynard the Fox she dropped her silence and became skeptical.

"You think our window-washing serial killer was schooled in medieval folklore?"

"I don't know," he answered. "Walling says

he could have picked it up from a children's book. Doesn't matter. There is enough there that I think we've got to look at birth certificates, make sure there is someone named Raynard Waits. In the first file, when he was popped for prowling in 'ninety-three, he was booked under the name Robert Saxon — the name he gave — but then they got Raynard Waits when his thumbprint hit the DMV computer."

"What are you seeing there, Harry? If they had his thumb on file back then, I'm thinking maybe the name isn't phony after all."

"Maybe. But you know it isn't impossible to get a DL with a false name on it in this state. What if Saxon actually was his real name but the computer spit out his alias and he just went with it? We've seen it happen before."

"Then why keep the name after? He had a record under Waits. Why not go back to Saxon or whatever his real name is?"

"Good questions. I don't know. But we've got to check it out."

"Well, we've got him no matter what his name is. I'll Google *Raynard the Fox* right now."

"Spell it with an *e.*"

He waited and could hear her fingers on the computer keyboard.

"Got it," she finally said. "There's a lot of stuff about Reynard the Fox."

"That's what Walling said."

There was silence for a long moment while Rider read. Then she spoke.

"Says here that part of the legend is that Reynard the Fox had a secret castle that nobody could find. He used all kinds of trickery to draw his victims close. Then he would take them back to the castle and eat them."

That hung out there untouched for a while. Finally Bosch spoke.

"Do you have time to run another Auto-Track and see if you can get anything on Robert Saxon?"

"Sure."

There was not a lot of conviction in her tone. But Bosch wasn't going to let her off the hook. He wanted to keep things in motion.

"Read me his DOB off the arrest report," Rider said.

"I can't. I don't have it here."

"Where is it? I don't see it on your desk."

"I gave the files to Agent Walling. I'll get

them back later tonight. You'll have to go on the computer to pull the arrest report."

A lengthy silence went by before Rider responded.

"Harry, those are official investigative files. You know you shouldn't have parted with them. And we're going to need them tomorrow for the interview."

"I told you, I'll have them back tonight."

"Let's hope so. But I've gotta tell you, partner, you're doing the cowboy thing again and I don't like it very much."

"Kiz, I'm just trying to keep things moving. And I want to be ready for this guy in that room tomorrow. What Walling is giving me will give us an edge."

"Fine. I trust you. Maybe at some point you will trust me enough to ask my opinion before you go off and make decisions that affect both of us."

Bosch felt his cheeks flare hot, mostly because he knew she was right. He didn't say anything because he knew that apologizing for leaving her out of the loop wasn't going to cut it.

"Call me back if Olivas gives us a time for tomorrow," she said.

"You got it."

After closing the phone Bosch thought about things for a moment. He tried to move on from his embarrassment over Rider's indignation. He focused on the case and what he had left out of the investigation so far. After a few minutes he reopened the phone, called Olivas and asked if a time and place had been set for the Waits interview.

"Tomorrow morning, ten o'clock," Olivas said. "Don't be late."

"Were you going to tell me, Olivas, or was I supposed to pick it up telepathically?"

"I just found out myself. You called me before I could call you."

Bosch ignored his excuse.

"Where?"

"The DA's office. We'll have him brought down from high-power and set him up in an interview room here."

"You're at the DA's now?"

"I had some things to go over with Rick."

Bosch let that float out there without a response.

"Anything else?" Olivas asked.

"Yeah, I have a question," Bosch said. "Where's your partner in all of this, Olivas? What happened to Colbert?"

"He's in Hawaii. He'll be back next week.

If this thing carries over till then he'll be part of it."

Bosch wondered if Colbert even knew what was happening or that he was missing out on a potentially career-making case while he was off on vacation. From everything Bosch knew about Olivas, there would be no surprise if he was scheming to ace out his own partner on a glory case.

"Ten o'clock, then?" Bosch asked.

"Ten."

"Anything else I should know, Olivas?"

He was curious about why Olivas was at the DA's office but didn't want to directly ask why.

"Matter of fact, there is one more thing. Sort of a delicate thing, you could say. I've been talking to Rick about it."

"What's that?"

"Well, take a guess at what I'm looking at here."

Bosch blew out his breath. Olivas was going to string it out. Bosch had known him less than one day and already knew without a doubt that he didn't like the man and never would.

"I have no idea, Olivas. What?"

"Your fifty-ones from Gesto."

He was referring to the Investigative Chronology, a master listing kept by date and time of all aspects of a case, ranging from an accounting of detectives' time and movements to notations on routine phone calls and messages to media inquiries and tips from citizens. Usually, these were hand-written with all manner of shorthand and abbreviations employed as they were updated throughout each day, sometimes hourly. Then, when a page became full, it was typed up on a form called a 51, which would be complete and legible when and if the case ever moved into the courts, and lawyers, judges and juries needed to review the investigative files. The original handwritten pages were then discarded.

"What about them?" Bosch asked.

"I'm looking at the last line on page fourteen. The listing is for September twenty-ninth, nineteen ninety-three, at six-forty p.m. Must've been quitting time. The initials on the entry are JE."

Bosch felt the bile rising in his throat. Whatever it was Olivas was getting at, he was enjoying milking it.

"Obviously," he said impatiently, "that

would've been my partner at the time, Jerry Edgar. What's the entry say, Olivas?"

"It says . . . I'll just read it. It says, 'Robert Saxon DOB eleven/three/'seventy-one. Saw *Times* story. Was at Mayfair and saw MG alone. Nobody following.' It gives Saxon's phone number and that's all it says. But that's enough, Hotshot. You know what it means?"

Bosch did. He had just given the name Robert Saxon to Kiz Rider to background. It was either an alias or perhaps the real name of the man known currently as Raynard Waits. That name on the 51s now connected Waits to the Gesto case. It also meant that thirteen years ago Bosch and Edgar had at least a shot at Waits/Saxon. But for reasons he didn't recall or didn't know about they never took it. He did not recall the specific entry in the 51s. There were dozens of pages in the Investigative Chronology filled with one- and two-line entries. Remembering them all — even with his frequent returns to the investigation over the years — would have been impossible.

It took him a long moment to find his voice.

"That's the only mention in the murder book?" he asked.

"That I've seen," Olivas said. "I've been through everything twice. I even missed it the first time through. Then the second time I said, 'Hey, I know that name.' It's an alias Waits used back in the early nineties. It should be in the files you have."

"I know. I saw it."

"It meant he called you guys, Bosch. The killer called you, and you and your partner blew it. Looks like nobody ever followed up with him or ran his name through the box. You had the killer's alias and a phone number and didn't do anything. 'Course, you didn't know he was the killer. Just some citizen calling in about what he saw. He must've been trying to play you guys in some way, trying to find out about the case. Only Edgar didn't play. It was late in the day and he probably wanted to get to that first martini."

Bosch said nothing and Olivas was only too happy to continue to fill the void.

"Too bad, you know? Maybe this whole thing could've ended right then. I guess we'll ask Waits about it in the morning."

Olivas and his petty world no longer mat-

tered to Bosch. The barbs couldn't pene-
trate the thick, dark cloud that was already
coming down on him. For he knew that if
the name Robert Saxon had come up in the
Gesto investigation, then it should have
been routinely run through the computer. It
would have scored a match in the alias
database and taken them to Raynard Waits
and his prior arrest for prowling. That would
have made him a suspect. Not just a person
of interest like Anthony Garland. A strong
suspect. And that would have undoubtedly
taken the investigation in a whole new direction.

But that never happened. Apparently neither Edgar nor Bosch had run the name
through the box. It was an oversight that
Bosch now knew had probably cost the
lives of the two women who ended up in
trash bags and the seven others Waits was
going to tell them about the next day.

"Olivas?" Bosch said.

"What, Bosch?"

"Make sure you bring the book with you
tomorrow. I want to see the fifty-ones."

"Oh, I will. We'll need it to do the interview."

Bosch closed his phone without another

word. He felt the pace of his breathing increase. Soon he was close to hyperventilating. His back felt hot against the car seat and he was starting to sweat. He opened the windows and tried to slow the measure of each breath. He was close to Parker Center but pulled to a stop at the curb.

It was every detective's nightmare. The worst-case scenario. A lead ignored or bungled, allowing something awful to be loose in the world. Something dark and evil, destroying life after life as it moved through the shadows. It was true that all detectives made mistakes and had to live with the regrets. But Bosch instinctively knew that this one was malignant. It would grow and grow inside until it darkened everything and he became the last victim, the last life destroyed.

He pulled out from the curb and into traffic to get air moving through the windows. He made a screeching U-turn and headed home.

7

From the rear deck of his house Bosch watched the sky start to dim. He lived up on Woodrow Wilson Drive in a cantilevered house that clung to the side of the hill like a cartoon character hanging on to the edge of a cliff. Sometimes Bosch felt like that character. Like on this night. He was drinking vodka sprinkled liberally over ice, the first time he'd gone with hard liquor since coming back on the job the year before. The vodka made his throat feel as though he had swallowed a torch, but that was okay. He was trying to burn away his thoughts and cauterize his nerve endings.

Bosch considered himself a true detective, one who took it all inside and cared. Everybody counts or nobody counts. That's what he always said. It made him good at the job but it also made him vulnerable. The mistakes could get to him and this one was the worst of all mistakes.

He shook the ice and vodka and took another deep drink until he finished the glass. How could anything so cold burn so intensely hot on the way down? He walked back inside the house to put more vodka on the ice. He wished he had some lemon or lime to squeeze in the drink but he had made no stops on his way home. In the kitchen, with fresh drink in hand, he picked up the phone and called Jerry Edgar's cell phone. He still knew the number by heart. A partner's number was something you never forgot.

Edgar answered and Bosch could hear TV noise in the background. He was at home.

"Jerry, it's me. I gotta ask you something."

"Harry? Where are you?"

"Home, man. But I'm working on one of our old ones."

"Oh, well let me go down the list of Harry Bosch obsessions. Let's see, Fernandez?"

"No."

"That kid, Spike whatever-her-name-was?"

"Nope."

"I give up, man. You've got too many ghosts for me to keep track of."

"Gesto."

"Shit, I should've gone with her first. I know you've been working it on and off since you've been back. What's the question?"

"There's an entry in the fifty-ones. It's got your initials on it. Says a guy named Robert Saxon called and said he saw her in the Mayfair."

Edgar waited a moment before replying.

"That's it? That's the entry?"

"That's it. You remember talking to the guy?"

"Shit, Harry, I don't remember entries in cases I worked last month. That's why we have the fifty-ones. Who is Saxon?"

Bosch shook his glass and took a drink before answering. The ice tumbled against his mouth, and vodka spilled down his cheek. He wiped it with the sleeve of his jacket and then brought the phone back to his mouth.

"He's the guy . . . I think."

"You've got the killer, Harry?"

"Pretty sure. But . . . we could've had him back then. Maybe."

"I don't remember anybody named Saxon calling me. He must've been trying to get his rocks off, calling us. Harry, are you drunk, man?"

"Gettin' there."

"What's wrong, man? If you got the guy it's better late than never. You should be happy. I'm happy. Did you call her parents yet?"

Bosch was leaning against the kitchen counter and felt the need to sit down. But the phone was on a cord and he couldn't go out to the living room or the deck. Being careful not to spill his drink, he slid down to the floor, his back against the cabinets.

"No, I haven't called them."

"What am I missing here, Harry? You're fucked up and that means something's wrong."

Bosch waited a moment.

"What's wrong is that Marie Gesto wasn't the first and she wasn't the last."

Edgar was silent as it registered. The background sound of television went quiet and he then spoke in the weak voice of a child asking what his punishment will be.

"How many came after?"

"Looks like nine," Bosch said in an equally quiet voice. "I'll probably know more tomorrow."

"Jesus," Edgar whispered.

Bosch nodded. Part of him was angry with Edgar and wanted to blame him for everything. But the other part said they were partners and they shared the good and the bad. Those 51s were in the murder book for both of them to read and react to.

"So you don't remember the call?"

"No, nothing. It's too far back. All I can say is that if there was no follow-up, then the call didn't sound legit or I got all there was to get from the caller. If he was the killer, he was probably just fucking with us anyway."

"Yeah, but we didn't put the name in the box. It would have drawn a match in the alias files. Maybe that's what he wanted."

They were both silent as their minds sifted the sands of disaster. Finally, Edgar spoke.

"Harry, did you come up with this? Who knows about it?"

"A Homicide guy from Northeast came up with it. He has the Gesto file. He knows and a DA working the suspect knows. It doesn't matter. We fucked up."

And people are dead, he thought but didn't say.

"Who is the DA?" Edgar asked. "Can this be contained?"

Bosch knew that Edgar had already moved on to thinking about how to limit the career damage something like this could cause. Bosch wondered whether Edgar's guilt over the nine victims that came after Marie Gesto had simply vanished or just been conveniently compartmentalized. Edgar was not a true detective. He kept his heart out of it.

"I doubt it," Bosch said. "And I don't really care. We should have been onto this guy in 'ninety-three but we missed it and he's been out there cutting up women ever since."

"What are you talking about, cutting up? Is this the Echo Park Bagman you're talking about? What's his name, Waits? *He* was our guy?"

Bosch nodded and held the cold glass against his left temple.

"That's right. He's going to confess tomorrow. Eventually it will get out because Rick O'Shea is going to run with it. There will be no way to hide it because some smart reporter is going to ask whether Waits ever came up way back when in the Gesto case."

"So we say no, because that's the truth. Waits's name never came up. It was an alias and we don't need to tell them about that. You have to make O'Shea see that, Harry."

His voice had an urgent tone to it. Bosch now regretted making the call. He wanted Edgar to share the burden of guilt with him, not figure out a way to avoid blame.

"Whatever, Jerry."

"Harry, that's easy for you to say. You're downtown on your second ride. I'm up for one of the D-two slots in RHD and this thing will fuck up any chance I have if it gets out."

Bosch now wanted to get off the line.

"Like I said, whatever. I'll do what I can, Jerry. But you know, sometimes when you fuck up you have to take the consequences."

"Not this time, partner. Not now."

It angered Bosch that Edgar had pulled the old "partner act," calling on Bosch to protect him out of loyalty and the unwritten rule that the bond of partnership lasts forever and is stronger than even a marriage.

"I said I'd do what I can," he told Edgar. "I have to go now, *partner.*"

He got up off the floor and hung the phone on the wall.

Before returning to the back deck he educated the ice in his glass once more with vodka. Outside, he went to the rail and leaned his elbows down on it. The traffic noise from the freeway far down the hill was a steady hiss that he was used to. He looked up at the sky and saw that the sunset was a dirty pink. He saw a red-tailed hawk floating on an upper current. It reminded him of the one he had seen way back on the day they had found Marie Gesto's car.

His cell phone started to chime and he struggled to pull it out of his jacket pocket. Finally, he got it out and opened it before he lost the call. He hadn't had time to look at the caller ID on the screen. It was Kiz Rider.

"Harry, did you hear?"

"Yeah, I heard. I just talked to Edgar about it. All he cares about is protecting his career and his chances at RHD."

"Harry, what are you talking about?"

Bosch paused. He was confused.

"Didn't that asshole Olivas tell you? I thought by now he would have told the whole world."

"Told me what? I was calling to see if you heard whether the interview's been set for tomorrow."

Bosch realized his mistake. He walked to the edge of the deck and dumped his drink over the side.

"Ten o'clock tomorrow at the DA's office. They'll put him in a room there. I'm sorry, Kiz, I guess I forgot to call you."

"Are you all right? It sounds like you've been drinking."

"I'm home, Kiz. I'm entitled."

"What did you think I was calling about?"

Bosch held his breath and composed his thoughts, then spoke.

"Edgar and I, we should have had Waits or Saxon or whatever his name is back in 'ninety-three. Edgar spoke to him on the phone and he used the name Saxon. But neither of us ran the name on the computer. We screwed up bad, Kiz."

Now she was silent as she tracked what he had said. It didn't take her long to realize the connection the alias would have given them to Waits.

"I'm sorry, Harry."

"Tell it to the nine victims that followed."

He was staring down at the brush beneath the deck.

"You going to be all right?"

"I'm all right. I just have to figure out how to get past this so I'm ready for tomorrow."

"Do you think you should stick with it at this point? Maybe one of the other OU teams should take over for us."

Bosch responded immediately. He wasn't sure how he was going to deal with the fatal mistake of thirteen years ago but he wasn't going to walk away now.

"No, Kiz, I'm not leaving the case. I might have missed him in 'ninety-three but I'm not going to miss him now."

"Okay, Harry."

She didn't hang up but she didn't say anything after that. Bosch could hear a siren from far down in the pass below.

"Harry, can I make a suggestion?"

He knew what was coming.

"Sure."

"I think you should put away the booze and start thinking about tomorrow. When we get into that room it's not going to matter what mistakes were made in the past. It will be all about the moment with this man. We'll need to be frosty."

Bosch smiled. He didn't think he'd heard that term since he'd been on a patrol in Vietnam.

"Stay frosty," he said.

"That's right. You want to meet in the squad and walk over from there?"

"Yeah. I'll be there early. I want to go by the Hall of Records first."

Bosch heard a knock at his front door and started into the house.

"Me, too, then," Rider said. "I'll meet you in the squad. Are you going to be all right tonight?"

Bosch opened the front door and Rachel Walling was standing there holding the files with both hands.

"Yes, Kiz," he said into the phone. "I'll be fine. Good night."

He closed the phone and invited Rachel in.

8

Since Rachel had been in his home before, she didn't bother looking around. She put the files down on the small table in the dining area and looked at Bosch.

"What's wrong? Are you all right?"

"I'm fine. I sort of forgot you were coming by."

"I can leave if —"

"No, I'm glad you're here. Did you find more time to look at the stuff?"

"A little bit. I have some notes and some thoughts that might help you tomorrow. And if you want me to be there, I can make arrangements to be there — unofficially."

Bosch shook his head.

"Officially, unofficially doesn't matter. This is Rick O'Shea's ticket and if I bring an FBI agent into it, then that will be my ticket out."

She smiled and shook her head.

"Everybody thinks that all the bureau wants are the headlines. It's not always like that."

"I know but I can't turn this into the test case for O'Shea. Do you want something to drink?"

He gestured to the table so that she could sit down.

"What are you having?"

"I was having vodka. I think I'm going to switch to coffee now."

"Can you make a vodka tonic?"

He nodded.

"I can make one without tonic," he said.

"Tomato juice?"

"Nope."

"Cranberry juice?"

"Just vodka."

"Hard-core Harry. I think I'll have coffee."

He went into the kitchen to get a pot brewing. He heard her pull out a chair at the table and sit down. When he came back he saw that she had spread the files out and had a page of notes in front of her.

"Did you do anything about the name yet?" she asked.

"In motion. We'll start early tomorrow and hopefully we'll know something before we get into the room with this guy at ten."

She nodded and waited for him to sit down across from her.

"Ready?" she asked.

"Ready."

She leaned forward and looked at her notes, talking at first without looking up from them.

"Whoever he is, whatever his name is, he's obviously smart and manipulative," she said. "Look at his size. Short and slightly built. This means he had a good act. He somehow was able to get these victims to go with him. That's the key thing. It is unlikely he used physical force — at least not at the start. He is too small for that. Instead, he employed charm and cunning and he was practiced and polished at it. Even if a girl is just off the bus on Hollywood Boulevard she is going to be wary and have some measure of street smarts. He was smarter."

Bosch nodded.

"The trickster," he said.

She nodded and referred to a short stack of documents.

"I did a little Internet work on that," she said. "In the Reynard epic he is often depicted as a member of the clergy and he is able to woo his audience closer to him that way so that he can grab them. The clergy at the time — we're talking about the twelfth century — was the ultimate authority. Today it would be different. The ultimate authority would be the government, notably represented by the police."

"You're saying he might have posed as a cop?"

"Just a thought, but it's possible. He had to have had something that worked."

"What about a weapon? Or money? He could have just flashed the green. These women . . . these girls would have gone for money."

"I think it was more than a weapon and more than money. To use either of them you still need to get close. Money doesn't lower the safety threshold. It had to be something else. His style or patter, something more than or in addition to money. When he got them close, then he would use the weapon."

Bosch nodded and wrote a few notes on

a page of a notebook he grabbed off a shelf behind where he sat.

"What else?" he asked.

"Do you know how long he's had his business?"

"No, but we'll know tomorrow morning. Why?"

"Well, because it shows another dimension of his skills. But my interest in it is not just because he ran his own business. I'm also curious about the choice of business. It allowed him to be mobile and to travel throughout the city. If you saw his van in your neighborhood, there would be no cause for concern — except late at night, which obviously led to his downfall. And the job also allowed him inside people's homes. I'm curious as to whether he started the job to help him fulfill his fantasies — the killings — or already had the business before he began acting on these impulses."

Bosch made a few more notes. Rachel had a good point with her questions about the job. He had questions that ran along the same lines. Could Waits have had his business thirteen years before? Had he cleaned windows at the High Tower and known about the vacant apartment? Maybe it was another mistake, a connection they had missed.

"I know I don't need to tell you this, Harry, but you are going to have to be careful and cautious with him."

He looked up from his notes.

"Why?"

"Something about what I see here — and obviously this is a very rushed response to a lot of material — but something doesn't fit right about this."

"What?"

She composed her thoughts before answering.

"You have to remember that it was a fluke that he was even caught. Officers looking for a burglar stumbled onto a killer. Up until the moment those officers found the bags in his van, Waits was completely unknown to law enforcement. He had been flying below the radar for years. As I said, it shows he had a certain level of cunning and skill. And it says something about the pathology as well. He wasn't sending notes to the police like the Zodiac or BTK. He wasn't displaying his victims as an affront to society or a taunt to police. He was quiet. He moved below the surface. And he chose victims, with the exception of the first two killings, who could be pulled under without leaving so much as a ripple behind. You understand what I mean?"

Bosch hesitated for a moment, not sure he wanted to tell her about the mistake he and Edgar had made so many years ago.

She read him.

"What?"

He didn't answer.

"Harry, I don't want to be spinning my wheels here. If there is something you know that I need to know, then tell me or I might as well get up and go."

"Just hold on until I get the coffee. I hope you like it black."

He got up and went into the kitchen and poured coffee into two mugs. He found some packets of sugar and sweetener in a basket where he threw condiments that came with to-go orders and brought them out for Rachel. She put sweetener in her mug.

"Okay," she said after the first sip. "What aren't you telling me?"

"My partner and I made a mistake back when we worked this in 'ninety-three. I don't know if it contradicts what you just said about Waits staying beneath the radar but it looks like he called us back then. About three weeks into the case. He talked to my partner on the phone and he used an alias. At least we think it was an alias. With this Reynard the Fox thing you've brought up, maybe he used his real name. Anyway, we blew it. We never checked him out."

"What do you mean?"

He slowly, reluctantly, told her in detail about the call from Olivas and his finding of Waits's alias in the 51s. She cast her eyes down at the table and nodded as he told it. She worked the pen she was holding in a circle on the page of notes in front of her.

"And the rest is history," he said. "He kept right on going . . . and killing people."

"When did you find this out?" she asked.

"Right after I left you today."

She nodded.

"Which explains why you were hitting the vodka so hard."

"I guess so."

"I thought . . . never mind what I thought."

"No, it wasn't because of seeing you, Rachel. Seeing you was — I mean, is — actually very nice."

She took up her mug and drank from it,

then looked down at her work and seemed to steel herself to move on.

"Well, I don't see how his calling you back then changes my conclusions," she said. "Yes, it does seem out of character for him to have made contact under any name. But you have to remember the Gesto case took place in the early stages of his formation. There are a number of aspects involving Gesto that don't fit with the rest. So for it to be the only case where he made contact would not be all that unusual."

"Okay."

She referred to her notes again, continuing to avoid his eyes since he had told her of the mistake.

"So where was I before you brought that up?"

"You said that after the first two killings he chose victims he could pull beneath the surface without notice."

"Exactly. What I'm saying is that he was getting his satisfaction in the work. He didn't need anybody else to know he was doing it. He wasn't getting off on the attention. He wanted no attention. His fulfillment was self-contained. It needed no outside or public component."

"So then, what bothers you?"

She looked up at him.

"What do you mean?"

"I don't know. But you look like something about your own profile of the guy bothers you. Something you don't believe."

She nodded, acknowledging that he had read her correctly.

"It's just that his profile doesn't support someone who would cooperate at this stage of the game, who would tell you about the other crimes. What I see here is someone who would never admit to it. Any of it. He would deny it, or at the very least keep quiet about it, until they put the needle in his arm."

"All right, so that's a contradiction. Don't all of these guys have contradictions? They're all messed up in some way. No profile is ever a hundred percent, right?"

She nodded.

"That's true. But it still doesn't fit and so I guess what I am trying to say is that from his point of view, there is something else. A higher goal, if you will. A plan. This whole confession thing is indicative of manipulation."

Bosch nodded like what she had said was obvious.

"Of course it is. He's manipulating O'Shea and the system. He's using this to avoid the needle."

"Maybe so, but there may be other motives as well. Be careful."

She said the last two words sternly, as if she were correcting a subordinate or even a child.

"Don't worry, I will," Bosch said.

He decided not to dwell on it.

"What do you think about the dismemberment?" he asked. "What's it say?"

"I actually spent most of my time studying the autopsies. I have always believed that you learn the most about a killer from his victims. Cause of death in each case was determined to be strangulation. There were no stab wounds on the bodies. There was just the dismemberment. These are two different things. I think the dismemberment was simply part of the cleanup. It was a way for him to easily dispose of the bodies. Again, it shows his skills, planning and organization. The more I read, the more I realized how lucky we were to get him that night."

She ran a finger down the sheet of notes she had written and then continued.

"I find the bags very intriguing. Three bags for two women. One bag held both heads and all four hands. It was as if he possibly had a separate destination or plan for the bag containing the identifiers; the heads and the hands. Have they been able to determine where he was going when they pulled him over?"

Bosch shrugged.

"Not really. The assumption was that he was going to bury the bags somewhere around the stadium, but that doesn't really work because they saw him drive off of Stadium Way and into a neighborhood. He was driving away from the stadium and the woods and the places he could bury the bags. There were some open lots down in the neighborhood and access to the hillsides below the stadium, but it seems to me that if he was going to bury them he would not have gone into a neighborhood. He would go deep into the park, where there was less chance of being noticed."

"Exactly."

She glanced at some of her other documents.

"What?" Bosch asked.

"Well, this Reynard the Fox thing might have nothing to do with all of this. It may all be coincidence."

"But in the epic Reynard had a castle that was his secret hideaway."

She raised her eyebrows.

"I didn't think you had a computer, let alone knew how to research on line."

"I don't. My partner did the search. But I gotta tell you, I was over in the neighborhood right before I called you today. I didn't see any castle."

She shook her head.

"Don't take everything so literally," she said.

"Well, there's still a big question about the Reynard stuff," he said.

"Which is?"

"Did you look at the booking sheet in the file? He wouldn't talk to Olivas and his partner but he did answer the protocol questions at the jail when he was booked. He listed his education level as high school. No higher education. I mean, look, the guy's a window washer. How would he even know about this medieval fox?"

"I don't know. But as I said, the character

has popped up repeatedly in all cultures. Children's books, television shows, there are any number of ways the character could have made an impact on this man. And don't underestimate this man's intelligence because he washed windows for a living. He owned and operated a business. That is significant in terms of showing some of his capabilities. The fact that he operated as a killer with impunity for so long is another strong indicator of intelligence."

Bosch wasn't completely convinced. He fired off another question that would take her in a new direction.

"How do the first two fit in? He went from public spectacle with the riots and then a big media splash with Marie Gesto to, as you say, diving completely beneath the surface."

"Every serial killer's MO changes. The simple answer is that he was on a learning curve. I think the first killing — with the male victim — was an opportunity killing. Like a spree killing. He had thought about killing for a long time but wasn't sure he could do it. He found himself in a situation — the chaos of the riots — where he could test himself. It was an opportunity to see if he could actually kill someone and then get away with it. The sex of the victim was not important. The identity of the victim was not important. At that moment he just wanted to find out if he could do it and almost any victim would do."

Bosch could see that. He nodded.

"So he did," he said. "And then we come to Marie Gesto. He picks a victim who draws the police and the media's attention."

"He was still learning, forming," she said. "He knew he could kill and now he wanted to go out and hunt. She was his first victim. She crossed his path, something about her fit his fantasy program and she simply became prey. At that time his focus was on victim acquisition and self-protection. In that case he chose badly. He chose a woman who would be sorely missed and whose disappearance would draw an immediate response. He probably didn't know this going into it. But he learned from it, from the heat he brought upon himself."

Bosch nodded.

"Anyway, after Gesto he learned to add a third element to his focus: victim back-grounding. He made sure that he chose victims who not only met the needs of his pro-

gram but who would also come from a so-
cietal fringe, where their comings and go-
ings would not be cause for notice, let alone
alarm."

"And he went beneath the surface."

"Exactly. He went under and he stayed
there. Until we got lucky in Echo Park."

Bosch nodded. All of this was helpful.

"It makes you wonder, doesn't it?" he
asked. "About how many of these guys are
out there. The under-the-surface killers."

Walling nodded.

"Yes. Sometimes it scares me to death.
Makes me wonder how long this guy would
have gone on killing if we hadn't gotten so
lucky."

She checked her notes and said nothing
further.

"Is that all you've got?" Bosch asked.

Walling looked up at him sharply and he
realized he had chosen his words poorly.

"I didn't mean it like that," he said quickly.
"This is all great and it's going to help me a
lot. I just meant is there anything else you
wanted to talk about?"

She held his eyes for a moment before replying.

"Yes, there is something else. It's not about this, though."

"Then, what is it?"

"You've got to give yourself a break on that phone call, Harry. You can't let that bring you down. The work ahead is too important."

Bosch nodded insincerely. It was easy for her to say that. She wouldn't have to live with the ghosts of all the women Raynard Waits would begin to tell them about the next morning.

"Don't just nod it off like that," Rachel said. "Do you know how many cases I worked in Behavioral where the guy kept killing? How many times we got calls and notes from these creeps but still couldn't get to them before the next victim was dead?"

"I know, I know."

"We all have ghosts. It's part of the job. With some jobs it's a bigger part than with others. I had a boss once, he used to say, if you can't stand the ghosts, get out of the haunted house."

He nodded again, this time while looking directly at her. He meant it this time.

"How many murders have you solved,

Harry? How many killers have you put away?"

"I don't know. I don't keep track."

"Maybe you should."

"What's the point?"

"The point is, how many of those killers would have done it again if you hadn't taken them down? More than a few, I bet."

"Probably."

"There you go. You're way ahead in the long run. Think about that."

"Okay."

His mind flashed on one of those killers. Bosch had arrested Roger Boylan many years before. He drove a pickup with a camper shell on the back. He had used marijuana to entice a couple young girls into the back while parked up at Hansen Dam. He raped and killed them, injecting them with an overdose of a horse tranquilizer. He then threw their bodies into the dry bed of the nearby slough. When Bosch put the cuffs on him Boylan had only one thing to say.

"Too bad. I was just getting started."

Bosch wondered how many victims there would have been if he hadn't stopped him. He wondered if he could trade Roger Boylan for Raynard Waits and call it even. On the one hand, he thought he could. On the other hand, he knew it wasn't a zero-sum game. The true detective knew that coming out even in homicide work was not good enough. Not by a long shot.

"I hope I've helped," Rachel said.

He looked up from the memory of Boylan to Rachel's eyes.

"I think you did. I think I'll know better who and what I am dealing with when I go into the room with him tomorrow."

She stood up from the table.

"I meant about the other thing."

Bosch stood.

"That, too. You've helped a lot."

He came around the table so he could walk her to the door.

"Be careful, Harry."

"I know. You said that. But you don't have to worry. It will be a full-security situation."

"I don't mean the physical danger as much as I mean the psychological. Guard yourself, Harry. Please."

"I will," he said.

It was time to go to the door but she was hesitating. She looked down at the contents of the file spread across the table and then at Bosch.

"I was hoping you would call me some-time," she said. "But not about a case."

Bosch had to take a few moments before coming back.

"I thought because of what I said — what we said — that . . ."

He wasn't sure how to finish. He wasn't sure what he was trying to say. She reached up and put her hand lightly on his chest. He took a step closer, coming into her space. He then put his arms around her and pulled her close.

9

Later, after they had made love, Bosch and Rachel remained in bed, talking about anything they could think of except what they had just done. Eventually they came back around to the case and the next morning's interview with Raynard Waits.

"I can't believe that after all this time I'm going to sit down face-to-face with her killer," Bosch said. "It's kind of like a dream. I actually have dreamed of catching the guy. I mean, it was never Waits in the dream but I dreamed about closing out the case."

"Who was it in the dream?" she asked.

Her head was resting on his chest. He couldn't see her face but he could smell her hair. Under the sheets she had one leg over one of his.

"It was this guy I always thought could be good for it. But I never had anything on him. I guess because he was always an asshole, I wanted it to be him."

"Well, did he have any connection to Gesto?"

Bosch tried to shrug but it was difficult with their bodies so entwined.

"He knew about the garage where we found the car and had an ex-girlfriend who was a ringer for Gesto. And he had anger-management issues. No real evidence. I just thought it was him. I followed him once way back during the first year of the investigation. He was working as a security guard up in the oil fields behind Baldwin Hills. You know where that is?"

"You mean where you see the oil pumps when you're coming in on La Cienega from the airport?"

"Yeah, right. That's the place. Well, this kid's family owned a chunk of those fields, and his old man was trying to straighten him out, I guess. You know, make him work for a living even though they had all the money in the world. So he was working security up there and I was watching him one day. He came across these kids who were fooling around up in there, just trespassing and messing around. They were just kids, maybe thirteen or fourteen. Two boys from the nearby neighborhood."

"What did he do to them?"

"He drew down on them, then handcuffed them to one of the pumps. Their backs were to each other and they were cuffed around this pole that was sort of like an anchor for the pump. And then he got back in his pickup and drove away."

"He just left them there?"

"That's what I thought he was doing but he was coming back. I was watching with binoculars from a ridge all the way across La Cienega and could see the whole oil field from up there. He had another guy with him and they drove over to this shack where I guess they kept samples of the oil they were pumping out of the ground. They went in there and came out with two buckets of this stuff, put 'em in the back of the pickup and drove back. They then dumped that shit all over the two kids."

Rachel got up on one elbow and looked at him.

"And you just watched this happen?"

"I told you, I was clear across La Cienega on the next ridge. Before they built houses up there. If he went any further I was going to try to intervene somehow, but then he let them go. Besides, I didn't want him to know I was watching him. At that point he didn't know I was thinking of him for Gesto."

She nodded like she understood and no longer questioned his lack of action.

"He just let them go?" she asked.

"He uncuffed them, kicked one of them in the butt and let them go. I could tell they were crying and scared."

Rachel shook her head in disgust.

"What's this guy's name?"

"Anthony Garland. His father is Thomas Rex Garland. You might have heard of him."

Rachel shook her head, not recognizing the name.

"Well, Anthony might not have been Gesto's killer but he sounds like a complete asshole."

Bosch nodded.

"He is. You want to see him?"

"What do you mean?"

"I've got a 'greatest hits' video. I've had

him in an interview room three times in thirteen years. Each interview was on tape."

"You have the tape here?"

Bosch nodded, knowing that she might find it strange or off-putting that he studied interrogation tapes at home.

"I had them copied onto one tape. I brought it home to watch the last time I worked the case."

Rachel seemed to consider his answer before she responded.

"Then pop it in. Let's take a look at this guy."

Bosch got out of bed, slipped on his boxer shorts and turned on the lamp. He went out to the living room and looked in the cabinet beneath the television. He had several crime scene tapes from old cases, as well as various other tapes and DVDs. He finally located a VHS tape marked GARLAND on the box and took it back to the bedroom.

He had a television with a built-in VCR on the bureau. He turned it on, slid in the tape and sat on the edge of the bed with the remote. He kept his boxers on now that he and Rachel were working. Rachel stayed under the covers and as the tape was cuing up she reached a foot toward him and tapped her toes on his back.

"Is this what you do with all the girls you bring here? Show them your interrogation techniques?"

Bosch glanced back at her and was almost serious with his response.

"Rachel, I think you're the only person in the world I could do this with."

She smiled.

"I think I get you, Bosch."

He looked back at the screen. The tape was playing. He hit the mute with the remote.

"This first one is March eleventh of 'ninety-four. It's about six months after Gesto disappeared and we were grasping for anything. We didn't have enough to arrest him — it wasn't even close — but I was able to convince him to come into the station to give a statement. He didn't know I had the bead on him. He thought he was just going to talk about the apartment where his ex-girlfriend had lived."

On the screen was a grainy color picture of a small room with a table at which two men sat. One was a much younger-looking Harry Bosch and the other was a man in his early twenties with wavy surfer-white hair. Anthony Garland. He was wearing a T-shirt that said *Lakers* across the chest. The sleeves were tight on his arms, and tattoo ink was visible on his left biceps. Black barbed wire wrapped the muscles of the arm.

"He came in voluntarily. He came in looking like he was headed to a day at the beach. Anyway . . ."

He brought up the sound. On the screen, Garland was looking all around the room with a slight smile on his face.

"So this is where it happens, huh?" he asked.

"Where what happens?" Bosch asked.

"You know, you break the bad guys down and they confess to all the crimes."

He smiled coyly.

"Sometimes," Bosch said. "But let's talk about Marie Gesto. Did you know her?"

"No, I told you I didn't know her. Never saw her before in my life."

"Before what?"

"Before you showed me her picture."

"So if somebody told me you knew her, then they'd be lying."

"Fucking-A right. Who told you that shit?"

"But you knew about the empty garage at the High Tower, right?"

"Yeah, well, my girlfriend had just moved

out and so, yeah, I knew the place was empty. That doesn't mean I stashed the car in there. Look, you asked me all of this stuff at the house. I thought there was something new going on here. Am I under arrest or something?"

"No, Anthony, you are not under arrest. I just wanted you to come down so we could go over some of this stuff."

"I've already gone over it with you."

"But that was before we knew some other things about you and about her. Now it's important to go over the same ground again. Make a formal record of it."

Garland's face seemed to momentarily contort in anger. He leaned across the table.

"What things? What the fuck are you talking about? I had nothing to do with this. I've told you that at least twice now. Why aren't you out there looking for the person who did it?"

Bosch waited until Garland calmed a bit before answering.

"Because maybe I think I'm with the person who did it."

"Fuck you, man. You've got nothing on me because there's nothing to get. I've told you this from day one. I'm not the guy!"

Now Bosch leaned across the table. Their faces were a foot apart.

"I know what you told me, Anthony. But that was before I went to Austin and talked to your girlfriend. She told me some things about you that, frankly, Anthony, require me to pay a little more attention."

"Fuck her. She's a whore!"

"Yeah? If she's all of that, then why'd you get angry with her when she left you? Why did she have to run from you? Why didn't you just let her go?"

"Because nobody leaves me. I leave them. Okay?"

Bosch leaned back and nodded.

"Okay. So in as much detail as you can remember, tell me what you did on September ninth of last year. Tell me where you went and who you saw."

Using the remote, Bosch started fast-forwarding the tape.

"He didn't have an alibi for the time we believed Marie was grabbed outside the supermarket. But we can skip ahead here because that part of the interview took forever."

Rachel was now sitting up in the bed behind him with the sheet wrapped around her. Bosch looked back at her.

"What do you think of this guy so far?"

She shrugged her bare shoulders.

"He seems like a typical rich asshole. But that doesn't make him a murderer."

Bosch nodded.

"This now is two years later. The lawyers from his daddy's firm slapped a TRO on me and I could only interview the kid if he had counsel present. So there's nothing much here but there's one thing I want you to see. His lawyer in this is Dennis Franks, an associate of Cecil Dobbs, a big-shot Century City guy who handles things for T. Rex."

"T. Rex?"

"The father. Thomas Rex Garland. Likes to be called T. Rex."

"Figures."

Bosch slowed the fast-forward down a notch so he could better see where the action on the tape was. On the screen was Garland sitting at a table with a man right next to him. As the image moved in fast motion the lawyer and his client conferred many times in mouth-to-ear communications. Bosch finally slowed it to normal speed and the audio came back up. It was Franks, the lawyer, doing the talking.

"My client has fully cooperated with you but you continue to harass him at work and home with these suspicions and questions that have not one ounce of evidentiary support."

"I'm working on that part of it, Counselor," Bosch said. "And when I get it, there won't be a lawyer in the world who can help him."

"Fuck you, Bosch!" Garland said. "You better hope you never come for me alone, man. I'll put you down in the dirt."

Franks put a calming hand on Garland's arm. Bosch was silent for a few moments before responding.

"You want to threaten me now, Anthony? You think I'm like one of those teenagers you cuff out in the oil fields and dump crude on? You think I'm going to go away with my tail between my legs?"

Garland's face pinched together and turned dark. His eyes looked like frozen black marbles.

Bosch hit the pause button on the VCR remote.

"There," he said to Rachel, pointing at the screen with the remote. "That's what I wanted you to see. Look at his face. Pure, perfect rage. That's why I thought it was him."

Walling didn't respond. Bosch glanced at her and she looked as though she had seen the face of pure, perfect rage before. She looked to be almost intimidated by it. Bosch wondered if she had seen it in one of the killers she had faced, or in someone else.

Bosch turned back to the television and hit the fast-forward button again.

"Now we jump almost ten years, to when I brought him in last April. Franks was gone and a new guy had the case in Dobbs's office. He dropped the ball and never went back to the judge when the first restraining order expired. So I took another shot at him. He was surprised to see me. I grabbed him when he came out of Kate Mantilini's at lunch one day. He probably thought I was long gone from his life."

He stopped the fast-forward and played the tape. On the screen Garland looked older and wider. His face had spread and he wore his now-thinning hair cropped short. He wore a white shirt with a tie. The taped interviews had followed him from the end of boyhood to well into manhood.

This time he sat in a different interview room. This one was at Parker Center.

"If I'm not under arrest, then I should be free to go," he said. "Am I free to go?"

"I was hoping you'd answer a few questions first," Bosch replied.

"I answered all your questions years ago. This is a vendetta, Bosch. You will not give up. You will not leave me alone. Am I free to go or not?"

"Where did you hide her body?"

Garland shook his head.

"My God, this is unbelievable. When will this end?"

"It will never end, Garland. Not until I find her and not until I lock you up."

"This is fucking crazy! *You're* crazy, Bosch. What can I say to make you believe me? What can —"

"You can tell me where she is and then I'll believe you."

"Well, that's the one thing I can't tell you, because I don't —"

Bosch suddenly killed the TV with the remote. For the first time, he realized how case-blind he had been, going after Garland as relentlessly as a dog chasing a car. He was unaware of the traffic, unaware that right in front of him in the murder book was the clue to the real killer. Watching the tape with Walling had heaped humiliation upon humiliation. He had thought by showing her the tape she would see why he had focused on Garland. She would understand and absolve him of the mistake. But now seeing it through the prism of Waits's impending confession he couldn't even absolve himself.

Rachel leaned toward him and touched his back, her soft fingers tracing down his spine.

"It happens to all of us," she said.

Bosch nodded. Not to me, he thought.

"I guess when this is all over I'm going to have to find him and apologize," he said.

"Fuck him. He's still an asshole. I wouldn't bother."

Bosch smiled. She was trying to make it easy for him.

"You think?"

She pulled back the elastic waistband on his boxers and then snapped them against his back.

"I think I have at least another hour before I should be thinking about getting home."

Bosch turned to look at her and she smiled.

10

The next morning Bosch and Rider walked from the Hall of Records to the CCB and despite the wait for an elevator still got to the DA's office twenty minutes early. O'Shea and Olivas were ready for them. Everyone took the same seats as before. Bosch noticed that the posters that had been leaning against the wall were gone. They had probably been put to good use somewhere, maybe sent to the public hall where the candidates' forum was scheduled for that night.

As he sat down Bosch saw the Gesto murder book on O'Shea's desk. He took it without asking and immediately opened it to the chronological record. He combed through the 51s until he found the page for September 29, 1993. He looked at the entry Olivas had told him about the evening before. It was, as it had been read to Bosch, the last entry of the day. Bosch felt the deep sense of regret tug at him all over again.

"Detective Bosch, we all make mistakes," O'Shea said. "Let's just move on from it and do the best we can today."

Bosch looked up at him and eventually nodded. He closed the book and put it back on the desk. O'Shea continued.

"I am told that Maury Swann is in the interview room with Mr. Waits and is ready to go. I have been thinking about this and I want to take the cases one at a time and in order. We start with Fitzpatrick and when we are satisfied by the confession, we move on to the Gesto case, and when we are satisfied there, we move on to the next one and so on."

Everybody nodded except for Bosch.

"I am not going to be satisfied until we have her remains," he said.

Now O'Shea nodded. He lifted a document off his desk.

"I understand that. If you can locate the

victim based on the statements from Waits, then fine. If it is a matter of him leading us to the body, I have a release order ready to go to the judge. I would say that if we reach a point where we are taking this man out of lockup, then the security should be extraordinary. There will be a lot riding on this and we cannot have any mistakes."

O'Shea took the time to look from detective to detective to make sure they understood the gravity of the situation. He would be gambling his campaign and political life on the security of Raynard Waits.

"We'll be ready for anything," Olivas said.

The look of concern on O'Shea's face didn't change.

"You're going to have a uniformed presence, right?" he asked.

"I don't think it is necessary — uniforms draw attention," Olivas said. "We can handle him. But if you want it we'll have it."

"I think it would be good to have, yes."

"No problem, then. We'll either get a car from Metro to go with us or a couple deputies from the jail."

O'Shea nodded his approval.

"Then, are we ready to start?"

"There's one thing," Bosch said. "We're

not sure who that is in the interview room waiting for us, but we're pretty sure his name isn't Raynard Waits."

A look of surprise played off O'Shea's face and immediately became contagious. Olivas dropped his mouth open an inch and leaned forward.

"We made him on fingerprints," Olivas protested. "On the prior."

Bosch nodded.

"Yes, the prior. As you know, when he was popped thirteen years ago for prowling, he first gave the name Robert Saxon along with the birth date of eleven/three/'seventy-five. This is the same name he used later that year when he called about Gesto, only then he gave the birth date of eleven/three/ 'seventy-one. But when he was pulled in on the prowling and they ran his prints through the computer, they matched the thumb to the DL of Raynard Waits, with a birth date of eleven/three/'seventy-one. So we keep getting the same month and day but different years. Anyway, when confronted with the thumbprint he copped to being Raynard Waits, saying he had given the false name and year because he was hoping to be handled as a juvenile. This is all in the file."

"But where does all of it go?" O'Shea said impatiently.

"Just let me finish. He got probation for the prowling because it was a first offense. In the probation report bio he said he was born and raised in L.A., okay? We just came from the Hall of Records. There is no record of Raynard Waits being born in L.A. on that date or any other. There have been a lot of Robert Saxons born in L.A. but none on November third of either of the years mentioned in the files."

"The bottom line," Rider said, "is we don't know who the man we are about to talk to is."

O'Shea pushed back from his desk and stood up. He paced around the spacious office as he thought and spoke about this latest information.

"Okay, so what are you saying, that the DMV had the wrong prints on file or there was some sort of a mix-up?"

Bosch turned in his seat so he could look at O'Shea while he answered.

"I'm saying that this guy, whoever he really is, could have gone to the DMV thirteen, fourteen, years ago to set up a false ID. What do you need to get a driver's license? Proof of age. Back then, you could buy phony IDs and birth certificates on Hollywood Boulevard, no problem. Or he could have bribed a DMV employee, could have done a lot of things. The point is, there is no record of him being born here in L.A., as he said he was. That puts all the rest in doubt."

"Maybe that's the lie," Olivas said. "Maybe he *is* Waits and he lied about being born here. It's like when you're born out in Riverside, you tell everybody you're from L.A."

Bosch shook his head. He didn't accept the logic Olivas was slinging.

"The name is false," Bosch insisted. "Raynard is a take on a character from medieval folklore known as Reynard the Fox. It's spelled with an e but it's pronounced the same. Put that with the last name and you have 'the little fox waits.' Get it? You can't convince me somebody gave him that name at birth."

That brought a momentary silence to the room.

"I don't know," O'Shea said, thinking out loud. "Seems a little far-fetched, this medieval connection."

"It's only far-fetched because we can't nail it down," Bosch countered. "You ask me, it's more far-fetched that this would be his given name."

"So what are you saying?" Olivas asked. "That he changed his name and continued to use it, even after he had an arrest tail on it? That doesn't make sense to me."

"Doesn't make a lot of sense to me, either. But we don't know the story behind it yet."

"Okay, so what are you suggesting we do?" O'Shea asked.

"Not much," Bosch said. "I'm just bringing it up. But I do think we ought to go on the record with it up there. You know, ask him to state his name, DOB, and place of birth. As if it is the routine way to start one of these interviews. If he gives us Waits, then we might be able to catch him in the lie down the road and prosecute him for everything. You said that was the deal; if he lies, he fries. We can turn it all against him."

O'Shea was standing by the coffee table behind where Bosch and Rider sat. Bosch turned again, to watch him take in the suggestion. The prosecutor was grinding it over and nodding.

"I don't see where it could hurt," he finally said. "Just get it on the record but let it go at that. Real subtle and routine. We can come back to him on it later — if we find out more about this."

Bosch looked at Rider.

"You'll be the one starting out with him, asking about the first case. Your first question can be about his name."

"Fine," she said.

O'Shea came back around the desk.

"Okay, then," he said. "Are we ready? It's time to go. I will try to stay with it as long as my schedule allows. Don't be offended if I jump in from time to time with a question."

Bosch answered by standing up. Rider followed suit and then Olivas.

"One last thing," Bosch said. "We picked up a Maury Swann story yesterday that maybe you guys ought to know."

Both Bosch and Rider took turns telling the story Abel Pratt had told them. By the end, Olivas was laughing and shaking his head and Bosch could tell by O'Shea's face that he was trying to count how many times he had shaken Maury Swann's hand in court. Maybe he was worrying about potential political fallout.

Bosch headed to the door of the office. He felt a mixture of excitement and dread rising. He was excited because he knew he was finally about to find out what had happened to Marie Gesto so long ago. At the same time, he dreaded finding out. And he dreaded the fact that the details he would soon learn would place a heavy burden on him. A burden he would have to transfer to a waiting mother and father up in Bakersfield.

11

Two uniformed sheriff's deputies stood at the door to the interview room in which sat the man who called himself Raynard Waits. They stepped aside and allowed the prosecutorial entourage to enter. The room contained one long table. Waits and his defense attorney, Maury Swann, were sitting on one side of it. Waits was directly in the middle and Swann was to his left. When the investigators and the prosecutor entered, only Maury Swann stood. Waits was held to the arms of his chair with plastic snap cuffs. Swann, a thin man with black-framed glasses and a luxurious mane of silver hair, offered his hand but no one shook it.

Rider took the chair directly across the table from Waits, and Bosch and O'Shea sat on either side of her. Since Olivas would not be up in the interview rotation for some time, he took the last remaining chair, which was next to the door.

O'Shea handled the introductions but again nobody bothered shaking anybody else's hand. Waits was in an orange jumpsuit that had black letters stenciled across the chest.

L.A. COUNTY JAIL
KEEP AWAY

The second line was not intended as a warning but it was just as good as one. It meant that Waits was on keep-away status within the jail, indicating he was housed by himself and not allowed into the general inmate population. This status was taken as a protective measure for both Waits and the other inmates.

As Bosch studied the man he had been hunting for thirteen years he realized that the most frightening thing about Waits was how ordinary he looked. Slightly built, he had an everyman's face. Pleasant, with soft features and short dark hair, he was the epitome of normality. The only hint of the evil that lay within was found in the eyes. Dark brown and deeply set, they carried an emptiness that Bosch recognized from other killers he had sat face-to-face with over the years. Nothing there. Just a hollowness that could never be filled, no matter how many other lives he stole.

Rider turned on the tape recorder that was on the table and started the interview perfectly, giving Waits no reason to suspect he was stepping into a trap with the very first question of the session.

"As was probably explained to you already by Mr. Swann, we are going to record each session with you and then turn the tapes over to your attorney, who will hold them until we have a completed agreement. Is that understood and approved by you?"

"Yes, it is," Waits said.

"Good," Rider said. "Then let's begin with an easy one. Can you state your name, birth date and place of birth for the record?"

Waits leaned forward and made a face like he was stating the obvious to schoolchildren.

"Raynard Waits," he said impatiently. "Born

November third, nineteen seventy-one, in the city of angles — oh, I mean angels. The city of angels."

"If you mean Los Angeles, could you please say it?"

"Yes, Los Angeles."

"Thank you. Your first name is unusual. Could you spell it for the tape?"

Waits complied. Again, it was a good move by Rider. It would make it even more difficult for the man in front of them to argue later that he had not knowingly lied during the interview.

"Do you know where the name came from?"

"My father pulled it out of his ass, I guess. I don't know. I thought we were here to talk about dead people, not the piddly basic shit."

"We are, Mr. Waits. We are."

Bosch felt an enormous sense of relief inside. He knew that they were about to sit through a retelling of horrors but he felt they already had Waits caught in a lie that might spring a fatal trap on him. There was now a chance that he was not going to walk away from this to a private cell and a life of public maintenance and celebrity.

"We want to take these in order," Rider said. "Your attorney's proffer suggests that the first homicide you were ever involved in was the death of Daniel Fitzpatrick in Hollywood on April thirtieth, nineteen ninety-two. Is that correct?"

Waits answered with the sort of matter-of-fact demeanor one would expect from someone giving directions to the nearest gas station. His voice was cold and calm.

"Yes, I burned him alive behind his security cage. It turned out that he wasn't so secure back there. Not even with all of his guns."

"Why did you do that?"

"Because I wanted to see if I could. I had been thinking about it for a long time and I just wanted to prove myself."

Bosch thought about what Rachel Walling had said to him the night before. She had called it a "spree killing." It looked like she had been right.

"What do you mean by 'prove yourself,' Mr. Waits?" Rider asked.

"I mean there is a line out there that everybody thinks about but not many have the guts to cross. I wanted to see if I could cross it."

"When you say you had been thinking about it for a long time, had you been thinking about Mr. Fitzpatrick in particular?"

Annoyance flared in Waits's eyes. It was as if he were putting up with her.

"No, you stupid cunt," he replied calmly. "I had been thinking about killing someone. You understand? All my life I had wanted to do it."

Rider shook off the insult without a flinch and kept moving.

"Why did you choose Daniel Fitzpatrick? Why did you choose that night?"

"Well, because I was watching TV and I saw the whole city coming apart. It was chaos out there and I knew the police couldn't do anything about it. It was a time when people were doing just what they wanted. I saw a guy on the tube talking about Hollywood Boulevard and how places were burning and I decided to go out to see it. I didn't want the TV showing it to me. I wanted to see it for myself."

"Did you drive there?"

"No, I could walk. Back then I lived on Fountain near LaBrea. I just walked up."

Rider had the Fitzpatrick file open in front of her. She glanced down at it for a moment while collecting her thoughts and formulating the next set of questions. That gave O'Shea the opportunity to jump in.

"Where did the lighter fluid come from?" he asked. "Did you take it with you from your apartment?"

Waits shifted his focus to O'Shea.

"I thought the dyke was asking the questions," he said.

"We're all asking the questions," O'Shea said. "And could you please keep the personal attacks out of your responses?"

"Not you, Mr. District Attorney. I don't want to talk to you. Only her. And them."

He pointed to Bosch and Olivas.

"Let me just back up a little bit before we get to the lighter fluid," Rider said, smoothly pushing O'Shea to the side. "You said you walked up to Hollywood Boulevard from Fountain. Where did you go and what did you see?"

Waits smiled and nodded at Rider.

"I got that right, didn't I?" he said. "I can always tell. I can always smell it on a woman, when she likes pussy."

"Mr. Swann," Rider said, "can you please tell your client that this is about him answering our questions, not the other way around?"

Swann put his hand on Waits's left forearm, which was bound to the arm of his chair.

"Ray," he said. "Don't play games. Just answer the questions. Remember, we want this. We brought it to them. It's our show."

Bosch saw a slow burn move across Waits's face as he turned and looked at his lawyer. But then it quickly disappeared and he looked back at Rider.

"I saw the city burning, that's what I saw."

He smiled after giving the answer.

"It was like a Hieronymus Bosch painting."

He turned to Bosch as he said this. It froze Bosch for a moment. How did he know?

Waits nodded toward Bosch's chest.

"It's on your ID card."

Bosch had forgotten that they'd had to clip their IDs on once they entered the DA's office. Rider moved in quickly with the next question.

"Okay, which way did you walk once you got to Hollywood Boulevard?"

"I took a right and headed east. The bigger fires were down that way."

"What was in your pockets?"

The question seemed to give him pause.

"I don't know. I don't remember. My keys, I guess. Cigarettes and a lighter, that was all."

"Did you have your wallet?"

"No, I didn't want to have ID with me. In case the police stopped me."

"Did you already have the lighter fluid with you?"

"That's right, I did. I thought I might join in the fun, help burn the city to the ground. Then I walked by that pawnshop and got a better idea."

"You saw Mr. Fitzpatrick?"

"Yeah, I saw him. He was standing inside his security fence holding a shotgun. He also was wearing a holster like he was Wyatt Earp or something."

"Describe the pawnshop."

Waits shrugged.

"A small place. It was called Irish Pawn. It had this neon sign out front that flashed a green three-leaf clover and then the three balls, you know, that are like the symbol for a pawnshop, I guess. Fitzpatrick was standing there, watching me when I passed by."

"And you kept walking?"

"At first I did. I passed by and then I

thought about the challenge, you know? How could I get to him without getting shot by that big fucking bazooka he was holding."

"What did you do?"

"I took the can of EasyLight out of my jacket pocket and filled my mouth with it. Squirted it right in, like those flame breathers do on the Venice boardwalk. I then put the can away and got out a cigarette and my lighter. I don't smoke anymore. It's a terrible habit."

He looked at Bosch as he said this.

"Then what?" Rider asked.

"I went back to the asshole's shop and walked into the alcove in front of the security fence. I acted like I was just looking for a blind to try to light my smoke. It was windy that night, you understand?"

"Yes."

"So he started yelling at me to get the fuck away. He came right up to the fence to yell at me. And I was counting on that."

He smiled, proud of how well his plan worked.

"The guy hit the stock of his shotty against the steel fence to get my attention. You see, he saw my hands, so he didn't realize the danger. And when he was about two feet away I got a flame on the lighter and looked him right in the eyes. I took the cigarette out of my mouth and spit all of that lighter fluid into his face. Of course, it hit the lighter on the way and I was a fucking flamethrower. He had a face full a' flames before he knew what hit him. He dropped the shotty pretty fast so he could try to slap at the flames. But his clothes went up and pretty soon he was one crispy critter. It was like being hit by napalm, man."

Waits tried to raise his left arm but couldn't. It was bound to the armrest at the wrist. He turned and raised his hand instead.

"Unfortunately, I burned my hand a little bit. Blisters, the whole thing. It really hurt, too. I can't imagine what that asshole Wyatt Earp felt. Not a good way to go, if you ask me."

Bosch looked at the upraised hand. He saw a discoloration in the skin tone, but not a scar. The burn had not gone deep.

After a long measure of silence, Rider asked another question.

"Did you seek medical attention for your hand?"

"No, I didn't think that would be too smart, considering the situation. And from what I heard, the hospitals were overflowing. So I went on home and took care of it myself."

"When did you place the can of lighter fluid in front of the store?"

"Oh, that was when I was walking away. I just took it out, wiped it off and put it down."

"Did Mr. Fitzpatrick call out for help at any time?"

Waits paused as if to ponder the question.

"Well, that's hard to say. He was yelling something, but I am not sure it was for help. He just kind of sounded like an animal to me. I closed the door on my dog's tail once when I was kid. It sort of reminded me of that."

"What were you thinking as you were walking home?"

"I was thinking, Far-fucking-out! I finally did it! And I knew I was going to get away with it, too. I felt like I was pretty goddamn invincible, if you want to know the truth."

"How old were you?"

"I was . . . I was twenty, man, and I fuckin' did it!"

"Did you ever think about the man you killed, who you burned to death?"

"No, not really. He was just there. There for the taking. Like the rest of them that came after. It was like they were there for me."

Rider spent another forty minutes questioning him, eliciting smaller details that nonetheless matched those contained in the investigative reports. Finally, at 11:15 she seemed to relax her posture and pull back from her place at the table. She turned to look at Bosch and then at O'Shea.

"I think I have enough for the moment," she said. "Maybe we could take a short break at this point."

She turned off the tape recorder, and the three investigators and O'Shea stepped out into the hallway to confer. Swann stayed in the interview room with his client.

"What do you think?" O'Shea said to Rider.

She nodded.

"I'm satisfied. I don't think there is any doubt that he did it. He solved the mystery of how he got to him. I don't think he's telling us everything but he knows enough of the details. He either did it or he was right there."

O'Shea looked at Bosch.

"Should we move on?"

Bosch thought about this for a moment. He was ready. As he had watched Rider interview Waits his anger and disgust had grown. The man in the interview room showed such a callous disregard for his victim that Bosch recognized it as the classic profile of a psychopath. As before, he dreaded what he would next hear from the man but he was ready to hear it.

"Let's do it," he said.

They all moved back into the interview room and Swann immediately suggested that they break for lunch.

"My client is hungry."

"Gotta feed the dog," Waits added with a smile.

Bosch shook his head, taking charge of the room.

"Not yet," he said. "He'll eat when we all eat."

He took the seat directly across from Waits and turned the recorder back on. Rider and O'Shea took the wing positions and Olivas sat once again in the chair by the door. Bosch had taken the Gesto file back from Olivas but had it closed in front of him on the table.

"We're going to move on now to the Marie Gesto case," he said.

"Ah, sweet Marie," Waits said.

He looked at Bosch with a brightness in his eyes.

"Your attorney's proffer suggests that you know what happened to Marie Gesto when she disappeared in nineteen ninety-three. Is that true?"

Waits frowned and nodded.

"Yes, I'm afraid so," he said with mock sincerity.

"Do you know the current whereabouts of Marie Gesto or the location of her remains?"

"Yes, I do."

Here it was, the moment Bosch had waited on for thirteen years.

"She's dead, isn't she?"

Waits looked at him and nodded.

"Is that a yes?" Bosch asked for the tape.

"That is a yes. She's dead."

"Where is she?"

Waits broke into a broad smile, the smile of a man who had not an atom of regret or guilt in his DNA.

"She's right here, Detective," he said. "She's right here with me. Just like all the others. Right here with me."

His smile turned into a laugh and Bosch almost went across the table at him. But Rider moved her hand under the table and put it on his leg. It immediately calmed him.

"Hold on a second," O'Shea said. "Let's step out again, and this time I would like you to join us, Maury."

12

O'Shea charged into the hallway first and managed to pace back and forth twice before all the others were out of the interview room. He then instructed the two deputies to go into the room and keep an eye on Waits. The door was then closed.

"What the fuck, Maury?" O'Shea barked. "We're not going to spend our time in there laying the groundwork for an insanity defense for you. This is a confession, not a defense maneuver."

Swann turned his palms up in a what-can-I-do gesture.

"The guy obviously has issues," he said.

"Bullshit. He's a stone-cold killer and he's

in there vamping like Hannibal Lecter. This
isn't a movie, Maury. This is real. You hear
what he said about Fitzpatrick? He was
more worried about a little burn on his hand
than he was about the guy whose face he
spit flames into. So I'll tell you what, you go
back in there and take five minutes with
your client. Set him straight or we walk
away from this and everybody takes their
chances."

Bosch was unconsciously nodding. He
liked the anger in O'Shea's voice. He also
liked the way this was going.

"I'll see what I can do," Swann said.

He went back into the interview room and
the deputies came back out to give the attorney and his client privacy. O'Shea continued to pace while he cooled down.

"Sorry about that," he said to no one in
particular. "But I'm not going to let them
control this thing."

"They already are," Bosch said. "Waits is,
at least."

O'Shea looked at him, ready for a fight.

"What are you saying?"

"I mean we're all here because of him. The
bottom line is, we are engaged in an effort
to save his life — at his own request."

O'Shea emphatically shook his head.

"I'm not going to go back and forth on that issue with you again, Bosch. The decision has been made. At this point, if you're not on board, the elevator's right down the hall to the left. I'll handle your part of the interview. Or Freddy will."

Bosch waited a beat before answering.

"I didn't say I wasn't on board. Gesto is my case and I will see it through."

"Nice to hear it," O'Shea said with full sarcasm. "Too bad you weren't so attentive back in 'ninety-three."

He reached over and knocked harshly on the interview room door. Bosch stared at his back with anger welling up from some place deep inside. Swann opened the door almost immediately.

"We're ready to continue," he said as he stepped back to let them in.

After everyone retook their seats, and the recorder was turned back on, Bosch shook off his anger at O'Shea and locked eyes with Waits again. He repeated the question.

"Where is she?"

Waits smiled slightly, like he was tempted to set things off again, but then the smile turned into a smirk and he answered.

"Up in the hills."

"Where in the hills?"

"Up near the stables. That's where I got her. Right when she was getting out of her car."

"Is she buried?"

"Yes, she is buried."

"Exactly where is she buried?"

"I would have to show you. It's a place I know but I can't describe . . . I would just have to show you."

"Try to describe it."

"It's just a place in the woods near where she parked. You go in and there's a path and then I went off the path. Way off the path. You could go look and either find it right away or maybe never find it. There's a lot of territory up there. You remember, they searched up there but they never found her."

"And after thirteen years you believe you could lead us to this spot?"

"It hasn't been thirteen years."

A sudden rush of horror came over Bosch. The idea that he had held her captive was too abhorrent to think about.

"It's not what you think, Detective," Waits said.

"How do you know what I am thinking?"

"I just do. But it's not what you think. Marie has been buried for thirteen years. But it has not been thirteen years since I was there. That's what I'm saying. I visited her, Detective. I visited her there quite often. So I can certainly lead you there."

Bosch paused, took out a pen and wrote a note on the inside flap of the Gesto file. It wasn't a note of any importance. It just gave him a moment to disengage from the emotions that were coming up.

"Let's go back to the beginning," he said. "Did you know Marie Gesto before September nineteen ninety-three?"

"No, I didn't."

"Had you ever seen her before the day you abducted her?"

"Not that I remember."

"Where did you first cross paths with her?"

"At the Mayfair. I saw her in there shopping and she was just my type. I followed her."

"Where?"

"She got in her car and drove up Beachwood Canyon. She parked in the gravel lot below the stables. I believe it is called Sunset Ranch. There was no one around when she was getting out, so I decided to take her."

"It wasn't planned before you saw her in the store?"

"No, I went there to buy some Gatorade. It was a hot day. I saw her and decided right then that I had to have her. You know, it was an impulse. I couldn't do anything about it, Detective."

"You approached her in the lot below the stables?"

He nodded.

"I pulled in right next to her in my van. She didn't think a thing about it. The parking area is down the hill from the ranch, from the stables. There was no one around, no one who could see. It was perfect. It was like God said I could have her."

"What did you do?"

"I went into the back of the van and I opened the sliding door on the side where she was. I had a knife and I just stepped out and told her to get in. She did. It was a simple operation really. She was no trouble at all."

He spoke as if he were a babysitter reporting on a child's behavior when the parents have returned home.

"Then what?" Bosch asked.

"I asked her to remove her clothes and she complied. She told me she would do whatever I wanted as long as I didn't hurt her. I agreed to that deal. She folded her clothes very nicely. As if she thought she would get the chance to put them back on again."

Bosch rubbed a hand over his mouth. The most difficult part of his job were the times he was face-to-face with a killer, when he saw firsthand the intersection of their warped and terrifying world with reality.

"Go on," he said to Waits.

"Well, you know the rest. We had sex but she was no good at it. She couldn't relax. So I did what I had to do."

"Which was what?"

Waits locked eyes with Bosch.

"I killed her, Detective. I put my hands around her neck and I squeezed and then I squeezed harder and I watched her eyes go still. Then I finished up."

Bosch stared at him but couldn't bring himself to open his mouth. It was moments like these that made him feel inadequate as a detective, moments when he was cowed by the depravity that was possible in the human form. They stared at each other for a long moment until O'Shea spoke.

"You had sex with her body?" he asked.

"That's right. While she was still warm. I always say a woman is at her best when she is dead but still warm."

Waits glanced at Rider to see if he had gotten a reaction. She showed nothing.

"Waits," Bosch said. "You are a worthless piece of trash."

Waits looked back at Bosch and put the smirk back on his face.

"If that is your best shot, Detective Bosch, then you'll have to do much better. Because it will only get worse for you from here. Sex is nothing. Alive or dead, it is transitory. But I took her soul and no one will ever get that back from me."

Bosch looked down at the open file in front of him but did not see the words printed on the documents.

"Let's move on," he finally said. "What did you do next?"

"I tidied up the van. I always had plastic drop sheets in the back. I wrapped her up and prepared her for burial. I then got out and locked the van. I took her things back to her car. I had her keys, too. I got in her car and drove it away. I thought that would be the best way to throw the police off."

"Where did you go?"

"You know where I went, Detective. The High Tower. I knew there was an empty garage that I could use there. A week or so before, I had gone to look for work there and the manager happened to mention there was an open apartment. He showed it to me because I acted like I was interested."

"He showed you the garage, too?"

"No, just pointed it out. On my way out I noticed that there was no lock on the latch."

"So you drove Marie Gesto's car there and stashed it in the garage."

"That's right."

"Did anyone see you? Did you see anyone?"

"No and no. I was very careful. Remember, I had just killed someone."

"What about your van? When did you go back up Beachwood to get it?"

"I waited until that night. I thought that would be better because I had some digging to do. You understand, I'm sure."

"Was this van painted with the name of your business?"

"No, not then. I had just started and was

not trying to draw attention yet. I worked mostly off referrals. I didn't have a city license yet. All of that came later. In fact, that was another van altogether. That was thirteen years ago. I've gotten a new van since then."

"How did you get back up to the stables to get your van?"

"Took a cab."

"You remember which cab company?"

"I don't remember because I didn't call for it. After dropping off the car at the High Tower I walked over to a restaurant I used to enjoy when I lived on Franklin. Bird's — have you ever been there? Good roasted chicken. Anyway, it was a long walk. I had dinner and when it was late enough I had them call me a cab. I went up to my van, only I had him drop me up at the stables so it wouldn't look like the van was mine. When I was sure there was no one around I went to the van and I found a nice private spot to plant my little flower."

"And this is a spot you will still be able to find?"

"Absolutely."

"You dug a hole."

"I did."

"How deep?"

"I don't know, not too deep."

"What did you use to dig it?"

"I had a shovel."

"You always carried a shovel in your window-washing van?"

"No, actually. I found it leaning against the barn up at the stables. I think it was for cleaning out the stalls, that sort of thing."

"You put it back when you were finished?"

"Of course, Detective. I steal souls, not shovels."

Bosch looked at the files in front of him.

"When was the last time you were at the place where you buried Marie Gesto?"

"Mmmm, a little over a year ago. I usually made the trip every September ninth. You know, to celebrate our anniversary. This year I was a bit tied up, as you know."

He smiled good-naturedly.

Bosch knew he had covered everything in general terms. It would all come down to whether Waits could lead them to the body and if Forensics would then match his story.

"There came a time after the murder when the media paid a lot of attention to Marie Gesto's disappearance," Bosch said. "Do you remember that?"

"Of course. That taught me a good lesson. I never acted so impulsively again. I was more careful about the flowers I picked after that."

"You called the investigators on the case, didn't you?"

"As a matter of fact I did. I remember that. I called and told them that I had seen her in the Mayfair store and that she hadn't been with anybody."

"Why did you call?"

Waits shrugged.

"I don't know. I just thought it would be fun. You know, to actually talk to one of the men who was hunting me. Was it you?"

"My partner."

"Yes, I thought I might be able to shift the focus away from the Mayfair. After all, I had been in there and I thought, who knows, maybe someone could describe me."

Bosch nodded.

"You gave the name Robert Saxon when you called. Why?"

Waits shrugged again.

"It was just a name I used from time to time."

"It's not your real name?"

"No, Detective, you know my real name."

"What if I told you I don't believe a fucking word you've said here today? What would you say to that?"

"I would say, take me to Beachwood Canyon and I will prove every word of what I have said here."

"Yeah, well, we'll see about that."

Bosch pushed back his chair and told the others he would like to confer with them in the hallway. Leaving Waits and Swann behind, they stepped out of the room into the cooler air of the hallway.

"Can you guys give us some space?" O'Shea said to the two deputies.

When everybody else was in the hallway and the interview room door was closed, O'Shea continued.

"Getting stuffy in there," he said.

"Yeah, with all of his bullshit," Bosch said.

"What now, Bosch?" the prosecutor asked.

"'What now' is that I don't believe him."

"Why not?"

"Because he knows every answer. And some of them don't work. We spent a week with the cab companies going over records for every pickup and drop. We knew that if the guy moved her car to the High Tower, then he needed some kind of ride back to his own car. The stables were one of the points we checked. Every cab company in the city. Nobody made a pickup or a drop-off up there that day or night."

Olivas injected himself into the conversation by stepping up next to O'Shea.

"That's not a hundred percent and you know it, Bosch," he said. "A cabbie could've given him a ride off the books. They do it all the time. There's also gypsy cabs. They hang outside restaurants all over the city."

"I still don't buy his bullshit stories. He's got an answer for everything. The shovel just happens to be leaning against the barn. How was he going to bury her if he didn't happen to see it?"

O'Shea spread his arms wide.

"There's one way to test him," he said. "We take him out on a field trip and if he leads us to that girl's body, then the little details that bother you aren't going to matter. On the other hand, if there is no body, then there is no deal."

"When do we go?" Bosch asked.

"I'll go see the judge today. We'll go tomorrow morning if you want."

"Wait a minute," Olivas said. "What about

the other seven? We still have a lot to talk to this bastard about."

O'Shea held one hand up in a calming motion.

"Let's make Gesto the test case. He either puts up or shuts up with this one. Then we'll go from there."

O'Shea turned and looked directly at Bosch.

"You going to be ready for this?" he asked.

Bosch nodded.

"I've been ready for thirteen years."

13

That night, Rachel brought dinner up to the house after calling first to see if Bosch was home. Bosch put some music on the stereo, and Rachel laid the dinner out on the dining room table on plates from the kitchen. The dinner was pot roast with a side of creamed corn. She'd brought a bottle of Merlot, too, and it took Bosch five minutes of hunting through kitchen drawers to find a cork-screw. They didn't talk about the case until they were sitting across from each other at the table.

"So," she said, "how did it go today?"

Bosch shrugged before answering.

"It went okay. Your take on everything was

very helpful. Tomorrow's the field trip, and in Rick O'Shea's words, it will be put-up or shut-up time."

"Field trip? Where to?"

"The top of Beachwood Canyon. He says that's where he buried her. I drove up there today after the interview and looked around — couldn't find anything, even using his description. Back in 'ninety-three we had the cadets looking in the canyon for three days and they found nothing. The woods are thick up there but he says he can find the spot."

"Do you believe he's the guy?"

"It looks like it. He's convinced everybody else and there's that call he made to us back then. That's pretty convincing."

"But what?"

"I don't know. Maybe it's my ego not being ready to accept I was so wrong, that for thirteen years I was looking at one guy and I was wrong about him. Nobody wants to face that, I guess."

Bosch concentrated on eating for a few moments. He then chased a mouthful of pot roast with some wine and wiped his mouth with a napkin.

"Man, this stuff is great. Where'd you get it?"

She smiled.

"Just another restaurant."

"No, this is the best pot roast I think I've ever had."

"It's a place called Jar. They say it stands for Just Another Restaurant."

"Oh, I get it."

"It's off Beverly near my place. They've got a long bar where you can eat. After moving out here I ate there a lot at first. Alone. Suzanne and Preech always take care of me. They let me take food to go and it's not that kind of place."

"They're the cooks?"

"Chefs. Suzanne's also the owner. I love sitting there at the bar and watching the people come in, watching their eyes scanning the place to see who's who. A lot of celebrities go there. You also get the foodies and you get the regular people. They're the most interesting."

"Somebody once said that if you circle around a murder long enough you get to know a city. Maybe it's the same with sitting at the counter in a restaurant."

"And easier to do. Harry, are you changing

the subject or are you going to tell me about Raynard Waits's confession?"

"I'm getting to it. I thought we'd finish eating first."

"That bad, huh?"

"It's not that. I think I just need a break from it. I don't know."

She nodded like she understood. She poured more wine into their glasses.

"I like the music. Who is this?"

Bosch nodded, his mouth full once again.

"I call this 'miracle in a box.' It's John Coltrane and Thelonious Monk at Carnegie Hall. The concert was recorded in nineteen fifty-seven and the tape sat in an unmarked box in archives for almost fifty years. Just sat there, forgotten. Then some Library of Congress guy was going through all the boxes and performance tapes and recognized what they had there. They finally put this out last year."

"It's nice."

"It's more than nice. It's a miracle to think it was there all that time. It took the right person to find it. To recognize it."

He looked at her eyes for a moment. He then looked down at his plate and saw he was down to his last bite.

"What would you have done for dinner if I hadn't called?" Rachel asked.

Bosch looked back at her and shrugged. He finished eating and started telling her about Raynard Waits's confession.

"He's lying," she said when he was finished.

"About the name? We've got that covered."

"No, about the plan. Rather, the lack of a plan. He tells you he just saw her in the Mayfair, followed her and grabbed her. Uh-uh, no way. I don't buy that. The whole thing doesn't feel like a spur-of-the-moment thing. There was a plan to this, whether he's telling you or not."

Bosch nodded. He had the same misgivings about the confession.

"We'll know more tomorrow, I guess," he said.

"I wish I could be there."

Bosch shook his head.

"I can't make a federal case out of this. Besides, it's not what you do anymore. Your own people wouldn't let you go, even if you were invited."

"I know. I can still wish."

Bosch got up and started clearing the

plates. They worked side by side at the sink and after everything was cleaned and put away they took the bottle out on the deck. There was enough left for them each to have a half glass.

The evening chill drew them close to one another as they stood at the railing and looked down at the lights in the Cahuenga Pass.

"Are you staying tonight?" Bosch asked.

"Yes."

"You don't have to call, you know. I'll give you a key. Just come up."

She turned and looked at him. He put his arm around her waist.

"That fast? Are you saying all is forgiven?"

"There's nothing to forgive. The past is past and life's too short. You know, all of those clichés."

She smiled and they sealed it with a kiss. They finished their wine and went inside to the bedroom. They made love slowly and quietly. At one point Bosch opened his eyes and looked at her and lost his rhythm. She noticed.

"What?" she whispered.

"Nothing. It's just that you keep your eyes open."

"I'm looking at you."

"No, you're not."

She smiled and turned her face away from him.

"This is sort of an awkward time for a discussion," she said.

He smiled and used his hand to turn her face to his. He kissed her and they both kept their eyes open now. Halfway through the kiss they started laughing.

Bosch craved the intimacy and reveled in the escape it brought. He knew she knew this, too. Her gift to him was in taking him away from the world. And that was why the past no longer mattered. He closed his eyes but didn't stop smiling.

Part Two

THE FIELD TRIP

14

It seemed to Bosch to take forever to amass the motorcade, but by 10:30 Wednesday morning the entourage was finally pulling out of the basement garage of the Criminal Courts Building.

The first car in line was unmarked. It was driven by Olivas. A sheriff's deputy from the jail division was riding shotgun, while in the back, Bosch and Rider were positioned on either side of Raynard Waits. The prisoner was in a bright orange jumpsuit and was bound by shackles on his ankles and wrists. The manacles on his wrists were secured in front to a chain that went around his waist.

Another unmarked car, driven by Rick

O'Shea and carrying Maury Swann and a DA's office evidence videographer, was second in the motorcade. It was followed by two vans, one from the LAPD's Scientific Investigation Division and the other from the coroner's office. The group was prepared to locate and disinter the body of Marie Gesto.

It was a perfect day for a field trip. A brief overnight rain shower had cleared the sky and it was a brilliant blue with just the last wisps of upper-level clouds in view. The streets were still wet and shiny. The precipitation had also kept the temperature from climbing with the sun's ascent. Though there can never be a good day to dig up the body of a twenty-two-year-old woman, the glory of the weather would offer a counterbalance to the grim duty at hand.

The vehicles stayed in a tight formation as they made their way onto the North 101 Freeway off the Broadway ramp. Traffic was heavy in downtown and moving at a slower than usual pace because of the wet streets. Bosch asked Olivas to crack a window to let in some fresh air and hopefully wash out the funk of Waits's body odor. It had become apparent that the admitted killer had not

been allowed a shower or issued a laun-
dered jumpsuit that morning.

"Why don't you just go ahead and light
up, Detective?" Waits said.

Since they were sitting shoulder to shoulder Bosch had to turn awkwardly to look at
Waits.

"I want the window open because of you,
Waits. You stink. I haven't had a smoke in
five years."

"I'm sure."

"Why do you think you know me? We've
never met. What makes you think you know
me, Waits?"

"I don't know you. I know your type. You
have an addictive personality, Detective.
Murder cases, cigarettes, maybe even the
alcohol I smell coming out of your pores.
You're not that hard to read."

Waits smiled and Bosch looked away. He
thought about things for a moment before
speaking again.

"Who are you?" he asked.

"Are you talking to me?" Waits asked.

"Yes, I'm talking to you. I want to know.
Who are you?"

"Bosch," Olivas quickly interjected from
the front. "The deal is, we don't question

him without Maury Swann being present. So leave him alone."

"This isn't an interrogation. I'm just making conversation back here."

"Yeah, well, I don't care what you want to call it. Don't."

Bosch could see Olivas looking at him in the rearview mirror. They held each other's stare until Olivas had to put his eyes back on the road.

Bosch leaned forward so that he could turn and look past Waits and over at Rider. She rolled her eyes at him. It was her don't-make-trouble look.

"Maury Swann," Bosch said. "Yeah, he's a good goddamn lawyer, all right. Got this man the deal of a lifetime."

"Bosch!" Olivas said.

"I'm not talking to him. I'm talking to my partner."

Bosch leaned back, deciding to drop it. Next to him the manacles clinked as Waits tried to adjust his position.

"You didn't have to take the deal, Detective Bosch," he said quietly.

"It wasn't my choice," Bosch said without looking at him. "If it had been, we wouldn't be doing this."

Waits nodded.

"An eye for an eye, man," he said. "I could have guessed. You're the kind of man who would —"

"Waits," Olivas said sharply. "Just keep your mouth shut."

Olivas reached toward the dash and turned on the radio. Loud mariachi music blared from the speakers. He immediately slapped the button to kill the sound.

"Who the fuck was driving this last?" he asked of no one in particular.

Bosch knew Olivas was covering up. He was embarrassed that he had not changed the channel or lowered the volume when he brought the car back last time.

The car remained silent. They were cutting through Hollywood now, and Olivas put on his turn signal and moved into the exit lane for Gower Avenue. Bosch turned around to look out the back window and see if they still had the other three vehicles with them. The group remained intact. But Bosch could now see a helicopter trailing above the motorcade. It had a large number 4 on its white underbelly. Bosch jerked back around and looked at Olivas in the rearview.

"Who called out the media, Olivas? Was that you or your boss?"

"My boss? I don't know what you're talking about."

Olivas glanced at him in the mirror but then quickly back at the road. It was too furtive a move. Bosch knew he was lying.

"Yeah, right. What's in this for you? Ricochet's going to make you chief of investigations after he wins? Is that it?"

Now Olivas held his eyes in the mirror.

"I'm not getting anywhere in the department. I might as well go where I'm respected and my skills are valued."

"What, is that the line you say to yourself in the mirror each morning?"

"Fuck you, Bosch."

"Gentlemen, gentlemen," Waits said. "Can't we all just get along here?"

"Shut up, Waits," Bosch said. "You might not care that this is being turned into a commercial for Candidate O'Shea, but I do. Olivas, pull over. I want to talk to O'Shea."

Olivas shook his head.

"No way. Not with a custody in the car."

They were coming down the exit ramp to Gower. Olivas took a quick right and they came to the light at Franklin. It turned green as they got there and they crossed Franklin and started up Beachwood Drive.

Olivas would not have to stop until they got to the top. Bosch pulled out his cell phone and called the number O'Shea had given everyone in the CCB garage that morning before heading off.

"O'Shea."

"It's Bosch. I don't think it was a smart thing to call the media out on this."

O'Shea held for a moment before answering.

"They're a safe distance. They're in the air."

"And who's going to be waiting for us at the top of Beachwood?"

"No one, Bosch. I was very specific with them. They could track us from the air but anyone on the ground would compromise the operation. You don't have to worry. They are working with me. They know they have to establish the relationship."

"Whatever."

Bosch closed his phone and jammed it back into his pocket.

"You need to calm down, Detective," Waits said.

"And, Waits, you need to keep quiet."

"Just trying to be helpful."

"Then shut the fuck up."

The car turned silent again. Bosch decided that his anger over the trailing media chopper and everything else was a distraction he didn't need. He tried to put it out of his mind and think about what was ahead.

Beachwood Canyon was a quiet neighborhood on the slope of the Santa Monica Mountains between Hollywood and Los Feliz. It didn't have the rustic, wooded charm of Laurel Canyon to the west but it was preferred by its inhabitants because it was quieter, safer, and self-contained. Unlike most of the canyon passes to the west, Beachwood reached a dead end at the top. It was not a route for going over the mountains, and consequently, the traffic in Beachwood did not consist of people just passing through. It consisted of people who belonged. That made it feel like a real neighborhood.

As they ascended, they saw that the Hollywood sign atop Mount Lee was directly in view through the windshield. It had been put up on the next ridge more than eighty years ago to advertise the Hollywoodland real-

estate development at the top of Beachwood. The sign was eventually shortened
and now advertised a state of mind more
than anything else. The only official indication left of Hollywoodland was the fortress-
like stone gateway halfway up Beachwood.

The gateway, with its historical plaque
commemorating the development, led to a
small village circle with shops, a neighborhood market and the enduring Hollywoodland real-estate office. Further up, at the
dead end at the top, was the Sunset Ranch,
the starting point of more than fifty miles of
horse trails that stretched over the mountains into and throughout Griffith Park. This
was where Marie Gesto traded menial work
in the stables for time on horseback. This
was where the grim motorcade of investigators, body recovery experts and a manacled
killer finally came to a stop.

The Sunset Ranch parking lot was merely
a level clearing located on the slope below
the ranch itself. Gravel had been dumped
and spread. Visitors to the ranch had to
park here and then leg it up to the stables at
the top. The parking lot was isolated and
surrounded by dense woods. It could not be
seen from the ranch and that was what

Waits had counted on when he had stalked and abducted Marie Gesto.

Bosch waited impatiently in the car until Olivas disabled the rear door locks. He then got out and looked up at the helicopter circling above. He had to work hard to keep his anger in check. He closed the car door and made sure it was locked. The plan was to leave Waits locked inside until everyone was sure the area was secure. Bosch walked directly to O'Shea as he was getting out of his car.

"Call your contact at Channel Four and ask them to take the chopper up another five hundred feet. The noise is a distraction we don't —"

"I already did, Bosch. Okay? Look, I know you don't like the media presence but it is an open society we live in and the public has a right to know what is going on here."

"Especially when it can help with your election, right?"

O'Shea spoke to him impatiently.

"Educating voters is what a campaign is all about. Excuse me, we have a body to find."

O'Shea abruptly walked away from him and over to Olivas, who was maintaining a vigil next to the car containing Waits. Bosch noticed that the sheriff's deputy was also standing guard at the rear of the car. He was holding a shotgun at ready position.

Rider came up to Bosch.

"Harry, are you all right?"

"Never better. Just watch your back with these people."

He was watching O'Shea and Olivas. They were now conferring about something. The sound of the helicopter's rotor blades prevented Bosch from hearing their exchange.

Rider put her hand on his arm in a calming gesture.

"Let's just forget about the politics and get this over with," Rider said. "There's something more important than all of that. Let's find Marie and bring her home. That's what is important."

Bosch looked down at her hand on his arm, realized she was right and nodded.

"Okay."

A few minutes later O'Shea and Olivas convened everyone except Waits in a circle in the gravel parking lot. In addition to the lawyers, investigators, and the sheriff's deputy, there were two body recovery experts from the coroner's office, along with a forensic archaeologist named Kathy Kohl and an LAPD forensic tech, as well as the videographer from the DA's office. Bosch had worked with almost all of them before.

O'Shea waited until the videographer had his camera going before he addressed the troops.

"Okay, people, we are here on a grim duty, to find and collect the remains of Marie Gesto," he said somberly. "Raynard Waits, the man in the car, is going to lead us to the place where he has told us he buried her. Our primary concern here is the security of the suspect and the safety of all of you people at all times. Be careful and be alert. Four of us are armed. Mr. Waits will be manacled and under the watchful eyes of the detectives and Deputy Doolan, with the shotgun. Mr. Waits will lead the way and we all will be watching his every move. I would like the video and the gas probe to go along with us while the rest of you wait here. When we find the location and confirm the body we will back away until we can secure Mr. Waits and then all of you will come to the location, which will, of course, be handled as the crime scene it is. Any questions so far?"

Maury Swann raised his hand.

"I am not staying here," he said. "I am going to be with my client at all times."

"That's fine, Mr. Swann," O'Shea said. "But I don't think you are dressed for it."

It was true. Inexplicably, Swann had worn a suit to a body excavation. Everyone else was dressed for the job. Bosch wore blue jeans, hiking boots, and an old academy sweatshirt with cut-off sleeves. Rider wore similar attire. Olivas was in jeans, a T-shirt, and nylon windbreaker that said LAPD across the back. The others in the troop were dressed the same way.

"I don't care," Swann said. "If I ruin my shoes I'll write them off as a business expense. But I stay with my client. Not negotiable."

"Fine," O'Shea said. "Just don't get too close or get in the way."

"Not a problem."

"Okay, then, people, let's do this."

Olivas and the deputy went to the car to retrieve Waits. Bosch heard the noise of the circling helicopter getting louder as the news crew came down for a better angle and a closer look with their camera.

After Waits was helped up out of the car, his manacles were checked by Olivas and he was led into the clearing. The deputy stayed six feet behind him at all times with the shotgun up and ready. Olivas kept a grip on Waits's upper left arm. They stopped when they reached the others in the group.

"Mr. Waits, fair warning," O'Shea said. "If you make an attempt to run, these officers will shoot you down. Do you understand that?"

"Of course," Waits said. "And they would do it gladly, I'm sure."

"Then we understand each other. Lead the way."

15

Waits led them toward a dirt path that fed off the lower end of the gravel parking lot. It disappeared beneath a canopy created by a grove of acacia trees, white oaks and heavy brush. He walked without hesitation, like he knew just where he was going. Soon the troop was in shadow and Bosch figured the cameraman in the helicopter wasn't getting much usable video from above the canopy. The only one who spoke was Waits.

"Not too much farther," he said, as though he were a nature guide leading them to a secluded waterfall.

The path became narrower as the trees and brush encroached and the trail evolved from the well-trodden to the seldom used. They were in a stretch where few hikers ventured. Olivas had to change position from holding Waits by the arm and walking next to him to following the killer, with a hand grasping the waist chain from behind. It was clear that Olivas was not going to let go of his suspect and this was comforting to Bosch. What wasn't comforting was that the new position blocked everybody else's shot at Waits should he try to run.

Bosch had traversed numerous jungles in his life. Most often they were the kind where you kept your eyes and ears on the distance, alert and waiting for ambush, and at the same time watched each step you took, wary of the booby trap. This time he kept his eyes focused on the two men moving in front of him, Waits and Olivas, without waver.

The terrain grew more difficult as the path followed the downslope of the mountain. The soil was soft and moist from the overnight precipitation as well as all the rain in the past year. In some places Bosch felt his hiking boots sink and catch. And at one point, there was the sound of breaking branches behind him and then the thud of a body hitting the mud. Though Olivas and Deputy Doolan stopped and turned to see what the commotion was about, Bosch never moved his eyes from Waits. From behind him he heard Swann curse and the others ask if he was okay as they helped him up.

After Swann stopped swearing and the troop regrouped, they moved farther down the slope. Progress was slow, as Swann's mishap caused everyone to step even more carefully than before. In another five minutes they stopped at the precipice of a steep drop-off. It was a place where the weight of water that pooled in the ground had caused a small mud slide in recent months. The ground had sheared away next to an oak tree, exposing half of its root system. The drop was almost ten feet down.

"Well, this wasn't here last time I came," Waits said in a tone that indicated he was put out by the inconvenience.

"Is that the way?" Olivas asked, pointing to the bottom of the drop-off.

"Yes," Waits confirmed. "We go down there."

"All right, wait a minute."

Olivas turned and looked at Bosch.

"Bosch, why don't you go down first and then I'll send him down to you."

Bosch nodded and moved past them. He grabbed one of the lower branches of the oak for balance as he tested the stability of the soil on the steep slope. It was loose and slippery.

"No good," he said. "This is going to be like a sliding board going down. And once we get down, how do we get back up?"

Olivas blew out his breath in frustration.

"Then what do —"

"There was a ladder on top of one of the vans," Waits suggested.

They all looked at him for a long moment.

"He's right. Forensics has a ladder on top of the truck," Rider said. "We get it, put it down on the incline and go up and down on it like stairs. Simple."

Swann broke into the huddle.

"Simple, except my client is not going up and down that slope or up and down a ladder with his hands chained to his waist," he said.

After a momentary pause everyone looked at O'Shea.

"I think we can work something out," he said.

"Wait a minute," Olivas said. "We're not taking the —"

"Then he's not going down there," Swann said. "It's that simple. I'm not allowing you to endanger him. He's my client and my responsibility to him is not only in the arena of the law but in all —"

O'Shea held his hands up in a calming manner.

"One of *our* responsibilities is the safety of the accused," he said. "Maury makes a point. If Mr. Waits falls going down the ladder without being able to use his hands, then we're responsible. And then we've got a problem. I am sure that with all of you people holding guns and shotguns, we can control this situation for the ten seconds it takes him to go down a ladder."

"I'll go get the ladder," said the forensic tech. "Can you hold this?"

Her name was Carolyn Cafarelli and Bosch knew most people called her Cal. She handed the gas probe, a yellow T-shaped device, to Bosch and started back through the woods.

"I'll help her with it," Rider said.

"No," Bosch said. "Everybody carrying a weapon stays with Waits."

Rider nodded, realizing he was right.

"I can handle it," Cafarelli called out. "It's lightweight aluminum."

"I just hope she can find her way back," O'Shea said after she was gone.

For the first few minutes they waited in silence, then Waits spoke to Bosch.

"Anxious, Detective?" he asked. "Now that we're so close."

Bosch didn't respond. He wasn't going to let Waits get inside his head.

Waits tried again.

"I think about all the cases you have worked. How many are like this one? How many are like Marie? I bet she —"

"Waits, shut the fuck up," Olivas commanded.

"Ray, please," Swann said in a soothing voice.

"Just making conversation with the detective."

"Well, make it with yourself," Olivas said.

The silence returned until a few minutes later, when they all heard the sound of Cafarelli carrying the ladder through the woods. She banged it a few times on low-level limbs but finally got it to their position. Bosch helped her slide it down the slope and they made sure it was steady on the steep incline. When he stood up and turned back to the group Bosch saw that Olivas was uncuffing one of Waits's hands from the chain running around the prisoner's waist. He left the other hand secured.

"The other hand, Detective," Swann said.

"He can climb with one hand free," Olivas insisted.

"I am sorry, Detective, but I am not going to allow that. He has to be able to hold on and break a fall if he happens to slip. He needs both hands free."

"He can do it with one."

While the posturing and debate continued, Bosch swung himself onto the ladder and went down the slope backwards. The ladder was steady. At the bottom he looked around and realized that there was no discernible path. From this point the trail to Marie Gesto's body was not as obvious as it had been above. He looked back up at the others and waited.

"Freddy, just do it," O'Shea instructed in an annoyed tone. "Deputy, you go down first and be ready with that shotgun in case Mr. Waits gets any ideas. Detective Rider, you have my permission to unholster your weapon. You stay up here with Freddy and be ready as well."

Bosch climbed back up a few steps on the ladder so the deputy could carefully hand him the shotgun. He then stepped back down and the uniformed man came down the ladder. Bosch gave him back the weapon and returned to the ladder.

"Toss me the cuffs," Bosch called up to Olivas.

Bosch caught the cuffs and then took a position two rungs up on the ladder. Waits began to go down while the videographer stood at the edge and recorded his descent. When Waits was three rungs from the bottom Bosch reached up and grabbed the waist chain to guide him the rest of the way to the lower ground.

"This is it, Ray," he whispered in his ear from behind. "Your only chance. You sure you don't want to make a run for it?"

Safely at the bottom, Waits stepped off the ladder and turned to Bosch, holding his hands up for the cuffs. His eyes held on Bosch's.

"No, Detective, I think I like living too much."

"I thought so."

Bosch cuffed his hands to the waist chain and looked back up the slope at the others.

"Okay, we're secure."

One by one the others came down the ladder. Once they had regrouped at the bottom O'Shea looked around and saw that there was no longer a path. They could go in any direction.

"Okay, which way?" he said to Waits.

Waits turned in a half circle as if seeing the area for the first time.

"Ummmm . . ."

Olivas almost lost it.

"You better not be pulling —"

"That way," Waits said coyly as he nodded to the right of the slope. "Lost my bearings there for a second."

"No bullshit, Waits," Olivas said. "You take us to the body right now or we go back, go to trial and you get the hot shot of Jesus juice you've got coming. You got that?"

"I got it. And like I said, this way."

The group moved off through the brush with Waits leading the way, Olivas clinging to the chain at the small of his back and the shotgun never more than five feet behind.

The ground on this level was softer and more muddy. Bosch knew that runoff from last spring's rains had likely gone down the slope and collected here. He felt his thigh muscles begin to tighten as every step was a labor to pull his work boots from the sucking mud.

In five minutes they came to a small clearing shaded by a tall, fully mature oak. Bosch saw Waits looking up and followed his eyes. A yellowish-white hair band hung limply from an overhead branch.

"It's funny," Waits said. "It used to be blue."

Bosch knew that at the time of Marie Gesto's disappearance she was believed to have had her hair tied back with a blue hair band known as a scrunchy. A friend who had seen her earlier on that last day had provided a description of what she was wearing. The scrunchy was not with the clothing found neatly folded in her car at the High Tower Apartments.

Bosch looked up at the hair band. Thirteen years of rain and exposure had taken its color.

Bosch lowered his eyes to Waits, and the killer was waiting for him with a smile.

"We're here, Detective. You've finally found Marie."

"Where?"

Waits's smile broadened.

"You're standing on her."

Bosch abruptly stepped back a pace and Waits laughed.

"Don't worry, Detective Bosch, I don't think she minds. What was it the great man wrote about sleeping the big sleep? About not caring about the nastiness of how you died or where you fell?"

Bosch looked at him for a long moment, wondering once again about the literary airs of the window washer. Waits seemed to read him.

"I've been in jail since May, Detective. I've done a lot of reading."

"Step back," Bosch said.

Waits opened his cuffed hands in a surrender move and stepped toward the trunk of the oak. Bosch looked at Olivas.

"You got him?"

"I got him."

Bosch looked down at the ground. He had left footprints in the muddy earth but it also looked like there was another, recent disturbance in the soil. It looked as though an animal had made a small dig in the ground, either foraging or burying its own dead.

Bosch signaled the forensics tech over to the center of the clearing. Cafarelli stepped forward with the gas probe and Bosch pointed to the spot directly below the color- less hair band. The tech pushed the point of the probe into the soft soil and easily sank it a foot into the earth. She clicked on the reader and began studying the electronic display. Bosch stepped toward her to look over her shoulder. He knew that the probe measured the level of methane in the soil. A buried body releases methane gas as it de- composes. Even a body wrapped in plastic.

"We're getting a read," Cafarelli said. "We're above normal levels."

Bosch nodded. He felt strange inside. Out of sorts. He had been with the case for more than a decade and a part of him liked holding on to the mystery of Marie Gesto. But, while he didn't believe in something called closure, he did believe in the need to know the truth. He felt that the truth was about to reveal itself, and yet it was discon- certing. He needed to know the truth to move on, but how could he move on once he no longer needed to find and avenge Marie Gesto?

He looked at Waits.

"How far down is she?"

"Not too far," Waits replied matter-of-factly. "Back in 'ninety-three we were in drought, remember? The ground was hard and, man, I wore my ass out digging a hole for her. I was lucky she was just a little thing. But, anyway, that's why I changed it up. No more digging big holes for me after that."

Bosch looked away from him and back at Cafarelli. She was taking another probe reading. She would be able to delineate the grave site by charting the highest methane readings.

They all watched the grim work silently. After taking several readings in a grid pattern Cafarelli finally moved her hand in a north-south sweep to indicate how the body was likely positioned. She then marked the limits of the grave site by dragging the point of the probe in the dirt. When she was finished she had marked out a rectangle about six feet by two feet. It was a small grave for a small victim.

"Okay," O'Shea said. "Let's get Mr. Waits back and secured in the car and then bring in the excavation group."

The prosecutor told Cafarelli that she should stay at the site so there would be no crime scene integrity issues. The rest of the group headed back toward the ladder. Bosch was last in the single-file line, his mind deep in thought about the ground they were traversing. There was something sacred about it. It was hallowed ground. He hoped that Waits had not lied to them. He hoped that Marie Gesto had not been forced to make the walk to her grave while alive.

At the ladder Rider and Olivas went up first. Bosch then walked Waits to the ladder, uncuffed him and started him up.

As the killer climbed, the deputy trained the shotgun, finger on the trigger, on his back. In that moment, Bosch realized he could slip on the muddy soil, fall into the deputy and possibly cause the shotgun to discharge and hit Waits with the deadly fusillade. He looked away from the temptation and up at the top of the sheer facing. His partner was looking down at him with eyes that told him she had just read his thoughts. Bosch tried to put an innocent look on his face. He spread his hands while mouthing the word *What?*

Rider shook her head with disapproval and moved back from the edge. Bosch noticed that she was holding her weapon at her side. As Waits got to the top of the ladder, he was welcomed by Olivas with opened arms.

"Hands," Olivas said.

"Certainly, Detective."

From Bosch's angle below he could only see Waits's back. He could tell by his posture that he had brought his hands together at his front for recuffing to the waist chain.

But then there was a sudden movement. A quick twist in the prisoner's posture as he leaned too far into Olivas. Bosch instinctively knew something was wrong. Waits was going for the gun holstered on Olivas's hip under the windbreaker.

"Hey!" Olivas shouted in panic. "Hey!"

But before Bosch or anyone else could react, Waits used his hold and leverage on Olivas to spin their bodies so that the detective's back was now at the top of the ladder. The deputy had no angle for a shot. Neither did Bosch. With a pistonlike move, Waits raised his knee and drove it twice into Olivas's crotch. Olivas started to collapse, and there were two quick gunshots, muffled by his body. Waits pushed the detective off the edge and Olivas came crashing down the ladder onto Bosch.

Waits then disappeared from view.

Olivas's weight took Bosch down hard into the mud. As he struggled to pull his weapon Bosch heard two more shots from above and shouts of panic from those on the lower ground. Behind him he heard the sound of running. With Olivas still on top of him, he looked up but could not see Waits or Rider. Then the prisoner appeared at the edge of the precipice, calmly holding a gun. He fired down at them and Bosch felt two impacts on Olivas's body. He had become Bosch's shield.

The blast of the deputy's shotgun split the air but the slug thwacked into the trunk of an oak tree to the left of Waits. Waits returned fire at the same moment and Bosch heard the deputy go down like a dropped suitcase.

"Run, you coward!" Waits yelled. "How's your bullshit deal looking now?"

He fired twice more indiscriminately into the woods below. Bosch managed to free his gun and fire up the ladder at Waits.

Waits ducked back out of sight as he used his free hand to grab the ladder by the top rung and yank it up to the top of the embankment. Bosch pushed Olivas's body off and got up, his gun aimed and ready for Waits to show again.

But then he heard the sound of running from above and he knew Waits was gone.

"Kiz!" Bosch yelled.

There was no reply. Bosch quickly checked both Olivas and the deputy but saw they were both dead. He holstered his weapon and scrambled up the incline, using ex- posed roots as handholds. The ground gave way as he dug his feet into it. A root snapped in his hand and he slid back down.

"Kiz, talk to me!"

Again no response. He tried again, this time going at an angle across the steep in- cline instead of by a straight-up assault. Grabbing roots and kicking his feet into the soft facing, he finally made it to the top and crawled over the edge. As he pulled himself up, he saw Waits moving off through the trees in the direction of the clearing, where the others waited. He pulled his gun again and fired five more shots but Waits never slowed.

Bosch got up, ready to give chase. But then he saw his partner's body lying crum- pled and bloody in the nearby brush.

16

Kiz Rider was faceup, clutching her neck with one hand while the other lay limp at her side. Her eyes were wide and searching but not focusing. It was as if she were blind. Her limp arm was so bloody it took a moment for Bosch to spot the bullet entrance in the palm of her hand, just below the thumb. It was a through-and-through shot and he knew it wasn't as serious as the neck wound. Blood was steadily seeping from between her fingers. The bullet must have hit the carotid artery, and Bosch knew that blood loss or depletion of oxygen in the brain could kill his partner in minutes, if not seconds.

"Okay, Kiz," he said as he knelt next to her. "I'm here."

He could see that her left hand, holding the wound on the right side of her neck, was creating insufficient pressure to stop the bleeding. She was losing the strength to hold on.

"Let me take over here," he said.

He moved his hand under hers and pressed against what he now realized were two wounds, bullet entry and exit. He could feel the blood pulsing against his palm.

"O'Shea!" he shouted.

"Bosch?" O'Shea called back from below the drop-off. "Where is he? Did you kill him?"

"He's gone. I need you to get on Doolan's rover and get us a medevac up here. Now!"

It took a moment before O'Shea responded, in a panicked voice.

"Doolan's shot! So is Freddy!"

"They're dead, O'Shea. You need to get on the radio. Rider is alive and we need to get her —"

In the distance there were two gunshots, followed by a shout. It was a female voice and Bosch thought about Kathy Kohl and the people up at the parking lot. There were two more shots and Bosch heard a change in the overhead sound of the helicopter. It was banking away. Waits was shooting at it.

"Come on, O'Shea!" he shouted. "We're running out of time."

When he heard nothing in response he brought Rider's hand back up and pressed in against the neck wounds again.

"Hold it there, Kiz. Press as hard as you can and I'll be right back."

Bosch jumped up and grabbed the ladder Waits had pulled up. He lowered it back into place between the bodies of Olivas and Doolan and quickly climbed down. O'Shea was on his knees next to Olivas's body. The prosecutor's eyes were as wide and as blank as those of the dead cop next to him. Swann was standing in the lower clearing with a dazed look on his face. Cafarelli had come from the grave site and was on her knees next to Doolan, trying to turn him over to get to the radio. The deputy had fallen chest down after being shot by Waits.

"Cal, let me do it," Bosch ordered. "You go up and help Kiz. We've got to stop the bleeding from her neck."

Without a word the Forensics tech scurried up the ladder and out of sight. Bosch turned Doolan over and saw that he had been hit in the forehead. His eyes were open and looked surprised. Bosch grabbed the radio off Doolan's equipment belt and made the "officer down" call and requested a medical airship and paramedics to the lower parking lot at Sunset Ranch. Once he was assured that medical help was on the way, he reported that an armed murder suspect had escaped custody. He gave a detailed description of Raynard Waits, then shoved the radio into his belt. He went to the ladder and as he climbed back up he called down to O'Shea, Swann and the videographer, who was still holding the camera up and recording the scene.

"All of you get up here. We need to carry her out to the parking lot for the evac."

O'Shea continued to look down in shock at Olivas.

"They're dead!" Bosch shouted from the top. "There's nothing we can do for them. I need you up here."

He turned back to Rider. Cafarelli was holding her neck but Bosch could see that time was growing short. The life was leaving his partner's eyes. Bosch bent down and grabbed and held her unhurt hand. He rubbed it between his two hands. He noticed that Cafarelli had used a hair band to wrap the wound on Rider's other hand.

"Come on, Kiz, hang in there. We've got an airship coming and we're going to get you out of here."

He looked around to see what was available to them and got an idea as he saw Maury Swann come up the ladder. He quickly moved to the edge and helped the defense attorney off the last rung. O'Shea was coming up behind him and the videographer was waiting his turn.

"Leave the camera," Bosch ordered.

"I can't. I'm respons —"

"You bring it up here and I'm going to take it and throw it as far as I can."

The cameraman reluctantly put his equipment on the ground, popped out the digital tape and put it in one of the big equipment pockets on his cargo pants. He then climbed up the ladder. Once everyone was on top Bosch pulled the ladder up and carried it over to Rider. He put it down next to her.

"Okay, we're going to use the ladder as a stretcher. Two men on each side and, Cal, I need you to walk beside us and keep that pressure on her neck."

"Got it," she said.

"Okay, let's put her on the ladder."

Bosch moved by Rider's right shoulder while the other three men took positions at her legs and other shoulder. They carefully lifted her onto the ladder. Cafarelli kept her hands in place on Rider's neck.

"We have to be careful," Bosch urged. "We tip the thing and she'll fall. Cal, keep her on the ladder."

"Got it. Let's go."

They raised the ladder and started moving back up the trail. Rider's weight, distributed among the four carriers, was not a problem. But the mud was. Two times Swann, in his courthouse shoes, slipped, and the make-shift stretcher almost went over. Each time Cafarelli literally hugged Rider to the ladder and kept her in place.

It took less than ten minutes to get to the clearing. Bosch immediately saw that the coroner's van was now missing, but Kathy Kohl and her two assistants were still there, standing unharmed by the SID van.

Bosch scanned the sky for a helicopter but saw none. He told the others to put Rider down next to the SID van. Carrying it the last distance with one hand hooked under the ladder, he used his free hand to operate the radio.

"Where's my airship?" he yelled at the dispatcher.

The response was that it was on the way with a one-minute ETA. They softly lowered the ladder to the ground and looked around to make sure there was enough open space in the lot to set a helicopter down. Behind him he heard O'Shea interrogating Kohl.

"What happened? Where did Waits go?"

"He came out of the woods and shot at the news helicopter. Then he took our van at gunpoint and headed down the hill."

"Did the chopper follow him?"

"We don't know. I don't think so. It flew away when he started shooting."

Bosch heard the sound of an approaching helicopter and hoped it wasn't the Channel 4 chopper coming back. He walked to the middle of the most open area of the parking lot and waited. In a few moments a silver-skinned medevac airship crested the mountaintop and he started waving it down.

Two paramedics jumped from the aircraft the moment it landed. One carried an equipment case, while the other brought a folding stretcher. They knelt on either side of Rider and went to work. Bosch stood and watched with his arms folded tightly across his chest. He saw one put a breathing mask over her face while the other inserted an IV into her arm. They then began to examine her wounds. To himself Bosch repeated the mantra, *Come on, Kiz, come on, Kiz, come on, Kiz . . .*

It was more like a prayer.

One of the paramedics turned toward the chopper and made a hand signal to the pilot, spinning an upraised finger in the air. Bosch knew it meant that they had to get going. Time would be of the essence on this run. The helicopter's engine started to rev higher. The pilot was ready.

The stretcher was unfolded and Bosch helped the paramedics move Rider onto it. He then took one of the handles and helped them carry it to the waiting airship.

"Can I go?" Bosch yelled loudly as they moved toward the open door of the helicopter.

"What?" yelled one of the paramedics.

"CAN I GO?"

The paramedic shook his head.

"No, sir. We need room to work on her. It's going to be close."

Bosch nodded.

"Where are you taking her?"

"St. Joe's."

Bosch nodded again. St. Joseph's was in Burbank. By air it was just on the other side of the mountain, five minutes' flying time at most. By car it would be a lengthy drive around the mountain and through the Cahuenga Pass.

Rider was carefully loaded into the airship and Bosch stepped back. As the door was being closed he wanted to yell something to his partner but he couldn't come up with any words. The door snapped closed and it was too late. He decided that if Kiz was conscious and even cared about such things, she would know what he had wanted to say.

The helicopter took off as Bosch was moving backwards, wondering if he would ever again see Kiz Rider alive.

Just as the airship banked away a patrol car came roaring up the hill to the parking lot, its blue lights flashing. Two uniforms out of Hollywood Division jumped out. One of them had his gun out and he pointed it at Bosch. Covered with mud and blood, Bosch understood why.

"I'm a police officer! My shield's in my back pocket."

"Then, let's see it," said the man with the gun. "Slowly!"

Bosch pulled out his badge case and flipped it open. It passed inspection and the gun was lowered.

"Get back in the car," he ordered. "We have to go!"

Bosch ran to the rear door of the car. The two officers piled in and Bosch told them to head back down Beachwood.

"Then where?" the driver asked.

"You have to take me around the mountain to St. Joe's. My partner was in that airship."

"You got it. Code three, baby."

The driver hit the switch that would add the siren to the already flashing emergency lights and pinned the accelerator. The car U-turned in a screech of tires and a spray of gravel, then headed downhill. The suspension was shot, as with most of the cars the LAPD put out on the street. The car swerved dangerously around the curves on the way down but Bosch didn't care. He had to get to Kiz. At one point they almost collided with another patrol car that was moving with the same speed up to the crime scene.

Finally, halfway down the hill the driver

slowed when they were passing through the pedestrian-crowded shopping area of the Hollywoodland village.

"Stop!" Bosch yelled.

The driver complied with screeching efficiency on the brakes.

"Back it up. I just saw the van."

"What van?"

"Just back it up!"

The patrol car reversed and moved back past the neighborhood market. There in the side lot Bosch saw the pale blue coroner's van parked in the back row.

"Our custody got loose and got a gun. He took that van."

Bosch gave them a description of Waits and the warning that he was unhesitant about using the weapon. He told them about the two dead cops back up the hill in the woods.

They decided to sweep the parking lot first and then enter the market. They called for backup but decided not to wait for it. They got out with their weapons drawn.

They searched and cleared the parking lot quickly, coming to the coroner's van last. It was unlocked and empty. But in the back Bosch found an orange jail-issue jumpsuit on the floor. Waits had either been wearing another set of clothes beneath the jumpsuit, or he had found clothes to change into in the back of the van.

"Be careful," Bosch announced to the others. "He could be wearing anything. Stay close to me. I know what he looks like."

In a tight formation they moved into the store through the automatic doors at the front. Once inside, Bosch quickly realized that they were too late. A man with a manager's tag on his shirt was consoling a woman who was crying hysterically and holding the side of her face. The manager saw the two uniforms and signaled them over. He didn't even seem to notice all the mud and blood on Bosch's clothes.

"We're the ones who called," the manager said. "Mrs. Shelton here just got carjacked."

Mrs. Shelton nodded tearfully.

"Can you give us a description of your car and what the man who did this was wearing?" Bosch asked.

"I think so," she whined.

"Okay, listen," Bosch said to the two officers. "One of you stays here, gets the description of what he's wearing and the car and puts it out on the air. The other leaves now and gets me to St. Joe's. Let's go."

The driver took Bosch, and the other patrolman stayed behind. In another three minutes they came screeching out of Beachwood Canyon and were moving toward the Cahuenga Pass. On the radio they heard a BOLO broadcast for a silver BMW 540 wanted in connection with a 187 LEO — murder of a law enforcement officer. The suspect was described as wearing a baggy white jumpsuit, and Bosch knew he had found the change of clothes in the back of the Forensics van.

The siren was clearing a path for them but Bosch estimated that they were still fifteen minutes away from the hospital. He had a bad feeling about it. He had a bad feeling about everything. He didn't think that they were going to get there in time. He tried to push that thought out of his mind. He tried to think about Kiz Rider alive and well and smiling at him, scolding him the way she always did. And when they got to the freeway, he concentrated on scanning all eight lanes of northbound traffic, looking for a carjacked silver BMW with a killer at the wheel.

17

Bosch strode through the emergency room entrance with his badge out. An intake receptionist sat behind a counter, taking information from a man huddled over on a chair in front of her. When Bosch came close he saw that the man was cradling his left arm like a baby. The wrist was bent at an unnatural angle.

"The police officer who was brought in on a medevac?" he said, not caring about interrupting.

"I have no information, sir," the desk woman said. "If you'll take —"

"Where can I get information? Where's the doctor?"

"The doctor is with the patient, sir. If I asked him to come out to speak to you, then he wouldn't be taking care of the officer, would he?"

"Then, she's still alive?"

"Sir, I can't give out any information at this time. If you'll —"

Bosch walked away from the counter and over to a set of double doors. He pushed a button on the wall that automatically swung them open. Behind him he heard the desk woman yelling to him. He didn't stop. He stepped through the doors into the emergency treatment area. There were eight curtained patient bays, four on each side of the room, and the nurses' and physicians' stations were in the middle. The place was abuzz. Outside a patient bay on the right Bosch saw one of the paramedics from the helicopter. He went to him.

"How is she?"

"She's holding on. She lost a lot of blood and —"

He stopped when he turned and saw that it was Bosch next to him.

"I'm not sure you're supposed to be in here, Officer. I think you better step out to the waiting room and —"

"She's my partner and I want to know what is happening."

"She's got one of the best ER attendings in the city trying to keep her alive. My bet is that he will do just that. But you can't stand here and watch."

"Sir?"

Bosch turned. A man in a private security uniform was approaching with the desk woman. Bosch held his hands up.

"I just want to be told what is happening."

"Sir, you will have to come with me, please," the guard said.

He put his hand on Bosch's arm. Bosch shrugged it off.

"I'm a police detective. You don't need to touch me. I just want to know what is happening with my partner."

"Sir, you will be told all you need to know in good time. If you will please come —"

The guard made the mistake of attempting to take Bosch by the arm again. This time Bosch didn't shrug it off. He slapped the man's hand away.

"I said, don't —"

"Hold on, hold on," said the paramedic. "Tell you what, Detective, let's go to the machines and get a coffee or something and I'll tell you everything that's happening with your partner, okay?"

Bosch didn't answer. The paramedic sweetened the offer.

"I'll even get you some clean scrubs so you can get out of those muddy and bloody clothes. Sound good?"

Bosch relented, the security man nodded his approval and the paramedic led the way, first to a supply closet where he looked at Bosch and guessed that he would need mediums. He pulled pale blue scrubs and booties off the shelves and handed them over. They then went down a hallway to the nurses' break room, where there were coin-operated machines serving coffee, sodas and snacks. Bosch took a black coffee. He had no change but the paramedic did.

"You want to clean up and change first? You can use the lav right over there."

"Just tell me what you know first."

"Have a seat."

They sat at a round table across from each other. The paramedic reached his hand across the table.

"Dale Dillon."

Bosch quickly shook his hand.

"Harry Bosch."

"Good to meet you, Detective Bosch. The first thing I need to do is thank you for your efforts out there in the mud. You and the others there probably saved your partner's life. She lost a lot of blood but she's a fighter. They're putting her back together and hopefully she'll be all right."

"How bad is it?"

"It's bad but it's one of those cases where they won't know until she stabilizes. The bullet hit one of her carotid arteries. That's what they are working on now — getting her ready to take to the OR so they can repair the artery. Meantime, since she lost a lot of blood, the risk right now is stroke. So she's not out of the woods yet, but if she avoids going into stroke she should come out of this okay. 'Okay' meaning alive and functioning with a lot of rehab ahead of her."

Bosch nodded.

"That's the unofficial version. I'm not a doctor and I shouldn't have told you any of that."

Bosch felt his cell phone vibrating in his pocket but he ignored it.

"I appreciate that you did," he said. "When will I be able to see her?"

"I have no idea, man. I just bring 'em in

here. I told you all I know and that was probably too much. If you're going to wait around I suggest you wash your face and change out of those clothes. You're probably scaring people with the way you look."

Bosch nodded and Dillon stood up. He had defused a potentially explosive ER situation and his work was done.

"Thanks, Dale."

"No problemo. Take her easy and if you see the security guard, you might want to . . ."

He left it at that.

"I will," Bosch said.

After the paramedic left, Bosch went into the lavatory and stripped off his sweatshirt. Because there were no pockets in the surgical clothes and no place for him to carry his weapon, phone, badge and other things, he decided to leave his dirty jeans on. He looked at himself in the mirror and saw that he had blood and dirt smeared on his face. He spent the next five minutes washing up, running the soap and water over his hands until he finally saw the water running clear into the drain.

When he stepped out of the lavatory he noticed that someone had come into the break room and either taken or thrown out his coffee. He checked his pockets again for change but still didn't find any.

Bosch walked back to the ER reception area and now found it crowded with police, both uniformed and not. His supervisor, Abel Pratt, was there among the suits. He looked as though the blood had completely drained from his face. He saw Bosch and immediately came over.

"Harry, how is she? What happened?"

"They're not giving me anything official. The paramedic who brought her in said it looks like she'll be okay, unless something new happens."

"Thank Christ! What happened up there?"

"I'm not sure. Waits got a gun and started shooting. Anything on whether they've got a bead on him?"

"He dumped the car he jacked by the Red Line station on Hollywood Boulevard. They don't know where the fuck he is."

Bosch thought about that. He knew that if Waits had gone underground on the Red Line, he could have gone anywhere from North Hollywood to downtown. The downtown line had a stop near Echo Park.

"Are they looking in Echo Park?"

"They're looking everywhere, man. OIS is

sending a team here to talk to you. I didn't think you'd be willing to leave to go to Parker."

"Right."

"Well, you know how to handle it. Just tell it like it was."

"Right."

The Officer Involved Shooting squad would not be a problem. As far as Bosch could see he had not personally done anything wrong in the handling of Waits. OIS was a rubber-stamp squad, anyway.

"They'll be a while," Pratt said. "They're up at Sunset Ranch right now interviewing the others. How the fuck did he get a gun?"

Bosch shook his head.

"Olivas got too close to him while he was coming up a ladder. He grabbed it then and started shooting. Olivas and Kiz were up top. It happened so fast and I was down below them."

"Jesus Christ!"

Pratt shook his head and Bosch knew he wanted to ask more questions about what had happened and how it could have happened. He was probably worried about his own situation as much as he was worried about Rider pulling through. Bosch decided he needed to tell him about the thing that could be a containment problem.

"He wasn't cuffed," he said in a low voice. "We had to take off the cuffs so he could go up a ladder. The cuffs were going to be off for thirty seconds at the max, and that's when he made his move. Olivas let him get too close. That's how it started."

Pratt looked stunned. He spoke slowly, as if not understanding.

"You took the cuffs off?"

"O'Shea told us to."

"Good. They can blame him. I don't want any blowback on Open-Unsolved. I don't want any on me. It's not my idea of the way to go out after twenty-five fucking years."

"What about Kiz? You're not going to cut her loose, are you?"

"No, I'm not going to cut her loose. I'll stand behind Kiz but I'm not standing behind O'Shea. Fuck him."

Bosch's phone vibrated again and this time he took it out of his pocket to check the screen. It said "Unknown Number." He answered it anyway to get away from Pratt's questions, judgments, and ass-covering strategies. It was Rachel.

"Harry, we just got the BOLO on Waits. What happened?"

Bosch realized he was going to be telling the story over and over for the rest of the day and possibly the rest of his life. He excused himself and stepped into an alcove where there were pay phones and a water fountain so he could speak privately. As concisely as possible he told her what had happened at the top of Beachwood Canyon and what the situation was with Rider. As he told the story he replayed the visual memories of the moment he saw Waits go for the gun. He replayed their efforts to stop the bleeding and save his partner.

Rachel offered to come to the ER but Bosch talked her out of it, saying he wasn't sure how long he would be there and reminding her he would likely be taken into a private interview with OIS investigators.

"Will I see you tonight?" she asked.

"If I get done with everything and Kiz is stable. Otherwise, I might stay here."

"I'm going to go to your place. Call me and let me know what you know."

"I will."

Bosch stepped out of the alcove and saw that the ER waiting room was beginning to fill with media now as well as cops. Bosch guessed this probably meant the word had gone out that the chief of police was on his way. Bosch didn't mind. Maybe the leverage of having the chief in the ER would get the hospital to open up with some information about his partner's condition.

He walked up to Pratt, who was standing with his boss, Captain Norona, the head of the Robbery-Homicide Division.

"What's going to happen with the excavation?" he asked both of them.

"I've got Rick Jackson and Tim Marcia headed up there," Pratt said. "They'll handle it."

"It's my case," Bosch said, a mild protest in his voice.

"Not anymore," Norona said. "You're with OIS until they finish this thing up. You're the only one with a badge who was up there and is still able to talk about it. That's front burner. The Gesto dig is back burner and Marcia and Jackson will handle it."

Bosch knew there would be no use arguing. The captain was right. Though there were four others present at the shooting who were unharmed, it would be Bosch's description and memory that would count the most.

There was a commotion at the ER entrance as several men with TV cameras on their shoulders jostled one another for position on either side of the double doors. When the doors came open, an entourage entered with the chief of police at the center. The chief strode to the reception desk, where he was met by Norona. They spoke to the same woman who had rejected Bosch earlier. This time she was the picture of cooperation, immediately picking up a phone and making a call. She obviously knew who counted and who didn't.

Inside of three minutes the hospital's chief surgeon came through the ER doors and invited the chief back for a private consultation. As they moved through the doors Bosch hitched a ride, joining the group of sixth-floor commanders and assistants in the chief's wake.

"Excuse me, Dr. Kim," a voice from behind the group called.

They all stopped and turned. It was the desk woman. She pointed at Bosch and said, "He's not with that group."

The chief noticed Bosch for the first time and corrected her.

"He most certainly is," he said in a tone that invited no disagreement.

The desk woman looked chastened. The group moved forward and Dr. Kim ushered them into an unused ER patient bay. They gathered around an empty bed.

"Chief, your officer is being —"

"Detective. She's a detective."

"I'm sorry. Your detective is being cared for in ICU by Drs. Patel and Worthing. I cannot interrupt their care to have them update you, so I am prepared to answer what questions you might have."

"Fine. Is she going to make it?" the chief said bluntly.

"We think so, yes. That is really not the question. The question is about permanent damage and we won't know that for some time. One of the bullets damaged one of the carotid arteries. The carotid delivers blood and oxygen to the brain. We don't know at this point what the interruption of the flow was or is, and what damage might have occurred."

"Aren't there tests that can be conducted?"

"Yes, sir, there are and, preliminarily, we are seeing routine brain activity at this time. That is very good news so far."

"Is she able to talk?"

"Not at this time. She was anesthetized during surgery and it is going to be several hours before she might be able to talk. Accent on 'might.' We won't know what we have until late tonight or tomorrow, when she comes out of it."

The chief nodded.

"Thank you, Dr. Kim."

The chief started to make a move toward the opening in the curtain and everyone else turned to leave as well. Then he turned back to the head surgeon.

"Dr. Kim," he said in a low voice. "At one time this woman worked directly for me. I don't want to lose her."

"We are doing our very best, Chief. We won't lose her."

The police chief nodded. As the group then shuffled toward the doors to the waiting room Bosch felt a hand grasp his shoulder. He turned to see that it was the chief. He pulled Bosch aside and into a private discussion.

"Detective Bosch, how are you doing?"

"I'm okay, Chief."

"Thank you for getting her here so quickly."

"It didn't seem that quick at the time, and it wasn't just me. There were a few of us. We worked together."

"Right, yes, I know. O'Shea's already on the news talking about carrying her out of the jungle. Making hay out of his part."

It didn't surprise Bosch to hear that.

"Walk with me for a moment, Detective," the chief said.

They walked through the waiting area and out to the ambulance drive-up area. The police chief didn't speak until they were out of the building and out of earshot of all others.

"We're going to take a big hit for this," he finally said. "We've got a goddamn admitted serial killer running around loose in the city. I want to know what happened up on that mountain, Detective. How did things go so awfully wrong?"

Bosch nodded his contrition. He knew that what had happened in Beachwood Canyon would be like a bomb detonating and sending a shock wave through the city and the department.

"That's a good question, Chief," he replied. "I was there but I'm not sure what happened."

Once again, Bosch began to tell the story.

18

Little by little the media and the police left the ER waiting room. In a way, Kiz Rider was a disappointment because she didn't die. If she had died, everything would have been an immediate sound bite. Get in, go live and then move on to the next spot and the next press conference. But she hung on and people couldn't wait around. As the hours went by, the number of people in the waiting room got smaller until only Bosch was left. Rider was not currently in a relationship and her parents had left Los Angeles after the death of her sister, so there was no one but Bosch to wait for the chance to see her.

Shortly before 5 p.m. Dr. Kim came through

the double doors looking for the chief of police or at least someone in uniform or above the rank of detective. He had to settle for Bosch, who stood up to receive the news.

"She's doing well. She's conscious, and nonverbal communication skills are good. She is not talking because of the trauma to the neck and we have her intubated, but the initial indications are all positive. No stroke, no infection, everything looks good. The other wound is stabilized and we'll deal further with that tomorrow. She's had enough surgery for one day."

Bosch nodded. He felt a tremendous relief begin to flood through him. Kiz was going to make it.

"Can I see her?"

"For a few minutes, but as I said, she's not talking at this time. Come with me."

Bosch followed the chief surgeon once more through the double doors. They walked through the ER to the intensive care unit. Kiz was in the second room on the right. Her body seemed small in the bed, surrounded with all the equipment and monitors and tubes. Her eyes were at half-mast and showed no change when he entered her focal range. He could tell she was conscious but just barely.

"Kiz," Bosch said. "How are ya, partner?"

He reached down and grabbed her good hand.

"Don't try to answer. I shouldn't have asked anything. I just wanted to see you. The chief surgeon just told me that you are going to be okay. You'll have some rehab but then you'll be as good as new."

She couldn't talk or make a sound because of the tube going down her throat. But she squeezed his hand, and Bosch took that as a positive response.

He pulled a chair over from the wall and sat down so he could keep her hand in his. Over the next half hour he said very little to her. He just held her hand and she squeezed it from time to time.

At 5:30 a nurse entered the room and told Bosch that two men had asked for him in the ER waiting room. Bosch gave Rider's hand a final squeeze and told her he would be back in the morning.

The two men waiting for him were OIS investigators. Their names were Randolph and Osani. Randolph was the lieutenant in charge of the unit. He had been investigating cop shootings so long that he had supervised the investigations the last four times Bosch had fired his weapon.

They took him out to their car so they could speak privately. With a tape recorder on the seat next to him, he told his story, beginning with the start of his part of the investigation. Randolph and Osani asked no questions until Bosch began recounting that morning's field trip with Waits. At that point they asked many questions obviously designed to elicit answers that went with the department's preconceived plan for dealing with the day's disaster. It was clear that they wanted to establish that the important decisions, if not *all* the decisions, came through the DA's office and Rick O'Shea. This was not to say that the department planned to announce that the disaster should be placed at the door of O'Shea's office. But the department was getting ready to defend itself against attack.

So when Bosch recounted the momentary disagreement over whether Waits should be uncuffed to descend the ladder, Randolph pressed him for exact quotes of what was said and by whom. Bosch knew that he was their last interview. They presumably had already talked to Cal Cafarelli, Maury Swann and O'Shea and his videographer.

"Have you looked at the video?" Bosch asked when he was finished telling his view of things.

"Not yet. We will."

"Well, it should have everything on it. I think the guy was rolling video when the shooting started. In fact, I'd like to see that tape myself."

"Well, to be honest, we are having a bit of a problem with that," Randolph said. "Corvin says he must have lost the tape in the woods."

"Corvin's the camera guy?"

"Right. Says it must've come out of his pocket when you people were carrying Rider on the ladder. We haven't found it."

Bosch nodded and did the political math. Corvin worked for O'Shea. The tape would show O'Shea instructing Olivas to take the handcuffs off Waits.

"Corvin's lying," Bosch said. "He was wearing the kind of pants with all the pockets, right? For carrying equipment. Cargo pants. I definitely saw him pop the tape out of the camera and put it in one of those pockets with the flap on the side of his leg.

It was when he was the last one left at the bottom. Only I saw it. But it wouldn't have fallen out. He closed the flap. He's got the tape."

Randolph just nodded as though he'd assumed all along that what Bosch had said was the situation, as though being lied to was simply par for the course in the OIS Unit.

"The tape's got O'Shea telling Olivas to take off the cuffs," Bosch said. "That's not the kind of video O'Shea would want on the news or in the LAPD's hands during an election year or any year. So it's a question of whether Corvin's keeping the tape to run his own play on O'Shea or O'Shea has told him to hang on to the tape. My bet would be on O'Shea."

Randolph didn't even bother nodding to any of that.

"Okay, let's go over it all once more from the top and then we can get you out of here," he said instead.

"Sure," Bosch said, understanding that he was being told that the tape was not his concern. "Whatever you need."

Bosch finished the second run-through of the story before seven o'clock and asked

Randolph and Osani if he could ride with them back to Parker Center so he could retrieve his car. On the ride back, the OIS men did not discuss the investigation. Randolph turned on KFWB at the top of the hour and they listened to the media version of the events in Beachwood Canyon and the latest update on the search for Raynard Waits.

A third report was on the growing political fallout from the escape. If the elections needed an issue, Bosch and company had certainly provided it. Everyone from city council candidates to Rick O'Shea's opponent weighed in with criticism of the way the LAPD and district attorney's office had handled the fatal field trip. O'Shea sought to distance himself from the potentially election-killing catastrophe by releasing a statement that characterized him as merely an observer on the trip, an observer who made no decisions concerning the security and transport of the prisoner. He said he relied on the LAPD for all of that. The report concluded with a mention of O'Shea's bravery in helping to save a wounded police detective, carrying her to safety while the armed fugitive was at large in the wooded canyon.

Having heard enough, Randolph turned the radio off.

"That guy O'Shea?" Bosch said. "He's got it down. He's going to make a great DA."

"No doubt," Randolph said.

Bosch said good night to the OIS men in the garage behind Parker Center and then walked to a nearby pay lot where he kept a parking space reserved to retrieve his car. He was drained from the day but there was almost an hour of daylight left. He headed back up the freeway toward Beachwood Canyon. Along the way he plugged his dead cell phone into its charger and called Rachel Walling. She was already at his house.

"It will be a while," he said. "I'm going back up to Beachwood."

"Why?"

"Because it's my case and they're up there working it."

"Right. You should be there."

He didn't respond. He just listened to the silence after that. It was comforting.

"I'll get home as soon as I can," he finally said.

Bosch closed the phone as he was exiting the freeway at Gower, and a few minutes later he was heading up Beachwood Drive.

Near the top he rounded a curve just as a pair of vans were passing on their way down. He recognized them as a body wagon followed by the SID van with the ladder on top. He felt a space open up in his chest. He knew they had come from the excavation. Marie Gesto was in that front van.

When he got to the parking lot he saw Marcia and Jackson, the two detectives who had been assigned to take over the excavation, peeling off the jumpsuits they had worn over their clothes and throwing them into the open trunk of their car. They were finished for the day. Bosch parked next to them and got out.

"Harry, how's Kiz?" Marcia asked immediately.

"They say she's going to be okay."

"Thank goodness."

"What a mess, huh?" Jackson said.

Bosch just nodded.

"What did you find?"

"We found her," Marcia said. "Or, I should say, we found a body. It's going to be a dental identification. You've got dental records, right?"

"In the file on the top of my desk."

"We'll get it and take it over to Mission."

The coroner's office was on Mission Road. A medical examiner with dental expertise would compare Marie Gesto's dental X-rays with those taken from the body reclaimed at the spot Waits had led them to that morning.

Marcia closed the trunk of the car and he and his partner looked at Bosch.

"You doing all right?" Jackson asked.

"Long day," Bosch said.

"And from what I hear, they might get longer," Marcia said. "Until they catch this guy."

Bosch nodded. He knew they wanted to know how it could have happened. Two cops dead and another in ICU. But he was tired of telling the story.

"Listen," he said, "I don't know how long I'm going to be hung up on this. I'm going to try to get clear tomorrow but obviously it's not going to be up to me. Either way, if you get the ID I'd appreciate it if you'd let me make the call to the parents. I've been talking to them for thirteen years. They'll want it to come from me. I want it to come from me."

"You got it, Harry," Marcia said.

"I've never complained about not having to make a notification," Jackson added.

They spoke for another few moments and then Bosch looked up and appraised the dying light of the day. In the woods the path would already be in deep shadows. He asked if they had a flashlight in the car that he could borrow.

"I'll bring it back tomorrow," he promised, though they all knew he might not be back the following day.

"Harry, there's no ladder in the woods," Marcia said. "SID took it with them."

Bosch shrugged and looked down at his mud-caked boots and pants.

"I might get a little dirty," he said.

Marcia smiled as he popped the trunk and reached in for a Maglite.

"You want us to stick around?" he asked as he gave Bosch the heavy light. "You slip in there and break an ankle, it'll be just you and the coyotes all night."

"No, I'll be fine. I've got my cell, anyway. And, besides, I like coyotes."

"Be careful in there."

Bosch stood by while they got into their car and drove off. He checked the sky again and headed down the path Waits had taken

them on that morning. It took him five minutes to get to the drop-off where the shooting had occurred. He turned on the flashlight and for a few moments played the
beam over the area. The place had been
trampled by the coroner's people, OIS investigators and Forensics techs. There was
nothing left to see. Eventually, he slid down
the incline using the same tree root he had
used to climb up that morning. In another
two minutes he came to the final clearing,
now delineated by yellow police-line tape
tied from tree to tree at the edges. In the
center was a rectangular excavation hole no
more than four feet deep.

Bosch ducked under the tape and entered
the hallowed ground of the hidden dead.

Part Three

HALLOWED GROUND

19

In the morning Bosch was making coffee for Rachel and himself when he got the call. It was his boss, Abel Pratt.

"Harry, you're not coming in. I just got the word."

Bosch had half expected it.

"From who?"

"The sixth floor. OIS hasn't wrapped it up and because the thing is so hot with the media, they want you to cool it on the sidelines for a few days until they see how it's going to go."

Bosch didn't say anything. The sixth floor was where the department administration was located. The "they" Pratt had referred

to was a collective of groupthink commanders who became frozen whenever a case hit
big on TV or in politics, and this one had hit
both. Bosch wasn't surprised by the call,
just disappointed. The more things changed,
the more they stayed the same.

"Did you watch the news last night?" Pratt
asked.

"No. I don't watch the news."

"Maybe you should start. We've now got
Irvin Irving all over the box weighing in on
this mess and he's zeroed in on you specifically. Gave a speech last night on the south
side, saying that hiring you back was an ex-
ample of the chief's ineptitude and the department's moral corruption. I don't know
what you did to the guy but he's got a real
hard-on for you, man. 'Moral corruption,'
that's taking the gloves off."

"Yeah, soon he'll be blaming me for his
hemorrhoids. Is the sixth floor sidelining me
in reaction to him or to OIS?"

"Come on, Harry, you think I'd be privy to
that conversation? I just got the call where I
was told to make the call, know what I
mean?"

"Yeah."

"But look at it this way — with Irving

punking you like that, the last thing the chief would do is cut you loose, because it would look like Irving was right. So the way I would read this thing is that they want to go by the numbers and nail it down tight before they close it down. So enjoy home duty and stay in touch."

"Yeah, and what do you hear about Kiz?"

"Well, they don't have to worry about home duty with her. She's not going any-where."

"That's not what I mean."

"I know what you mean."

"And?"

It was like peeling a label off a beer bottle. It never came all at once.

"And I think Kiz could be in some trouble. She was up on top with Olivas when Waits made his move. The question is, why didn't she take *his* ass out when she had the chance? It looks like she froze, Harry, and that means she could get hurt in this thing."

Bosch nodded. Pratt's political take on the situation seemed on target. It made Bosch feel bad. Right now Rider had to fight to stay alive. Later she'd have to fight to keep her job. He knew that no matter what the fight was he would stand beside her the whole way.

"Okay," he said. "Anything new on Waits?"

"Nothing, man. He's in the wind. Probably down in Mexico by now. If that guy knows what's best for him, he'll never raise his head above sea level again."

Bosch wasn't so sure about that but didn't express his disagreement. Something, some instinct, told him that Waits was lying low, yes, but that he had not gone very far. He thought about the Red Line subway Waits had apparently disappeared into and its many stops between Hollywood and downtown. He remembered the legend of Reynard the fox and the secret castle.

"Harry, I gotta go," Pratt said. "You cool?"

"Yeah, right, cool. Thanks for running it down for me, Top."

"All right, man. Technically, you are supposed to check in with me every day until we get the word you're back on active."

"You got it."

Bosch hung the phone up. A few minutes later when Rachel came into the kitchen, he poured coffee into an insulated cup that came with the Lexus she had leased when she transferred to L.A. She had brought the cup in with her the night before.

She was dressed and ready for work.

"I don't have anything here for breakfast," he said. "We could go down the hill to Du-par's if you have time."

"No, that's okay. I need to get going."

She tore open a pink packet of sugar sub-stitute and dumped it into the coffee. She opened the refrigerator and took out a quart of milk she had brought with her the night before as well. She whitened the coffee and put the top on the cup.

"What was the call you just got?" she asked.

"My boss. I just got sidelined while all of this is going on."

"Oh, baby . . ."

She came over and hugged him.

"In a way it's routine. The media and poli-tics of the case make it a necessity. I'm on home duty until the OIS wraps things up and clears me of any wrongdoing."

"You going to be okay?"

"I already am."

"What are you going to do?"

"I don't know. Home duty doesn't mean I have to stay home. So I'm going to the hospital to see if they'll let me hang with my partner for a while. Take it from there, I guess."

"Want to have lunch?"

"Yeah, sure, that sounds good."

They had quickly slipped into a domestic comfort that Bosch liked. It was almost as though they didn't have to talk.

"Look, I'm fine," he said. "You go to work and I'll try to come down around lunchtime. I'll call you."

"Okay, I'll talk to you."

She kissed him on the cheek before leaving through the kitchen door to the carport. He had told her to use the space in the carport on the days she came to stay with him.

Bosch drank a cup of coffee on the back deck while looking over the Cahuenga Pass. The skies were still clear from the rain two days earlier. It would be another beautiful day in paradise. He decided to go to Du-par's on his own to eat breakfast before heading to the hospital to check on Kiz. He could pick up the papers, see what was reported about the events of the day before and then bring them to Kiz, maybe read them to her if she wanted.

He walked back inside and decided to

leave on the suit and tie he had dressed in that morning before getting the call from Pratt. Home duty or not, he was going to act and look like a detective. He did, however, go into the closet in the bedroom and from the shelf above pull down the box containing the case file copies he had made four years earlier, when he had retired. He looked through the stacks until he found the copy of the Marie Gesto murder book. Jackson and Marcia would have the original, since they were running with the investigation now. He decided to take the copy with him in case he needed something to read while visiting with Rider or if Jackson or Marcia called with any questions.

He drove down the hill and up to Ventura Boulevard and followed it west into Studio City. At Du-par's he bought copies of the Los Angeles Times and the Daily News out of racks in front of the restaurant, then went in and ordered French toast and coffee at the counter.

The Beachwood Canyon story was on the front page of both papers. Both displayed color booking photos of Raynard Waits, and the articles played up the hunt for the mad killer, the formation of an LAPD task force,

and a toll-free telephone tip line just for finding Waits. The editors of the newspapers
apparently considered that angle more important to the readers and a better selling
point than the killing of two cops in the line
of duty and the wounding of a third.

The stories contained information released during the numerous press confer-
ences held the day before but very few details about what had actually happened in
the woods at the top of Beachwood Canyon.
According to the stories it was all under
continuing investigation and information
was being jealously guarded by those in
charge. The short bios of the officers involved in the shooting and Deputy Doolan
were sketchy at best. Both of the victims
killed by Waits had been family men. The
wounded detective, Kizmin Rider, had recently separated from a "life partner" —
code for reporting that she was gay. Bosch
didn't recognize the names of the reporters
on the stories and thought maybe they were
new to the police beat and without sources
close enough to the investigation to reveal
the inside details.

On the jump pages of both papers he
found sidebar stories that focused on the

political response to the shooting and escape. Both papers quoted a variety of local
pundits who for the most part said it was
too early to tell whether the Beachwood incident would help or hinder Rick O'Shea's
candidacy for district attorney. While it was
his case that went horribly awry, the reports
of his selfless efforts to help save the
wounded law officer while an armed killer
was loose in the very same woods could be
a balancing positive.

Said one pundit: "In this city, politics are
like the movie business; nobody knows
anything. This could be the best thing that
happens to O'Shea. It could be the worst."

Of course, O'Shea's opponent, Gabriel
Williams, was quoted liberally in both papers, calling the incident an unpardonable
disgrace and laying all blame at O'Shea's
feet. Bosch thought about the missing videotape and wondered how much it would
be worth to the Williams camp. Perhaps, he
thought, Corvin the videographer had already found out.

In both papers Irvin Irving got his licks in
and in doing so took a specific swipe at
Bosch for being the epitome of what was
wrong in the police department, something

Irving as a city councilman would right. He said Bosch should never have been hired back into the department the year before and that Irving, as a deputy chief at the time, had lobbied hard against it. The papers said Bosch was under investigation by the department's OIS squad and could not be reached for comment. Neither noted that the OIS routinely conducted an investigation of every shooting that involved a police officer, so what was presented to the public seemed unusual and therefore suspicious.

Bosch noticed that the sidebar in the *Times* had been written by Keisha Russell, who had worked the cop beat for a number of years before finally reaching a level of burnout that led her to ask for a new beat. She had landed in politics — a beat with its own high burnout rate. She had called and left a message for Bosch the night before but he had been in no mood to talk to a reporter, even one he trusted.

He still had her numbers programmed in his cell. When she worked cops he had been her source on a number of occasions, and she had provided him with help several times in return. He put the papers aside and took his first bites of French toast. His breakfast had both powdered sugar and maple syrup on it and he knew the sugar high would help charge him into the day.

After getting through about half of the meal he pulled out his cell and called the reporter's number. She answered right away.

"Keisha," he said. "It's Harry Bosch."

"Harry Bosch," she said. "Well, long time no see."

"Well, with you being a big shot on the political scene now . . ."

"Ah, but now it is politics *and* police coming together in a violent collision, isn't it? How come you didn't call me back yesterday?"

"Because you know I can't comment on an ongoing investigation, especially an investigation involving myself. Besides that, you called after my phone died. I didn't get your message until I got home, and it was probably after your deadline."

"How is your partner?" she said, putting the banter aside for a serious tone.

"Hanging in."

"And you came away unscathed as reported?"

"In the physical sense."

"But not the political."

"That's right."

"Well, the story is already in the paper. Calling to comment and defend yourself now doesn't exactly work."

"I'm not calling to comment or defend myself. I don't like my name in the paper."

"Oh, then I get it. You want to go off the record and be my Deep Throat on this."

"Not quite."

He heard her blowing out her breath in frustration.

"Then why are you calling, Harry?"

"First of all, I always like hearing your voice, Keisha. You know that. And second, on the political beat, you probably have direct lines to all of the candidates. You know, so you can get them to give a quick comment on any issue that comes up in the course of a day. Right? Just like yesterday?"

She hesitated before answering, trying to get a read on where this was going.

"Yes, we're known to be able to get hold of people when we have to. Except cantankerous police detectives. Sometimes they can be a problem."

Bosch smiled.

"There you go," he said.

"Which brings us to the reason you are calling."

"Right. I want the number that will get me directly to Irvin Irving."

This time the pause was longer.

"Harry, I can't give you that number. It was entrusted to me and if he knows I gave —"

"Come on. Entrusted to you and every other reporter covering the campaign and you know it. He wouldn't know who gave it to me unless I told him, and I'm not going to tell him. You know you can trust me when I say that."

"Still, I just don't feel comfortable giving it out without his permission. If you want me to call him and ask if I can —"

"He won't want to talk to me, Keisha. That's the point. If he wanted to talk to me I could leave a message at campaign head-quarters — which is where, by the way?"

"On Broxton in Westwood. I still don't feel comfortable just giving you the number."

Bosch quickly grabbed the *Daily News,* which was folded to the page with the polit-ical fallout story. He read the byline.

"Okay, well maybe Sarah Weinman or Du-ane Swierczynski will feel comfortable giv-ing it to me. They might want to have an

IOU from somebody who's in the middle of this thing."

"All right, Bosch, all right, you don't have to go to them, okay? I can't believe you."

"I want to talk to Irving."

"All right, but you don't say where you got the number."

"Obviously."

She gave him the number and he committed it to memory. He promised to call her back when there was something relating to the Beachwood Canyon incident that he could give her.

"Look, it doesn't have to be political," she urged. "Anything to do with the case, okay? I can still write a cop story if I'm the one who gets the story."

"Got it, Keisha. Thanks."

He closed his phone and left money for the bill and tip on the counter. As he stepped out of the restaurant he reopened the phone and punched in the number the reporter had just given him. Irving answered after six rings without identifying himself.

"Irvin Irving?"

"Yes, who is this?"

"I just wanted to thank you for confirming everything I always thought about you. You are nothing but a political opportunist and hack. That's what you were in the department and that's what you are out of it."

"Is this Bosch? Is this Harry Bosch? Who gave you this number?"

"One of your own people. I guess somebody in your own camp doesn't like the message you're putting out."

"Don't worry about it, Bosch. Don't worry about a thing. When I get in, you can start counting the days until you —"

Message delivered, Bosch closed his phone. It felt good to have said what he said, and to not worry that Irving was a superior officer who could say and do whatever he wanted without retribution from those he slighted.

Happy with his response to the newspaper stories, Bosch got in his car and drove to the hospital.

20

On the way down the hallway in ICU Bosch passed a woman who had just left Kiz Rider's room. He recognized her as Rider's former lover. They had met briefly a few years earlier when Bosch happened to see Rider at the Playboy Jazz Festival at the Hollywood Bowl.

He nodded to the woman as she passed but she didn't stop to talk. He knocked once on Rider's door and went in. His partner looked much better than she had the day before but still not even close to a hundred percent. She was conscious and alert when Bosch entered her room and her eyes tracked him to the side of her bed. There was no longer a tube in her mouth but the right side of her face drooped and Bosch immediately feared that she had suffered a stroke during the night.

"Don't worry," she said in slow, slurred words. "They've made my neck numb and it's working on half of my face, too."

He squeezed her hand.

"Okay," he said. "Other than that how do you feel?"

"Not so good. It hurts, Harry. It really hurts."

He nodded.

"Yeah."

"I have surgery on my hand in the afternoon. That's going to hurt, too."

"But then you'll be on the road to recovery. Rehab and all of that good stuff."

"I hope so."

She sounded depressed and Bosch didn't know what to say. Fourteen years earlier, when he had been about her age, Bosch had woken up in the hospital after taking a bullet in his left shoulder. He still remembered the screaming pain that had set in every time the morphine started to wear off.

"I brought the papers," he said. "You want me to read 'em to you?"

"Yeah. Nothing good, I suppose."

"No, nothing good."

He held the *Times* front page up so she could see the mug shot of Waits. He then read the lead story and then the sidebar. When he was finished he looked over at her. She looked distressed.

"You okay?"

"You should've left me, Harry, and gone after him."

"What are you talking about?"

"In the woods. You could've gotten him. Instead you saved me. Now look at the shit you're in."

"It comes with the territory, Kiz. The only thing I could think about out there was getting you to the hospital. I feel really guilty about everything."

"What exactly do you have to feel guilty about?"

"A lot. When I came out of retirement last year I made you leave the chief's office and partner with me again. You wouldn't have been there yesterday if I —"

"Oh, please! Would you shut your fucking mouth!"

He didn't remember ever hearing her use such language. He did what she told him.

"Just shut up," she said. "No more of that. What else did you bring me?"

Bosch held up the copy of the Gesto murder book.

"Oh, nothing. I brought this for me. To read if you were asleep or something. It's the copy of the Gesto file I made back when I retired the first time."

"So what are you going to do with that?"

"Like I said, I was just going to read it. I keep thinking there's something we missed."

"'We'?"

"Me. Something I missed. I've been listening a lot lately to a recording of Coltrane and Monk playing together at Carnegie Hall. It was right there in the Carnegie archives for like fifty years until somebody found it. The thing is, the guy who found it had to know their sound to know what they had in that box in the archives."

"And that relates to the file how?"

Bosch smiled. She was in a hospital bed with two bullet wounds and she was still giving him shit.

"I don't know. I keep thinking there's something in here and I'm the only one who can find it."

"Good luck. Why don't you sit on that

chair and read your file. I think I'm going to go to sleep for a while."

"Okay, Kiz. I'll be quiet."

He pulled the chair away from the wall and brought it closer to the bed. As he sat down she spoke again.

"I'm not coming back, Harry."

He looked at her. It was not what he wanted to hear but he wouldn't object. Not now, at least.

"Whatever you want, Kiz."

"Sheila, my old girl, was just visiting. She saw the news and came in. She says she'll take care of me until I get better. But she doesn't want me going back to the cops."

Which explained why she hadn't wanted to talk to Bosch out in the hallway.

"That was always a point of contention with us, you know?"

"I remember you told me. Look, you don't have to tell me any of this stuff now."

"It's not just Sheila, though. It's me. I shouldn't be a cop. I proved that yesterday."

"What are you talking about? You are one of the best cops I know."

He saw a tear roll down her cheek.

"I froze out there, Harry. I fucking froze and I let him . . . just shoot me."

"Don't do this to yourself, Kiz."

"Those men are dead because of me. When he grabbed Olivas, I couldn't move. I just watched. I should have put him down, but I just stood there. I just stood there and I let him shoot me next. Instead of raising my gun I raised my hand."

"No, Kiz. You didn't have an angle on him. If you had fired you might have hit Olivas. After that it was too late."

He hoped she understood that he was telling her what to say when the OIS came around.

"No, I have to own up to it. I —"

"Kiz, you want to quit, that's fine. I'll back you one hundred percent. But I won't back you on this other shit. You understand?"

She tried to turn her face away from him but the bandages on her neck prevented her from turning.

"Okay," she said.

More tears came down and Bosch knew that she had wounds that were far deeper than those in her neck and hand.

"You know, you should have gone up top," she said.

"What are you talking about?"

"Out there with the ladder. If you had been

up top instead of me none of this would've happened. Because you wouldn't have hesitated, Harry. You would've blown his shit away."

Bosch shook his head.

"Nobody knows how they're going to react in a situation until they're in that situation."

"I froze."

"Look, go to sleep, Kiz. Get better and then make your decision. If you don't come back I will understand. But I'm always going to be your backup, Kiz. No matter what happens and where you go."

She used her left hand to wipe her face.

"Thanks, Harry."

She closed her eyes and he watched as she finally gave it up. She mumbled something he couldn't understand and then was asleep. Bosch watched her for a while and thought about not having her as a partner anymore. They had worked well together, like family. He would miss it.

He didn't want to think about the future right now. He opened the murder book and decided to start reading about the past. He started from page one, the initial crime report.

A few minutes later he had it covered and was about to turn to the witness reports when his phone began vibrating in his pocket. He walked out of the room to answer the call in the hallway. It was Lieutenant Randolph from the Officer Involved Shooting Unit.

"Sorry we're holding you off active while we take our time with this thing," he said.

"It's all right. I know why."

"Yeah, a lot of pressure."

"What can I do for you, Lieutenant?"

"I was hoping maybe you'd take a ride down here to Parker Center and look at this videotape we've got."

"You have the tape from O'Shea's cameraman?"

There was a pause before Randolph answered.

"We have a tape from him, yes. I'm not sure it's a complete tape and that's what I want you to look at. You know, tell us what might be missing. Can you come down?"

"I'll be there in forty-five minutes."

"Good. I'll be waiting. How's your partner?"

Bosch wondered if Randolph knew where he was.

"She's still hanging in. I'm at the hospital now but she's still out of it."

He hoped to delay Rider's OIS interview as long as possible. In a few days, once she was off the painkillers and clear of mind, maybe she'd think better of volunteering that she had frozen when Waits made his move.

"We're waiting to hear when we can interview her," Randolph said.

"Probably be a few days, I would think."

"Probably. Anyway, see you soon. Thanks for coming down."

Bosch closed the phone and went back into the room. He picked the murder book up off the chair where he had left it and checked on his partner. She was asleep. He quietly left the room.

He made good time on the drive in and called Rachel to tell her that lunch looked good, since he was already going to be downtown. They agreed to go fancy and she said she would make a reservation at the Water Grill for noon. He said he would see her there.

The OIS squad was on the third floor at Parker Center. It was at the opposite end of the building from the Robbery-Homicide Division. Randolph had a private office with video equipment set up on a stand. He was sitting behind the desk, while Osani was working with the equipment and getting ready to play the tape. Randolph motioned Bosch to the only other seat.

"When did you get the tape?" Bosch asked.

"It was delivered this morning. Corvin said it took him twenty-four hours to remember he had put it in one of those cargo pockets you mentioned. This, of course, came after I had reminded him I had a witness who saw the tape go in the pocket."

"And you think it's been doctored?"

"We'll know for sure after I give it to SID but, yeah, it's been edited. We found his camera at the crime scene, and Osani here was bright enough to write down the number on the counter. When you roll this tape the counter on the tape doesn't match. About two minutes of tape are missing. Why don't you roll it, Reggie."

Osani started the tape and Bosch watched as it began with the huddle of investigators and techs in the Sunset Ranch parking lot. Corvin had stayed close to O'Shea at all times and there was an uninterrupted flow of raw video footage which seemed to always keep the candidate for district attorney at center. This continued as the group followed Waits into the woods and until they all stopped at the top of the steep drop-off. Then it was clear there was a cut where it was to be presumed that Corvin had turned the camera off and then back on again. There was no discussion on the tape of whether the handcuffs should be removed from Waits's wrists. The video cut from Kiz Rider saying they could use the SID ladder to Cafarelli returning to the spot with the ladder.

Osani stopped the tape so they could discuss it.

"It's likely that he did stop the camera while we were waiting for the ladder," Bosch said. "That probably took ten minutes max. But he probably didn't stop it until after the back and forth about the cuffs on Waits."

"Are you sure?"

"No, I'm just assuming. But I wasn't watching Corvin. I was watching Waits."

"Right."

"Sorry."

"Don't be. I don't want you to give me anything that wasn't there."

"Did any of the other witnesses back me on this? Did they say they heard the discussion about uncuffing him?"

"Cafarelli, the SID tech, heard it. Corvin said he didn't and O'Shea said it never happened. So you got two from the LAPD saying yes and two from the DA's office saying no. And no tape to back it up either way. Classic pissing match."

"What about Maury Swann?"

"He'd be the tiebreaker except he's not talking to us. Says it is in his client's best interest to remain mute."

That didn't surprise Bosch, coming from a defense lawyer.

"Is there another edit you wanted to show me?"

"Possibly. Go ahead, Reggie."

Osani started the video again and it took them through the descent on the ladder and then to the clearing where Cafarelli methodically used the probe to mark the location of the body. The shot was uninterrupted. Corvin simply turned the camera on and shot everything, probably with the idea that he would edit it later if the tape was ever needed in a court hearing. Or possibly a campaign documentary.

The tape continued and documented the group's return to the ladder. Rider and Olivas went up to the top and Waits was uncuffed by Bosch. But as the prisoner started his climb up the ladder, the tape cut off just as he reached the upper rungs and Olivas was leaning down to grab him.

"That's it?" Bosch asked.

"That's it," Randolph said.

"I remember after the shooting, when I told Corvin to leave the camera and come up the ladder to help with Kiz, he had it on his shoulder. He was rolling."

"Yeah, well, we asked about why the tape ended and he claimed that he thought he was going to run short on tape. He wanted to keep some for when the diggers came in and excavated the body. So he turned the camera off when Waits was going up the ladder."

"That make sense to you?"

"I don't know. You?"

"Nope. I think that's bullshit. He had the whole thing on tape."

"That's just an opinion."

"Whatever," Bosch said. "The question is, why cut the tape at this point? What was on it?"

"You tell me. You were there."

"I told you everything I could remember."

"Well, you better remember more. You're not in such good shape here."

"What are you talking about?"

"There's no discussion on the tape of whether the man should or shouldn't be cuffed. What is on the tape is Olivas uncuffing him for the climb down and you uncuffing him for the climb back up."

Bosch realized that Randolph was right and that the tape made him look like he had uncuffed Waits without even discussing it with the others.

"O'Shea's setting me up."

"I don't know if anyone is setting anyone up. Let me ask you something. When the shit hit the fan out there and Waits grabbed the gun and started shooting, do you remember seeing O'Shea at that point?"

Bosch shook his head.

"I ended up on the ground with Olivas on top of me. I was worried about where Waits was, not O'Shea. I don't know where O'Shea was. All I can tell you is that he wasn't in my picture. He was behind me somewhere."

"Maybe that's what Corvin had on the tape. O'Shea running away like a coward."

Randolph's use of the word *coward* sparked something in Bosch.

He now remembered. From on top of the embankment Waits had called someone, presumably O'Shea, a coward. Bosch remembered hearing the sound of running behind him. O'Shea had run.

Bosch thought about this. First of all, O'Shea had no weapon with which to protect himself from the man he was going to put in prison for life. By all rights, running from the gun would not be unexpected or unreasonable. It would have been an act of self-preservation, not cowardice. But since O'Shea was a candidate for top prosecutor in the county, running away under any circumstances would probably not look so good — especially if it was on video on the six o'clock news.

"I remember now," Bosch said. "Waits called somebody a coward for running. It must've been O'Shea."

"Mystery solved," Randolph said.

Bosch turned back to the monitor.

"Can we back it up and look at that last part again?" he asked. "Just before it cuts off, I mean."

Osani worked the video and they watched

it silently from the moment Waits was un-cuffed for the second time.

"Can you stop it right before the cut?" Bosch asked.

Osani froze the image on the screen. It showed Waits past the halfway point on the ladder and Olivas reaching down to grab him. The angle of Olivas's body had caused his windbreaker to fall open. Bosch could see his pistol in a pancake holster on his left hip, grips out so that he could take the gun with an across-the-body pull.

Bosch stood up and walked to the moni-tor. He took out a pen and tapped it on the screen.

"You notice that?" he said. "It looks like he's got the snap on his holster open."

Randolph and Osani studied the screen. The safety snap was something they obvi-ously hadn't noticed before.

"Could've been that he wanted to be ready if the prisoner made a move," Osani said. "It's within regs."

Neither Bosch nor Randolph responded. Whether it fell within department regulations or not, it was a curiosity that could not be explained, since Olivas was dead.

"You can turn it off, Reg," Randolph finally said.

"No, can you show it one more time?" Bosch asked. "Just this part at the ladder."

Randolph nodded to Osani and the tape was backed up and replayed. Bosch tried to use the images on the monitor to build momentum and carry him into his own memory of what happened when Waits got to the top. He remembered looking up and watching Olivas being swung around so that his back was to those below and there was no clear shot at Waits. He now remembered wondering where Kiz was and why she wasn't reacting.

Then there were shots and Olivas was falling backwards down the ladder toward him. Bosch raised his hands to try to lessen the impact. On the ground with Olivas on top of him he heard more shots and then the yelling.

The yelling. Forgotten in all the adrenaline rush and panic. Waits had come to the precipice and fired down at them. And he had yelled. He called O'Shea a coward for running. But he had said more than just that.

"Run, you coward! How's your bullshit deal looking now?"

Bosch had forgotten the taunt in the commotion and confusion of the shooting, escape and effort to save Kiz Rider. In the charge of fear that came with those moments.

What did that mean? What was Waits saying by calling the agreement a "bullshit deal"?

"What is it?" Randolph asked.

Bosch looked at him, coming out of his thoughts.

"Nothing. I was just trying to concentrate on what happened during the moments where there's no tape."

"It looked like you remembered something."

"I just remembered how close I came to getting killed like Olivas and Doolan. Olivas landed on me. He ended up shielding me."

Randolph nodded.

Bosch wanted to get out of there. He wanted to take his discovery — *"How's your bullshit deal looking now?"* — and work it. He wanted to grind it down to a powder and analyze it under the microscope.

"Lieutenant, you have anything else for me right now?"

"Not right now."

"Then I'm going to go. Call me if you need me."

"You call me when you remember what you can't remember."

He gave Bosch a knowing look. Bosch looked away.

"Right."

Bosch left the OIS office and went out to the elevator lobby. He should have left the building then. But instead he pushed the button to go up.

21

Remembering what Waits had yelled changed things. To Bosch it meant something had been going on up there in Beachwood Canyon and it was something he'd had no clue about. His first thought now was to retreat and consider everything before making a move. But the appointment at OIS had given him a reason to be in Parker Center and he planned to make the most of it before leaving.

He entered room 503, the offices of the Open-Unsolved Unit, and headed toward the alcove where his desk was located. The squad room was almost vacant. He checked the workstation shared by Marcia and Jackson and saw that they were out. Bosch had to walk by the open door of Abel Pratt's office to get to his own workstation, so he decided to be up-front. He stuck his head in the door and saw his boss ensconced at his desk. He was eating raisins out of a little red box that looked like it was meant for a child. He looked surprised to see Bosch.

"Harry, what are you doing here?" he asked.

"OIS called me down to look at the video O'Shea's guy took of the Beachwood field trip."

"He's got the shooting on it?"

"Not quite. He claimed the camera was off."

Pratt's eyebrows arched.

"Randolph doesn't believe him?"

"Hard to tell. The guy sat on the tape until this morning and it looks like it might have been altered. Randolph's going to have SID check it. Anyway, listen, I thought that while I was here I would take a bunch of files and stuff back to Archives so it's not all lying around. Kiz had some files out, too, and it will be a while before she gets back to them."

"That's probably a good idea."

Bosch nodded.

"Hey," Pratt said, his mouth full of raisins. "I just heard from Tim and Rick. They're leaving Mission right now. The autopsy was this morning and they got the ID. Marie Gesto, confirmed. They got it on the dental."

Bosch nodded again as he considered the finality of this news. The search for Marie Gesto was over.

"I guess that's it, then."

"They said you were going to make the next-of-kin call on it. You wanted to do it."

"Yeah. But I'll probably wait until tonight, when Dan Gesto comes home from work. It'll be better if both parents are together."

"However you want to handle it. We'll keep the lid on it from this end. I'll call the ME and tell them not to put it out until tomorrow."

"Thanks. Did Tim or Rick tell you if they got a cause of death?"

"Looks like manual strangulation. Hyoid was fractured."

He touched the front of his neck in case Bosch didn't remember where the fragile hyoid bone was located. Bosch had only worked about a hundred strangulation cases in his time but he didn't bother saying anything.

"Sorry, Harry. I know you're close to this one. When you started pulling the file every couple of months, I knew it meant something to you."

Bosch nodded more to himself than to Pratt. He went to his desk, thinking about the confirmation of the body's identification and remembering how thirteen years earlier he had been all but convinced that Marie Gesto would never be found. It was always strange how things turned out. He started gathering all the files associated with the Waits investigation. Marcia and Jackson had the Gesto murder book but this didn't bother Bosch, because he had his own copy in his car.

He walked around to his partner's desk to gather the files she had on Daniel Fitzpatrick, the Hollywood pawnbroker Waits said he murdered during the 1992 riots, and saw two plastic cartons on the floor. He opened one and found it contained the pawn records salvaged from the burned-out pawnshop. Bosch remembered Rider mentioning these. The musty smell of the once-wet documents hit him and he quickly

snapped the top back on the carton. He decided he would take these as well, but it
would mean two trips past Pratt's open
door to get everything down to his car, and
that would give his boss two opportunities
to become curious about what Bosch was
really up to.

Bosch was considering leaving the cartons behind when he got lucky. Pratt stepped
out of his office and looked over at him.

"I don't know who decided raisins are a
good snack food," he said. "I'm still hungry.
You want anything from downstairs, Harry?
A doughnut or something?"

"No thanks, I'm fine. I'm going to take this
stuff over and then get out of here."

Bosch noticed that Pratt was holding one
of the guidebooks usually stacked on his
desk. It said *West Indies* on the cover.

"Doing some research?" he asked.

"Yeah, checking things out. You ever
heard of a place called Nevis?"

"Uh-uh."

Bosch had heard of few of the places
Pratt asked about during his researches.

"Says here you can buy an old sugar mill
on eight acres for less than four hundred.

Shit, I'll clear more than that on my house alone."

It was probably true. Bosch had never been to Pratt's home but knew that he owned a property up in Sun Valley that was big enough to keep a couple horses on. He'd lived there nearly twenty years and was sitting on a gold mine in real-estate value. There was only one problem, though. A few weeks earlier Rider had been at her desk and had overheard Pratt on the phone in his office asking questions about child custody and communal property. She told Bosch about the call and they both assumed that Pratt had been talking to a divorce lawyer.

"You want to make sugar?" Bosch asked.

"No, man, it's just what the property was used for at one time. Now you'd probably buy it, fix it up, and make it a bed-and-breakfast or something."

Bosch just nodded. Pratt was moving into a world he knew and cared nothing about.

"Anyway," Pratt said, sensing he didn't have an audience, "I'll see you. And by the way, it's nice that you got dressed up for the OIS. Most guys on home duty would've slogged in here in jeans and a

T-shirt, looking more like a suspect than a cop."

"Yeah, no problem."

Pratt left the office and Bosch waited thirty seconds for him to get the elevator. He then put a stack of files on one of the evidence cartons and carried it all out the door. He was able to take it down and out to his car and get back before Pratt returned from the cafeteria. He then took the second carton and left. No one questioned what he was doing or where he was going with the materials.

After pulling out of the pay lot Bosch checked his watch and saw that he had less than an hour to kill before he was supposed to meet Rachel for lunch. It wasn't enough time to drive home, drop the documents and come back — besides, that would be a waste of time and gas. He thought about canceling the lunch so he could go home right away and get going on the review of the records, but he decided against it because he knew Rachel would be a good sounding board and might even have some ideas about what Waits had meant when he yelled during the shooting.

He could also get to the restaurant early

and start his review while waiting at the table for Rachel. But he knew that might cause a problem if a customer or waiter happened to catch a glimpse of some of the photos in the murder books.

The city's main library was located in the same block as the restaurant, and he decided he would go there. He could do some file work in one of the private cubicles and then meet Rachel on time at the restaurant.

After parking in the garage beneath the library he carried the murder books from the Gesto and Fitzpatrick cases with him onto the elevator. Once inside the confines of the sprawling library, he found an open cubicle in a reference room and set to work reviewing the documents he had brought. Since he had begun rereading the Gesto files in Rider's hospital room, he decided to stick with them and finish his review.

Moving through the book in the order the documents and reports were filed, he didn't reach the Investigative Chronology — usually filed at the back of a murder book — until the end. He casually read through the 51 forms, and nothing about the investigative moves made, the subjects interviewed or the calls received hit him as any more important than when they had been originally added to the chrono.

Then suddenly he was struck by what he had not seen in the chronology. He quickly flipped pages backwards until he came to the 51 for September 29, 1993, and looked for the entry on the call Jerry Edgar had taken from Robert Saxon.

It wasn't there.

Bosch leaned forward to read the document more clearly. This made no sense. In the official murder book the entry was there. Raynard Waits's alias, Robert Saxon. The entry date was September 29, 1993, and the time of the call was 6:40 p.m. Olivas had found it during his review of the case and the next day in O'Shea's office Bosch had seen it clear as day. He had studied it, knowing that it was confirmation of an error that allowed Waits another thirteen years of freedom to kill.

But the entry was not in Bosch's copy of the murder book.

What the hell?

At first Bosch couldn't put it together. The copy of the chronology in front of him was made four years earlier, when Bosch had decided to retire. He had secretly copied murder books from a handful of open cases that still gnawed at his insides. They were his retirement cases. His plan had been to work them on his own and at his leisure, to solve them before he could finally let the mission go and sit on a beach in Mexico with a fishing pole in one hand and a Corona in the other.

But it didn't work out that way. Bosch learned that the mission was best served with a badge and he came back to the job. After he was assigned with Rider to the Open-Unsolved Unit, one of the first murder books he pulled out of Archives was the Gesto case. The book he pulled was the live record, the investigative file that was updated each time he or anybody else worked it. What he had in front of him was a copy that had sat on a shelf in his closet and had not been updated in four years. Even so, how could one have a notation entered on a 51 form in 1993, while the other one didn't?

The logic of it dictated only one answer.

The official record of the investigation had been tampered with. The notation entering the name Robert Saxon into the murder book was added after Bosch had made his copy of the book. That of course left a four-year window during which the false notation could have been added, but common sense told Bosch he was dealing with days, not years.

Just a few days earlier Freddy Olivas had called him, looking for the murder book. Olivas took possession of the book and then became the one who discovered the Robert Saxon entry. It was Olivas who had brought it to light.

Bosch flipped through the chronology. Almost all of the pages corresponding with the dates of the initial investigation were filled in completely with time-marked notations. Only the page marked September 29 had space at the bottom. This would have allowed Olivas to remove the page from the binder, type in the Saxon entry and then return it to its place, setting the stage for his supposed discovery of this link between Waits and Gesto. Back in 1993 Bosch and Edgar did the 51s on a typewriter in the Hollywood squad room. It was all done on computer now but there were still plenty of typewriters around most squad rooms for the old-school cops — like Bosch — who couldn't quite grasp the idea of working on a computer.

Bosch felt a heavy mixture of relief and anger start to overtake him. The burden of guilt over the mistake he and Edgar had supposedly made was lifting. They were in the clear and he needed to tell Edgar as soon as he could. But Bosch couldn't embrace the feeling — not yet — because of the growing rage he felt at being victimized by Olivas. He stood up and walked away from the cubicle. He stepped out of the reference room and into the library's main rotunda, where a circular mosaic high up on the walls told the story of the city's founding.

Bosch felt like yelling something, exorcising the demon, but he kept quiet. A security guard walked quickly across the floor of the cavernous structure, maybe on his way to put the collar on a book thief or a flasher in the stacks. Bosch watched him go and then went back to his own work.

Back in the cubicle he tried to think through what had happened. Olivas had tampered with the murder book, typing a two-line entry into the chronology that would make Bosch believe he had made a profound mistake in the early stages of the investigation. The entry said that Robert

Saxon had called to report seeing Marie Gesto at the Mayfair Supermarket on the afternoon she had disappeared.

That was all. It wasn't the content of the call that was important to Olivas. It was the caller. Olivas had wanted to somehow get Raynard Waits into the murder book. Why? To put Bosch on some sort of a guilt trip that would allow Olivas the upper hand and control of the current investigation?

Bosch dismissed this. Olivas already had the upper hand and control. He was lead investigator in the Waits case and Bosch's proprietary hold on the Gesto case would not change that. Bosch was along for the ride, yes, but he wasn't steering the car. Olivas was steering, and therefore the Robert Saxon name plant was not necessary.

There had to be another reason.

Bosch worked it over for a while but only came to the weak conclusion that Olivas needed to connect Waits to Gesto. By putting the killer's alias into the book, he was going back thirteen years in time and firmly tying Raynard Waits to Marie Gesto.

But Waits was about to admit he murdered Gesto. There could be no stronger tie than an uncoerced confession. He was even going to lead authorities to the body. The notation in the chronology would be a minor connection compared with these two. So then why put it in?

Ultimately, Bosch was confounded by the risk Olivas had taken. He had tampered with the official record of the murder investigation for seemingly little reason or gain. He had run the risk that Bosch would discover the deceit and call him on it. He had run the risk of the deceit possibly being revealed by a smart lawyer like Maury Swann in court one day. And he did all of this knowing that he didn't have to, knowing that Waits would be tied solidly into the case with a confession.

Now Olivas was dead and could not be confronted. There was no one to answer why.

Except maybe Raynard Waits.

"How's your bullshit deal looking now?"

And maybe Rick O'Shea.

Bosch thought about everything and all in a moment it came together. Bosch suddenly knew why Olivas had taken the risk and put the specter of Raynard Waits into the Marie Gesto murder book. He saw it with a clarity that left him no room for doubt.

Raynard Waits didn't kill Marie Gesto.

He jumped up and started gathering the files together. Clutching them with both hands, he hurried through the rotunda toward the exit. His footfalls echoed behind him in the great room like a crowd of people chasing him. He looked back but there was nobody there.

22

Bosch had lost track of time while in the library. He was late. Rachel was already seated and waiting for him. She was holding a large one-sheet menu that obscured the look of annoyance on her face as Bosch was led to the table by a waiter.

"Sorry," Bosch said as he sat down.

"It's okay," she replied. "But I already ordered for myself. I didn't know if you were going to show or not."

She handed the menu across to him. He immediately handed it to the waiter.

"I'll have what she's having," he said. "And just the water is fine."

He drank from the glass already poured

for him while the waiter hurried away. Rachel smiled at him, but not in a nice way.

"You're not going to like it. You'd better call him back."

"Why? I like seafood."

"Because I ordered the sashimi. You told me the other night that you like your sea-food cooked."

The news gave him momentary pause but he decided he deserved to pay for his mis-take of arriving late.

"It all goes to the same place," he said, dismissing the issue. "But why do they call this place the Water *Grill* if they're not grilling the food?"

"Good question."

"Forget about it. We need to talk. I need your help, Rachel."

"With what? What's wrong?"

"I don't think Raynard Waits killed Marie Gesto."

"What do you mean? He led you to her body. Are you saying that wasn't Marie Gesto?"

"No, ID was confirmed today at the au-topsy. It was definitely Marie Gesto in that grave."

"And Waits was the one who led you to it, right?"

"Right."

"And Waits was the one who confessed to killing her, right?"

"Right."

"At autopsy, was the cause of death in agreement with that confession?"

"Yeah, from what I hear, it was."

"Then, Harry, you're not making sense. With all of that, how can he not be the killer?"

"Because something is going on that we don't know about, that I don't know about. Olivas and O'Shea had some sort of play going with him. I'm not sure what it was but it all went to shit in Beachwood Canyon."

She held up her hands in a hold-it-right-there gesture.

"Why don't you start at the beginning. Only tell me facts. No theory, no conjecture. Just give me what you've got."

He told her everything, starting with the tampering with the murder book by Olivas and concluding with the detail-by-detail accounting of what had happened when Waits started to climb up the ladder in Beachwood Canyon. He told her what Waits had yelled at O'Shea and what had been edited out of the field trip video.

It took him fifteen minutes and during that time their lunch was served. Of course it came fast, Bosch thought. It didn't have to be cooked! He felt lucky to be the one doing all the talking. It gave him a ready excuse not to eat the raw fish put down in front of him.

By the time he was finished recounting the story he could see that Rachel's mind had gone to work on everything. She was grinding it down.

"Putting Waits in the murder book doesn't make sense," she said. "It connects him to the case, yes, but he is already connected through his confession and his leading you to the body. So why bother with the murder book?"

Bosch leaned across the table to respond.

"Two things. One, Olivas thought he might need to sell the confession. He had no idea if I'd be able to punch holes in it, so he wanted some insurance. He put Waits in the file. And it put me in a position of being preconditioned to believe the confession."

"Okay, and two?"

"This is where it gets tricky," he said.

"Putting Waits in the book was a way of pre-conditioning me but it was also about knocking me off my game."

She looked at him, but what he was saying didn't register.

"You'd better explain that."

"This is where we go off the known facts and talk about what the facts might mean. Theory, conjecture, whatever you want to call it. Olivas put that line in the chronology and then threw it in my face. He knew that if I saw it and believed it, then I would believe that my partner and I had horribly messed up back in 'ninety-three, that I would believe people were dead because of our mistake. The weight of all those women Waits killed since then would be on me."

"Okay."

"And it would connect me with Waits on an emotional level of pure hate. Yes, I've wanted the guy who killed Marie Gesto for thirteen years. But adding in all those other women and putting their deaths on me would bring things to a raw edge when I finally came face-to-face with the guy. It would distract me."

"From what?"

"From the fact that Waits didn't kill her. He

was confessing to killing Marie Gesto but he didn't kill her. He made some sort of deal with Olivas and probably O'Shea to take the fall for it because he was already going down for all the others. I was so overcome with my hatred that I didn't have my eyes on the prize. I wasn't paying attention to the details, Rachel. All I wanted to do was jump across the table and choke the guy out."

"You are forgetting something."

"What?"

Now she leaned across the table, keeping her voice down so as not to disturb the other diners.

"He *led* you to her body. If he didn't kill her, how did he know where to go in the woods? How did he lead you right to her?"

Bosch nodded. It was a good point but one he had already thought about.

"It could have been done. He could have been schooled in his cell by Olivas. It could've been a Hansel and Gretel trick, a trail marked in such a way that only he would notice the markers. I'm going back up to Beachwood this afternoon. My guess is that when I go through there this time, I'll find the markers."

Bosch reached over and took her empty

plate and exchanged it with his untouched plate. She didn't object.

"So you're saying that the whole field trip was a setup to convince you," she said. "That Waits was fed the basic information about the Marie Gesto murder and he just regurgitated it all in the confession, then happily led you like Little Red Riding Hood through the woods to the spot where she was buried."

He nodded.

"Yeah, that's what I am saying. When you boil it all down to that, it sounds a little far-fetched, I know, but —"

"More than a little."

"What?"

"More than a little far-fetched. First of all, how did Olivas know the details to give Waits? How did he know where she was buried so he could mark a trail for Waits to follow? Are you saying *Olivas* killed Marie Gesto?"

Bosch shook his head emphatically. He thought she was going over the top with her devil's advocate logic and he was getting annoyed.

"No, I'm not saying that Olivas was the killer. I am saying he was gotten to by the killer. He and O'Shea. The real killer came to them and made some sort of a deal."

"Harry, this just sounds so . . ."

She didn't finish. She pushed the sashimi on her plate around with her chopsticks but ate very little of it. The waiter used the moment to approach the table.

"You didn't like your sashimi?" he said to her in a trembling voice.

"No, I —"

She stopped when she realized she had almost a full portion on the plate in front of her.

"I guess I wasn't very hungry."

"She doesn't know what she's missing," Bosch said, smiling. "I thought it was great."

The waiter took the plates off the table and said he would be back with dessert menus.

"'I thought it was great,'" Walling said in a mocking voice. "You jerk."

"Sorry."

The waiter brought the dessert menus and they both handed them back and ordered coffee. Walling remained quiet after that and Bosch decided to wait her out.

"Why now?" she finally asked.

Bosch shook his head.

"I don't know exactly."

"When was the last time you pulled the case and actively worked it?"

"About five months ago. The last video I showed you the other night — that was the last time I worked it. I was just about to make another run at it."

"What did you do besides pull Garland in again?"

"Everything. I talked to everybody. I knocked on all the same doors again. I only brought Garland in at the end."

"You think it was Garland who got to Olivas?"

"For Olivas and maybe O'Shea to make a deal, it would have had to be somebody with juice. Lots of money and power. The Garlands have both."

The waiter came with their coffee and the check. Bosch put a credit card on it but the waiter had already left.

"You want to at least split it?" Rachel asked. "You didn't even eat."

"It's okay. Hearing what you have to say makes it worth it."

"I bet you say that to all the girls."

"Only the ones who are federal agents."

She shook her head. He saw the doubt creep back into her eyes.

"What?"

"I don't know, it's just . . ."

"Just what?"

"What if you look at it from Waits's view of things?"

"And?"

"It's such a long shot, Harry. It's like one of those mumbo-jumbo conspiracies. You take all the facts after it's over and move them around to fit some far-fetched theory. Marilyn Monroe didn't overdose, the Kennedys used the mob to kill her. Like that."

"So what about Waits's point of view?"

"I'm just saying, why would he do it? Why would he confess to a murder he didn't commit?"

Bosch made a dismissive gesture with his hands, as if he were pushing something away.

"That's an easy one, Rachel. He would do it because he had nothing to lose. He was already going down as the Echo Park Bagman. If he went to trial, he was no doubt going to get the Jesus juice, just like Olivas reminded him out there yesterday. So his only shot at living was to confess to his crimes, and if, say, the investigator and the prose-cutor wanted him to add another killing in for good measure, what was Waits going to say about that? No deal? Don't kid yourself, they had the leverage and if they told Waits to jump, he would've nodded his head and said, 'On who?'"

She nodded.

"And there was something else," Bosch added. "He knew there would be a field trip and I'll bet that gave him hope. He knew he might get a shot at an escape. Once they told him that he'd be leading us through the woods, that shot got a little bigger and no doubt his cooperation got a little better. His whole motivation was probably getting to the field trip."

She nodded again. He couldn't tell whether he had convinced her of anything. They were silent for a long moment. The waiter came and took his credit card. Lunch was over.

"So what are you going to do?" she asked.

"Like I told you, next stop Beachwood Canyon. After that, I'm going to find the man who can explain everything to me."

"O'Shea? He'll never talk to you."

"I know. That's why I'm not going to talk to him. Not yet, at least."

"You're going to find Waits?"

He could hear the doubt in her voice.

"That's right."

"He's long gone, Harry. You think he would stay around here? He killed two cops. His life expectancy in L.A. is zero. You think he'd stick around with every person with a gun and badge in this county looking for him with a license to kill?"

He nodded slowly.

"He's still here," he said with conviction. "Everything you said is right, except you forgot one thing. He's got the leverage now. When he escaped, the leverage shifted to Waits. And if he is smart, and it appears he is, he'll use it. He'll stick around and he'll use O'Shea to maximum potential."

"You mean blackmail?"

"Whatever. Waits carries the truth. He knows what went down. If he can make it believable that he's a danger to O'Shea and his whole election machine, and if he can contact O'Shea, he can now make the candidate do the jumping."

She nodded.

"You raise a good point about leverage,"

she said. "What if this grand conspiracy of yours had gone down as planned? You know, Waits takes the fall for Gesto and all the others and heads off to Pelican Bay or San Quentin to do his life without. Then the conspirators have this guy sitting in a cell and he has all the answers — and the leverage. He's still a danger to O'Shea and his whole political machine. Why would the future district attorney of Los Angeles County put himself in that position?"

The waiter brought back the credit card and the final bill. Bosch added a tip and signed it. It had to be the most expensive lunch he had never eaten.

He looked up at Rachel when he was finished scribbling his name.

"Good question, Rachel. I don't know the exact answer to it but I assume O'Shea or Olivas or somebody had a plan for an endgame. And maybe that's why Waits decided to run."

She frowned.

"You can't be talked out of this, can you?"

"Not yet."

"Well, good luck. I think you are going to need it."

"Thanks, Rachel."

He stood up and so did she.

"Did you valet?" she asked.

"No, I'm over in the library garage."

It meant they would leave the restaurant by different doors.

"Will I see you tonight?" he asked.

"If I'm not held up. There's word of a case coming our way from Washington head-quarters. How about if I call you?"

He said that was fine and walked with her to the door that led to the garage where the valets waited. He hugged her there and said good-bye.

23

On the way out of downtown Bosch took Hill Street up to Caesar Chavez and turned left. It soon became Sunset Boulevard and he drove it through Echo Park. He wasn't expecting to see Raynard Waits crossing at the light or coming out of a *medicina* clinic or one of the *migra* offices that lined the street. But Bosch was running way out on his instincts on this case and they told him Echo Park was still in play. The more he drove through, the more he would get a feel for the neighborhood and the better he would be at his search. Instincts or not, he was sure of one thing. Waits had originally been arrested while on his way to a specific destination in Echo Park. Bosch was going to find it.

He pulled into a no-parking zone near Quintero Street and walked up to the Pescado Mojado grill. He ordered *camarones a la diabla* and showed the booking photo of Waits to the man who took his order and to the patrons waiting in line. He got the usual shake of the head from each customer, and the Spanish conversation among them died off. Bosch took his shrimp plate to a table and finished his food quickly.

From Echo Park he drove home to change from his suit into jeans and a pullover shirt. Then he drove over to Beachwood Canyon and made his way to the top of the hill. The parking clearing below Sunset Ranch was empty and Bosch wondered if all the activity and media attention from the day before had kept riders away. He got out of his car and went to its trunk. He pulled out a coiled thirty-foot length of rope and headed into the brush on the same path he had taken behind Waits the day before.

He was only a few steps down the path when his cell phone started vibrating. He stopped, dug the phone out of his blue jeans and saw on the screen that it was

Jerry Edgar calling. Bosch had left him a message earlier while driving home.

"How's Kiz?"

"Doing better. You ought to go visit her, man. Get over whatever it is you two need to get over and visit her. You didn't even call yesterday."

"Don't worry, I will. In fact, I was thinking about cutting out of here early and dropping by. You going to be there?"

"I might. Give me a call when you're going and I'll try to meet you. Anyway, that's not really why I called. There's a couple things I wanted to tell you. First, they got a confirmation on the ID at the autopsy today. It was Marie Gesto."

Edgar was silent a moment before responding.

"Have you talked to her parents?"

"No, not yet. Dan's got that job selling tractors. I was going to call up there tonight when he's home and they're together."

"That's what I'd do. What else you got, Harry? I got a guy in a room here and I'm about to go in and break his ass down on a murder-rape we're working."

"Sorry to interrupt. I thought you called me."

"I did, man, but I was calling you back real quick in case it was important."

"It is important. I thought you'd want to know, I think that line that was found in the fifty-ones on this case was phonied. I think when it all shakes out we'll be clear on it."

This time there was no hesitation in his old partner's response.

"What are you saying, Waits never called us back then?"

"That's right."

"Then how'd that entry get in the chrono?"

"Somebody added it. Recently. Somebody trying to fuck with me."

"Goddamn it!" Bosch could hear the anger and relief in Edgar's voice. "I haven't slept since you called me up and told me that shit, Harry. They didn't only fuck with you, man."

"That's what I figured. That's why I called. I haven't figured it all out, but that's the way it's looking. When I get the whole story I'll let you know. Now go back to your interview and nail that guy."

"Harry, my man, you just made my day. I'm going to go into the room and crunch this asshole's bones."

"I'm glad to hear that. Call me if you're going to see Kiz."

"You got it."

But Bosch knew Edgar was just paying lip
service to the idea. He wouldn't be visiting
Kiz, not if he was in the middle of a breaking case like he said. After closing and
pocketing the phone, Bosch looked around
and took in his surroundings. He looked
high and low, from the ground to the overhead canopy, and didn't see any obvious
markings. He guessed that there would've
been no need for a Hansel and Gretel trail
while Waits had been on the clearly defined
path. If there were markers, they would be
at the bottom of the mud slide embankment. He headed that way.

At the top of the precipice he looped the
rope around the trunk of the white oak at
the top and was able to rappel down the
sheer surface to the lower level. He left the
rope in place and once again assessed the
area from floor to canopy. He saw nothing
that readily marked the way to the grave
site, where Marie Gesto had been found. He
started walking toward the grave site, looking for carvings in the trunks of the trees,

ribbons in the branches, anything that Waits might have used to lead the way.

Bosch got to the grave site without seeing a single indication of a marked trail. He was disappointed. His lack of findings went against the theory he had outlined for Rachel Walling. But Bosch was sure he was right in his thinking and he refused to believe there was no trail. He thought it was possible that whatever markings had been there had been trampled over and obliterated by the army of investigators and technicians who had descended on the woods the day before.

Refusing to give up, he made his way back to the embankment and then turned and looked toward the grave site. He tried to put his mind into the position Waits was in. He had never been to the spot before, yet he had to readily choose a direction to go in while everyone else watched.

How did he do it?

Bosch stood motionless, thinking and looking off into the woods in the direction of the grave site. He did not move for five minutes. After that he had the answer.

In the middle distance on the sight line to the grave site was a tall eucalyptus tree. It was split at ground level and two fully mature trunks rose at least fifty feet through the canopy of other trees. In the split, about ten feet off the ground, was a branch that had fallen and become lodged horizontally between the trunks. The formation of split trunk and branch created an inverted A that was clearly recognizable and could have been noticed quickly by someone scanning the woods and looking specifically for it.

Bosch headed toward the eucalyptus, certain that he had the first marker that Waits had followed. When he reached the position, he looked again in the direction of the grave site. He slowly scanned until he again picked up on an anomaly that was obvious and unique in terms of the immediate vicinity. He walked toward it.

It was a young California oak. What made it noticeable to Bosch from a distance was that its natural balance was off. It had lost the symmetrical spread of its branches because one of the lower limbs was missing. Bosch walked to it and looked up at a broken outcropping on the trunk where a four-inch-thick limb had been attached about eight feet up. By grabbing a lower branch and pulling himself up into the tree he was able to examine the break more closely and found that it was not a natural break. The outcropping showed a smooth cut through the top half of the branch. Someone had sawed across the top of the branch and then pulled down on it to break it. Bosch was no tree surgeon but he thought the cut and break looked recent. The exposed inner wood was light in color and there was no indication of regrowth or natural repair.

Bosch dropped to the ground and looked around in the brush. The fallen limb was nowhere to be found. It had been dragged away so as not to be noticed and cause suspicion. To him it was further proof that a Hansel and Gretel trail had been left for Waits to follow.

He turned and looked in the direction of the final clearing. He was less than twenty yards from the grave site and he was easily able to pick out what he believed to be the last marker. High up in the oak tree that shaded the grave site was a nest that looked like the home of a large bird, an owl or a hawk.

He walked to the clearing and looked up. The hair scrunchy Waits had said marked the spot had been removed by the Forensics team. Looking further up into the tree, Bosch could not see the nest from directly beneath. Olivas had planned it well. He had used three markers recognizable only from a distance. Nothing that would draw a second glance from those following Waits, yet three markers that could easily lead him to the grave site.

As his eyes dropped to the open grave at his feet he remembered that he had noticed a disturbance in the soil the day before. He had credited it to animals foraging in the dirt. Now he believed the disturbance had been left by the first digging into the soil to confirm the grave site. Olivas had been out here before any of them. He had come out to mark the trail and confirm the grave. He had either been told where to find it or had been led to it by the real killer.

Bosch had been staring at the grave and putting the scenario together for several seconds before he realized he was hearing voices. At least two men in conversation, their voices approaching. Bosch could hear them moving through the brush, their footfalls heavy in the mud and on the bed of fallen leaves. They were coming from the same direction Bosch had come from.

He moved quickly across the small clearing and got behind the massive trunk of the oak tree. He waited and soon he could tell that the men had reached the clearing.

"Right here," said the first voice. "She was right here for thirteen years."

"No shit! This is spooky."

Bosch didn't dare look around the tree and risk exposing himself. No matter who it was — media, cops or even tourists — he didn't want to be seen here.

The two men stayed in the clearing and batted meaningless conversation back and forth for a few moments. Luckily, neither approached the trunk of the oak and Bosch's position. Then finally Bosch heard the first voice say, "Well, let's go get this done and get out of here."

The men trod off in the direction from which they had come. Bosch looked around the tree and caught a glimpse of them just before they disappeared back into the brush. He saw Osani and another man he assumed was also from the OIS Unit. After giving them a head start Bosch moved from around the tree and crossed the clearing.

He took a position behind an old eucalyptus and watched as the OIS men walked back to the sheer facing left by the mud slide.

Osani and his partner made so much noise walking through the brush that it was quite easy for Bosch to pick and move his way toward the embankment as well. Under cover of their noise he got to the eucalyptus that was Waits's first marker and watched the two men as they set up to take measurements from the bottom of the embankment to the top. There was a ladder on the facing now, positioned much like the ladder had been the day before. Bosch realized that the two men were cleaning up the official report. They were taking distance measurements that had either been forgotten or deemed unnecessary the day before. Today, in light of the political fallout involved, everything was necessary.

Osani climbed the ladder to the top while his partner remained below. He then took a tape measure off his belt and pulled out several lengths, passing the end down to his partner. They took measurements with Osani calling out the lengths and his partner writing them down in a notebook. It looked to Bosch as though they were measuring various lengths from the spot on the ground where he had been the day before to the positions where Waits, Olivas and Rider had been. Bosch had no idea what the importance of such measurements would be to the investigation.

Bosch's phone started to vibrate in his pocket and he quickly pulled it out and shut it off. As the screen died he saw that the incoming number had a 485 prefix, which he knew meant Parker Center.

A few seconds later Bosch heard the ringing of a cell phone in the clearing where Osani and the other man were working. Bosch peeked around the tree and saw Osani take a phone off his belt. He listened to the caller and then took a sweeping look around the woods, doing a 360-degree turn. Bosch ducked back.

"No, Lieutenant," Osani said. "We don't see him. The car's in the lot but we don't see him. We don't see anybody out here."

Osani listened some more and said yes several times before closing the phone and returning it to his belt. He went back to work with the tape measure and within another minute or so the two OIS men had what they needed.

Osani climbed the ladder and then both men pulled it up the embankment. It was at that moment that Osani noticed the rope looped around the trunk of the white oak at the edge of the embankment. He put the ladder down on the ground and went to the tree. He pulled the rope from around the trunk and started coiling it. He looked out into the woods as he did this and Bosch moved back behind one of the eucalyptus's two trunks.

A few minutes later they were gone, loudly trudging back through the woods to the parking clearing, the ladder carried between them. Bosch went to the embankment but waited until he could no longer hear the OIS men before using the roots as handholds to climb up.

When he got to the parking clearing, there was no sign of Osani and his partner. Bosch turned his phone back on and waited for it to boot up. He wanted to see if the caller from Parker Center had left a message. Before he could listen, the phone started vibrating in his hand. He recognized the number as one of the lines from the Open-Unsolved Unit. He took the call.

"This is Bosch."

"Harry, where are you?"

It was Abel Pratt. There was an urgency in his voice.

"Nowhere. Why?"

"Where *are* you?"

Something told Bosch that Pratt knew exactly where he was.

"I'm in Beachwood Canyon. What's going on?"

There was a moment of silence before Pratt responded, the urgent tone replaced with one of annoyance.

"What's going on is that I just got a call from Lieutenant Randolph at OIS. He says there's a Mustang registered to you sitting in the lot up there. I tell him that's really strange, because Harry Bosch is on home duty and is supposed to be staying a million miles away from the investigation in Beachwood Canyon."

Thinking quickly, Bosch came up with what he thought was a way out.

"Look, I'm not investigating anything. I'm looking for something. I lost my challenge coin out here yesterday. I'm just looking for it."

"What?"

"My RHD chip. It must've come out of my

pocket when I was sliding down the embankment or something. I got home last night and it wasn't in my pocket."

As he spoke Bosch reached into his pocket and pulled out the coin he was claiming to have lost. It was a heavy metal coin about the size and width of a casino chip. One side showed a gold detective's badge and the other side showed the caricature of a detective — suit, hat, gun and exaggerated chin — set against an American flag background. It was known as a challenge coin or chip and was a carryover from the practice of elite and specialized military units. Upon acceptance into the unit a soldier is given a challenge coin and is expected to carry it always. At any time or place a fellow unit member can ask to see the coin. This most often takes place in a bar or canteen. If the soldier fails to be carrying the coin, then he picks up the tab. The tradition had been observed for several years in the RHD. Bosch had been given his coin upon returning from retirement.

"Fuck the coin, Harry," Pratt said angrily. "You can replace it for ten bucks. *Stay away* from the investigation. Go home and stay home until you hear from me. Am I clear?"

"You're clear."

"Besides, what the fuck? If you lost your coin out there the Forensics people would have found it already. They went over that scene with a metal detector looking for cartridges."

Bosch nodded.

"Yeah, I sort of forgot about that."

"Yeah, Harry, you forgot? Are you bullshitting with me?"

"No, Top, I'm not. I forgot. I was bored and decided to come look for it. I saw Randolph's people and decided to keep my head down. I just didn't think they'd call in my plate."

"Well, they did. And then I got the call. I don't like blowback like this, Harry. You know that."

"I'm going home right now."

"Good. Stay there."

Pratt didn't wait for Bosch's response. He clicked off and Bosch closed his phone. He flipped the heavy coin into the air, caught it in his palm, badge side up, and pocketed it. He then walked to his car.

24

Something about being told to go home made Bosch not go home. After leaving Beachwood Canyon he made a stop at St. Joe's to check in on Kiz Rider. She had changed locations again. She was now out of ICU and on a regular patient floor. She didn't have a private room but the other bed in the room was empty. They often did that for cops.

Speaking was still difficult for her and the malaise of depression she exhibited that morning had not lifted. Bosch didn't stay long. He passed on a get-well from Jerry Edgar and then left, finally going home as instructed and hauling in the two cartons and files he had collected earlier from the Open-Unsolved Unit.

He put the cartons on the floor in the dining room and spread the files out on the table. There was a lot and he knew he could probably occupy himself for at least a couple days with what he had taken from the office. He went over to the stereo and turned it on. He knew that he already had the Coltrane-Monk collaboration from Carnegie Hall in the machine. The player was on shuffle and the first song out was called "Evidence." Bosch took that as a good sign as he went back to the table.

To begin he had to take an inventory of exactly what he had so he could decide how to approach his review of the material. First and foremost was the copy of the investigative record in the current case Raynard Waits was being prosecuted for. This had been turned over by Olivas but not studied closely by Bosch and Rider because their assignments and priorities were the Fitzpatrick and Gesto cases. On the table Bosch also had the Fitzpatrick murder book Rider had pulled out of Archives as well as his secret copy of the Gesto murder book, of which he had already completed a review.

Finally, on the floor were the two plastic cartons containing whatever pawn records had been salvaged after Fitzpatrick's business was torched and then soaked by fire hoses during the 1992 riots.

There was a small drawer in the side of the dining room table. Bosch figured that it had been designed for silverware but since he used the table more often to work on than to eat on, the drawer contained an assortment of pens and legal pads. He withdrew one of each, deciding that he needed to write down the important aspects of the current investigation. After twenty minutes and three torn-off and crumpled pages, his free-form thoughts had filled less than half a page.

/ arrest
Echo Park
    \ escape (Red Line)
Who is Waits? Where is the castle?
  (destination: Echo Park)
Beachwood Canyon — setup, false
  confession
Who benefits? Why now?

Bosch studied the notes for a few moments. He knew that the last two questions he had written were actually the starting point. If things had gone according to plan, who would have benefited from Waits's false confession? Waits, for one, by avoiding a death sentence. But the real winner was the real killer. The case would have been closed, all investigations halted. The real killer would escape justice.

Bosch looked at the two questions again. *Who benefits? Why now?* He considered them carefully and then reversed their order and considered them again. He came to a single conclusion. His continued investigations of the Marie Gesto case had created a need for something to be done now. He had to believe that he had knocked too hard on someone's door and that the entire Beachwood Canyon plan had come about because of pressure he was continuing to exert on the case.

This conclusion led to the answer to the other question at the bottom of the sheet. *Who benefits?* Bosch wrote:

Anthony Garland — Hancock Park

For thirteen years Bosch's instinct had told him Garland was the one. But beyond his instincts there was no evidence directly connecting Garland to the murder. Bosch had not yet been made privy to the evidence, if any, that was developed during the excavation of the body and the autopsy, but he doubted that after thirteen years there would be anything usable — no DNA or forensics that could tie the killer to the body.

Garland was a suspect under the "replacement victim" theory. That is, his rage toward the woman who had dropped him led him to kill a woman who reminded him of her. The shrinks would call it a long-shot theory but Bosch now moved it front and center. Do the math, he thought. Garland was the son of Thomas Rex Garland, wealthy oil baron from Hancock Park. O'Shea was in a highly contested election battle, and money was the gasoline that kept a campaign engine running. It was not inconceivable that a quiet approach had been made to T. Rex, a deal struck and a plan enacted. O'Shea gets the money he needs to win the election, Olivas gets the head investigator nod in O'Shea's office and Waits takes the fall for Gesto while Garland takes a ride on it.

It was said that L.A. was a sunny place for

shady people. Bosch knew that better than most. He had no hesitation in believing Olivas had been part of such a scheme. And the thought of O'Shea, a career prosecutor, selling his soul for a shot at the top slot didn't give him pause for very long either.

"Run, you coward! How's your bullshit deal looking now?"

He opened his phone and called Keisha Russell at the *Times.* After several rings he checked his watch and saw it was a few minutes after five. He realized she was probably on deadline and ignoring her calls. He left a message at the prompt, asking her to call back.

Since it was so late in the day Bosch decided he had earned a beer. He went to the kitchen and got an Anchor Steam out of the box. He was happy he had gone high end the last time he bought beer. He took the bottle out on the deck and watched as the heart of rush hour gripped the freeway below. The traffic slowed to a crawl and the incessant sound of car horns of every variety began. It was just far enough away to be less than intrusive. Bosch was glad he was not down there in the fight.

His phone buzzed and he pulled it out of

his pocket. It was Keisha Russell calling back.

"Sorry, I was going over tomorrow's story with the copyeditor."

"I hope you spelled my name right."

"Actually, you're not in this one, Harry. Surprise."

"Glad to hear it."

"What can you do for me?"

"Uh, I was actually going to ask you to do something for me."

"Of course you were. What could it be?"

"You're a political reporter now, right? Does that mean you look at campaign contributions?"

"I do. I review every filing by every one of my candidates. Why?"

He walked back inside and muted the stereo.

"This is off the record, Keisha. I'd like to know who has been supporting Rick O'Shea's campaign."

"O'Shea? Why?"

"I'll tell you when I can tell you. I just need the information right now."

"Why do you always do this to me, Harry?"

It was true. They had danced like this

many times in the past. But their history was that Bosch was always true to his word when he said he would tell her when he could tell her. He hadn't double-crossed her once. And so her protests were banter, a mere prequel to her doing what Bosch wanted her to do. That was part of the dance as well.

"You know why," he said, playing his part. "Just help me out and there will be something for you when the time is right."

"Someday I want to decide when the time is right. Hold on."

She clicked off and was gone for almost a minute. As he waited Bosch stood over the spread of documents on the dining room table. He knew that he was spinning his wheels with this angle on O'Shea and Garland. They could not be touched at the moment. They were guarded by money and the law and the rules of evidence. Bosch knew the correct angle of investigation was to go at Raynard Waits. His job was to find him and break open the case.

"Okay," Russell said after getting back on the line. "I have the most up-to-date filing. What do you want to know?"

"How up-to-date is up-to-date?"

"This was filed last week. Friday."

"Who are his main contributors?"

"There's nobody who is really big, if that is what you mean. He's mostly running a grassroots campaign. Most of his contributors are fellow lawyers. Almost all of them."

Bosch thought of the Century City law firm that handled things for the Garland family and had gotten the court orders preventing Bosch from questioning Anthony Garland about Marie Gesto without an attorney present. The head of the firm was Cecil Dobbs.

"Is one of those lawyers Cecil Dobbs?"

"Um . . . yes, C. C. Dobbs, Century City address. He gave a thousand."

Bosch remembered the lawyer in his collection of videotaped interviews with Anthony Garland.

"What about Dennis Franks?"

"Franks, yes. A lot of people from that firm contributed."

"What do you mean?"

"Well, according to election law, you give your home and work address when you make a contribution. Dobbs and Franks have a Century City work address and, let's see, nine, ten, eleven other people gave the same address. They each gave a thousand, too. It's probably all the lawyers in the same firm."

"So thirteen thousand dollars from there. Is that it?"

"That's it from there, yes."

Bosch thought about whether to specifically ask if the name Garland was on the contributors list. He didn't want her making phone calls or snooping around in his investigation.

"No big corporate contributors?"

"Nothing of major consequence. Why don't you tell me what you are looking for, Harry? You can trust me."

He decided to go for it.

"You have to hold on to it until you hear from me. No phone calls, no inquiries. You just sit on this, right?"

"Right, until I hear from you."

"Garland. Thomas Rex Garland, Anthony Garland, anybody like that on there?"

"Mmmm, no. Isn't Anthony Garland the kid you were looking at once for Marie Gesto?"

Bosch almost cursed out loud. He was hoping she wouldn't make the connection. A decade earlier, when she was a hellion on the cop beat, she had come across a search warrant application he had filed in an effort to search Anthony Garland's home. The application had been rejected for lack of probable cause but the filing was public record, and at the time, Russell, the ever industrious reporter, routinely combed through the search warrants at the courthouse. Bosch had talked her out of writing a story identifying the scion of the local oil family as a suspect in the Gesto murder but here it was a decade later and she remembered the name.

"You can't do anything with this, Keisha," he responded.

"What are you doing? Raynard Waits confessed to Gesto. Are you saying that was bullshit?"

"I'm not saying anything. I was simply curious about something, that's all. Now, you cannot do anything with this. We have a deal. You sit on this until you hear from me."

"You're not my boss, Harry. How come you are talking to me like you're my boss?"

"I'm sorry. I just don't want you running off and going crazy on this. It could hurt what I've got going. We have a deal, right? You just said I can trust you."

It was a long time before she answered.

"Yes, we have a deal. And, yes, you can trust me. But if this is going where I think you are going with it, I want updates and reports. I'm not just going to sit around waiting to hear from you after you get the full package put together. If I don't hear from you, Harry, I'm going to get nervous. When I get nervous I do some crazy things, make some crazy phone calls."

Bosch shook his head. He should never have made the call to her.

"I understand, Keisha," he said. "You'll be hearing from me."

He closed the phone, wondering what fresh hell he might have just unleashed on earth and when it would come back to bite him. He trusted Russell but only to the limit he could trust any reporter. He finished his beer and went to the kitchen for another. As soon as he popped the top his phone buzzed.

It was Keisha Russell again.

"Harry, have you ever heard of GO! Industries?"

He had. GO! Industries was the current corporate titling of a company started eighty years earlier as Garland Oil Industries. The company had a logo in which the word GO! had wheels and was slanted forward to look as if it were a speeding car.

"What about it?" he responded.

"Headquartered downtown in the ARCO plaza. I count twelve employees of GO! making one-thousand-dollar contributions to O'Shea. How's that?"

"That's fine, Keisha. Thanks for calling back."

"Did O'Shea take a payoff to put Gesto on Waits? Is that it?"

Bosch groaned into the phone.

"No, Keisha, that's not what happened and that's not what I am looking at. If you make any calls in this regard you will compromise what I am doing and could be putting yourself, me, and others in danger. Now would you please drop it until I can tell you exactly what is going on and when you can run with it?"

Once again she hesitated before answering, and it was in that space of silence that Bosch began to wonder if he could still trust her. Maybe her move from police to politics had changed something in her. Maybe, as with most who worked in the realm of politics, her sense of integrity had been sanded

down by exposure to the world's oldest pro-
fession: political whoring.

"Okay, Harry, I got it. I was just trying to
help. But you remember what I said. I want
to hear from you. Soon!"

"You will, Keisha. Good night."

He closed the phone and tried to shake off
his concerns about the reporter. He thought
about the information he had gotten from
her. Between GO! and the law firm of Cecil
Dobbs, O'Shea had received at least twenty-
five thousand in campaign contributions
from people who could be directly tied to
the Garlands. It was spread out and legal,
but nevertheless, it was a strong indication
that Bosch was on the right track.

He felt a satisfying tug in his guts. He had
something to work with now. He just had
to find the right angle from which to work it.
He went to the table in the dining room and
looked at the array of police reports and
records spread out in front of him. He
picked up the file marked WAITS — BACK-
GROUND and started to read.

25

From the standpoint of law enforcement, Raynard Waits was a rarity as a murder suspect. When his van was pulled over in Echo Park, the LAPD in effect had captured a killer the department wasn't even looking for. In fact, Waits was a killer no department or agency was looking for. There was no file on him in any drawer or computer anywhere. No FBI profile or background briefing existed to refer to. They had a killer and they had to start from scratch with him.

This presented a whole new angle of investigation for Detective Freddy Olivas and his partner, Ted Colbert. The case came to them with a momentum that simply dragged them with it. Everything was about moving forward, toward prosecution. There was little time or inclination to go backwards. Waits was arrested in possession of bags containing the parts of two murdered women. It was a slam dunk, and that precluded the need to know exactly who they had in custody and what had brought him to be in that van on that street at that time.

Consequently, little in the file on the present case helped Bosch. The file contained records of the investigative work related to attempts to identify the victims and drawing the physical evidence together for the impending prosecution.

The background information in the file was simply basic data on Waits either provided by the suspect himself or culled by Olivas and Colbert during routine computer searches. The bottom line was that they knew little about the man they were prosecuting, but what they knew was enough.

Bosch completed his read-through of the file in twenty minutes. When he was finished, once again he had less than a half page of notes on his pad. He had constructed a short timeline that charted the suspect's arrests, admissions, and use of

the names Raynard Waits and Robert
Saxon.

4/30/92 — Daniel Fitzpatrick
murdered, Hollywood
5/18/92 — Raynard Waits, dob
11/3/71, DL issued,
Hollywood
2/01/93 — Robert Saxon, dob
11/3/75 — arrested,
prowling
— IDed as Raynard Waits,
dob 11/3/71, through DL
thumbprint
9/09/93 — Marie Gesto abducted,
Hollywood
5/11/06 — Raynard Waits, dob
11/3/71, arrested 187
Echo Park

Bosch studied the timeline. He found two
things worth noting. Waits supposedly didn't
get a driver's license until he was twenty,
and no matter which name he used, he always gave the same month and day of
birth. While he once offered 1975 as his
year of birth in an attempt to be considered
a juvenile, he uniformly gave 1971 at other

times. Bosch knew that the latter was a practice often employed by people switching identities. Change the name but keep some of the other details the same to avoid getting confused or forgetting basic information — an obvious giveaway, especially if it's a cop asking for it.

Bosch knew from the record searches earlier in the week that there was no birth record of Raynard Waits or Robert Saxon with the corresponding 11/03 birth date in Los Angeles County. The conclusion he and Kiz Rider had reached from this was that both names were false. But now Bosch considered that maybe the birth date of 11/03/71 was not false. Maybe Waits, or whoever he was, kept his real date of birth as he changed his name.

Bosch now looked at the close proximity between the date of the Fitzpatrick murder and the date of issue of Waits's driver's license. It was less than a month. He added to this the fact that according to the records Waits did not apply for a driver's license until he was twenty. He thought it was unlikely that a boy growing up in the autotopia of L.A. would wait until he was twenty to get his driver's license. It was yet one more indication that Raynard Waits was not his name.

Bosch started to feel it. Like a surfer waiting for the right swell before starting to paddle, he felt his wave coming in. He thought that what he was looking at was the birth of a new identity. Eighteen days after he murdered Daniel Fitzpatrick under cover of the riots, the man who killed him walked into a DMV office in Hollywood and applied for a driver's license. He gave November 3, 1971, as a date of birth and the name Raynard Waits. He would have had to provide a birth certificate, but that would not have been too hard to come up with if he knew the right people. Not in Hollywood. Not in L.A. Getting a phony birth certificate would have been an easy, almost risk-free task.

Bosch believed that the Fitzpatrick murder and the change of ID were connected. It was a cause-and-effect. Something about the murder caused the killer to change his identity. This belied the confession given two days earlier by Raynard Waits. He had characterized the murder of Daniel Fitzpatrick as a thrill kill, an opportunity to indulge a long-held fantasy. He went out of his way to depict Fitzpatrick as a victim chosen at random, chosen simply because he was there.

But if that was truly the case and if the killer had no previous connection to the victim, then why did the killer act almost immediately to reinvent himself with a new identity? Within eighteen days the killer procured a false birth certificate and got a new driver's license. Raynard Waits was born.

Bosch knew there was a contradiction in what he was considering. If the killing of Fitzpatrick had taken place as Waits had confessed, then there would have been no reason for him to quickly create a new identity. But the facts — the timeline of the murder and the issuance of the driver's license — contradicted this. The conclusion to Bosch was obvious. There *was* a connection. Fitzpatrick was not a random victim. He could, in fact, be linked in some way to his killer. And that was why his killer changed his name.

Bosch got up and took his empty bottle to the kitchen. He decided that two beers was enough. He needed to stay sharp and up on the wave. He went back out to the stereo and put in the masterpiece. *Kind of Blue.* It never failed to give him the charge. "All

Blues" was the first song out of the shuffle, and it was like being dealt blackjack at a twenty-five-dollar table. It was his favorite and he let it ride.

Back at the table he opened the Fitzpatrick murder book and started to read. Kiz Rider had handled it earlier but she had simply been engaged in a review to prepare for taking Waits's confession. She wasn't looking for the hidden connection Bosch was now seeking.

The investigation of Fitzpatrick's death had been carried out by two detectives temporarily assigned to the Riot Crimes Task Force. Their work was cursory at best. Few leads were followed, because there weren't many to follow in the first place and because of the overriding pall of futility that fell over all the cases associated with the riots. Almost all acts of violence associated with the three days of widespread unrest were random. People robbed, raped and murdered indiscriminately and at will — simply because they could.

No witnesses to the attack on Fitzpatrick were located. No forensic evidence was found other than the can of lighter fluid —

and it had been wiped clean. Most of the shop's records had been destroyed by fire or water. What was left was put in two cartons and ignored. The case was treated as a dead end from the moment it was born. It was orphaned and archived.

The murder book was so thin that Bosch finished his front-to-back read-through in less than twenty minutes. He had taken no notes, gotten no ideas, seen no connections. He felt the tide ebbing. His ride on the wave was coming to an end.

He thought about getting another beer out of the box and attacking the case all over again the next day. Then the front door opened and Rachel Walling walked in, carrying takeout cartons from Chinese Friends. Bosch stacked the reports on the dining room table so there would be room to eat. Rachel brought plates from the kitchen and opened the cartons. Bosch got the last two Anchors out of the refrigerator.

They small-talked for a while and then he told her what he had been doing since lunch and what he had learned. He could tell by her reserved comments that she was not convinced by his description of the trail he had found in Beachwood Canyon. But when he showed her the timeline he had worked up, she readily agreed with his conclusions about the killer's changing of ID after the Fitzpatrick murder. She also agreed that, while they didn't have the killer's real name, they might have his real birth date.

Bosch looked down at the two plastic cartons on the floor.

"Then I guess it's worth the shot," he said.

She leaned to the side so she could see what he was looking at.

"What are those?"

"Pawn slips mostly. All the records salvaged after the fire. Back in 'ninety-two they were all wet. They dropped them in these boxes and forgot about them. Nobody's ever looked through them all."

"Is that what we're doing tonight, Harry?"

He looked up at her and smiled. He nodded.

After they were finished eating they decided that they would take a carton each. Bosch suggested that they take them out onto the back deck because of the musty smell that would come from the cartons once they were opened. Rachel readily agreed. Bosch lugged the cartons out and then got two empty cardboard boxes from the carport. They sat down in deck chairs and began the work.

Taped to the top of the carton Bosch chose was a 3 × 5 card that said MAIN FILE CABINET. Bosch took the top off and used it to try to wave away the fumes that came out. The carton contained mostly pink pawn slips and 3 × 5 cards that had been haphazardly put in the container as if with a shovel. There was nothing ordered or neat about the records.

Water damage was high. Many of the slips had stuck together while wet, and the ink on others was smeared and unreadable. Bosch looked over at Rachel and saw her dealing with the same issues.

"This is bad, Harry," she said.

"I know. Just do the best you can. It might be our last hope."

There was no way to begin but simply to dig in. Bosch pulled out a wad of slips, brought them up to his lap and started going through them, attempting to make out the name, address and birth date of each customer who had pawned something through Fitzpatrick. Each time he looked at a slip, he checked the top corner with a red pencil from the dining room table drawer and dropped it into the cardboard box on the other side of his chair.

They were at it a solid half hour, working without conversation, when Bosch heard the phone in the kitchen ring. He thought about letting it go but knew it might be a call from Hong Kong. He got up.

"I didn't even know you had a landline," Walling said.

"Not many people do."

He grabbed the phone on the eighth ring. It wasn't his daughter. It was Abel Pratt.

"Just checking on you," he said. "I figure if I get you on the house line and you say you are home, then you're really home."

"What, am I under house arrest now?"

"No, Harry, I'm just worried about you, that's all."

"Look, there will be no blowback from me, okay? But home duty does not mean I have to be at home twenty-four-seven. I checked with the union."

"I know, I know. But it does mean you do not take part in any job-related investigation."

"Fine."

"What are you doing, then?"

"I'm sitting on the back deck with a friend. We're having a beer and enjoying the night air. Is that okay with you, Top?"

"Anybody I know?"

"I doubt it. She doesn't like cops."

Pratt laughed and it seemed that Bosch had finally put him at ease about what he was doing.

"Then, I'll let you get back to it. Have a good one, Harry."

"I will if I can stay off the phone. I'll call in tomorrow."

"I'll be there."

"And I'll be here. Good night."

He hung up, checked the refrigerator for hidden or lost beers and returned to the deck empty-handed. Rachel was waiting for him with a smile on her face and a water-stained 3 × 5 card in her hand. Attached to it with a paper clip was a pink pawn slip.

"Got it," she said.

She handed it to him and Bosch stepped back inside the house, where the lighting was better. He read the card first. It was written on with blue ink that was partially smeared by water but still legible.

Unsatisfied Customer — 02/12/92
Customer complained that property
was sold before 90-day pawn period
expired. Shown pawn slip and
corrected. Customer complained
that 90 days should not have included weekends and holidays.
Cursed/ slammed door.

DGF

The pink pawn slip attached to the com-
plaint card carried the name Robert Foxworth, the DOB 11/03/71 and an address
on Fountain in Hollywood. The item pawned
on October 8, 1991, was listed as an "heirloom medallion." Foxworth had been given
eighty dollars for it. There was a fingerprint
square at the bottom right corner of the slip.
Bosch could see the ridges of a fingerprint
but the ink had either worn away or leached
out of the paper because of the moisture
contained in the storage carton.

"The DOB is a match," Rachel said. "Plus
the name connects on two levels."

"What do you mean?"

"Well, he took Robert forward when he
used the name Robert Saxon and he took
the Fox in Foxworth forward when he used

Raynard. Maybe that's where this whole Raynard thing came from. If his real name is Foxworth, maybe when he was a kid, his parents told him stories about a fox named Reynard."

"If his real name is Foxworth," Bosch repeated. "Maybe we just found another alias."

"Maybe. But at least it's something you didn't have before."

Bosch nodded. He could feel his excitement building. She was right. Finally they had a new angle to pursue. Bosch pulled out his phone.

"I'm going to run the name and see what happens."

He called central dispatch and asked a service operator to run the name and birth date they had found on the pawn slip. It came back clean and with no record of a current driver's license. He thanked the operator and hung up.

"Nothing," he said. "Not even a driver's license."

"But that's good," Rachel said. "Don't you see? Robert Foxworth would be about to turn thirty-five right now. If there's no history or current license, then that is further confirmation that he is no more, that he's either dead or he became someone else."

"Raynard Waits."

She nodded.

"I guess I was hoping for a DL with an Echo Park address," Bosch said. "I guess that's too much to ask for."

"Maybe not. Is there a way in this state to check defunct driver's licenses? Robert Foxworth, if that's his real name, probably got a license when he turned sixteen in nineteen eighty-seven. When he switched identities it would have expired."

Bosch considered this. He knew that the state did not start requiring a thumbprint from licensed drivers until the early nineties. It meant Foxworth could have gotten a driver's license in the late eighties and there would be no way to connect him to his new identity as Raynard Waits.

"I could check with DMV in the morning. It's not something I can get through communications dispatch tonight."

"There is something else you can check tomorrow," she said. "Remember the quick and dirty profile I did the other night? I said these early crimes weren't aberrations. He built up to them."

Bosch understood.

"A juvy jacket."

She nodded.

"You might find a juvenile record on Robert Foxworth — again, if that's his real name. It wouldn't have been accessible through dispatch either."

She was right. State law kept juvenile records from trailing an offender into adulthood. The name may have come up clean when Bosch called dispatch to run it but that didn't mean it was squeaky clean. As with the driver's license information, Bosch would have to wait until morning, when he could get into the juvenile records at the Department of Probation.

But as soon as his hopes were lifted he knocked them down again.

"Wait a minute, that doesn't work," he said. "His prints would have drawn a match. When they ran his prints as Raynard Waits, they would have hit the prints taken from Robert Foxworth as a juvenile. His record might not be available but the prints stay in the system."

"Maybe, maybe not. Two separate systems. Two separate bureaucracies. The crossover doesn't always work."

That was true, but it was more wishful thinking than anything else. Bosch now reduced the juvenile angle to a long shot. It was more likely that Robert Foxworth had never been in the juvenile system. Bosch was beginning to think the name was just another false identity in a string of them.

Rachel tried to change the subject.

"What do you think about this heirloom medallion he pawned?" she asked.

"I have no idea."

"The fact that he wanted to get it back is interesting. Makes me think maybe it wasn't stolen. Like maybe it belonged to someone in his family and he needed to get it back."

"It would explain him cursing and slamming doors, I guess."

She nodded.

Bosch yawned and all at once he realized how tired he was. He had been running all day just to get to this name and the uncertainties that accompanied it. The case was crowding his brain. Rachel seemed to read him.

"Harry, I say we quit while we're ahead and have another beer."

"I don't know how far ahead we are but

I could use another beer," Bosch said. "There's only one problem with that."

"What?"

"No more beer."

"Harry, you invited a girl over to do your dirty work and help you crack the case and all you give her is one beer? What's wrong with you? What about wine? You have some wine?"

Bosch shook his head sadly.

"But I'm on my way to the store."

"That's good. I'm on my way to the bed-room. I'll be waiting for you there."

"Then, I won't delay."

"Make mine a red wine, will you?"

"I'm on it."

Bosch hurried from the house. He had parked earlier at the front curb so that Rachel could use the carport if she came over. As he walked out the front door he no-ticed a vehicle sitting at the opposite curb two houses down. The vehicle, a silver SUV, caught his eye because it was parked in a red zone. There was no parking allowed along that curb, since it was too close to the next curve in the road. A car could come around the bend and easily collide with any car parked there.

As Bosch looked up the street the SUV suddenly took off without its lights on. It sped north around the bend and disappeared.

Bosch ran to his car, jumped in and headed north after the SUV. He drove as fast as he could safely go. Within two minutes he had followed the curving street around to the four-way stop at Mulholland Drive. There was no sign of the SUV and it could have gone in any of three directions from the stop.

"Shit!"

Bosch sat at the intersection for a long moment, thinking about what he had just seen and what it might mean. He decided that it either meant nothing or it meant someone was watching his house and therefore watching him. But at the moment there was nothing he could do. He let it go. He turned left and drove Mulholland at a safe speed all the way down to Cahuenga. He knew there was a liquor store near Lankershim. He headed there, checking the rearview mirror for a trailer the whole way.

26

Home duty or not, Bosch dressed in a suit the next morning before heading out. He knew it would give him an aura of authority and confidence while dealing with government bureaucrats. And by twenty minutes after nine it had paid off. He had a solid lead. The Department of Motor Vehicles' archives had produced a driver's license issued to a Robert Foxworth on November 3, 1987, the day he turned sixteen and was eligible to drive. The license was never renewed in California but there was no DMV record of the holder being deceased. This meant Foxworth had either moved to another state and was licensed there, decided he no longer wanted to drive or changed identities. Bosch was betting on the third option.

The address on the license was the lead. It listed Foxworth's residence as the Los Angeles County Department of Children and Family Services, 3075 Wilshire Blvd., Los Angeles. In 1987 he had been a juvenile ward of the county. He either had no parents or they had been declared unfit to raise him and he was removed from them. The designation of DCFS as his address meant that he was either housed in one of the department's youth halls or had been placed in its foster care program. Bosch knew all of this because he, too, had had such a designation on his first driver's license. He, too, had been a ward of the county.

As Bosch stepped out of the DMV offices on Spring Street he felt a renewed surge of energy. He had broken through what had seemed to be a dead end the night before and had turned it into a solid lead. As he headed to his car his cell phone vibrated and he answered it without breaking stride or looking at the screen, hoping that it would be Rachel and that he'd be able to share the good news.

"Harry, where are you? No one answered the home line."

It was Abel Pratt. Bosch was getting tired of his constant checking up on him.

"I'm on my way in to visit Kiz. Is that all right with you?"

"Sure, Harry, except you're supposed to check in with me."

"Once a day. It's not even ten o'clock!"

"I want to hear from you every morning."

"Whatever. Tomorrow's Saturday, should I call you? What about Sunday?"

"Don't go overboard. I'm just trying to look out for you, you know."

"Sure, Top. Whatever you say."

"You heard the latest, I take it."

Bosch stopped in his tracks.

"They caught Waits?"

"No, I wish."

"Then, what?"

"It's all over the news. Everybody's worked up about it down here. Some girl got snatched off the street in Hollywood last night. Pulled into a van on Hollywood Boulevard. The division had those new street cameras installed last year and one of the cameras caught part of the abduction. I haven't seen it but they say it's Waits. He's changed his look — shaved his head, I think — but they're saying it was him. There's a press conference at eleven and they're going to show the tape to the world."

Bosch felt a dull thud pound in his chest. He had been right about Waits not leaving town. He wished now he had been wrong. As he had these thoughts he realized that he still thought of the killer as Raynard Waits. It didn't matter if he was truly Robert Foxworth, Bosch knew he would always think of him as Waits.

"Did they get a plate off the van?" he asked.

"No, it was covered. All they put out was that it was a plain white Econoline van. Like the other one he used but older. Look, I've gotta go. I just wanted to check in. Hopefully, this is the last day. OIS will finish up and you'll be back in the unit."

"Yeah, that would be good. But listen, during his confession, Waits said he had a different van in the nineties. Maybe the task force should get somebody to look through old DMV registrations under his name. They might come up with a plate to go with the van."

"It's worth a shot. I'll tell them."

"Okay."

"Stay close to home, Harry. And give my regards to Kiz."

"Right."

Bosch closed the phone, happy that he'd been able to come up with the Kiz line on the spot like that. But he also knew that he was becoming a good liar with Pratt, and that didn't make him very happy.

Bosch got into his car and headed toward Wilshire Boulevard. The call from Pratt had increased his sense of urgency. Waits had abducted another woman, but there had been nothing in the files to indicate that he killed his victims immediately. That meant the latest victim might still be alive. Bosch knew that if he could get to Waits he could save her.

The DCFS offices were crowded and loud. He waited at a records counter for fifteen minutes before he got the attention of a clerk. After taking Bosch's information and typing it into a computer, she told him that there was indeed a juvenile file relating to Robert Foxworth, DOB 11/03/71, but that to see it he would need a court order authorizing his search of the records.

Bosch just smiled. He was too excited by the fact that a file was actually still in existence to be upset by one more frustration. He thanked her and told her he would be back with the court order.

Bosch stepped back out into the sunlight. He knew he was at a crossroads now. Dancing around the truth of where he was during phone calls with Abel Pratt was one thing. But if he was to apply for a search warrant seeking the DCFS records without departmental approval — coming in the form of a supervisor's okay — then he would be completely going off the reservation. He would be conducting a rogue investigation and committing a firing offense.

He figured he could take what he had into Randolph at OIS or the Fugitive Task Force and let them run with it, or he could go the rogue route and accept the possible consequences. Since coming back from retirement Bosch had felt less constricted by the rules and regulations of the department. He had already walked out the door once and knew that if push came to shove he would be able to do it again. The second time would be easier. He didn't want it to come to that but he could do it if he had to.

He pulled out his phone and made the one call he knew might save him from making a choice between two bad options. Rachel Walling answered her cell on the second ring.

"So what's happening over there in Tactical?" he asked.

"Oh, we always have something happening here. How did it go downtown? Did you hear that Waits abducted another woman last night?"

She had a habit of asking more than one question at a time, especially when she was excited. Bosch told her that he had heard about the abduction and then related the tale of his morning's activities.

"So what are you going to do?"

"Well, I'm thinking about seeing if the FBI might be interested in joining the case."

"And what about the case would carry it across the federal threshold?"

"You know, corruption of public officials, campaign finance violations, kidnapping, cats and dogs living together — the usual stuff."

She stayed serious.

"I don't know, Harry. You open that door and there's no telling where it will go."

"But I've got an insider. Somebody who will watch out for me and safeguard the case."

"Wrong. They probably wouldn't let me anywhere near this. It's not my group and there's the conflict of interest."

"What conflict? We've worked together before."

"I'm just telling you how this will likely be received."

"Look, I need a search warrant. If I go off the reservation to get one I probably won't be able to come back on again. I know it will be the last straw with Pratt, that's for sure. But if I can say that I was brought into a federal investigation, then that would give me a valid explanation. It would give me an out. All I want is to look at Foxworth's DCFS file. I think it will lead us to whatever's in Echo Park."

She was quiet for a long moment before responding.

"Where are you right now?"

"I'm still at DCFS."

"Go get a doughnut or something. I'll be there as soon as I can."

"You sure?"

"No, but that's what we're going to do."

She hung up the phone. Bosch closed his and looked around. Instead of a doughnut he went over to a newspaper box and got the morning edition of the *Times.* He took a seat on the planter that ran along the front length of the DCFS building and looked through the paper for stories on the Raynard Waits and Beachwood Canyon investigations.

There was no story on the abduction on Hollywood Boulevard because that had occurred during the night and long after the paper's deadline. The coverage of the Waits story had moved off the front page to the state and local section but it was still extensive. There were three stories in all. The most prominent report was on the so-far-unsuccessful nationwide search for the escaped serial killer. Most of the information had already been rendered obsolete by the events of the night. There was no nationwide search anymore. Waits was still here in the city.

This story jumped inside the section and was framed by two sidebars. One was an update on the investigation that filled in some of the details of what had happened during the shoot-out and escape, and the other story was a political update. This latter story was written by Keisha Russell and Bosch quickly scanned it to see if anything they had discussed about Rick O'Shea's campaign financing had gotten into the paper. Luckily there was nothing, and he felt his trust in her rising.

Bosch finished reading the stories and there was still no sign of Rachel. He moved into other sections of the paper, studying the box scores of sporting events he cared nothing about and reading reviews of movies he would never see. When there was nothing left for him to read he put the paper aside and started pacing in front of the building. He became anxious, worried that he'd lose the edge the morning's discoveries had given him.

He got out his phone to call her but decided instead to call St. Joseph's Hospital and check on Kiz Rider's condition. He was transferred to the third-floor nursing station and was then put on hold. While he was waiting to be connected he saw Rachel finally pull up in a federal cruiser. He closed the phone, crossed the sidewalk and met her as she was getting out.

"What's the plan?" he said by way of greeting.

"What, no 'how are you doing' or 'thanks for coming'?"

"Thanks for coming. What's the plan?"

They started walking into the building.

"The plan is the federal plan. I go in and draw down on the man in charge the full force and weight of the government of this great country. I raise the specter of terrorism and he gives us the file."

Bosch stopped.

"You call that a plan?"

"It's worked pretty well for us for more than fifty years."

She didn't stop. He now had to hurry to catch up.

"How do you know it's a man in charge?"

"Because it always is. Which way?"

He pointed straight ahead in the main hallway. Rachel didn't break stride.

"I didn't wait around for forty minutes for this, Rachel."

"You have a better idea?"

"I *had* a better idea. A federal search warrant, remember?"

"That was a nonstarter, Bosch. I told you, I open that door and you get trampled. This is better. In and out. If I get you the file, I get you the file. Doesn't matter how."

She was two paces in front of him now, moving with federal momentum. Bosch secretly started to believe. She moved through the double doors beneath the sign that said RECORDS with an authority and command presence that could not be questioned.

The clerk Bosch had dealt with was at the counter speaking with another citizen. Walling stepped right up and didn't wait for an invitation to speak. She drew her credentials from her suit jacket pocket in one smooth move.

"FBI. I need to see your office manager in regard to a matter of urgency."

The clerk looked at her with an unimpressed face.

"I will be with you as soon as I fin—"

"You're with me now, honey. Go get your boss or I'll go get him. This is life-or-death urgent."

The woman made a face that seemed to indicate she had never encountered such rudeness before. Without a word to the citizen in front of her or anyone else she stepped away from the counter and walked to a door behind a row of cubicles.

They waited less than a minute. The clerk stepped back out through the door, followed by a man wearing a white, short-sleeved shirt and a maroon tie. He came directly to Rachel Walling.

"I'm Mr. Osborne. How can I help you?"

"We need to step into your office, sir. This is a highly confidential matter."

"Over this way, please."

He pointed to a swing door at the far end of the counter. Bosch and Walling walked down to it and its lock was buzzed open. They followed Osborne back through the rear door to his office. Rachel let him get a look at her credentials once he was seated behind a desk festooned with dusty Dodgers memorabilia. There was a wrapped sandwich from Subway front and center on his desk.

"What's this all —"

"Mr. Osborne, I work for the Tactical Intelligence Unit here in Los Angeles. I'm sure you understand what that means. And this is Detective Harry Bosch of the LAPD. We're working a joint investigation of high importance and urgency. We've learned from your clerk that there exists a file pertaining to an individual named Robert Foxworth, date of birth eleven/three/'seventy-one. It is vitally important that we be allowed to review that file immediately."

Osborne nodded, but what he said didn't go with a nod.

"I understand. But here at DCFS we work under very precise laws. State laws that protect the children. The records of our juvenile wards are not open to the public without court order. My hands are —"

"Sir, Robert Foxworth is no longer a juvenile. He is thirty-four years old. The file might contain information that will lead us to the containment of a very grave threat to this city. It will undoubtedly save lives."

"I know, but you have to understand that we are not —"

"I do understand. I understand perfectly that if we don't see that file now, we could be talking about a loss of human life. You don't want that on your conscience, Mr. Osborne, and neither do we. That's why we are on the same team. I'll make a deal with you, sir. We will review the file right here in your office with you watching. In the meantime, I will get on the phone and instruct a member of my team at Tactical to draw up a search warrant. I will see to it that it is signed by a judge and furnished to you before the end of business today."

"Well . . . I'd have to call it up from Archives."

"Are the archives here in the building?"

"Yes, down below."

"Then, please call Archives and get that file up here. We don't have a lot of time, sir."

"Just wait here. I will handle it personally."

"Thank you, Mr. Osborne."

The man left the office and Walling and Bosch sat down in chairs in front of his desk. Rachel smiled.

"Now let's hope he doesn't change his mind," she said.

"You're good," he responded. "I tell my daughter that she could talk a zebra out of its stripes. I think you could talk a tiger out of its."

"If I get this, you owe me another lunch at Water Grill."

"Fine. Just no sashimi."

They waited for Osborne's return for nearly fifteen minutes. When he came back to the office he was carrying a file folder that was nearly an inch thick. He presented it to Walling, who took the file as she was standing up. Bosch took the cue and stood as well.

"We'll get this back to you as soon as possible," she said. "Thank you, Mr. Osborne."

"Wait a minute! You said you were going to look at it here."

Rachel was heading toward the office door, gathering that momentum again.

"There's no longer time, Mr. Osborne. We have to move. You'll have the file back by tomorrow morning."

She was already through the door. Bosch followed, closing it behind him on Osborne's final words.

"What about the court ord —"

As they passed behind the clerk, Walling asked her to buzz them out. Rachel kept a two-pace lead on Bosch as they headed out into the hallway. He liked walking behind her and admiring how she handled herself. Command presence in spades.

"Is there a Starbucks around here where we could sit and look at this thing? I'd like to look before heading back."

"There's always a Starbucks around."

Out on the sidewalk they walked east until they came to a tiny luncheonette that had a small inside counter with stools. It beat looking for a Starbucks, so they went in. While Bosch ordered two coffees from the man behind the counter Rachel opened the file.

By the time the coffees were put down on the counter and paid for she had a one-page lead on him. They sat side by side and she passed each page to him after she was finished with her review of it. They worked silently and neither one drank their coffee. Buying the coffee had merely bought them the work space at the counter.

The first document in the file was a copy of Foxworth's birth certificate. He was born at Queen of Angels Hospital. The mother was listed as Rosemary Foxworth, DOB 6/21/54, Philadelphia, Pa., and the father was listed as unknown. The mother's address was an apartment on Orchid Avenue in Hollywood. Bosch placed the address in the middle of what was now called the Kodak Center, part of the Hollywood renovation and rebirth plan. It was all glitz and glass and red carpets now, but back in 1971 it would have been a neighborhood patrolled by streetwalkers and hypes.

The birth certificate also listed the doctor

who delivered the child and a hospital social worker involved in the case.

Bosch did the math. Rosemary Foxworth was seventeen years old when she gave birth to her son. No father listed or in attendance. No father known. The listing of a social worker meant the county was picking up the tab on the delivery, and the home address did not bode well for a happy start for baby Robert.

All of this led to a picture developing like a Polaroid in Bosch's mind. He guessed that Rosemary Foxworth had been a runaway from Philadelphia, that she hit Hollywood and shared a flop apartment with others like her. She probably worked the nearby streets as a prostitute. She probably used drugs. She gave birth to the boy and then the county eventually stepped in and took him away.

As Rachel passed him more documents, the sad story was borne out. Robert Foxworth was removed from his mother's custody at age two and taken into the DCFS system. For the next sixteen years of his life he was in and out of foster homes and youth halls. Bosch noted that among the facilities where he had spent time was the McLaren Youth Hall in El Monte, a place where Bosch himself had spent a number of years as a child.

The file was replete with psychiatric evaluations conducted annually or upon Foxworth's frequent returns from foster care homes. In total the file charted the journey of a broken life. Sad, yes. Unique, no. It was the story of a child taken from his one parent and then equally mistreated by the institution that had taken him. Foxworth floated from place to place. He had no real home or family. He probably never knew what it was like to be wanted or loved.

Reading through the pages brought up memories in Bosch. Two decades before Foxworth's journey through the system Bosch had charted his own path. He had survived with his own set of scars, but the damage was nothing compared with the extent of Foxworth's injuries.

The next document Rachel handed him was a copy of a death certificate for Rosemary Foxworth. She died March 5, 1986, of complications stemming from drug use and hepatitis C. She had died in the jail ward at County-USC Medical Center. Robert Foxworth would have been fourteen.

"Here we go, here we go," Rachel suddenly said.

"What?"

"His longest stay in any foster home was in Echo Park. And the people he stayed with? Harlan and Janet Saxon."

"What's the address?"

"Seven-ten Figueroa Lane. He was there from 'eighty-three to 'eighty-seven. Almost four years total. He must have liked them and I guess they liked him back."

Bosch leaned over to look at the document in front of her.

"He was on Figueroa Terrace, only a couple blocks from there, when he got pulled over with the bodies," he said. "If they had followed him for just one more minute they would've had the place!"

"If that's where he was going."

"It's got to be where he was going."

She handed him the page and moved on to the next. But Bosch stood up and walked away from the counter. He had read enough for the time being. He had been looking for the connection to Echo Park and now he knew he had it. He was ready to put the book work aside. He was ready to make a move.

"Harry, these shrink reports from when he was a teenager — he was talking about some sick shit here."

"Like what?"

"A lot of anger toward women. Young promiscuous women. Prostitutes, drug users. You know what the psychology is here? You know what I think he ended up doing?"

"No and no. What?"

"He was killing his mother over and over again. All those missing women and girls they've hung on him? The one last night? To him they were like his mother. And he wanted to kill her for abandoning him. And maybe kill them before they did the same thing — brought a child into the world."

Bosch nodded.

"That's a nice shake-and-bake shrink job. If we had the time, you could probably find his Rosebud memory, too. But she didn't abandon him. They took him away from her."

She shook her head.

"Doesn't matter," she said. "Abandonment through lifestyle. The state had no choice but to step in and take him away from her. Drugs, prostitution, the whole thing. By being an unfit mother she abandoned him to this deeply flawed institution where he was trapped until he was old enough to walk away on his own. In his brain chart, that constituted abandonment."

Bosch nodded slowly. He guessed that she was right but the whole situation made him uncomfortable. It felt too personal to Bosch, too close to his own path. Except for a turn here or there, Bosch and Foxworth had made similar journeys. Foxworth was doomed to kill his own mother over and over again. A police shrink had once told Bosch that he was doomed to solve his own mother's murder over and over again.

"What is it?"

Bosch looked at her. He had not yet told Rachel his own sordid history. He didn't want her profiling skills turned on him.

"Nothing," he said. "I'm just thinking."

"You look like you've seen a ghost, Bosch."

He shrugged. Walling closed the file on the counter and finally raised her coffee cup to sip from it.

"So what now?" she asked.

Bosch looked at her for a long moment before answering.

"Echo Park," he said.

"What about backup?"

"I'm going to check it out first, then call backup."

She nodded.

"I'm going with you."

Part Four

THE DOG YOU FEED

27

Bosch and Walling used Bosch's Mustang, since it would give them at least a small degree of cover compared with her federal cruiser, which screamed law enforcement. They drove to Echo Park but did not approach the Saxon house at 710 Figueroa Lane. There was a problem. Figueroa Lane was a short turnaround street that extended for a block off the end of Figueroa Terrace and curved up along the ridge below Chavez Ravine. There was no cruising by it without being obvious about it. Even in a Mustang. If Waits was there and watching for law enforcement, he would have the advantage of seeing them first.

Bosch stopped the car at the intersection of Beaudry and Figueroa Terrace and drummed his fingers on the steering wheel.

"He picked a good place for the secret castle," he said. "There's no getting close to it without being picked up on radar. Especially in daylight."

Rachel nodded.

"Medieval castles were built on hilltops for the same reason."

Bosch looked to his left, toward downtown, and saw the tall buildings rising over the roofs of the homes on Figueroa Terrace. One of the closest and tallest buildings was the Department of Water and Power headquarters. It was directly across the freeway.

"I've got an idea," he said.

They drove out of the neighborhood and back into downtown. Bosch entered the DWP garage and parked in one of the visitor slots. He popped the trunk and went to the surveillance kit he always kept in the car. He got out a pair of high-powered binoculars, a surveillance camera and a rolled-up sleeping bag.

"What are you going to take pictures of?" Walling asked.

"Nothing. But it's got a long lens and you

might want to look through it while I use the binocs."

"And the sleeping bag?"

"We might be lying on the roof. I don't want your fancy federal suit to get dirty."

"Don't worry about me. Worry about yourself."

"I'm worried about that girl Waits grabbed. Let's go."

They headed across the garage floor toward the elevators.

"Did you notice that you still call him Waits, even though we are now sure his name is Foxworth?" she asked when they were going up.

"Yeah, I have noticed. I think it's because when we were face-to-face he was Waits. When he started shooting, he was Waits. And it just sort of stuck."

She nodded and didn't say anything else about it, though he guessed that she probably had a psychological angle on it.

When they reached the lobby Bosch went to an information desk, showed his badge and credentials and asked to see a security supervisor. He told the desk man that it was urgent.

In less than two minutes a tall black man

in gray pants and a navy blazer over his white shirt and tie came through a door and directly toward them. This time Bosch and Walling both showed their creds and the man appeared properly impressed by the federal-local tandem.

"Hieronymus," he said, reading Bosch's police ID. "Do you go by Harry?"

"That's right."

The man put out his hand and smiled.

"Jason Edgar. I believe you and my cousin were partners once."

Bosch smiled, not just because of the coincidence but because he knew it meant that he would have this man's cooperation. He put the sleeping bag under his other arm and shook his hand.

"That's right. He told me he had a cousin with DWP. You used to get him billing info when we needed it. Nice to meet you."

"Likewise, man. What do we have here? If the FBI's involved, are we talking about a terrorism situation?"

Rachel raised a hand in a calming gesture.

"Not quite," she said.

"Jason, we're just looking for a place where we can look down on a neighborhood across the freeway in Echo Park. There's a house we're interested in and we can't get close to it without being obvious about it, know what I mean? We were thinking that maybe from one of the offices here or from the roof we could get an angle and just see what's happening over there."

"I've got just the spot," Edgar said without hesitation. "Follow me."

He led them back to the elevators and had to use a key to get the fifteenth-floor button to light. On the way up he explained that the building was going through a floor-by-floor renovation. At the moment the work had moved to the fifteenth floor. The floor had been gutted and was empty, waiting for the contractor to come in to rebuild according to the renovation plan.

"You can have the whole floor to your-selves," he said. "Pick any angle you want for an OP."

Bosch nodded. OP, as in observation point. That told him something about Jason Edgar.

"Where'd you serve?" he asked.

"Marines, Desert Storm, the whole she-bang. That's why I didn't join the PD. Had my fill of war zones. This gig is pretty much nine to five, low stress and just interesting enough, if you know what I mean."

Bosch didn't but nodded anyway. The elevator doors opened and they stepped out onto a floor that was wide open from glass exterior to glass exterior. Edgar led them toward the glass wall that would look down on Echo Park.

"What's the case about, anyway?" Edgar asked as they approached.

Bosch knew it would come to this. He was ready with an answer.

"There's a place down there we think is being used as a safe house for fugitives. We just want to see if there is anything there to be seen. You know what I mean?"

"Sure do."

"There's something else you can do to help us," Walling said.

Bosch turned to her along with Edgar. He was just as curious.

"What do you need?" Edgar said.

"Could you run the address through your computers and tell us who is paying for utilities?"

"Not a problem. Let me just get you situated here first."

Bosch nodded to Rachel. It was a good move. It would not only get the inquisitive Edgar out of the way for a while, but it could also provide them with some valuable information about the house on Figueroa Lane.

At the floor-to-ceiling glass wall on the north side of the building, Bosch and Walling looked down and across the 101 Freeway at Echo Park. They were farther from the hillside neighborhood than Bosch had thought they would be, but they still had a good vantage point. He pointed out the geographic markers to Rachel.

"There's Fig Terrace," he said. "Those three houses up above it on the curve are on Fig Lane."

She nodded. Figueroa Lane had only the three houses on it. From this height and distance it looked like an afterthought, a developer's discovery that he could jam three more houses onto the hillside after the main street grid had already been laid out.

"Which one is seven-ten?" she asked.

"Good question."

Bosch dropped the sleeping bag and raised the binoculars. He studied the three houses, looking for an address. He finally zeroed in on a black trash can sitting out front of the house in the middle. In large white numerals someone had painted 712 on the can in an effort to safeguard it from theft. Bosch knew the address numbers would rise as the street extended away from downtown.

"The one on the right is seven-ten," he said.

"Got it," she said.

"So that's the address?" Edgar asked. "Seven-ten Fig Lane?"

"Figueroa Lane," Bosch said.

"Got it. Let me go see what I can find. If anybody comes up here and asks what you are doing, just tell them to call me on three-three-eight. That's my page."

"Thanks, Jason."

"You got it."

Edgar started walking back to the elevators. Bosch thought of something and called after him.

"Jason, this glass has got film on it, right? Nobody can see us looking out, right?"

"Yeah, no problem. You could stand there naked and nobody would see you from the outside. But don't try that at night, 'cause it's a different story. Internal light changes things and you can look right in."

Bosch nodded.

"Thanks."

"When I come back, I'll bring a couple chairs."

"That would be good."

After Edgar disappeared into the elevator, Walling said, "Good, at least we'll be able to *sit* naked at the window."

Bosch smiled.

"Sounded like he knew all that from experience," he said.

"Let's hope not."

Bosch raised the binoculars and looked down at the house at 710 Figueroa Lane. It was of similar design to the other two on the street; built high on the hillside with steps leading down to a street-front garage cut into the embankment below the house. It had a red barrel-tile roof and a Spanish motif. But while the other houses on the street were neatly painted and cared for, 710 appeared run-down. Its pink paint had faded. The embankment between the garage and the house was overrun with weeds. The flagpole that stood at the corner of the front porch flew no flag.

Bosch fine-tuned the focus of the field glasses and moved them from window to window, looking for indications of occupancy, hoping to get lucky and see Waits himself looking back out.

Next to him he heard Walling click off a few photos. She was using the camera.

"I don't think there's any film in that. It's not digital."

"It's all right. Just force of habit. And I wouldn't expect a dinosaur like you to have a digital camera."

Beneath the binoculars, Bosch smiled. He tried to think of a rejoinder but let it go. He focused his attention back on the house. It was of a style commonly seen in the city's older hillside neighborhoods. While with newer construction the contour of the land dictated design, the houses on the inclined side of Figueroa Lane were of a more conquering design. At street level the embankment was excavated for a garage. Then, above this, the hillside was terraced and a small single-level home had been constructed. The mountains and hillsides all over the city were molded this way in the forties and fifties as the city sprawled through the flats and grew up the hillsides like a rising tide.

Bosch noticed that at the top of the stairs that ran from the side of the garage up to the front porch there was a small metal platform. He checked the stairs again and saw the metal guide rails.

"There's a lift on the stairs," he said. "Whoever's living there now is in a wheelchair."

He saw no movement behind any window viewable from the angle they had. He dropped his focus down to the garage. It had a pedestrian entrance door and double garage doors that had been painted pink a long time before. The paint, what was left of it, was gray now and the wood was splintering in many places from direct exposure to the afternoon sun. One garage door looked as though it had closed at an uneven angle to the pavement. It didn't look operational anymore. The pedestrian entrance door had a window, but a shade was pulled down behind it. Across the top panel of each of the garage doors was a row of small square windows, but they were being hit with direct sunlight and the dazzling reflection prevented Bosch from seeing in.

Bosch heard the elevator ding and put the binoculars down for the first time. He checked behind him and saw Jason Edgar carrying two chairs toward them.

"Perfect," Bosch said.

He took one of the chairs and positioned it near the glass so he could sit on it backwards and prop his elbows on the seat back — classic surveillance form. Rachel positioned her chair so she could sit normally in it.

"Did you get a chance to check with records, Jason?" she asked.

"I did," Edgar said. "Services to that address are billed to a Janet Saxon and have been for twenty-one years."

"Thank you."

"No problem. I take it that's all you need from me right now?"

Bosch looked up at Edgar.

"Jerry, you — I mean, Jason — you've been a great help. We appreciate it. We'll probably stick around a little bit and then split. You want us to let you know or drop these chairs off somewhere?"

"Uh, just tell the guy in the lobby on your way out. He'll get a message to me. And leave the chairs. I can take care of that."

"Will do. Thanks."

"Good luck. Hope you get your man."

Everybody shook hands and Edgar returned to the elevator. Bosch and Walling

went back to watching the house on Figueroa Lane. Bosch asked Rachel if she
would prefer taking shifts and she said no.
He asked if she would rather use the binoculars and she said she would stick with the
camera. Its long lens actually allowed her a
closer focus than the binoculars did.

Twenty minutes went by and no movement at the house was seen. Bosch had
spent the time moving back and forth between the house and the garage but was
now training his focus on the heavy brush
on the ridgeline up above, looking for another possible observation position that
would put them closer. Walling spoke ex-
citedly.

"Harry, the garage."

Bosch lowered his focus and picked up
the garage. The sun had moved behind a
cloud and the glare had dropped off the line
of windows across the top panel of each
garage door. Bosch saw Rachel's discovery.
Through the windows of the garage door
that appeared to still be functional he could
see the back of a white van.

"I heard that a white van was used in the
abduction last night," Walling said.

"That's what I heard, too. It's part of the BOLO."

He was excited. A white van in a house where Raynard Waits had lived.

"That's it!" he called out. "He has to be in there with the girl. Rachel, we gotta go!"

They got up and hurried to the elevator.

28

They debated backup as they sped out of the DWP garage. Walling was for it. Bosch was against.

"Look, all we have is a white van," he said. "She might be in that house, but he might not be. If we storm in there with the troops, we could lose him. So all I want to do is check it out up close. We can call for backup when we get there. *If* we need it."

He believed his view was certainly reasonable, but so was hers.

"And what if he is in there?" she asked. "The two of us could be walking into an ambush. We need at least one team of backup, Harry, to do this correctly and safely."

"We'll call them when we get there."

"That will be too late. I know what you're doing. You want this guy for yourself and you're willing to risk that girl — and us — to get it."

"You want me to drop you off, Rachel?"

"No, I don't want you to drop me off, Harry."

"Good. I want you to be there."

Decision made, they ended the discussion. Figueroa Street ran behind the DWP Building. Bosch took it east under the 101 Freeway, crossed Sunset and then followed it as it jogged north and under the 110 Freeway. Figueroa Street became Figueroa Terrace, and they drove to where it ended and Figueroa Lane curved up to the crest of the hillside. Bosch pulled the car to the curb before driving up it.

"We walk up and then we stay close to the line of garages until we get to seven-ten," he said. "If we stay in close, he won't have an angle on us from the house."

"What if he isn't in the house? What if he's in the garage waiting for us?"

"Then we deal with it. We clear the garage first and then go up the stairs to the house."

"The houses are on the hillside. We still need to cross the street."

He looked at her across the top of the car as they got out.

"Rachel, are you with me or not?"

"I told you, I'm with you."

"Then, let's go."

Bosch got out and started trotting up the sidewalk leading up the hill. He pulled out his phone and turned it off so it wouldn't possibly vibrate while they were sneaking the house.

He was huffing by the time he got to the top. Rachel was right behind him and didn't show the same level of oxygen depletion. Bosch hadn't smoked in years but the damage of twenty-five years before that had been done.

Their only visual exposure to the pink house at the end of the street came when they got to the top and had to cross over to the garages that lined the east side of the street. They walked it, Bosch casually holding Walling by the arm and whispering in her ear.

"I'm using you to block my face," he said. "He's seen me but he's never seen you."

"It doesn't matter," she said when they got

across. "If he saw us, you can expect he knows what's happening."

He ignored the warning and started moving in front of the garages, which were built right along the sidewalk line. They got to 710 quickly and Bosch went to the panel of windows over one of the doors. Cupping his hands against the dirty glass, he looked in and saw that the interior was crowded by the van and stacks of boxes, barrels and other junk. He saw no movement and heard no sound. A door at the back wall of the garage was closed.

He stepped over to the garage's pedestrian door and checked the knob.

"Locked," he whispered.

He stepped back and looked at the two pull-up doors. Rachel was now standing by the far door and leaning in close to it to listen for sounds from inside. She looked at Bosch and shook her head. Nothing. He looked down and saw that there was a handle at the bottom of each pull-up door but no exterior locking mechanism. He went to the first one, bent down and tried to pull the door open. It came about an inch and then stopped. It was locked from the inside. He tried the second door and encountered the same response. The door gave for a few inches but then stopped. Because of the minimal movement each door allowed, Bosch guessed that they were secured inside by padlocks.

Bosch stood up and looked at Rachel. He shook his head and pointed upward, meaning it was time to go up to the house.

They moved to the concrete stairs and quietly started up. Bosch led the way and stopped four steps from the top. He crouched and tried to catch his breath. He looked at Rachel. He knew they were winging it. *He* was winging it. There was no way to approach the house but to go directly to the front door.

He turned from her and studied the windows one by one. He saw no movement, but he thought he could hear the sound of a television or radio coming from inside. He pulled his gun — it was a backup he had gotten out of the hallway closet that morning — and went up the final steps, holding the weapon down at his side as he quietly crossed the porch to the front door.

Bosch knew that a search warrant was not at issue here. Waits had abducted a woman, and the life-and-death nature of the situation assuredly pushed them into no-warrant, no-knock territory. He put his hand on the knob and turned. The door was un-locked.

Bosch slowly pushed the door open, noticing that a two-inch ramp had been placed over the threshold to accommodate a wheelchair. As the door came open the sound of the radio became louder. An evan-gelical station, a man talking about the im-pending rapture.

They stepped into the house's entry area. To the right it opened into a living room with a dining area to the back. Directly ahead through an arched opening was the kitchen. A hallway to the left led to the rest of the house. Without looking back at Rachel he pointed to the right, meaning she would go that way while he moved forward and cleared the kitchen before taking the hall-way to the left.

As he reached the archway Bosch glanced at Rachel and saw her moving through the living room, weapon up in a two-handed grip. He stepped into the kitchen and saw that it was clean and neat, without a dish in the sink. The radio was on the counter. The speaker was telling his listeners that those who did not believe would be left behind.

There was another archway leading from the kitchen to the dining room. Rachel came through it, pointed her gun up when she saw Bosch and shook her head.

Nothing.

That left the hallway leading to the bedrooms and the rest of the house. Bosch turned and went back through the archway to the entry area. When he turned toward the hallway he was startled to see an old woman sitting in a wheelchair in the threshold to the hallway. On her lap she was holding a long-barrel revolver. It looked like it was too heavy for her frail arm to hold up.

"Who's there?" she said forcefully.

Her head was turned at an angle. Though her eyes were open they were focused on the floor instead of Bosch. It was her ear that was trained toward him and he knew she was blind.

He raised his gun and pointed it at her.

"Mrs. Saxon? Take it easy. My name is Harry Bosch. I'm just looking for Robert."

A look of puzzlement played on her features.

"Who?"

"Robert Foxworth. Is he here?"

"You've got the wrong place, and how dare you come in here without knocking."

"I —"

"Bobby uses the garage. I don't let him use the house. All those chemicals, it smells awful."

Bosch started edging toward her, his eyes on the gun the whole time.

"I'm sorry, Mrs. Saxon. I thought he was up here. Has he been here lately?"

"He comes and goes. He comes up here to give me the rent, that's all."

"For the garage?"

He was getting closer.

"That's what I said. What do you want him for? Are you his friend?"

"I just want to talk to him."

Bosch reached down and took the gun out of her hand.

"Hey! That's my protection."

"It's all right, Mrs. Saxon. I'll give it back. I just think it needs to be cleaned up a little. And oiled. This way it will be sure to work in case you ever really need to use it."

"I need it."

"I'm going to take it down to the garage

and get Bobby to clean it. Then I'll bring it back."

"You better."

Bosch checked the gun. It was loaded and appeared operational. He put it into the waistband at the back of his pants and looked at Rachel. She was standing three feet behind him in the entryway. She made a movement with her hand, pantomiming turning a key. Bosch understood.

"Do you have a key to the garage door, Mrs. Saxon?" he asked.

"No. Bobby came and got the extra key."

"Okay, Mrs. Saxon. I'll check with him."

He moved toward the front door. Rachel joined him and they went out. Halfway down the steps to the garage, Rachel grabbed his arm and whispered.

"We have to call backup. Now!"

"Go ahead and call but I'm going into the garage. If he's in there with the girl, we can't wait."

He shook off her grip and continued down. When he got to the garage he looked once again through the windows on the top panels and saw no movement inside. His eyes focused on the door on the rear wall. It was still closed.

He moved over to the pedestrian door and opened the blade of a small folding knife that was attached to his key ring.

Bosch went to work on the door's lock and got the blade across the tongue. He nodded to Rachel to be ready and pulled the door open. But it didn't come. He tried it again and pulled hard. Again the door would not come open.

"There's an inside lock," he whispered. "It means he's in there."

"No, it doesn't. He could've come out through one of the garage doors."

He shook his head.

"They're locked from the inside," he whispered. "All the doors are locked from the inside."

Rachel understood and nodded.

"What do we do?" she whispered back.

Bosch thought about things for a moment and then handed her his keys.

"Go back and get the car. When you get up here, park it with the rear end right here. Then pop the trunk."

"What are you —"

"Just do it. Go!"

She ran down the sidewalk in front of the garages and then crossed the street and dropped from sight down the hill. Bosch moved toward the pull-up door that looked like it had closed awkwardly. It was out of alignment and he knew it would be the better of the two doors to try to breach.

Bosch heard the Mustang's big engine before he saw his car come over the hill. Rachel drove toward him fast. He stepped back against the garage to give her maximum room to maneuver. She made almost a complete turn in the street and then backed toward the garage. The trunk was popped and Bosch immediately reached in for the rope he kept in the back. It was gone. He then remembered that Osani had taken it after discovering it on the tree in Beachwood Canyon.

"Shit!"

He quickly looked through the trunk and found a shorter length of clothesline he had used once to tie down the trunk lid when he was moving a piece of furniture to the Salvation Army. He quickly tied one end of the cord to a steel towing loop underneath the car's bumper and then the other end to the handle at the bottom of the garage door. He knew that something would have to give. The door, the handle or the rope. They had a one-in-three shot at getting the door open.

Rachel had gotten out of the car.

"What are you doing?" she asked.

Bosch quietly closed the car's trunk.

"We're going to pull it open. Get back in the car and go forward. Go slow. A sudden jerk will snap the line. Go ahead, Rachel. Hurry."

Without a word she got back in the car, dropped it in drive and started moving forward. She watched in the rearview and he rolled a finger to keep her moving. The cord pulled taut and then Bosch could hear the sound of the garage door groaning as the pressure mounted. He stepped back and at the same time drew his gun again.

The garage door gave way all at once and popped up and out three feet.

"Stop!" Bosch yelled, knowing there was no longer any need for whispers.

Rachel stopped pulling but the line remained taut and the garage door was held open. Bosch moved forward quickly and used his momentum to duck and roll beneath it. He came up inside the garage with his gun up and ready. He swept the space but saw no one. Keeping his eyes on the door at the rear wall, he sidestepped over to the van. He jerked one of the side doors open and quickly checked the interior. It was empty.

Bosch moved toward the back wall, making his way around an obstacle course of upright barrels, rolls of plastic, bales of towels, squeegee blades and other window-washing equipment. There was a strong smell of ammonia and other chemicals. Bosch's eyes were beginning to water.

The hinges on the door at the rear wall were visible and Bosch knew it would swing toward him when he opened it.

"FBI!" Walling yelled from outside. "Coming in!"

"Clear!" Bosch yelled back.

He heard her scrabble under the garage door but kept his attention on the door in the back wall. He moved toward it, listening all the time for any sound.

Taking a position to the side of the door Bosch put his hand on the doorknob and turned it. It was unlocked. He looked back for the first time at Rachel. She was in a combat stance at an angle from the door. She nodded and in one quick move he flung the door open and moved across the threshold.

The room was dark and windowless and he saw no one. He knew he was a target standing in the light in the doorway and quickly sidestepped into the room. He saw a string from an overhead light and reached out and yanked on it. The string snapped in his hand but the light came on, the hanging bulb jumping and swinging in response. He was in a crowded work and storage room that was about ten feet deep. There was no one in the room.

"Clear!"

Rachel entered and they stood there scanning the room. A bench cluttered with old paint cans, household tools and flashlights was on the right. Four old and rusting bikes were stacked against the left wall, along with folding chairs and a pile of collapsed cardboard boxes. The back wall was concrete block. Hung on it was the dusty old flag for the pole up on the front terrace of the house. On the floor in front of it was a stand-up electric fan, its blades caked with dust and crud. It looked like at one time somebody had tried to blow the fetid, damp smell out of the room.

"Shit!" Bosch said.

He lowered his gun, turned and walked past Rachel back into the garage. She followed him.

Bosch shook his head and tried to rub some of the chemical sting out of his eyes. He didn't understand. Were they too late? Were they following the wrong lead altogether?

"Check the van," he said. "See if there is any sign of the girl."

Rachel crossed behind him to the van, and Bosch went to the pedestrian door to check for the flaws in his belief that someone had to be in the garage.

He had to be right. There was a deadbolt on the door, meaning it could only have been locked from the inside. He moved over to the garage doors and stooped down to look at their locking mechanisms. He was right again. Both had padlocks on interior slide locks.

He tried to puzzle it out. All three doors had been locked from the inside. It meant that either someone was inside the garage or there was an exit point he hadn't identified yet. But this seemed impossible. The garage was dug directly into the hillside embankment. There was no possibility of a rear exit.

He was checking the ceiling, wondering if it was possible that there was a passageway up to the house, when Rachel called from inside the van.

"I've got a roll of duct tape," she said. "I've got used strips on the floor with hair."

It boosted Bosch's belief that they had the right place. He stepped over to the open side door of the van. He looked in at Rachel while he pulled out his phone. He noticed the wheelchair lift in the van.

"I'll call for backup and Forensics," he said. "We missed him."

He had to turn the phone back on, and while he waited for it to boot up he realized something. The stand-up fan in the back room wasn't pointed toward the garage doors. If you were going to air the room out, you would point the fan toward the door.

His phone buzzed in his hand and it distracted him. He looked down at the screen. It told him he had a message waiting. He clicked a button to check the call record and saw that he had just missed a call from Jerry Edgar. He'd get to it later. He punched in a number for Communications and told the dispatcher to connect him with the Raynard Waits Fugitive Task Force. An officer identifying himself as Freeman picked up.

"This is Detective Harry Bosch. I have —"

"Harry! Gun!"

It was Rachel who had yelled. Time slowed down. All in a second Bosch looked at her in the van's doorway, her eyes focused over his shoulder at the back of the garage. Without thinking, he jumped forward and into her, pulling his arms around her and taking her to the floor of the van in a crushing tackle. Four shots came from behind him followed by the instantaneous sound of bullets striking metal and glass breaking. Bosch rolled off Rachel and came up with his gun in hand. He caught a glimpse of a figure ducking into the rear storage room. He fired six shots through the doorway and raking across the wall to its right.

"Rachel, okay?"

"I'm okay. Are you hit?"

"I don't think so!"

"It was him! Waits!"

They paused and watched the door to the rear room. No one came back through.

"Did you hit him?" Rachel whispered.

"I don't think so."

"I thought we cleared that room."

"I thought we did, too."

Bosch stood up, keeping his aim on the doorway. He noticed that the light from within was now off.

"I dropped my phone," he said. "Call for backup."

He started moving toward the door.

"Harry, wait. He could —"

"Call for backup! And remember to tell them I'm in there."

He cut to his left and approached the door from an angle that would give him the widest vision of the interior space. But without the overhead light the room was cast in shadows and he could see no movement. He started taking small steps using his right foot first and maintaining a firing position. Behind him he heard Rachel on her phone identifying herself and asking for a transfer to LAPD dispatch.

Bosch got to the threshold and swung the gun across his body to cover the part of the room he had not had an angle on. He stepped in and sidestepped to the right. There was no movement, no sign of Waits. The room was empty.

He looked at the fan and confirmed his
mistake. It was pointed toward the flag
hanging on the back wall. It had not been
used to blow damp air out. The fan had
been used to blow air in.

Bosch took two steps toward the flag. He
reached forward, grabbed it by the edge
and ripped it down.

In the wall, three feet off the ground, was
a tunnel entrance. About a dozen concrete
blocks had been removed to create an
opening four feet square and the excavation
into the hillside continued from there.

Bosch crouched to look into the opening
from the safety of the right side. The tunnel
was deep and dark, but he saw a glimmer of
light thirty feet in. He realized that the tunnel
made a turn and that there was a source of
light around the bend.

Bosch leaned closer and realized he could
hear a sound from the tunnel. It was a low
whimpering. It was a terrible sound but it
was beautiful just the same. It meant that no
matter what horrors she had experienced
through the night, the woman Waits had abducted was still alive.

Bosch reached back over to the work-
bench and picked up the shiniest flashlight

he saw. He turned it on. It was dead. He tried another and got a weak beam of light. It would have to do.

He flashed the beam into the tunnel and confirmed that the first leg was clear. He took a step toward the tunnel.

"Harry, wait!"

He turned and saw Rachel in the doorway.

"Backup's on the way!" she whispered.

Bosch shook his head.

"She's in there. She's alive."

He turned back to the tunnel and flashed the light in once more. It was still clear up to the turn. He turned the light off to conserve it. He glanced back at Rachel and then stepped into the darkness.

29

Bosch hesitated a moment in the mouth of the tunnel to let his eyes adjust. He then started moving. He didn't have to crawl. The tunnel was large enough for him to move through in a crouch. Flashlight in his right hand and gun up in his left, he kept his eyes on the dim light ahead. The sound of the woman crying grew louder as he moved forward.

Ten feet into the tunnel the musty smell that he had noticed outside turned into the deeper stench of decay. As rancid as it was, it was not something new to him. Almost forty years before, he had been a tunnel rat with the U.S. Army, taking part in more than a hundred missions in the tunnels of Vietnam. The enemy sometimes buried their dead in the clay walls of their tunnels. That hid them from sight but the odor of decay was impossible to hide. Once it got into your nose it was equally impossible to forget.

Bosch knew that he was headed toward something horrific, that the missing victims of Raynard Waits were ahead somewhere in the tunnel. This had been the destination on the night Waits was pulled over in his work van. But Bosch couldn't help but think that maybe it was his own destination as well. He had come many years and many miles but it seemed to him that he had never really left the tunnels behind, that his life had always been a slow movement through darkness and tight spaces on the way to a flickering light. He knew he was then, now, and forever a tunnel rat.

His thigh muscles burned from the strain of moving in a crouched position. Sweat began to sting his eyes. And as he got closer to the turn in the tunnel Bosch saw the light changing and rechanging and knew that this was caused by the undulation of a flame. Candlelight.

Five feet from the turn Bosch slowed to a

stop and rested on his heels as he listened. Behind him, he thought he could hear sirens. Backup on the way. He tried to concentrate on what could be heard from the tunnel ahead but there was only the intermittent sound of the woman crying.

He raised himself up and started forward again. Almost immediately the light ahead went out and the whimpering took on a new energy and urgency.

Bosch froze. He then heard nervous laughter from ahead, followed by the familiar voice of Raynard Waits.

"Is that you, Detective Bosch? Welcome to my foxhole."

There was more laughter and then it stopped. Bosch let ten seconds go by. Waits said nothing else.

"Waits? Let her go. Send her out to me."

"No, Bosch. She's with me now. Anybody comes in here, I'll kill her on the spot. I'll save the last bullet for myself."

"Waits, no. Listen. Just let her come out and I will come in. We'll trade."

"No, Bosch. I like the situation the way it is."

"Then what are we doing? We need to talk and you need to save yourself. There's not a lot of time. Send the girl out."

A few seconds went by and then the voice came out of the darkness.

"Save myself from what? For what?"

Bosch's muscles were on the verge of cramping. He carefully lowered himself to a seated position against the right side of the tunnel. He was sure that the candlelight had been coming ahead from the left. The tunnel turned to the left. He kept his gun up but was now employing a cross-wrists bracing with the flashlight up and ready as well.

"There's no way out," he said. "Give it up and come out. Your deal is still in play. You don't have to die. Neither does the girl."

"I don't care about dying, Bosch. That's why I'm here. Because I don't fucking care. I just want it to be on my own terms. Not the state's or anybody else's. Just mine."

Bosch noticed that the woman had gone silent. He wondered what had happened. Had Waits silenced her? Had he just . . . ?

"Waits, what's wrong? Is she all right?"

"She passed out. Too much excitement, I guess."

He laughed and then was silent. Bosch decided that he needed to keep Waits talking. If he was engaged by Bosch he would be distracted from the woman and what was assuredly being planned outside the tunnel.

"I know who you are," he said quietly.

Waits didn't take the bait. Bosch tried again.

"Robert Foxworth. Son of Rosemary Foxworth. Raised by the county. Foster homes, youth halls. You lived here with the Saxons. For a time you lived at the McLaren Youth Hall out in El Monte. So did I, Robert."

Bosch was met with a long silence. But then the voice came quietly out of the darkness.

"I'm not Robert Foxworth anymore."

"I understand."

"I hated that place. McLaren. I hated them all."

"They closed it down a couple years ago. After some kid died in there."

"Fuck them and fuck that place. How did you find Robert Foxworth?"

Bosch felt a rhythm building in the conversation. He understood the cue Waits was giving by speaking of Robert Foxworth as someone other than himself. He was Raynard Waits now.

"It wasn't that hard," Bosch answered. "We figured it out through the Fitzpatrick case. We found the pawn slip in the records and matched birth dates. What was the heirloom medallion that had been pawned?"

There was a long silence before an answer.

"It was Rosemary's. It was all he had from her. He had to pawn it and when he went back to get it, that pig Fitzpatrick had already sold it."

Bosch nodded. He had Waits answering questions but there wasn't a lot of time. He decided to jump to the present.

"Raynard. Tell me about the setup. Tell me about Olivas and O'Shea."

There was only silence. Bosch tried again.

"They used you. O'Shea used you and he's going to just walk away from it. Is that what you want? You die here in this hole and he just walks away?"

Bosch put the flashlight down so he could wipe the sweat out of his eyes. He then had to feel around on the floor of the tunnel to find it again.

"I can't give you O'Shea or Olivas," Waits said in the darkness.

Bosch didn't get it. Was he wrong? He doubled back in his head and started at the beginning.

"Did you kill Marie Gesto?"

There was a long silence.

"No, I didn't," Waits finally said.

"Then how was this set up? How could you know where —"

"Think about it, Bosch. They're not stupid. They would not directly communicate with me."

Bosch nodded. He understood.

"Maury Swann," he said. "He brokered the deal. Tell me about it."

"What's to tell? It was a setup, man. He said the whole thing was to make you a believer. He said you were bothering the wrong people and had to be convinced."

"What people?"

"He didn't tell me that."

"This is Maury Swann saying this?"

"Yes, but it doesn't matter. You can't get to him either. This is communication between a lawyer and his client. You can't touch it. It's privileged. Besides, it would be my word against his. That won't go anywhere and you know it."

Bosch did know it. Maury Swann was a tough lawyer and a respected member of the bar. He was also a media darling. There was no way to go after him with just the words of a criminal client — and a serial killer at that. It had been a masterstroke by O'Shea and Olivas to use him as the go-between.

"I don't care," Bosch said. "I want to know how it all went down. Tell me."

A long silence went by before Waits responded.

"Swann went to them with the idea of making a deal. My clearing the books in exchange for my life. He did this without my knowledge. If he had asked me I would have said, don't bother. I'd rather take the needle than forty years in a cell. You understand that, Bosch. You're an eye-for-an-eye guy. I like that about you, believe it or not."

He ended it there and Bosch had to prompt him again.

"So then what happened?"

"One night in the jail, I was taken to the attorney room and there was Maury. He told me there was a deal on the table. But he said it would only work if I threw in a freebie. Admit to one I didn't do. He told me that there would be a field trip and I would have to lead a certain detective to the body. This detective had to be convinced, and leading him to the body would be the only way to do it. That detective was you, Bosch."

"And you said yes."

"When he said there would be a field trip, I said yes. That was the only reason. It meant daylight. I saw a chance at daylight."

"And you were led to believe that this of-fer, this deal — that it came directly from Olivas and O'Shea?"

"Who else would it come from?"

"Did Maury Swann ever use their names in connection with the deal?"

"He said this is what they wanted me to do. He said it came directly from them. They would not make a deal if I didn't throw in the freebie. I had to throw in Gesto and take you to her or there was no fucking deal. You get it?"

Bosch nodded.

"Yeah, I got it."

He felt his face getting hot with anger. He tried to channel it, put it aside so that it was ready to be used, but not at this moment.

"How did you get the details you gave me during the confession?"

"Swann. He got them from them. He said they had the records from the original inves-tigation."

"And he told you how to find the body up there in the woods?"

"Swann told me there were markers in the woods. He showed me pictures and told me how to lead everybody there. It was easy. The night before my confession I studied up on everything."

Bosch was silent as he thought about how easily he had been led down the path. He had wanted something so badly and for so long that it had made him blind.

"And what were you supposed to get out of all of this, Raynard?"

"You mean, what was in it for me from their point of view? My life, man. They were offering me my life. Take it or leave it. But the truth is, I didn't care about that. I told you, man, when Maury said there'd be a field trip, I knew that I might have a chance to get away . . . and to visit my . . . my fox-hole one last time. That was enough for me. I didn't care about anything else. I didn't care if I died trying, either."

Bosch tried to think of what he should do or ask next. He thought about using his cell to call the district attorney or a judge and have Waits confess over the phone. He put the flashlight down again and reached into his pocket but then he remembered he had dropped his phone when he had jumped onto Rachel as the shooting broke out in the garage.

"Are you still there, Detective?"

"I'm here. What about Marie Gesto? Did Swann tell you why you had to confess to the Marie Gesto killing?"

Waits laughed.

"He didn't have to. It was pretty obvious that the fix was in. Whoever did Gesto was trying to get you off his back."

"No name was mentioned?"

"No, no name."

Bosch shook his head. He had nothing. Nothing on O'Shea or Anthony Garland or anybody else. He looked down the tunnel in the direction of the garage. He could see nothing but he knew that there would be people there. They had blacked out that end to prevent backlighting. He knew they would be coming at any moment.

"What about your escape?" he asked in order to keep the dialogue going. "Was that planned or were you just improvising?"

"A little of both. I met with Swann the night before the field trip. He told me how I would lead you to the body. He showed me the photos and told me about the markings in the trees and how they would begin after we came to where there had been a mud slide and we would have to climb down. That's when I knew. I knew I might have a chance then. So I told him to make them uncuff me if I had to do any climbing. I told him that I wouldn't follow through on the deal if I had to do any climbing with my hands cuffed to my sides."

Bosch remembered O'Shea overruling Olivas and telling him to take the cuffs off. Olivas's reluctance had all been a play for Bosch's benefit. Everything had been a play for his benefit. Everything was phony and he had been played perfectly.

Bosch heard the sound of men crawling behind him in the tunnel. He turned the flashlight on and saw them. It was the SWAT team. Black Kevlar, automatic rifles, night-vision goggles. They were coming. Any moment they would launch a flash-bang grenade into the tunnel and start coming. He turned the light out. He thought about the woman. He knew Waits would kill her the moment they made the move.

"Were you really at McLaren?" Waits asked.

"I was there. It was before your time but I was there. I was in B dorm. It was closest to the baseball fields so we always got there first at rec time and got the best equipment."

It was a you-had-to-be-there story, the best Bosch could think of in the moment. He had spent most of his life trying to forget about McLaren.

"Maybe you were there, Bosch."

"I was."

"And look at us now. You went your way and I went mine. I guess I fed the wrong dog."

"What do you mean? What dog?"

"You don't remember. At McLaren they used to pass around that saying about every man having two dogs inside. One good and one bad. They fight all the time because only one can be the alpha dog, the one in charge."

"And?"

"And the one that wins is always the dog you chose to feed. I fed the wrong one. You fed the right one."

Bosch didn't know what to say. He heard a click from behind him in the tunnel. They were going to launch the grenade. He quickly stood up, hopeful that they would not shoot him in the back.

"Waits, I'm coming in."

"No, Bosch."

"I'll give you my gun. Watch the light. I'll give you my gun."

He switched on the flashlight and played its beam on the turn in the tunnel ahead. He moved forward and when he got to the turn extended his left hand into the cone of light. He held his gun by the barrel so Waits could see it was no threat.

"I'm coming in now."

Bosch took the turn and entered the final chamber of the tunnel. The space was at least twelve feet wide but still not tall enough for him to stand in. He dropped to his knees and swept the chamber with his light. The dim amber beam revealed a ghastly sight of bones and skulls and decaying flesh and hair. The stench was overpowering and Bosch had to hold himself from gagging.

The beam came to the face of the man Bosch had known as Raynard Waits. He was propped against the far wall of his foxhole, sitting on what looked like a throne carved into the rock and clay. To his left the woman he had abducted lay naked and unconscious on a blanket. Waits held the barrel of Freddy Olivas's gun to her temple.

"Easy now," Bosch said. "I'll give you my gun. Just don't hurt her anymore."

Waits smiled, knowing he was in complete control of the situation.

"Bosch, you are a fool to the end."

Bosch lowered his arm and tossed the gun to the right side of the throne. As Waits reached down to grab it he lifted the muzzle of the other gun off the woman. Bosch dropped the flashlight and reached behind him at the same time, his hand finding the grip of the revolver he had taken from the blind woman.

The long barrel made his aim true. He fired twice, hitting Waits in the center of the chest with both rounds.

Waits was knocked back against the wall. Bosch saw his eyes go wide, then they lost that light that separates life from death. His chin dropped and his head tilted forward.

Bosch crawled to the woman and checked her for a pulse. She was still alive. He covered her with the blanket she was lying on. He then called out to the others in the tunnel.

"This is Bosch — RHD! It's clear! We are clear! Raynard Waits is dead!"

A bright light flashed on around the corner in the entrance tunnel. It was a blinding light and he knew the men with guns would be waiting on the other side of it.

No matter, he felt safe now. He slowly moved toward the light.

30

After emerging from the tunnel Bosch was led out of the garage by two SWAT officers wearing gas masks. He was delivered into the hands of the waiting members of the Fugitive Task Force and others associated with the case. Randolph and Osani from OIS were on hand as well as Abel Pratt from the Open-Unsolved Unit. Bosch looked around for Rachel Walling but didn't see her anywhere on the scene.

Next out of the tunnel was Waits's last victim. The young woman was carried to a waiting ambulance and immediately transported to County-USC Medical Center for assessment and treatment. Bosch was pretty sure his own imagination couldn't top the real horrors she had lived through. But he knew the important thing was that she was alive.

The task force leader wanted Bosch to sit in a van and tell his story but Bosch said he didn't want to be in a closed space. Even out in the open air on Figueroa Lane he couldn't get the smell of the tunnel out of his nose and he noticed that the task force members who had crowded around him at first had now all taken a step or two back. He saw a garden hose attached to a faucet alongside the stairway of the house next to 710. He went over, turned it on and then bent over as he ran the water through his hair, on his face and down his neck. It pretty much soaked his clothes but he didn't care. It washed away a good deal of the dirt and sweat and stench and he knew the clothes were trash now anyway.

The task force top was a sergeant named Bob McDonald who had been pulled in from Hollywood Division. Luckily, Bosch knew him from past days in the division and that set the stage for a cordial debriefing. Bosch realized it was just a warmup. He would have to submit to a formal interview with

Randolph and the OIS before the end of the day.

"Where's the FBI agent?" Bosch asked. "Where's Rachel Walling?"

"She's being interviewed," McDonald said. "We're using a neighbor's house for her."

"And the old lady upstairs in the house?"

McDonald nodded.

"She's fine," McDonald said. "She's blind and in a wheelchair. They're still talking to her but it turns out Waits lived here when he was a kid. It was a foster home and his real name is Robert Foxworth. She can't get around by herself anymore, so she pretty much stays up there. County assistance brings in her food. Foxworth helped her out financially by renting the garage. He kept supplies for window washing in there. And an old van. It's got a wheelchair lift in it."

Bosch nodded. He guessed that Janet Saxon had no idea what else her former foster son used her garage for.

McDonald told Bosch it was time to tell his story, and so he did, giving the step-by-step playback of the moves he had made after discovering the connection between Waits and the pawnbroker Fitzpatrick.

There were no questions. Not yet. Nobody

asked why he never called the task force or Randolph or Pratt or anybody else. They listened and simply locked in his story. Bosch was not too concerned. He and Rachel had saved the girl and he had killed the bad guy. He was sure that these two accomplishments would allow him to rise above all transgressions upon protocol and regulations and save his job.

It took him twenty minutes to tell the story, and then McDonald said they should take a break. As the group around him splintered, Bosch saw his boss waiting to get to him. Bosch knew this conversation would not be easy.

Pratt finally saw an opening and walked up. He looked anxious.

"Well, Harry, what did he tell you in there?"

Bosch was surprised Pratt wasn't jumping all over him for acting on his own, without authority. But he wasn't going to complain about it. In abbreviated form he outlined what he had learned from Waits about the setup in Beachwood Canyon.

"He told me it was all orchestrated through Swann," he said. "Swann was the go-between. He took the deal from Olivas and O'Shea to Waits. Waits didn't kill Gesto but agreed to take the fall for her. It was part of the deal for avoiding the death penalty."

"That's it?"

"That's enough, isn't it?"

"Why would Olivas and O'Shea do this?"

"The oldest reasons in the book. Money and power. And the Garland family has plenty of both."

"Anthony Garland was the person of interest on Gesto, right? The guy who got the court orders keeping you away."

"Yeah, until Olivas and O'Shea used Waits to convince me otherwise."

"You got anything besides what Waits said in there?"

Bosch shook his head.

"Not much. I traced twenty-five thousand in contributions to O'Shea's campaign back to T. Rex Garland's lawyers and oil company. But it was all done legally. It proves a connection, nothing else."

"Twenty-five seems cheap to me."

"It is. But the twenty-five is all we know about. We do some digging and there'll probably be more."

"You tell all of this to McDonald and his crew?"

"Only what Waits told me in there. I didn't

tell them about the contributions. Only what Waits said."

"You think they'll go after Maury Swann for this?"

Bosch thought a moment before answering.

"Not a chance. Whatever was said between them was privileged information. Besides that, nobody would go after him based on the word of a dead madman like Waits."

Pratt kicked the ground. He had nothing else to say or ask.

"Look, Top, I'm sorry about this," Bosch said. "About not being up-front with you on what I was doing, the home duty and everything."

Pratt waved it off.

"It's okay, man. You got lucky. You ended up doing some good and taking out the bad guy. What am I going to say to that?"

Bosch nodded his thanks.

"Besides, I'm coasting," Pratt continued. "Another three weeks and you'll be someone else's problem. He can decide what to do with you."

Whether Kiz Rider came back or not, Bosch didn't want to leave the unit. He'd heard that David Lambkin, the new top coming up from RHD, was a good man to work for. Bosch hoped when all of this shook out, he'd still be part of the Open-Un-solved Unit.

"Holy shit!" Pratt whispered.

Bosch followed his eyes to a car that had just parked on the perimeter near where the media trucks were and the reporters were setting up for standups and sound bites. Rick O'Shea was getting out of the passen-ger side. Bosch felt the bile immediately rise in his throat. He made a move to walk toward the prosecutor but Pratt caught his arm.

"Harry, take it easy."

"What the fuck is he doing here?"

"It's his case, man. He can come if he wants. And you better play it cool. Don't show your hand with him or you might never be able to get to him."

"And what, meantime he does his dance in front of the cameras and turns this into another campaign commercial? Bullshit. What I ought to do is go over there and kick his ass right in front of the cameras."

"Yeah, that would be real smart, Harry. Very subtle. That will help the situation a lot."

Bosch broke free of Pratt's grasp but simply stepped over and leaned against one of the police cars. He folded his arms and kept his head down until he was calmer. He knew Pratt was right.

"Just keep him away from me."

"That will be kind of hard because he's coming right to you."

Bosch looked up just as O'Shea and the two men that made up his entourage got to him.

"Detective Bosch, are you okay?"

"Never better."

Bosch kept his arms folded across his chest. He didn't want one of his hands getting loose and involuntarily taking a swing at O'Shea.

"Thank you for what you have done here today. Thank you for saving the young woman."

Bosch just nodded while looking down at the ground.

O'Shea turned to the men with him and to Pratt, who had remained nearby in case he had to pull Bosch off the prosecutor.

"Could I speak to Detective Bosch alone?"

O'Shea's minions walked off. Pratt hesitated until Bosch nodded to him, telling him everything was cool. Bosch and O'Shea were left to themselves.

"Detective, I've been briefed on what Waits — or, I should say, Foxworth — revealed to you in the tunnel."

"Good."

"I hope you do not give any credence to what an admitted and confirmed serial killer would say about the men who were prosecuting him, especially one who cannot even be here to defend himself?"

Bosch stepped away from the patrol car's fender and finally dropped his arms to his sides. His hands were balled into fists.

"You're talking about your pal Olivas?"

"Yes, I am. And I can tell by your posture that you actually believe what Foxworth allegedly told you."

"Allegedly? What, now I'm the one making it up?"

"Someone is."

Bosch leaned a few inches toward him and spoke in a low voice.

"O'Shea, get away from me. I might hit you."

The prosecutor took a step backwards as if he had already been punched.

"You're wrong, Bosch. He was lying."

"He was confirming what I already knew before I even went into that tunnel. Olivas was dirty. He put the entry in the murder book that falsely tied Raynard Waits to Gesto. He went out there and marked a trail for Waits to follow and lead us to the body. And he wouldn't have done any of it without somebody telling him to do it. He wasn't that kind of guy. He wasn't smart enough."

O'Shea stared at him for a long moment. The implication in Bosch's words was clear.

"I can't dissuade you from this bullshit, can I?"

Bosch looked at him and then looked away.

"Dissuade? Not a chance. And I don't care what it does or doesn't do for the campaign, Mr. Prosecutor. Those are the undisputed facts and I don't need Foxworth or what he said to prove them."

"Then, I guess I'll have to appeal to a higher authority than you."

Bosch took half a step closer to him. This time he really got into his space.

"You smell that? You smell that on me? That's the fucking putrid smell of death. I've got it all over me, O'Shea. But at least I can wash it off."

"What is that supposed to mean?"

"Whatever you want it to mean. Who's your higher authority? You going to call T. Rex Garland up in his shiny office?"

O'Shea took a deep breath and shook his head in confusion.

"Detective, I don't know what happened to you in that tunnel but you aren't making much sense."

Bosch nodded.

"Yeah, well, it will make sense soon enough. Before the election, that's for sure."

"Help me out, Bosch. What exactly am I missing here?"

"I don't think you're missing anything. You know it all, O'Shea, and before it's all over, so will the whole wide world. Somehow, some way, I'm going to take down you and the Garlands and everybody else who had a part in this. Count on it."

Now O'Shea took a step toward Bosch.

"Are you saying that I did this, that I set all of this up, for T. Rex Garland?"

Bosch started laughing. O'Shea was the consummate actor to the end.

"You're good," he said. "I'll give you that. You're good."

"T. Rex Garland is a valid contributor to

my campaign. Up-front and legal. How you can tie that into —"

"Then, why the fuck didn't you mention he was a valid and legal contributor when I brought up his son the other day and told you he was my suspect on Gesto?"

"Because it would have complicated things. I have never met or even spoken to either of the Garlands. T. Rex contributed to my campaign. So what? The guy spreads money through every election in the county. For me to bring it up at that point would have been to invite your suspicion. I didn't want that. Now I see I have it anyway."

"You are so full of shit. You —"

"Fuck you, Bosch. There is no connection."

"Then, we've got nothing else to say."

"Yes, we do. I've got something to say. Take your best shot with this bullshit and we'll see who comes out at the end still standing."

He turned and walked away, barking an order to his men. He wanted a telephone with a secured line. Bosch wondered who the first call would go to, T. Rex Garland or the chief of police.

Bosch made a snap decision. He would

call Keisha Russell and turn her loose. He would tell her she was clear to look into those campaign contributions Garland had funneled to O'Shea. He put his hand into his pocket and then remembered that his phone was still somewhere in the garage. He walked that way and stopped at the yellow tape that was strung across the now fully opened door behind the white van.

Cal Cafarelli was in the garage, directing the forensic analysis of the scene. She had a breathing-filter mask down around her neck. Bosch could tell by her face that she had been to the macabre scene at the end of the tunnel. And she would never be the same again. He waved her over.

"How's it going, Cal?"

"It's going about as well as you'd expect after seeing something like that."

"Yeah. I know."

"We're going to be here long into the night. What can I do for you, Harry?"

"Have you found a cell phone somewhere in here? I lost my phone when things started happening."

She pointed to the floor near the front tire of the van.

"Is that it over there?"

Bosch looked over and saw his phone lying on the concrete. The red message light was blinking. He noticed that someone had circled it on the concrete with chalk. That was not good. Bosch didn't want his phone inventoried as evidence. He might never get it back.

"Can I get it back? I need it."

"I'm sorry, Harry. Not yet. This place hasn't been photographed. We're starting with the tunnel and moving out from there. It will be a while."

"Then how about if you give it to me and I use it right here and then I give it back when it's time to take photos. It looks like I've got messages waiting."

"Harry, come on."

He knew that his suggestion would break about four rules of evidence.

"Okay, just let me know when I can get it back. Hopefully before the battery's dead."

"You got it, Harry."

He turned away from the garage and saw Rachel Walling walking toward the yellow tape that delineated the outside perimeter of the crime scene. There was a federal cruiser there and a man in a suit and sunglasses was waiting for her. She had apparently called for a ride.

Bosch trotted toward the tape, calling her name. She stopped and waited for him.

"Harry," she said. "Are you all right?"

"I am now. How about you, Rachel?"

"I'm fine. What happened to you?"

She indicated his wet clothes with her hand.

"I had to hose off. It was bad. I need about a two-hour shower. Are you leaving?"

"Yes. They're done with me for the time being."

Bosch nodded toward the man in the sunglasses ten feet behind her.

"Are you in trouble?" he asked quietly.

"I don't know yet. I should be all right. You got the bad guy and saved the girl. How can that be a bad thing?"

"*We* got the bad guy and saved the girl," Bosch corrected. "But there are people in every institution and bureaucracy who can find a way to turn something good into shit."

She looked him in the eyes and nodded.

"I know," she said.

Her look froze him and he knew they were now different.

"Are you mad at me, Rachel?"

"Mad? No."

"Then, what?"

"Then, nothing. I have to go."

"Will you call me, then?"

"When I can. Good-bye, Harry."

She took two steps toward the waiting car but then stopped and turned back to him.

"That was O'Shea you were talking to out by the car, wasn't it?"

"Yeah."

"Be careful, Harry. If you let your emotions run you the way they did out here today, O'Shea could put you in a world of pain."

Bosch smiled slightly.

"You know what they say about pain, don't you?"

"No, what?"

"They say pain is weakness leaving the body."

She shook her head.

"Well 'they' are full of shit. Don't put it to the test unless you have to. Good-bye, Harry."

"I'll see you, Rachel."

He watched as the man in sunglasses held the tape up for her to duck under. She got into the front passenger seat and Sunglasses drove them off. Bosch knew that something had changed in the way she saw him. His actions in the garage and going into the tunnel had made her change her mind about him. He accepted it and guessed that he might never see her again. He decided that it would be one more thing that he would blame on Rick O'Shea.

He turned back to the scene, where Randolph and Osani were standing waiting for him. Randolph was putting away his cell phone.

"You two again," Bosch said.

"Gettin' to be like déjà vu all over again, isn't it?" Randolph said.

"Something like that."

"Detective, we are going to need to take you over to Parker Center and conduct a more formal interview this time around."

Bosch nodded. He knew the drill. This time it wasn't about shooting into the trees or the woods. He had killed somebody, so this time it would be different. They would need to nail down every detail.

"I'm ready to go," he said.

31

Bosch was seated in an interview room in the Officer Involved Shooting Unit at Parker Center. Randolph had allowed him to shower in the basement locker room and he'd changed into blue jeans and a black West Coast Choppers sweatshirt, clothing he kept in a locker for the times he was downtown and unexpectedly needed to fly below the radar that a suit would bring. On the way out of the locker room he had dumped his contaminated suit into a trash can. He would now be down to two.

The tape recorder on the table was turned on, and from separate sheets of paper, Osani read to him his constitutional rights as well as the police officer's bill of rights. The double insulation of protections was designed to safeguard the individual and police office from the unfair assault of the government, but Bosch knew that when push came to shove, in one of these little rooms neither piece of paper would do much to protect him. He had to fend for himself. He said he understood his rights and agreed to be interviewed.

Randolph took over from there. At his request Bosch once more told the story of the shooting of Robert Foxworth, aka Raynard Waits, beginning with the discovery made during the review of records from the Fitzpatrick case and ending with the two bullets he fired into Foxworth's chest. Randolph asked few questions until Bosch was finished going through the story. Then he asked many detailed questions about the moves Bosch had made in the garage and then the tunnel. More than once he asked Bosch why he didn't listen to the cautioning words of FBI agent Rachel Walling.

This question told Bosch not only that Rachel had been interviewed by the OIS but also that she had not said things particularly favorable to his case. This disappointed

Bosch greatly but he tried to keep his thoughts and feelings about Rachel out of the interview room. To Randolph he repeated as a mantra a sentence that he believed would ultimately win the day for him, no matter what Randolph or Rachel or anyone else thought of his actions and procedures.

"It was a life-or-death situation. A woman was in jeopardy and we had been fired upon. I felt that I could not wait around for backup or anybody else. I did what I had to do. I used as much caution as I could and used deadly force only when necessary."

Randolph moved on and focused many of the next questions on the actual shooting of Robert Foxworth. He asked Bosch what he was thinking when Foxworth revealed that Bosch had been set up to believe that the Gesto case was solved. He asked Bosch what he was thinking when he saw the remains of Foxworth's victims positioned in the chamber at the end of the tunnel. He asked Bosch what he was thinking when he pulled the trigger and killed the defiler and murderer of those victims.

Bosch patiently answered each question but finally hit his limit. Something was off-kilter about the interview. It was almost as if Randolph were working from a script.

"What's going on here?" Bosch asked. "I'm sitting here telling you people everything. What aren't you telling me?"

Randolph looked at Osani and then back at Bosch. He leaned forward, arms on the table. He had a habit of turning a gold ring on his left hand. Bosch had noticed him doing it last time. He knew it was a USC ring. Big deal. A lot of the department's ruling class had gone through night school at USC.

Randolph looked back at Osani and reached over to turn the tape recorder off but held his fingers on the buttons.

"Detective Osani, could you go get us a couple bottles of water? All this talking and my voice is about to go. Probably the same with Detective Bosch, too. We'll hold up until you get back."

Osani got up to leave and Randolph turned off the recorder. He didn't speak until the interview room door was closed.

"The thing is, Detective Bosch, we only have your word on what happened in that tunnel. The female was unconscious. There were only you and Foxworth, and he didn't make it out alive."

"That's right. Are you saying my word is not acceptable?"

"I'm saying that your description of events might be perfectly acceptable. But the forensics might come in with an interpretation that varies from your statement. You see? It can get messy very quickly. Things can be left open to interpretation and misinterpretation. Public and political interpretation as well."

Bosch shook his head. He didn't understand what was happening.

"So what?" he said. "I don't care what the public or politicians think. Waits pushed the action in that tunnel. It was clearly a kill-or-be-killed situation and I did what I had to do."

"But there is no witness to your description of events."

"What about Agent Walling?"

"She didn't go into the tunnel. She warned you not to go in."

"You know, there's a woman over at County-USC who probably wouldn't be alive right now if I hadn't gone in. What is going on here, Lieutenant?"

Randolph started playing with his ring again. He looked like a man with a distaste for what his duty called on him to do.

"That's probably enough for today. You've been through a lot. What we're going to do is keep things open for a few days while we wait for the forensics to come in. You'll continue on home duty. Once we have everything in order I'll bring you in to read and sign your statement."

"I asked what's going on, Lieutenant."

"And I told you what's going on."

"You didn't tell me enough."

Randolph took his hand away from his ring. It had the effect of underlining with importance what he would say next.

"You rescued the hostage and brought a resolution to the case. That's good. But you were reckless in your actions and got lucky. If we believe your story, then you shot a man who was threatening the lives of you and others. The facts and forensics, however, might just as easily lead to another interpretation, perhaps one that indicates the man you shot was attempting to surrender. So what we're going to do is take our time with it. In a few days we'll get it right. And then we'll let you know."

Bosch studied him, knowing that he was delivering a message that was not so hidden in his words.

"This is about Olivas, isn't it? The funeral's set for tomorrow, the chief is going to be there and you want to keep Olivas a hero killed in the line of duty."

Randolph went back to turning his ring.

"No, Detective Bosch, you have that wrong. If Olivas was dirty, then nobody is going to bend over backwards to worry about his reputation."

Bosch nodded. He now had it.

"Then it's about O'Shea. He reached out to a higher authority. He told me he would. That authority then reached out to you."

Randolph leaned back in his chair and seemed to search the ceiling for a proper reply.

"There are a great number of people in this department as well as the community who believe Rick O'Shea would make a fine district attorney," he said. "They also believe he would be a good friend to have on the side of the LAPD."

Bosch closed his eyes and slowly shook his head. He couldn't believe what he was hearing. Randolph continued.

"His opponent, Gabriel Williams, has allied himself with an anti–law enforcement constituency. It would not be a good day for the LAPD if he were to be elected."

Bosch opened his eyes and stared at Randolph.

"You're actually going to do this?" he asked. "You're going to let this guy skate because you think he could be a friend to the department?"

Randolph shook his head sadly.

"I don't know what you are talking about, Detective. I'm simply making a political observation. But I do know this. There is no evidence real or imagined of this conspiracy you speak of. If you think that Robert Foxworth's attorney will do anything other than deny the conversation you have outlined here, then you would be a fool. So don't be a fool. Be wise. Keep it to yourself."

Bosch took a moment to compose himself.

"Who made the call on this?"

"Excuse me?"

"How high up did O'Shea reach? It couldn't have been directly to you. He would have gone higher. Who told you to knock me down?"

Randolph spread his hands and shook his head.

"Detective, I have no idea what you are talking about."

"Right. Of course not."

Bosch stood up.

"Then, I guess you'll write it up the way you've been told and I'll either sign it or I won't. Simple as that."

Randolph nodded but said nothing. Bosch leaned down and put both hands on the table so he could get close to his face.

"You going to Deputy Doolan's funeral, Lieutenant? It's right after they put Olivas in the ground. Remember him, the one Waits shot in the face out there? I thought maybe you'd be going to the funeral to explain to his family about how choices had to be made and how the man directly behind that bullet could be a friend to the department and therefore doesn't need to face the consequences of his actions."

Randolph stared straight ahead at the wall across the table. He said nothing. Bosch straightened up and pulled open the door, startling Osani, who had been standing just outside. He wasn't holding any water bottles. Bosch pushed past him and left the squad room.

At the elevator Bosch pushed the up button. He waited and paced and thought about taking his grievance up to the sixth floor. He envisioned himself charging into the chief of police's suite and demanding to know if he was aware of what was being done in his name and under his command.

But as the elevator opened he dismissed the idea and pushed the 5 button. He knew that the Byzantine levels of bureaucracy and politics in the department were impossible to fully understand. If he didn't watch himself he could end up complaining about all the bullshit to the very person who created it.

The Open-Unsolved Unit was deserted when he got there. It was just after four and most detectives worked seven-to-four shifts that put them on the road home before rush hour. If something wasn't breaking, they left at four on the dot. Even a fifteen-minute delay could cost them an hour on the freeways. The only one still around was Abel Pratt, and that was because as a supervisor he had to work eight to five. Company rules. Bosch waved as he walked by the open door of Pratt's office on the way to his desk.

Bosch dropped into his chair, exhausted by the day's events and the weight of the departmental fix. He looked down and saw that his desk was littered with pink phone message slips. He started looking through them. Most were from colleagues in different divisions and stations. They were all call-backs. Bosch knew they wanted to say nice shooting or words to that effect. Anytime anybody got a clean kill the phones lit up.

There were several messages from reporters, including Keisha Russell. Bosch knew he owed her a call but would wait until he got home. There was also a message from Irene Gesto, and Bosch guessed that she and her husband wanted to know if there was any update on the investigation. He had called them the night before to tell them that their daughter had been found and the ID confirmed. He put that slip in his pocket. Home duty or not, he would make the call back to them. With the autopsy completed the body would be released and at the very least they could finally, after thirteen years, claim their daughter and take her home. He could not tell them that their daughter's killer had been brought to justice, but at least he could help them get her home.

There was also a message from Jerry Edgar, and Bosch remembered that his old partner had called his cell right before the shooting had gone down in Echo Park. Whoever had taken the message had written *Says it's important* on the slip and underlined it. Bosch checked the time on the slip and noted that this call had come in before the shooting as well. Edgar had not been calling to congratulate him on taking out a bad guy. He assumed that Edgar had heard that Harry had met his cousin and that he wanted to chew the fat about it. At the moment Bosch didn't feel up for that.

Bosch wasn't interested in any of the other messages, so he stacked them and put them in a desk drawer. Nothing else to do, he then started straightening the papers and files on his desk. He thought about whether he should call Forensics and see about getting his phone and car back from the Echo Park crime scene.

"I just got the word."

Bosch looked up. Pratt was standing in

the doorway of his office. He was in shirt-
sleeves, his tie loose at his neck.

"What word?"

"From OIS. You haven't cleared home
duty, Harry. I gotta send you home."

Bosch looked back down at his desk.

"So what's new? I'm leaving."

Pratt paused as he tried to interpret
Bosch's tone of voice.

"Everything okay, Harry?" he asked tentatively.

"Nope, everything's not okay. The fix is in
and when the fix is in, then everything's not
okay. Not by a long shot."

"What are you talking about? They're going to cover up Olivas and O'Shea?"

Bosch looked up at him.

"I don't think I should talk to you about it,
Top. It could put you in a spot. You wouldn't
want the blowback."

"They're that serious about it, huh?"

Bosch hesitated but then answered.

"Yeah, they're serious. They're willing to
jam me up if I don't play the game."

He stopped there. He didn't want to be
having this conversation with his supervisor.
In Pratt's position loyalties went both up
and down the ladder. It didn't matter if he

was only a few weeks from retirement. Pratt had to play the game until the buzzer sounded.

"My cell is back there, part of the crime scene," he said, reaching for the phone. "I just came in to make a phone call and then I'm out of here."

"I was wondering about your phone," Pratt said. "Some of the guys have been trying to call you and they said you weren't answering."

"Forensics wouldn't let me take it from the scene. The phone or my car. What did they want?"

"I think they wanted to take you out for a drink at Nat's. They might still be heading over there."

Nat's was a dive off Hollywood Boulevard. It wasn't a cop bar but a fair number of off-duty cops passed through there on any given night. Enough for the management to keep The Clash's hard-edged version of "I Fought the Law" on the jukebox for going on twenty years now. Bosch knew that if he showed up at Nat's the punk anthem would be in heavy if not inappropriate rotation in salute to the recently dispatched Robert Foxworth, aka Raynard Waits. *I fought the law but the law won* . . . Bosch could almost hear them all singing the chorus.

"You going?" he asked Pratt.

"Maybe later. I've got something to do first."

Bosch nodded.

"I don't think I feel like it," he said. "I'm going to pass."

"Suit yourself. They'll understand."

Pratt didn't move from the doorway so Bosch picked up his phone. He called Jerry Edgar's number just so he could follow through on the lie he had told about having to make a call. But Pratt remained in the doorway, his arm leaning against the jamb as he surveyed the empty squad room. He was really trying to get Bosch out of there. Maybe he had gotten the word from higher up the ladder than Lieutenant Randolph.

Edgar answered the call.

"It's Bosch, you called?"

"Yeah, man, I called."

"I've been a little busy."

"I know. I heard. Nice shooting today, partner. You okay?"

"Yeah, fine. What were you calling about?"

"Just something I thought you might want to know. I don't know if it matters anymore."

"What was it?" Bosch said impatiently.

"My cousin Jason called me from DWP. He said you saw him today."

"Yeah, nice guy. He helped a lot."

"Yeah, well, I wasn't checking on how he treated you. I'm trying to tell you that he called me and said there was something you might want to know but you didn't give him a business card or a number or anything. He said that about five minutes after you and the FBI agent you were with left, another cop came and asked for him. Asked at the lobby desk for the guy who was just helping the cops."

Bosch leaned forward at his desk. He was suddenly very interested in what Edgar was telling him.

"He said this guy showed a badge and said he was monitoring your investigation and he asked Jason what you and the agent had wanted. My cousin took him up to the floor you people had gone to and walked this guy out to the window. They were standing there looking down on the house in Echo Park when you and the lady agent showed up down there. They watched you go into the garage."

"Then what happened?"

"The guy ran out of there. Grabbed an elevator and went down."

"Did your cousin get a name off this guy?"

"Yeah, the guy said his name was Detective Smith. When he held up his ID he sort of had his fingers over the part with his name."

It was an old ploy, Bosch knew, used mostly when detectives were going off the reservation and didn't want their real name out in circulation. Bosch had used it himself on occasion.

"What about a description?" he asked.

"Yeah, he gave me all that. He said white guy, about six feet and one-eighty. The guy had silver-gray hair he kept cut short. Let's see, midfifties and he was wearing a blue suit, white shirt and a striped tie. He had an American flag on the lapel."

The description matched about fifty thousand men in the immediate vicinity of downtown. And Bosch was looking at one of them. Abel Pratt was still standing in his office doorway. He was staring at Bosch with eyebrows raised in question. He wasn't wearing his suit jacket but Bosch could see it on a hook on the door behind him. There was an American flag pinned to the lapel.

Bosch looked back down at his desk.

"How late does he work to?" he asked quietly.

"Normally, I think he stays till five. But there's a bunch of people hanging up there, watching the scene in Echo Park."

"Okay, thanks for the tip. I'll call you later."

Bosch hung up before Edgar could say anything else. He looked up and Pratt was still staring at him.

"What was that?" he asked.

"Oh, just something on the Matarese case. The one we filed this week. It looks like we might have a witness after all. It will help at trial."

Bosch said it as nonchalantly as he could. He stood up and looked at his boss.

"But don't worry. It will hold until I get back from home duty."

"Good. Glad to hear it."

32

Bosch walked toward Pratt. He came too close to him, invading his personal space, which caused Pratt to back into his office and move back to his desk. This was what Bosch wanted. He said good-bye and have a good weekend. He then headed toward the door of the squad room.

The Open-Unsolved Unit had three cars assigned to its eight detectives and one supervisor. The cars were used on a first-come first-served basis and the keys hung on hooks next to the squad room door. The procedure was for a detective taking a car to write his or her name and the estimated time of return on an erasable white board

that hung below the keys. When Bosch got
to the door he opened it wide to block the
view from Pratt's office of the key hooks.
There were two sets of keys on the hooks.
Bosch grabbed one and left.

A few minutes later he pulled out of the
garage behind Parker Center and headed
toward the DWP Building. The mad rush to
empty downtown by sunset was only just
beginning and he made it the seven blocks
in quick time. He parked illegally in front of
the fountain at the entrance to the building and jumped out of his car. He checked
his watch as he approached the front door.
It was twenty minutes to five.

A uniformed security guard came through
the doors, waving at him.

"You can't park —"

"I know."

Bosch showed him his badge and pointed
to the radio on the man's belt.

"Can you get Jason Edgar on that thing?"

"Edgar? Yeah. What's this —"

"Get him on there and tell him Detective
Bosch is waiting out front. I need to see him
as soon as possible. Do it now, please."

Bosch turned and headed back to his car.
He got in and waited five minutes before he

saw Jason Edgar come through the glass doors. When he got to the car he opened the passenger door to look in, not get in.

"What's up, Harry?"

"I got your message. Get in."

Edgar reluctantly got in the car. Bosch pulled away from the curb as he was closing his door.

"Wait a minute. Where are we going? I can't just leave."

"This should only take a few minutes."

"Where are we going?"

"Parker Center. We won't even get out of the car."

"I have to let them know."

Edgar took a small two-way off his belt. He called in at the DWP security center and said he would be off-location on a police matter for a half hour. He received a 10-4 and put the radio back on his belt.

"You should've asked me first," he said to Bosch. "My cousin said you had a habit of acting first and asking questions later."

"He said that, huh?"

"Yeah, he did. What are we doing at Parker Center?"

"Making an ID of the cop who talked to you after I left today."

Traffic had already gotten worse. A lot of nine-to-fivers getting an early jump on the commute home. Friday afternoons were particularly brutal. Bosch finally pulled back into the police garage at ten to five and hoped they wouldn't be too late. He found a parking space in the first row. The garage was an open-air structure and the space afforded them a view of San Pedro Street, which ran between Parker Center and the garage.

"You have a cell phone?" Bosch asked.

"Yeah."

Bosch gave him the general number for Parker Center and told him to call it and ask for the Open-Unsolved Unit. Calls transferred from the main number did not carry forward caller ID. Edgar's name and number would not show up on the OU lines.

"I just want to see if somebody answers," Bosch said. "If somebody does, just ask for Rick Jackson. When you're told that he's not there, don't leave a message. Just say you'll get him on his cell and hang up."

Edgar's call was answered and he went through the routine Bosch had outlined. When he was finished he looked over at Bosch.

"Somebody named Pratt answered."

"Good. He's still there."

"So what's that mean?"

"I wanted to make sure he hadn't left. He'll leave at five, and when he does he'll cross the street right over there. I want to see if he's the guy who told you he was monitoring my investigation."

"Is he IAD?"

"No. He's my boss."

Bosch slapped the visor down as a precaution against being seen. They were parked a good thirty yards from the crosswalk Pratt would use to get to the garage but he didn't know which way Pratt would go once he was inside the structure. As a squad supervisor he had the perk of being able to park a personal car in the police garage, and most of those assigned spaces were on the second level. There were two sets of stairs and the ramp up. If Pratt walked up the ramp he would come right by Bosch's position.

Edgar asked questions about the Echo Park shooting and Bosch answered them in short sentences. He didn't want to talk about it but he had just yanked the guy off post and had to respond in some way. It was only being courteous. Finally, at 5:01 he saw Pratt come through the back doors of Parker Center and down the ramp by the jail's intake doors. He walked out to San Pedro and started to cross with a group of four other detective supervisors who were heading home as well.

"Okay," Bosch said, cutting Edgar off in the middle of a question. "See those guys crossing the street. Which one came to DWP today?"

Edgar studied the pack crossing the street. He had an unobstructed view of Pratt, who was walking next to another man at the back of the group.

"Yeah, the last guy," Edgar said without hesitation. "The one puttin' on the shades."

Bosch looked over. Pratt had just put on his Ray-Bans. Bosch felt a deep pressure in his chest, like the worst case of heartburn he'd ever had. He kept his eyes on Pratt and watched him turn away from their position once he crossed the street. He was heading toward the far stairwell.

"Now what? You going to follow him?"

Bosch remembered Pratt saying he had something to do after work.

"I want to but I can't. I've got to shoot you back to DWP."

"Don't worry about it, man. I can walk it. Probably be faster with this traffic, anyway."

Edgar cracked his door and turned to get out. He looked back at Bosch.

"I don't know what's going on but good luck, Harry. I hope you get who you're looking for."

"Thanks, Jason. Hope to see you again."

After Edgar was clear Bosch backed out and left the garage. He took San Pedro over to Temple because he assumed that Pratt would take that route on his way to the freeway. Whether he was going home or not, the freeway was the likely choice.

Bosch crossed Temple and pulled to the curb in a red zone. It gave him a good angle on the exit to the police garage.

In two minutes a silver SUV came out of the garage and headed toward Temple. It was a Jeep Commander with a retro boxy design. Bosch identified Pratt behind the wheel. He immediately fit the dimensions and color of the Commander to those of the mystery SUV he had seen take off from the street near his house the night before.

Bosch leaned down across the seat as the Commander approached Temple. He heard it make the turn and after a few seconds he got back up behind the wheel. Pratt was on Temple up at the light at Los Angeles Street and he was turning right. Bosch waited until he completed the turn and then took off to follow.

Pratt entered the crowded northbound lanes of the 101 Freeway and joined the crawl of rush-hour traffic. Bosch came down the ramp and pushed into the line of cars about six vehicles behind the Jeep. He got lucky in that Pratt's vehicle had a white ball with a face on it atop the radio antenna. It was a giveaway promotion from a fast-food chain. It allowed Bosch to track the Jeep without having to get too close. He was in an unmarked Crown Vic which might as well have had a neon sign on its roof that flashed POLICE!

Slowly but surely Pratt made his way north with Bosch following at a distance. When the freeway cut past Echo Park he looked up to the ridgeline and saw that the crime scene and media soirée on Figueroa Lane was still in full swing. He counted two media choppers still circling overhead. He wondered if his car would be towed from the scene or if he would be able to go back and retrieve it later.

As he drove, Bosch tried to piece together what he had on Pratt. There was little doubt that Pratt had been following him while he was on home duty. His SUV matched the SUV that had been on his street the night before, and Pratt had been IDed by Jason Edgar as the cop who had followed him into the DWP Building. It was not feasible to think that he had been following Bosch simply to see if he was abiding by the rules of home duty. There had to be another reason and Bosch could think of only one thing.

The case.

Once he'd made this assumption, other things quickly came together and they served to only stoke the fire that was burning in Bosch's chest. Pratt had told the story about Maury Swann earlier in the week, and that made it clear they knew each other. While he had relayed a negative story about the defense attorney, that could have been a cover or an attempt to distance himself from someone he was actually close to and possibly working with.

Also obvious to Bosch was the fact that Pratt was intimately aware that Bosch had regarded Anthony Garland as a person of interest in the Gesto case. Bosch had routinely informed Pratt of his activities in re-opening the case. Pratt was also notified when Garland's lawyers successfully reac-quired a court order restraining Bosch from talking to Garland without one of his law-yers present.

Last, and perhaps most important, Pratt had access to the Gesto murder book. It sat most of the time on Bosch's desk. It could have been Pratt who put in the phony con-nection to Robert Saxon, aka Raynard Waits. He could have planted the connection long before the book was given to Olivas. He could have planted it so Olivas would dis-cover it.

Bosch realized that the whole plan for Raynard Waits to confess to the murder of Marie Gesto and to lead investigators to the body could have completely originated with Abel Pratt. He was in a perfect position as a go-between who could monitor Bosch as well as all the other parties involved.

And he realized that with Swann part of the plan, Pratt wouldn't need Olivas or O'Shea. The more people in a conspiracy, the more likely it is that it will fail or fall apart. All Swann had to do was tell Waits that the prosecutor and investigator were behind it and he would have planted a false trail for someone like Bosch to follow.

Bosch felt the hot flash of guilt start to burn at the back of his neck. He realized that he could be wrong about everything he had been thinking until a half hour before. Totally wrong. Olivas might not be dirty after all. Maybe he had been used as skillfully as Bosch had been used himself, and maybe O'Shea was guilty of nothing more than political maneuvering — taking credit where it was not due him, redirecting blame away from where it was due. O'Shea could have called for the department fix simply to contain Bosch's accusations because they would be politically damaging, not because they were true.

Bosch thought this new theory through again and it held up. He found no air in the brake lines, no sand in the gas tank. It was a car that could drive. The only thing missing was motive. Why would a guy who banked twenty-five years with the department and was looking at retiring at fifty risk it all on a scheme like this? How could a guy who had spent twenty-five years chasing bad guys let a killer go free?

Bosch knew from working a thousand

murders that motive was often the most elu-
sive component of crime. Obviously, money
could motivate, and the disintegration of a
marriage could play a part. But those were
unfortunate common denominators in many
people's lives. They could not readily explain why Abel Pratt had broken across the
line.

Bosch banged the palm of his hand hard
on the steering wheel. The question of motive aside, he was embarrassed and angry
with himself. Pratt had played him perfectly
and the betrayal was deep and painful. Pratt
was his boss. They had eaten together,
worked cases together, told jokes and
talked about their kids together. Pratt was
heading toward a retirement that no one in
the department believed was anything other
than well-earned and well-deserved. It was
time to double-dip, collect a department
pension and grab a lucrative security job in
the islands where the pay was high and the
hours low. Everybody was shooting for that
and no one would begrudge it. It was blue
heaven, the policeman's dream.

But now Bosch saw through all of that.

"It's all bullshit," he said out loud in the
car.

33

Thirty minutes into the drive Pratt exited the freeway in the Cahuenga Pass. He took Barham Boulevard northeast into Burbank. The traffic was still thick and Bosch had no trouble following and maintaining his distance and cover. Pratt drove past the back entrance to Universal and the front entrance to Warner Bros. He then made a few quick turns and pulled to the curb in front of a row of town houses on Catalina near Verdugo. Bosch drove on by quickly, took his first right and then another and then another. He killed his lights before taking one more right and coming up on the town houses again.

He pulled to the curb a half block behind Pratt's SUV and slid down in his seat.

Almost immediately Bosch saw Pratt standing in the street, looking both ways before crossing. But he was taking too long to do it. The street was clear but Pratt kept looking back and forth. He was looking for someone or checking to see if he had been followed. Bosch knew that the hardest thing in the world to do was to follow a cop who was looking for it. He slouched down lower in the car.

Finally, Pratt started across the street, still looking back and forth continuously, and when he got to the other curb he turned and stepped up onto it backwards. He took a few steps back, surveying the area in both directions. When his scan came to Bosch's car his eyes held on it for a long moment.

Bosch froze. He didn't think Pratt had seen him — he was slouched too far down — but he might have recognized the car as either an unmarked police cruiser or one of the cars specifically assigned to the Open-Unsolved Unit. If he walked down the street to check it out Bosch knew he would be caught without much of an explanation. And without a gun. Randolph had routinely confiscated his backup weapon for a ballistics analysis in regard to the shooting of Robert Foxworth.

Pratt started walking toward Bosch's car. Bosch grabbed the door handle. If he needed to, he would bail out of the car and run toward Verdugo, where there would be traffic and people.

But suddenly Pratt stopped, his attention drawn to something behind him. He turned around and looked up the steps of the town house he had been standing in front of. Bosch tracked his eyes and saw the front door of the town house was partially open and a woman was looking out and calling to Pratt while smiling. She was hiding behind the door but one of her bare shoulders was exposed. Her expression changed as Pratt said something and signaled her back inside. She put a pout on her face and stuck her tongue out at him. She disappeared from the door, leaving it open six inches.

Bosch wished he had his camera but it was back in his car in Echo Park. However, he didn't need photographic evidence to know that he recognized the woman in the doorway and that she was not Pratt's wife — Bosch had met his wife at the recent squad room party when he had announced his retirement.

Pratt looked toward Bosch's car again, hesitated but then turned back to the town house. He strode up the stairs, went through the open door and shut it behind him. Bosch waited and, as he expected, saw Pratt pull back a curtain and look out at the street. Bosch stayed down as Pratt's eyes lingered on the Crown Vic. There was no doubt that the car had drawn Pratt's suspicion but Bosch guessed that the lure of illicit sex had overpowered his instinct to check the car out.

There was a commotion as Pratt was grabbed from behind and he turned away from the window, and the curtain fell back into place.

Bosch immediately sat up, started the car and made a U-turn away from the curb. He took a right on Verdugo and headed toward Hollywood Way. No doubt the Crown Vic had been blown. Pratt would be actively looking for it when he came back out of the town house. But the Burbank Airport was close. Bosch figured he could dump the Crown Vic at the airport, pick up a rental car and be back to the town house in less than a half hour.

As he drove he tried to place the woman he had seen looking out the door of the town house. He used a few mind-relaxation drills he had employed back when hypnotizing witnesses was accepted by the courts. Soon he was keying in on the woman's nose and mouth, the parts of her that had triggered his recognition center. And soon after that he had it. She was an attractive, young civilian employee of the department who worked in the office down the hall from Open-Unsolved. It was a personnel office, known by the rank and file as Hiring & Firing because it was the place where both things happened.

Pratt was fishing off the company dock, waiting out the rush hour in a Burbank shack-up spot. Not bad work if you could get it and get away with it. Bosch wondered if Mrs. Pratt knew of her husband's extracurricular activities.

He pulled into the airport and entered the valet parking lanes, thinking that that would be fastest. The man in the red coat who took the Crown Vic from him asked when he would be returning.

"I don't know," Bosch said, not having considered it.

"I need to write something on the ticket," the man said.

"Tomorrow," Bosch said. "If I'm lucky."

34

Bosch got back to Catalina Street in thirty-five minutes. He drove his rented Taurus past the row of town houses and spotted Pratt's Jeep still at the curb. This time he found a spot on the north side of the town house and parked there. While he slouched down in the car and watched for activity, he turned on the cell phone he had rented with the car. He called Rachel Walling's cell number but got her voice mail. He ended the call without leaving a message.

Pratt didn't come out until it was full-on dark outside. He stood in front of the complex beneath a streetlight and Bosch noticed he was wearing different clothes now.

He had on blue jeans and a dark, long-sleeved pullover shirt. The change of attire told Bosch that the liaison with the woman from Hiring & Firing was probably more than a casual shack-up. Pratt kept clothes at her place.

Pratt once again looked up and down the street, his eyes lingering longest on the south side where earlier the Crown Vic had drawn his attention. Apparently satisfied that the car was gone and he wasn't being watched, Pratt went to his Commander and soon pulled away from the curb. He made a U-turn and headed south to Verdugo. He then turned right.

Bosch knew that if Pratt was looking for a tail he would slow on Verdugo and watch his rearview mirror for any vehicle turning off Catalina in his direction. So he U-turned from the curb and went north a block to Clark Avenue. He turned left and gunned the car's weak engine. He drove five blocks to California Street and took a quick left. At the end of the block he would come to Verdugo. It was a risky move. Pratt could be long gone but Bosch was playing a hunch. Seeing the Crown Vic had spooked his boss. He would be on full alert.

Bosch had called it right. Just as he got to Verdugo he saw Pratt's silver Commander go by in front of him. He had obviously delayed on Verdugo, watching for a follower. Bosch let him get some distance and then turned right to follow.

Pratt made no evasive moves after that first effort to smoke out a tail. He stayed on Verdugo into North Hollywood and then turned south on Cahuenga. Bosch almost lost him at the turn but he went through the light on red. It was clear to him now that Pratt was not going home — Bosch knew that he lived in the opposite direction in the northern valley.

Pratt was heading toward Hollywood, and Bosch guessed that he was simply planning to join the other members of the squad at Nat's. But halfway through the Cahuenga Pass he turned right onto Woodrow Wilson Drive and Bosch felt his pulse kick up a notch. Pratt was now heading toward Bosch's own house.

Woodrow Wilson wound up the side of the Santa Monica Mountains, one deep curve after another. It was a lonely street and the only way to follow a vehicle was to do it without headlights and to keep at least one curve behind the brake lights of the lead car.

Bosch knew the curves intimately. He had lived on Woodrow Wilson for more than fifteen years and could make the drive half asleep — which he had done on occasion. But following Pratt, a police officer wary of a tail, was a unique difficulty. Bosch tried to stay two curves back. This meant he lost sight of the lights on Pratt's car from time to time but never for very long.

When he was two curves away from his house, Bosch started to coast and the rental car eventually came to a stop before the final bend. Bosch got out, quietly closed the door and trotted up the curve. He stayed close to the hedge that guarded the home and studio of a famous painter who lived on the block. He edged around it until he could see Pratt's SUV up ahead. He had pulled to the curb two houses before Bosch's house. Pratt's lights were now off and he seemed to be just sitting there and watching the house.

Bosch looked up at his house and saw lights on behind the kitchen and dining room windows. He could see the tail end of a car protruding from his carport. He recognized the Lexus and knew that Rachel Walling was in his home. Even as he was buoyed by the prospect of her being there waiting for him, Bosch was concerned about what Pratt was up to.

It appeared that he was doing exactly what he had been doing the night before, just watching and possibly trying to determine if Bosch was home.

Bosch heard a car coming behind him. He turned and started walking back toward his car as if he were on an evening walk. The car drove by slowly and Bosch then turned and headed back to the hedge. As the car came up behind Pratt's Jeep, rather than pull to the side, Pratt took off again, the lights of his SUV coming on as he sped away.

Bosch turned and ran back toward his rental car. He jumped in and pulled away from the curb. As he drove he hit redial on the rental phone and soon Rachel's line was ringing. This time she answered.

"Yes?"

"Rachel, it's Harry. Are you in my house?"

"Yes, I've been wait —"

"Come outside. I'm going to pick you up. Hurry."

"Harry, what is —"

"Just come out and bring your gun. Right now."

He clicked off and pulled to a stop in front of his house. He could see the glow of brake lights disappearing around the curve ahead. But he knew those belonged to the car that had spooked Pratt. Pratt was farther ahead.

Bosch turned and looked at his front door, ready to hit the horn, but Rachel was coming out.

"Close the door," Bosch yelled through the open passenger window.

Rachel pulled the door closed and hurried out to the car.

"Get in. Hurry!"

She jumped into the car and Bosch took off before she had the door closed.

"What is going on?"

He gave her the shorthand as he sped through the curves on the way up to Mulholland. He told her that his boss, Abel Pratt, was the setup man, that what had happened in Beachwood Canyon had been his plan. He told her that for the second night in a row he had been outside Bosch's home.

"How do you know all of this?"

"I just know. I'll be able to prove it all later. For now, it's a fact."

"What was he doing outside?"

"I don't know. Trying to see if I was home, I think."

"Your phone rang."

"When?"

"Right before you called my cell. I didn't answer it."

"It was probably him. Something's going on."

They came around the last bend, and the four-way stop at Mulholland was ahead. Bosch saw the taillights of a large vehicle just as they disappeared to the right. Another car moved up to the stop. It was the car that had made Pratt move on. It went straight through the intersection.

"The first one must have been Pratt. He turned right."

Bosch got to the stop and also turned right. Mulholland was the winding snake that followed the crest line of the mountains across the city. Its curves were smoother and not as deep as Woodrow Wilson's. It was also a busier street, with plenty of night cruisers. He would be able to follow Pratt without causing much suspicion.

They quickly caught up to the vehicle that had turned and confirmed that it was Pratt's Commander. Bosch then dropped back and for the next ten minutes tailed Pratt along the crest line. The sparkling lights of the Valley sprawled below on the north side. It was a clear night and they could see all the way to the shadowy mountains on the far side of the sprawl. They stayed on Mulholland through the intersection with Laurel Canyon Boulevard and continued west.

"I was waiting at your house to say goodbye," Rachel suddenly said.

After a moment of silence, Bosch responded.

"I know. I understand."

"I don't think you do."

"You didn't like the way I was today, the way I went after Waits. I'm not the man you thought I was. I've heard it before, Rachel."

"It's not that, Harry. Nobody is ever the man you think they are. I can live with that. But a woman has to feel safe with a man. And that includes when they are not together. How can I feel safe when I've seen firsthand how you work? It doesn't matter whether it is the way I would do it or not. I'm not talking about us cop to cop. What I'm talking about is that I could never feel comfortable and safe. I'd wonder every night if it's the night you won't be coming home. I can't do that."

Bosch realized he was giving the car too much gas. Her words had made him unconsciously press the pedal down harder. He was getting too close to Pratt. He slowed down and pulled back from the taillights a hundred yards.

"It's a dangerous job," he said. "I thought you more than anybody would know that."

"I do. I do. But what I saw out there today with you was recklessness. I don't want to have to worry about someone who is reckless. There's enough to worry about out there without that."

Bosch blew out his breath. He gestured toward the red lights moving in front of them.

"Okay," he said. "Let's talk about it later. Let's just concentrate on this for tonight."

As if on cue, Pratt hooked a hard left onto Coldwater Canyon Drive and started dropping down toward Beverly Hills. Bosch delayed as long as he believed he could and made the same turn.

"Well, I'm still glad I've got you with me," he said.

"Why?"

"Because if he ends up in Beverly Hills I won't need to call the locals because I'm with a fed."

"Glad I could do something."

"You have your gun with you?"

"Always. You don't have yours?"

"It was part of the crime scene. I don't know when I'll get it back. And that's the second gun they've taken from me this week. It's gotta be a record of some kind. Most guns lost during reckless gunplay."

He looked over to see if he was getting under her skin. She showed nothing.

"He's turning," she said.

Bosch snapped his attention back to the road and saw the left-turn signal on the Commander blinking. Pratt made the turn and Bosch went on by. Rachel bent down so she could see out the window and up at the street sign.

"Gloaming Drive," she said. "Are we still in the city?"

"Yeah. Gloaming goes way back in there but there's no way out. I've been in there before."

The next street down was Stuart Lane. Bosch used it to turn around in and headed back up to Gloaming.

"Do you know where he could be going?" Rachel asked.

"No idea. Another girlfriend's place, for all I know."

Gloaming was another curving mountain road. But that's where the similarity to Woodrow Wilson Drive ended. The homes here ran a minimum seven figures, easy, and all had nicely manicured lawns and hedges with not so much as a leaf out of place. Bosch drove it slowly, looking for the silver Jeep Commander.

"There," Rachel said.

She pointed out her window at a Jeep parked in the turnaround of a mansion with a French provincial design. Bosch drove by and parked two houses away. They got out and walked back.

"West Coast Choppers?"

She hadn't been able to see the front of his shirt while he was driving.

"It helped me blend in on a case once."

"Nice."

"My daughter saw me in this one time. I told her it was from my dentist."

The gate to the driveway was open. The cast-iron mailbox had no name on it. Bosch opened it and looked inside. They were in luck. There was mail, a small stack held together with a rubber band. He pulled it out and angled the top envelope toward a nearby streetlight in order to read it.

"'Maurice' — it's Maury Swann's place," he said.

"Nice," Rachel said. "I guess I should've been a defense attorney."

"You'd've been good working with criminals."

"Fuck you, Bosch."

The banter ended with a loud voice coming from behind a tall hedge that ran along the far side of the turnaround and on the left side of the house.

"I said get in there!"

There was a splash and Bosch and Walling headed toward the sound.

35

Bosch searched the hedge with his eyes, looking for an opening. There didn't appear to be one from the front. When they got close he wordlessly signaled Rachel to follow the hedge to the right while he went left. He noticed that she was carrying her weapon down at her side.

The hedge was at least ten feet high and so thick that Bosch could see no light from the pool or house through it. But as he moved along it he heard the sound of splashing and voices, one of which he recognized as belonging to Abel Pratt. The voices were close.

"Please, I can't swim. I can't touch the bottom!"

"Then what d'you have a swimming pool for? Keep paddling."

"Please! I'm not going to — why would I tell a soul about —"

"You're a lawyer, and lawyers like to play the angles."

"Please."

"I'm telling you, if I get even a hint that you're playing an angle on me, then next time it won't be a pool. It will be the fucking Pacific Ocean. You understand that?"

Bosch came to an alcove where the pool's filter pump and heater were located on a concrete pad. There was also a small opening in the hedge for a pool maintenance man to squeeze through. He slipped into the opening and stepped onto the tile surrounding a large oval pool. He was twenty feet behind Pratt, who was standing at the edge, looking down at a man in the water. Pratt held a long blue pole with a curved extension. It was for pulling people in trouble to the side but Pratt was holding it just out of reach of the man. He grabbed at it desperately but each time Pratt jerked it away.

It was hard to identify the man in the water as Maury Swann. The pool was dark with the lights off. Swann's glasses were gone and his hair looked like it had slipped off his scalp to the back of his head like a mud slide. On his gleaming bald dome was a strip of tape for holding his hairpiece in place.

The sound of the pool filter gave Bosch cover. He was able to walk unnoticed to within six feet of Pratt before speaking.

"What's happening, Top?"

Pratt quickly lowered the pole so that Swann could grab the hook.

"Hang on, Maury!" Pratt yelled. "You're all right."

Swann grabbed on and Pratt started pulling him toward the side of the pool.

"I gotcha, Maury," Pratt said. "Don't worry."

"You don't have to bother with the life-guard act," Bosch said. "I heard it all."

Pratt paused and looked down at Swann in the water. He was three feet from the side.

"In that case," Pratt said.

He let go of the pole and whipped his right hand behind his back to the belt line.

"Don't!"

It was Walling. She had found her own

way through the hedge. She was on the other side of the pool, pointing her weapon at Pratt.

Pratt froze and seemed to be making a decision about whether to draw or not. Bosch moved in behind him and yanked the gun out of his pants.

"Harry!" Rachel called. "I've got him. Get the lawyer."

Swann was sinking. The blue pole was going down with him. Bosch quickly went to the pool's edge and grabbed it. He pulled Swann to the surface. The lawyer started coughing and spitting water. He held tight to the pole and Bosch walked him down to the shallow end. Rachel came around to Pratt and ordered him to put his wrists behind his head.

Maury Swann was naked. He came up the steps in the shallow end cupping his shriveled balls with one hand and trying to pull his toupee back on with the other. Giving up on the hairpiece, he tore it all the way off and threw it down on the tile, where it landed with a splat. He went directly to a pile of clothes by a bench and started getting dressed while still soaking wet.

"So what was going on here, Maury?" Bosch asked.

"Nothing that concerns you."

Bosch nodded.

"I get it. A guy comes here to put you in the pool and watch you drown, maybe make it look like suicide or an accident, and you don't want anybody concerned about it."

"It was a disagreement, that's all. He was scaring me, not drowning me."

"Does that mean you and he had an agreement before you then had this disagreement?"

"I'm not answering that."

"Why was he scaring you?"

"I don't have to answer any of your questions."

"Then maybe we should back on out of here and leave you two to finish your disagreement. Maybe that would be the best thing to do here."

"Do what you want."

"You know what I think? I think that with your client Raynard Waits dead, there's only one person who can link Detective Pratt to the Garlands. I think your partner over there was getting rid of that link because he was getting scared. You'd be at the bottom of that pool if we hadn't happened by here."

"You can do *and* think what you want. But what I am telling you is that we had a disagreement. He happened by while I was taking my nightly swim and we disagreed about something."

"I thought you didn't know how to swim, Maury. Isn't that what you said?"

"I'm finished talking to you, Detective. You can leave my property now."

"Not yet, Maury. Why don't you finish getting dressed and join us at the deep end."

Bosch left him there as he struggled to get his wet legs into a pair of silk pants. At the other end of the pool Pratt was now handcuffed and sitting on a concrete bench.

"I'm not saying anything until I talk to a lawyer," he said.

"Well, there's one over there putting his clothes on," Bosch said. "Maybe you can hire him."

"I'm not talking, Bosch," Pratt repeated.

"Good decision," Swann called from the far end. "Rule number one: Never talk to the cops."

Bosch looked at Rachel and almost laughed.

"Can you believe this? Two minutes ago he was trying to drown the guy, and now the guy's giving him free legal advice."

"*Sound* legal advice," Swann said.

Swann walked over to where the others were waiting. Bosch noticed that his clothes were sticking to his wet body.

"I wasn't trying to drown him," Pratt said. "I was trying to help him. But that's all I'm going to say."

Bosch looked at Swann.

"Pull your zipper up, Maury, and sit down over here."

Bosch pointed to a spot on the bench next to Pratt.

"No, I don't think I will," Swann replied.

He took a step toward the house but Bosch took two steps and cut him off. He redirected him to the bench.

"Sit down," he said. "You're under arrest."

"For *what?*" Swann said indignantly.

"Double murder. Both of you are under arrest."

Swann laughed as though he were dealing with a child. Now that he had his clothes on he was recovering some of his swagger.

"And what murders would these be?"

"Detective Fred Olivas and Deputy Derek Doolan."

Now Swann shook his head, the smile intact on his face.

"I'm assuming these charges fall under the felony-homicide rule, since there is ample evidence that we did not actually pull the trigger that fired the bullets that killed Olivas and Doolan."

"It's always good to deal with a lawyer. I hate having to explain the law all the time."

"It's a pity you need the law explained to *you,* Detective Bosch. The felony-homicide rule comes into play only when someone is killed during the commission of a serious crime. If that threshold is satisfied, then co-conspirators in the criminal enterprise may be charged with murder."

Bosch nodded.

"I got that," he said. "And I've got you."

"Then be so kind as to tell me what the threshold crime is that I have conspired to commit."

Bosch thought for a moment before answering.

"How about suborning perjury and obstruction of justice? We could start there and move up to corruption of a public official, maybe aiding and abetting an escape from lawful custody."

"And we could end there as well," Swann said. "I was representing my client. I committed none of those crimes and you have not a shred of evidence that I did. If you arrest me, it will simply prove your own undoing and embarrassment."

He stood up.

"Good evening to you all."

Bosch stepped over and put his hand on Swann's shoulder. He drove him back down onto the bench.

"Sit the fuck down. You are under arrest. I'll leave it to the prosecutors to decide about threshold crimes. I don't give a shit about that. As far as I'm concerned, two cops are dead and my partner is going to end her career because of you, Maury. So fuck you."

Bosch looked over at Pratt, who sat with a slight smile on his face.

"It's good to have a lawyer in the house, Harry," he said. "I think Maury makes a good point. Maybe you should think about this before doing anything rash."

Bosch shook his head.

"You aren't walking away from this," he said. "Not by a long shot."

He waited a moment but Pratt said nothing.

"I know you're the setup man," Bosch said. "The whole thing up in Beachwood Canyon was yours. It was you who made the deal with the Garlands, then you went to Maury here, who took it to Waits. You doctored the murder book after Waits gave you an alias to stick in it. Maury might have a point about the felony-murder rap but there's more than enough there for obstruction, and if I get that, then I've got you. That means no island and no pension, Top. That means you go down in flames."

Pratt's eyes dropped from Bosch to the dark waters of the pool.

"I want the Garlands, and you can give them to me," Bosch said.

Pratt shook his head without turning his eyes from the water.

"Then, have it your way," Bosch said. "Let's go."

He signaled Pratt and Swann to stand up. They complied. Bosch turned Swann around so he could cuff him. As he did so he looked over the lawyer's shoulder at Pratt.

"After we book you, who're you going to call about bail, your wife or the girl from Hiring and Firing?"

Pratt immediately sat back down as if hit by a sucker punch. Bosch had been saving it for his last shot. He kept the pressure on.

"Which one was going to go with you to the island? To your sugar plantation? My guess is it was what's-her-name."

"Her name is Jessie Templeton. And I made you on the tail at her place tonight."

"Yeah, and I made you making me. But tell me, how much does Jessie Templeton know, and is she going to be as strong as you when I go see her after I book you?"

"Bosch, she doesn't know anything. Leave her out of it. Leave my wife and kids out of it, too."

Bosch shook his head.

"Doesn't work that way. You know that. We're going to turn everything upside down and shake it to see what falls out. I'm going to find the money the Garlands paid you and I'll tie it back to you, to Maury Swann, everybody. I just hope you didn't use your girlfriend to hide it. Because if you did, she goes down, too."

Pratt leaned forward on the bench. Bosch got the impression that if his hands hadn't been cuffed behind his back, he'd have been using them at that moment to hold his head and hide his face from the world. Bosch had kept at him like a man with an axe chopping at a tree. It was barely standing now. It needed one little push and it would go down.

Bosch walked Swann over to Rachel, who took him by one of his arms. Bosch then turned back to Pratt.

"You fed the wrong dog," Bosch said.

"What's that supposed to mean?"

"Everybody's got choices and you made the wrong one. Problem is, we don't pay for our mistakes alone. We take people down with us."

Bosch walked to the edge of the pool and looked down into the water. It shimmered on top but was impenetrably dark beneath the surface. He waited but it didn't take long for the tree to fall.

"Jessie doesn't need to be part of this and my wife doesn't need to know about her," Pratt said.

It was an opening offer. Pratt was going to talk. Bosch kicked his foot on the tile edging and turned back to face him.

"I'm not a prosecutor but I'll bet something could be worked out."

"Pratt, you are making a big mistake!" Swann said urgently.

Bosch reached down to Pratt and patted his pockets until he located the keys to the Commander and pulled them out.

"Rachel, take Mr. Swann to Detective Pratt's car. It will be better for transporting him. We'll be right there."

He threw her the keys and she started walking Swann to the opening in the hedge she had come through. Swann had to be pushed. He looked over his shoulder as he went and called back to Pratt.

"Do not talk to that man," he yelled. "Do you hear me? Do not talk to anyone! You will talk us all into prison!"

Swann kept yelling legal advice through the hedge. Bosch waited until he heard the car door close on his voice. He then stood in front of Pratt and noticed that sweat was dripping from his hairline and down his face.

"I don't want Jessie or my family involved," Pratt said. "And I want a deal. No jail time, I'm allowed to retire *and* I get to keep my pension."

"You want a lot for somebody who got two people killed."

Bosch started to pace, trying to figure out a way of making it all work for both of them. Rachel came back through the hedge. Bosch looked at her and was about to ask why she had left Swann unattended.

"Child-proof locks," she said. "He can't get out."

Bosch nodded and gave his attention back to Pratt.

"Like I said, you want a lot," he said. "What are you giving back?"

"I can give you the Garlands, easy," Pratt said desperately. "Anthony took me up there two weeks ago and led me to the girl's body. And Maury Swann, I can give you him on a platter. The guy's as dirty as . . ."

He didn't finish.

"You?"

Pratt lowered his eyes and slowly nodded his head.

Bosch tried to put everything aside so that he could think clearly about Pratt's offer. The blood of Freddy Olivas and Deputy Doolan was on Pratt's hands. Bosch didn't know whether he'd be able to sell the deal to a prosecutor. He didn't know if he could even sell it to himself. But in that moment, he was willing to try if it meant he would finally get to the man who killed Marie Gesto.

"No promises," he said. "We'll go see a prosecutor."

Bosch moved to the last important question.

"What about O'Shea and Olivas?"

Pratt shook his head once.

"They were clean on this."

"Garland funneled at least twenty-five grand to O'Shea's campaign. That's documented."

"He was just covering his bets. If O'Shea got suspicious, T. Rex could keep him in line because it would look like a payoff."

Bosch nodded. He felt the burn of humiliation over what he had thought about O'Shea and said to him.

"That wasn't the only thing you got wrong," Pratt said.

"Yeah, what else?"

"You said I went to the Garlands with this thing. I didn't. They came to me, Harry."

Bosch shook his head. He didn't believe Pratt for the simple reason that if the Garlands had had the idea to buy off a cop, their first overture would have been to the source of their problem: Bosch. That never happened and that made Bosch feel confident that the scheme had been hatched by Pratt as he tried to juggle retirement, a possible divorce, a mistress and whatever other secrets his life held. He had gone to the Garlands with it. He had gone to Maury Swann, too.

"Tell it to the prosecutor," Bosch said. "Maybe he'll care."

He looked at Rachel and she nodded.

"Rachel, you take the Jeep with Swann. I'll take Detective Pratt in my car. I want to keep them separated."

"Good idea."

Bosch signaled Pratt up.

"Let's go."

Pratt stood up again and came face-to-face with Bosch.

"Harry, you've got to know something first."

"What's that?"

"Nobody was supposed to get hurt, okay? It was a perfect plan with nobody getting hurt. It was Waits — he turned it all to shit out there in the woods. If he had just done what he'd been told, everybody would still be alive and everybody'd be happy. Even you. You would've solved the Gesto case. End of story. That's how it was supposed to be."

Bosch had to work to hold back his anger.

"Nice fairy tale," he said. "Except for the part of the story where the princess never wakes up and the real killer walks, everybody lives happily ever after. Keep telling yourself that one. You might actually be able to live with it someday."

Bosch roughly took him by the arm and led him toward the opening in the hedge.

Part Five

ECHO PARK

36

At 10 a.m. on Monday Abel Pratt walked from his car across the green lawn of Echo Park to a bench where an old man was sitting beneath the protective arms of the *Lady of the Lake.* There were five pigeons resting on her shoulders and upturned hands and one on her head but she showed no sign of annoyance or fatigue.

Pratt shoved the folded newspaper he carried into the overly full trash can by the statue and then sat on the bench next to the old man. He looked out at the smooth waters of Lake Echo in front of them. The old man, who held a cane down by his knee and wore a tan business suit with a maroon handkerchief in the breast pocket, spoke first.

"I remember when you could take your family here on a Sunday and not have to worry about being shot up by gang-bangers."

Pratt cleared his throat.

"Is that what you're worried about, Mr. Garland? The gangbangers? Well, I'll give you a little tip. Right now is one of the safest hours in any neighborhood in the city. Most of your gangbangers don't roll out of bed until the afternoon. That's why whenever we go out with warrants we go in the morning. We always catch them in bed."

Garland nodded approvingly.

"That's good to know. But that's not what I am worried about. I'm worried about you, Detective Pratt. Our business was con-cluded. I was not expecting to hear from you ever again."

Pratt leaned forward and scanned the park. He studied the rows of tables on the other side of the lake, where the old men played dominoes. His eyes then moved along the cars parked at the curb that edged the park.

"Where's Anthony?" he asked.

"He'll be along. He's taking precautions."
Pratt nodded.

"Precautions are good," he said.

"I don't like this place," Garland said. "It's full of ugly people, and that includes you. Why are we here?"

"Wait a minute," a voice said from behind them. "Don't say another word, Dad."

Anthony Garland had approached from their blind side. He came around the statue to the bench at the water's edge. He stood in front of Pratt and signaled him to stand up.

"Up," he said.

"What is this?" Pratt protested mildly.

"Just stand up."

Pratt did as he was asked and Anthony Garland produced a small electronic wand from the pocket of his blazer. He began moving it up and down in front of Pratt from head to toe.

"If you're transmitting an RF signal this will tell me."

"Good. I always wondered if I had RF. You never know with those women down in Tijuana."

Nobody laughed. Anthony Garland seemed satisfied with the scan and started putting his magic wand away. Pratt started to sit down.

"Wait," Garland said.

Pratt remained standing and Garland started running his hands over Pratt's body, a second precaution.

"Can't be too sure with a slimeball like you, *Detective*."

He moved his hands to Pratt's waist.

"That's my gun," Pratt said.

Garland kept searching.

"That's my cell phone."

The hands went lower.

"And those are my balls."

Garland then went down both legs and when he was satisfied, he told Pratt he could sit down. The detective returned to his seat next to the old man.

Anthony Garland remained standing in front of the bench, his back to the lake, his arms folded across his chest.

"He's clean," he said.

"Okay, then," T. Rex Garland said. "We can talk. What's this about, Detective Pratt? I thought it was made clear to you: You don't call us. You don't threaten us. You don't tell us where to be and when."

"If I hadn't threatened you, would you have come?"

Neither of the Garlands answered and Pratt smiled smugly and nodded.

"I rest my case."

"Why are we here?" the old man asked. "I made it quite clear before. I don't want my son touched by any of this. Why did he have to be here?"

"Well, because I sort of missed him since our little walk in the woods. We've got a bond, don't we, Anthony?"

Anthony said nothing. Pratt pressed on.

"I mean, a guy leads you to a body in the woods, I'd say normally they'd stay pretty tight. But I haven't heard from Anthony since we were up at the top of Beachwood together."

"I don't want you talking to my son," T. Rex Garland said. "You don't talk to my son. You're bought and paid for, Detective, you get that? This is the only time you will ever call a meeting with me. I call you. You don't call me."

The old man never looked at Pratt as he spoke. His eyes were cast toward the lake. The message was clear. Pratt wasn't worth his attention.

"Yeah, all that was fine, but things have changed," Pratt said. "In case you haven't been reading the papers or watching the news, things have gone to shit out there."

The old man remained seated but stretched his arms forward and put both palms on the polished gold dragon's head at the top of his cane. He spoke calmly.

"And whose fault is that? You told us you and the lawyer could keep Raynard Waits in line. You told us no one would get hurt. You called it a clean operation. Now look at what you've involved us in."

Pratt took a few moments to respond.

"You involved yourself. You wanted something and I was the provider. No matter whose fault it is, the bottom line is I now need more money."

T. Rex Garland shook his head slowly.

"You were paid one million dollars," he said.

"I had to cut it up with Maury Swann," Pratt responded.

"Your subcontractor costs were not and are not my concern."

"The fee was based on everything working smoothly. Waits taking the fall for Gesto, case closed. Now there are complications, ongoing investigations to contend with."

"Again, not my concern. Our deal is done."

Pratt leaned forward on the bench and put his elbows on his knees.

"It's not quite done yet, T. Rex," he said. "And maybe you *should* be concerned. Because you know who paid me a visit on Friday night? Harry Bosch, and he had an FBI agent with him. They took me to a little meeting with Mr. Rick O'Shea. Turns out that before Bosch capped Waits the little bastard told him that he didn't kill Marie Gesto. So that puts Bosch back on your ass, Junior. And it puts all of them on mine. They've damn near worked the whole story out — connecting me and Maury Swann. They just need somebody to fill in the blanks and, since they can't get to Swann, they want that somebody to be me. They're starting to apply the pressure."

Anthony Garland groaned and kicked at the ground with his expensive loafers.

"Goddamn it! I knew this whole thing would —"

His father put a hand up for quiet.

"Bosch and the FBI don't matter," the old man said. "It's all about what O'Shea will do, and O'Shea is taken care of. He's bought and paid for. Only he doesn't know it yet. Once I apprise him of his situation, he will do what I tell him to do. If he wants to be district attorney."

Pratt shook his head.

"Bosch isn't going to let go of this. He hasn't for thirteen years. He's not going to now."

"Then, you take care of it. That's your end of the deal. I took care of O'Shea. You take care of Bosch. Let's go, son."

The old man started to get up, using the cane to push up on. His son stepped over to help him.

"Wait a minute," Pratt said. "You aren't going anywhere. I said I want more money and I'm serious. I'll take care of Bosch, but then I need to check out and disappear. I need more money to do that."

Anthony Garland angrily pointed down at Pratt on the bench.

"You goddamn piece of shit," he said. "You were the one who came to us. This whole goddamn thing is your plan from start to finish. You go out there and get two people killed, and then you have the balls to come back to us for more money?"

Pratt shrugged and spread his hands.

"I'm looking at a choice here, same as you. I could sit tight with the way things are and see how close they come to me. Or I could disappear right now. The thing you should know is that they always make deals with the little fish to get to the bigger fish. I'm a little fish, Anthony. The big fish? That would be you."

He turned to look at the old man.

"And the biggest fish? That would be you."

T. Rex Garland nodded. He was a pragmatic businessman. He seemed to now understand the gravity of the situation.

"How much?" he asked. "How much to disappear?"

Pratt didn't hesitate.

"I want another million dollars and it will be well worth it to you to give it to me. They can't get to either of you without me. If I'm gone, the case is gone. So it's a million and the price is nonnegotiable. Anything less and it is not worth it for me to run. I'll make a deal and take my chances."

"What about Bosch?" the old man asked. "You already said he won't give up. Now that he knows Raynard Waits didn't —"

"I'll take care of him before I split," Pratt said, cutting him off. "I'll throw that in for free."

He reached into his pocket and took out a piece of paper with numbers printed on it. He slid it across the bench to the old man.

"There's the bank account and wiring code. Same as before."

Pratt stood up.

"Tell you what, talk amongst yourselves. I'm going over to the boathouse to take a leak. When I come back I'll need an answer."

Pratt walked past Anthony, coming close, each man holding the other's eyes in a hard stare of hatred.

37

Harry Bosch studied the monitors in the surveillance van. The FBI had worked through the night setting cameras in eight locations at the park. One whole side of the interior of the van was covered with an array of digital screens that showed a multitude of visual angles on the bench where T. Rex Garland sat and his son stood waiting for Abel Pratt to return. The cameras were located on four of the park's path lights, in two of its flower beds, in the mock lighthouse atop the boathouse and in the fake pigeon perched on top of the *Lady of the Lake*'s head.

Added to this, the bureau techs had set up microwave sound receivers triangulated on the bench. The sound sweep was aided by directional mikes located in the fake pigeon, a flower bed and the folded newspaper Pratt had placed in the nearby trash can. A bureau sound tech named Jerry Hooten sat in the van, wearing a huge set of earphones and manipulating the audio feeds in order to produce the cleanest sound. Bosch and the others had been able to watch Pratt and the Garlands and hear their conversation word for word.

The others were Rachel Walling and Rick O'Shea. The prosecutor was sitting front and center, the video screens spread before him. This was his show. Walling and Bosch sat on either side of him.

O'Shea pulled off his earphones.

"What do we think?" he asked. "He's going to call. What do I tell him?"

Three of the screens showed Pratt about to enter the park's restroom. According to the plan, he would wait until the room was clear and then call the surveillance van's number on his cell phone.

Rachel pulled her earphones down around her neck and so did Bosch.

"I don't know," she said. "It's your call but

we don't have much of an admission from the son in regard to Gesto."

"That's what I was thinking," O'Shea responded.

"I don't know," Bosch said. "When Pratt talked about him leading him through the woods to the body, Anthony didn't deny it."

"But he didn't admit it either," Rachel said.

"But if a guy was sitting there talking to you about finding a body you buried and you didn't know what he was talking about, I think you'd say something."

"Well, that can be an argument for the jury," O'Shea said. "I'm just saying that he hasn't yet made anything I would call a statement of admission. We need more."

Bosch nodded, conceding the point. It had been decided on Saturday morning that Pratt's word was not going to be good enough. His testimony that Anthony Garland had led him to Marie Gesto's body and that he had taken a payoff from T. Rex Garland would not be sufficient to build a solid prosecution on. Pratt was a crooked cop and building a case on his testimony was too risky in an age when juries were highly suspicious of police integrity and behavior. They needed to get admissions from both of the Garlands for the case to move onto solid ground.

"Look, all I'm saying is, I think it's good but we're not quite there yet," O'Shea said. "We need to get a direct —"

"What about the old man?" Bosch asked. "I think Pratt got him to shit all over himself."

"I agree," Rachel said. "He's toast. If you send him back, tell him to work on Anthony."

As if on cue there was a low-level buzzing sound that indicated an incoming call. O'Shea, unfamiliar with the equipment, raised a finger over the console and looked for the right button to push.

"Here," Hooten said.

He punched a button that opened the cell line.

"This is the van," O'Shea said. "You're on speaker."

"How'd I do?" Pratt said.

"It's a start," O'Shea said. "What took you so long to call?"

"I actually did have to take a leak."

While O'Shea talked to Pratt about going back to the bench and trying once more for an admission from Anthony Garland, Bosch slipped his earphones back on to hear the conversation taking place at the bench.

From the visuals on the screens it looked like Anthony Garland was arguing with his father. The old man was pointing a finger at him.

Bosch picked it up in the middle.

"It's our only out," Anthony Garland said.

"I said no!" the old man commanded. "You cannot do this. You *will* not do this."

On the screen Anthony stepped away from his father and then stepped right back. It looked like he was on an invisible leash. He bent down close to his father and this time he pointed the finger. What he said was spoken so low that the FBI microphones picked up only a mumble. Bosch pressed his hands over the earphones but couldn't get it.

"Jerry," he said. "Can you work on this?"

Bosch pointed to the screens. Hooten pulled on his earphones and went to work on the audio dials. But it was too late. The close conversation between father and son was over. Anthony Garland had just straightened up in front of his father and turned his back to him. He was silently looking out across the lake.

Bosch leaned back so that he could see the screen that showed an angle on the bench from one of the path lights at the water's edge. It was the only screen that showed Anthony's face at the moment. Bosch saw the rage in his eyes. He had seen it before.

Anthony set his jaw tightly and shook his head. He turned back to his father.

"Sorry, Dad."

With that he started walking toward the boathouse. Bosch watched him take forceful strides toward the door of the restrooms. He saw his hand go inside his blazer.

Bosch slapped off his earphones.

"Anthony's headed to the men's room!" he said. "I think he's got a gun!"

Bosch jumped up and shoved past Hooten to get to the van's door. Unfamiliar with it, he fumbled with the handle trying to get it open. Behind him he heard O'Shea barking commands into the radio mike.

"Everybody move in! Move in! Suspect is armed. Repeat, suspect is armed!"

Bosch finally got out of the van and started running toward the boathouse. There was no sign of Anthony Garland. He was already inside.

Bosch was on the far side of the park and

more than a hundred yards away. Other agents and district attorney's office investigators had been deployed closer and Bosch saw them running with weapons out toward the boathouse as well. Just as the first man, an FBI agent, got to the doorway the sound of gunfire echoed from within the restroom. Four quick shots.

Bosch knew that Pratt's weapon was dry. It was a prop. He had needed to have a gun in case the Garlands checked him. But Pratt was in custody and facing charges. They had taken away his bullets.

As Bosch watched, the agent at the doorway dropped into a combat stance, shouted, "FBI!" and entered. Almost immediately, there were more shots but these were of a different timbre than the first four. Bosch knew these were from the agent's gun.

As Bosch got to the restroom the agent stepped out, gun at his side. He held a radio to his mouth.

"We have two down in the restroom," he said. "Scene is secured."

Winded from his run, Bosch gulped down some air and walked toward the doorway.

"Detective, that's a crime scene in there," the agent said.

He put his hand up in front of Bosch's chest. Bosch pushed it aside.

"I don't care."

He entered the restroom and saw the bodies of Pratt and Garland on the dirty concrete floor. Pratt had been shot twice in the face and twice in the chest. Garland had taken three chest shots. The fingers of Pratt's right hand were touching the sleeve of Garland's blazer. Pools of blood on the floor were blossoming from both bodies and soon would mingle.

Bosch watched for a few moments, studying Anthony's open eyes. The rage Bosch had seen moments before was gone, replaced by the empty look of death.

He stepped out of the restroom and looked over at the bench. The old man, T. Rex Garland, sat leaning forward with his face in his hands. The cane with the polished dragon's head had been dropped to the grass.

38

The entirety of Echo Park was closed for the investigation. For the third time in a week Bosch was interviewed about a shooting, only this time it was the feds doing the questioning and his part was peripheral because he had not fired a weapon. When he was finished he walked over to a *mariscos* truck that was parked at the curb and open for business to the crowd of onlookers outside the yellow tape. He ordered a shrimp taco and a Dr Pepper and took them over to one of the nearby federal cruisers. He was leaning on the front fender eating his lunch when Rachel Walling approached.

"Turns out Anthony Garland had a con-

cealed-weapon permit," she said. "His security job required it."

She leaned casually on the fender next to
him. Bosch nodded.

"I guess we should've checked," he said.

He took his last bite, wiped his mouth with
a napkin and then balled it up in the aluminum foil the taco came in.

"I remembered your story," she said.

"What story?" he asked.

"The one you told me about Garland
rousting those kids in the oil field."

"What about it?"

"You said he drew down on them."

"That's right."

She didn't say anything. She looked out at
the lake. Bosch shook his head like he wasn't
sure what was going on. She finally spoke.

"You knew about the permit and you knew
Anthony would be carrying, didn't you?"

It was a question but she meant it as a
statement.

"Rachel, what are you saying?"

"I'm saying you knew. You knew from way
back that Anthony carried a gun. You knew
what could happen today."

Bosch spread his hands wide.

"Look, that thing with the kids was twelve

years ago. How would I know that he would have a gun today?"

She got off the fender and turned to face him.

"How many times did you talk to Anthony over the years? How many times did you shake him down?"

Bosch squeezed the ball of aluminum foil tighter in his fist.

"Look, I never —"

"Are you telling me that in all those times you never once came up with a gun? That you didn't check permits? That you didn't know that there was a very high probability that he would bring a gun — and his uncontrolled rage — to a meeting like this? If we had known this guy carried a gun, we would never have set this thing up in the first place."

Bosch smiled unpleasantly and shook his head in a disbelieving sort of way.

"What was it you said about mumbo-jumbo conspiracies the other day? Marilyn didn't overdose; the Kennedys had her killed. Bosch knew Anthony would bring a gun to the meeting and would start shooting? Rachel, it all sounds like —"

"And what about what *you* said about being a true detective?"

She stared pointedly at him.

"Rachel, listen to me. There was no way anybody could have predicted this. There was no —"

"Predicted, hoped, accidentaly set in motion — what's the difference? You remember what you said to Pratt the other night by the pool?"

"I said a lot of things to him."

Her voice took on a tone of sadness.

"You told him about the choices we all make."

She pointed across the grass at the boathouse.

"And, well, Harry, I guess this is the dog you chose to feed. I hope you're happy with it. And I hope it fits in perfectly well with the way of the true detective."

She turned and walked back toward the boathouse and the knot of investigators crowding the crime scene.

Bosch let her go. For a long time he didn't move. Her words had gone through him like the sounds of a roller coaster. Low rumbling and high shrieks. He squeezed the ball of aluminum foil in his hand and shot it toward a trash can sitting next to the *mariscos* truck.

He missed by a mile.

39

Kiz Rider came through the double doors in a wheelchair. She found it embarrassing but that was the hospital rule. Bosch was waiting for her with a smile and a bouquet of flowers he had bought from a vendor at the freeway exit near the hospital. As soon as she was allowed by the nurse, she got up and out of the chair. She tentatively hugged Bosch as though she felt fragile, and thanked him for coming to take her home.

"I'm right out front," he said.

With his arm across her back he walked her out to the waiting Mustang. He helped her get in, then put a bag of cards and gifts she had received into the trunk and came around to the driver's side.

"You want to go anywhere first?" he asked once he was in the car.

"No, just home. I can't wait to sleep in my own bed."

"I hear you."

He started the car and pulled out, heading back to the freeway. They drove silently. When he got back to the 134 the flower vendor was still in the median. Rider looked down at the bouquet in her hand, realized that Bosch had gotten them as an afterthought and started laughing. Bosch joined in.

"Oh, shit, that hurts!" she said, touching her hand to her neck.

"Sorry."

"It's all right, Harry. I need to laugh."

Bosch nodded his agreement.

"Is Sheila going to come by today?" he asked.

"Yeah, after work."

"Good."

He nodded because there wasn't anything else to do. They lapsed back into silence.

"Harry, I took your advice," Rider said after a few minutes.

"What was that?"

"I told them I didn't have a shot. I told them I didn't want to hit Olivas."

"That's good, Kiz."

He thought about things for a few moments.

"Does that mean you're going to keep your badge?" he asked.

"Yes, Harry, I'm keeping the badge . . . but not my partner."

Bosch looked over at her.

"I talked to the chief," Rider said. "After I finish rehab I'm going to go back to work in his office, Harry. I hope that will be all right with you."

"Whatever you want to do is all right with me. You know that. I'm glad you're staying."

"Me, too."

A few more minutes went by and when she spoke again it was as if the conversation had never lagged.

"Besides, up there on the sixth floor, I'll be able to watch out for you, Harry. Maybe keep you out of all the politics and bureaucratic scrapping. Lord knows you're still going to need me from time to time."

Bosch smiled broadly. He couldn't help it. He liked the idea of her being up there one floor above him. Watching out and watching over.

"I like it," he said. "I don't think I've ever had a guardian angel before."

Acknowledgments

The author gratefully acknowledges a number of people who greatly helped in the research and writing of this book. They include Asya Muchnick, Michael Pietsch, Jane Wood, Pamela Marshall, Shannon Byrne, Terrill Lee Lankford, Jan Burke, Pam Wilson, Jerry Hooten and Ken Delavigne. Also of great help to the author were Linda Connelly, Jane Davis, Maryelizabeth Capps, Carolyn Chriss, Dan Daly, Roger Mills and Gerald Chaleff. Also many thanks to Sgt. Bob McDonald and Detectives Tim Marcia, Rick Jackson and David Lambkin of the Los Angeles Police Department.

About the Author

Michael Connelly is the author of the best-selling Harry Bosch series of novels as well as the recent #1 *New York Times* bestseller *The Lincoln Lawyer.* He is a former newspaper reporter who has won numerous awards for his journalism and his novels. He spends his time in California and Florida.